THE
PERFECT
CORPSE

GILES MILTON

PROSPERO

First published in Great Britain by Prospero Press

www.prosperopress.net

A CIP catalogue record for this book is available from the British Library.

ISBN: 978-0-9928972-2-2

Set in Adobe Caslon Pro 11 pt

Cover design: Laura Bamber

ABOUT THE AUTHOR

Giles Milton is a writer and historian. He is the internationally bestselling author of *Nathaniel's Nutmeg*, *Big Chief Elizabeth*, *Samurai William*, *White Gold*, *The Riddle and the Knight*, *Paradise Lost*, *Wolfram* and, most recently, *Russian Roulette*.

His books have been translated into twenty languages. *White Gold* is currently being piloted as a major Channel 4 series.

He has also written two novels, *Edward Trencom's Nose* and *According to Arnold*, and three children's books, two of them illustrated by his wife, Alexandra.

He writes a regular history blog:
http://surviving-history.blogspot.co.uk/

He lives in London.

http://www.gilesmilton.com
@SurviveHistory

ALSO BY GILES MILTON

Non-Fiction
The Riddle and the Knight
Nathaniel's Nutmeg
Big Chief Elizabeth
Samurai William
White Gold
Paradise Lost: Smyrna 1922
Wolfram
Russian Roulette

Fiction
Edward Trencom's Nose
According to Arnold

Children's Books
Zebedee's Zoo
Call Me Gorgeous
Good Luck, Baby Owls

PRAISE FOR GILES MILTON

'To write a book which makes the reader, after finishing it, sit in a trance, lost in his passionate desire to pack a suitcase and go, somehow, to the fabulous place – that, in the end, is something one would give a sack of nutmegs for.' Philip Hensher, *The Spectator* (Nathaniel's Nutmeg).

'Giles Milton's research is impeccable and his narrative reads in part like a modern-day Robert Louis Stevenson novel.' Martin Booth, *The Times* (Nathaniel's Nutmeg).

'This book is a magnificent piece of popular history. It is an English story, but its heroism is universal. This is a book to read, reread, then, aside from the X-rated penultimate chapter, read again to your children.' Nicholas Fearn, *The Independent on Sunday* (Nathaniel's Nutmeg)

'In an exceptionally pungent, amusing and accessible historical account, Giles Milton brings readers right into the midst of the colonists and their daunting American adventure... there's no question that Mr Milton's research has been prodigious and that it yields an entertaining, richly informative look at the past.' Janet Maslin, *The New York Times* (Big Chief Elizabeth).

'Milton has a terrific eye for the kind of detail that can bring the past vividly to life off the page. He revels in the grim realities of the early colonists' experience. There's disease, famine, torture, cannibalism and every kind of deprivation imaginable. Compelling reading.' *The Spectator* (Big Chief Elizabeth).

'Giles Milton is a man who can take an event from history and make it come alive... He has a genius for lively prose, and an appreciation for historical credibility. With *Samurai William*, he has crafted an inspiration for those of us who believe that history can be exciting and entertaining.' Matthew Redhead, *The Times* (Samurai William).

'Giles Milton has once again shown himself to be a master of historical narrative. The story of William Adams is a gripping tale of Jacobean derring-do, a fizzing, real-life Boy's Own adventure underpinned by genuine scholarship.' Katie Hickman, *The Sunday Times* (Samurai William)

'A sheer pleasure to read.' Susan Chira, *The New York Times* (Samurai William).

'A romping tale of 18th-century sailors enslaved by Barbary seafarers and sold to a Moroccan tyrant. It has all the usual Miltonian ingredients: swift narrative and swashbuckling high-drama laid on a bed of historical grit. Benedict Allen, *The Independent* (White Gold).

'Milton's story could scarcely be more action-packed and its setting and subsidiary characters are as fantastic as its events... Milton conjures up a horrifying but enthralling vision of the court of Moulay Ismail.' Lucy Hughes-Hallett, *The Sunday Times* (White Gold)

'Milton brings the past alive in this vivid, detailed and poignant book.' Adam Le Bor, *Literary Review* (Paradise Lost)

'It is the lives of the Levantine dynasties that form the focus for Giles Milton's brilliant re-creation of the last days of Smyrna ... Milton has written a grimly memorable book... well paced, even-handed and cleverly focused.' William Dalrymple, *The Sunday Times* (Paradise Lost)

'Idiosyncratic and utterly fascinating.' James Delinpole, *The Daily Mail* (Wolfram)

'Milton has synthesized and filleted a mass of material - old memoirs, official archives and newly released intelligence files - to produce a rollicking tale... which explains the long war against Russia with verve, wit and colour. It reads like fiction, but it is, astonishingly, history.' Michael Binyon, *The Times* (Russian Roulette).

'Readers will find themselves as gripped as they would be by the very best of Fleming or Le Carré.' *The Sunday Times* (Russian Roulette)

'Milton is a compulsive storyteller whose rattling style ensures this is the antithesis of a dry treatise on espionage. And unlike 007, it's all true.' *The Daily Express* (Russian Roulette).

For Alexandra

PART ONE

GREENLAND, JUNE, 1944

Ferris Clark had grown so used to solitude that he no longer realised when he was talking to himself. Even now, as he stared blankly out of the window, he was only dimly aware of the voice in his head.

Only thirteen more days, Ferris, and then you're off for a month. A whole goddam month!

The isolation had preyed on his mind at first. Here he was, six hundred miles from nowhere, his pre-fab cabin anchored with wires to a lonely outcrop of icy-rock. What if he fell into a crevasse? What if his wireless failed? What if? In the early days, any number of disasters had run through his head. But as each day passed and there were no mishaps, he decided that he hadn't pulled the short straw after all.

Jeez Ferris, there's plenty worse places to be sent. Lester and Gerald and the others, probably right now being bombed to shit by some band of squint-eyed Japs.

He glanced out of the cabin window and slowly shook his head. The sky was stained like an ashtray and storm clouds were banking up on the horizon. He knew those clouds. They'd bring eight hours of snow and send the mercury plunging to twenty below.

He reached for his matches and lit the kerosene lamp. A yellow glow filled the small room, slowly brightening to metallic white as the flame took hold of the wick. The light sent shadows scuttling into the darkened corners. As he glanced around, he glimpsed the shadow of his head and shoulders looming improbably huge on the wall behind him.

He stoked the Tromso stove and felt the clothes that he had hung up to dry. His woollen socks, all steaming, were strung up like a row of so many kippers. Then he reached for the nightclothes that he kept folded on his army camp bed. Pyjamas, slipper-socks and long woollen scarf. Even with the stove burning it got bitterly cold at night.

He undressed, got into his night-gear and sat down on the bed. It was so low on the floor that it was almost touching the floorboards. Then he pushed his legs under the covering and drew the blankets upwards until they were tight around his chest.

A final glance around the cabin before extinguishing the lamp.

* * *

He had no idea what time it was when he was jolted from his sleep. It was pitch black in the cabin and there was no hint of light from the window. He could hear the wind driving horizontal, scouring the surface of the ice field. It whipped the roof of the cabin and hit the window like a muffled machine gun. Tak-tak-tak-tak.

But it was not the storm that had woken him. Rather, it was the noise of the huskies roped up outside. They were barking loudly.

Why are they doing that?

He sat up in the darkness. Shivered. Couldn't be because they were unsettled by the storm. They liked it best when it was biting cold and the snow was chucking it down.

Instinctively he reached for the kerosene lamp, pushing his

hand outwards from underneath the blanket. He always kept it close to his pillow.

It wasn't there.

He felt again, his hand tapping lightly across the floorboards. He could have sworn that's where he left it, next to his head. He could even smell the scent of kerosene.

But it was gone.

He pushed his hand further into the darkness and as he did so he felt his innards shrink in on themselves, like a fist squeezing his gut.

Jesus –

There was the faint sound of breathing.

He shivered. Felt a lump in his throat. He pushed himself downwards into the camp bed, as if it might protect him from danger. And then gingerly, without making a sound, he drew the blanket over his head.

Get a grip, Ferris. You're imagining things. You've been too long alone. That's why they never let you do shifts longer than eight weeks.

Thinking like that, it made him feel better.

There's no one outside. There's no one breathing. And in just a few hours it'll be morning again.

He lay absolutely still, listening intently. Inched his head to one side and drew back the blanket a fraction so that his right ear was exposed.

There. See. It's gone. You woke from a nightmare, that's all.

He was hot under the blanket yet he could feel that his skin was cold with sweat. He took three deep breaths to relax himself.

That's better.

The dogs had stopped barking and the night was returning to normal. He hated what tricks the darkness could play.

Reassured, he rolled slowly onto his back and tightened the blanket around his chest. Must be the early hours. He'd try to get some more sleep.

But just as he did so he heard it again. The faint sound of breathing. And now – *oh Jesus God* – he could feel the floorboards under his camp bed shifting and squeaking ever so gently, as if they were moving on heavy springs. And this time – *help me God* - it was for real. Someone, somehow, had got inside his cabin.

He felt the footfall coming towards him. Coming closer. And then it stopped. Came to an abrupt halt. Right by his head.

He dared to open his eyes a fraction. It was still completely dark yet he could just make out the blur of a heavy white boot, inches from his face. It smelled musty, wet, like it was splashed with snow-melt and slush.

And then -

Jesus.

There was a violent crunch of bone and a burst of stars shattered across his eyes. The boot slammed deep into his right temple and a shaft of agony lurched through his neck.

He screamed, crumpled his head into his arms. He yanked the blanket over his pulsing head. Another kick and a second welter of stars played tricks with his eyes.

Jesus – Jesus –

There was a shaft of freezing air as the latch to the cabin door snapped open. In an instant everything was moving and there was noise and shouting and the clatter of guns. Flashlights sent a chaos of light through the darkness. Their hands ripped off the covering and tore at his pyjamas. One of them wrenched away the sleeves. Another forced off his scarf and socks. Suddenly he was naked.

Three flashlights exposed his body, a fourth shone into his eyes.

Please God.

An iron grip wrapped round his ankles and the room spun upside down. They dragged him over to a lump of frozen driftwood and tied up his wrists and ankles. Then they seized the wood, wrenched him over the high step and out into the blinding snowstorm. His head hit the ice with a solid crack.

Jesus.

He felt his body shudder uncontrollably, lungs, kidneys,

shaking in rhythmic spasm.
Then a desperate cry.
'*Why – ?*'

ONE

J ack Raven stood by the open window of his study and drained his coffee in a single slug. There was still a glimmer of daylight in the London sky, even though it was almost eleven, and the air was full of summer warmth. In the garden square opposite, groups of people were sitting on the grass and drinking wine and beer.

He closed the window with a downwards thrust, locked it and drew down the blind. Then he turned back to face the room, still distracted by his thoughts. On his desk, neatly packed in a box, was a plaster replica of Napoleon's death mask. On the screen of his computer, blown up to scale, was an image of the same mask.

Jack sat down and pulled the keyboard towards him. He clicked on the Resurrect icon, typed in a code and then shifted the cursor slightly. He paused for a moment, his finger held in suspended animation. And then he hit the return key.

'Go for it, you bastard.'

He studied the screen intently.

'Go.'

It began so slowly that at first it was almost imperceptible. Yet he could see that something was starting to happen. The image of the death mask was beginning to inflate. The cheeks were swelling slightly as if they were being pumped with air and the drawn features were losing their creases and lines. The plaster-grey pallor of the death mask was transforming itself into pinkish flesh.

'Go my beauty.'

He stretched his fingers towards the screen. The mask was resurrecting itself into a living face. The rigid angularity of death was falling away and in its place there was a fleshly presence. Napoleon was being conjured back from the dead. No longer was he the hollow-cheeked cadaver of his deathbed. This was Napoleon, but alive.

The image stalled for a moment.

'No, no. Don't stop now baby.'

He clicked the keyboard.

There was a ripple in the upper face and he noticed the brow contract slightly. He hit another key. As he did so, the eyelids blinked open one by one.

'Huh!'

Napoleon was staring him directly in the eye, his chilling blue-grey pupils glinting sharply in the light of the anglepoise.

'Beautiful. Just beautiful.'

Death masks were a lie. Jack had known that for years. Even if wet plaster was slapped onto a face within an hour of death, it never captured the genuine, living face. Within minutes of a person dying, the muscles collapse and the flesh sinks like a soufflé, turning the cheekbones into high and bony ridges.

He turned his gaze from the screen to the death mask, still tucked neatly into its box. Napoleon's face was shrunk into a wizened old hag, with airless cheeks and tight-pinched lips.

The idea had come to him twelve months earlier. If you filmed enough people dying, filmed the hours that took them from living soul to lifeless cadaver, then you could find patterns in the collapse of a face. Feed this into a computer and you could design a programme that would accurately reverse the process.

It was a simple idea, one that could conjure the past to life. He could take any death mask, scan its image into a computer and use the programme to recreate the living face. If it worked for Napoleon, there was no reason why it wouldn't work for Beethoven, Tolstoy, Robespierre, Cromwell. There were thousands of death masks in existence. Half the most famous people in history had been moulded after their deaths. And now he, Jack, could breath life back into their features.

Tennyson. He knew there was a death mask of Tennyson. He also knew there were recordings of him reading his poems. If he lip-synched the recordings to the reanimated mask, he could watch Tennyson himself reading the Charge of the Light Brigade.

'Frigging macabre, Jack.' That's what Karin had said when he'd first told her about the project. 'Next you'll be digging up old graves.'

He got up from his chair, walked over to the fireplace. Above the mantelpiece hung the hugely magnified scan of a human brain. A parting gift from the Innsbruck team, digitalized, all green and red pixels, with specks of brain coloured lighter than the rest. He knew those specks better than anyone else in the world. Each one was an ice crystal of shattered blood – cells that had frozen and exploded into microscopic fragments.

He went back to his desk and drew the keyboard towards him. Napoleon was still staring at him in 3-D. Alarmingly, his eyes had started to blink. He saved the face into a new file and switched screens in order to check his emails. A new message flashed up on screen. Subject: Greenland Corpse. Sender: Tammy Fox.

Dear Doctor Raven,

Apologies for this unsolicited mail but I am writing to you for possible assistance. ZAKRON Inc., Nevada, (see attachment) has recently taken delivery of a corpse that was found entombed in the Greenland ice. The identity of this corpse is as yet unknown, as is the cause of death. But it seems certain he died in suspicious circumstances, not least because his body was found naked. I was wondering if you might be able to help us with our investigations.

The glimmer of a smile registered on Jack's face as he sat back in his chair, leaning just enough weight against the backrest to hear it crack. An unidentified corpse. Suspicious circumstances. And naked. Just perfect.

ZAKRON will, of course, pay you for your time and reimburse you for travel expenses for the duration of your stay. There is now considerable urgency to this matter and your response would be much appreciated.

It was so exactly what he needed at this moment in his life that he immediately reached for his electronic diary and began flicking through it, double-checking to see that he had nothing on. A lecture in Durham in the second week of August and a pathology conference in Stratford on the Friday of that week. And then there was the whole press business in Leicester for King Richard III. He *had* to be there for that, but it wasn't for another three weeks. Otherwise, every day until the end of August was still marked *Italy hols*.

He leaned back in his chair again and stared blankly into space. Italy hols. If only Karin hadn't done what she'd done.

He shifted the anglepoise lamp a fraction in order to remove the glare from the screen. Then he re-read the email a second time. Nevada. He'd never been there. It was where Aureol Kampfner had found those three American Indian mummies. He remembered reading it in *Scientific American*. That was back in the seventies.

He clicked on the email's attachment and waited a few

seconds while it downloaded. It provided a little background information about ZAKRON and gave a link to the company website.

'ZAKRON Inc. is the world's leader in cryonics, including cryonic research and technology. Our principal goal is to use ultra-cold temperature to conserve and preserve human life.'

The final page was ZAKRON Research. 'For some years ZAKRON has been occasionally involved with the FBI and other agencies, charged with undertaking scientific and forensic analysis on unidentified bodies in order to help these agencies with their enquiries. Most notably, we were involved in the recovery and subsequent identification of three American pilots whose *George One* plane crashed in 1946 in West Antarctica.'

The George One case. He remembered it well. As a matter of fact he'd been asked to help out on that occasion too, but he was halfway up the Tyrolean Alps at the time, working on the Utzi case. He clicked back onto his mailbox and started typing.

Dear Ms Fox,

Many thanks for your email. The Greenland corpse sounds fascinating. It's absolutely my specialist field. As it happens, my diary is completely blank for the next few weeks due to the last minute cancellation of my holiday. I'd be most interested in taking up your proposal. Please let me know how we should proceed. I look forward to hearing back from you and, I hope, meeting you in the near future.

Dr. Jack Raven,
Bsc., (hons) Msc., Forensic Archaeology, IfA.

A reply came back almost immediately.

Great news. Will get provisional times and dates for tickets and get back to you. Many thanks, Tammy.

He was about to close the laptop when he had another thought. He typed Tammy Fox into Google to see what came up. There was a link back to the ZAKRON website. 'Tammy Fox is ZAKRON's senior lab technician with responsibility for the long term care of our cryo-preserved patients. She worked on the *George One* Antarctic case. She is an honorary member of the ZAKRON board and her grandfather, Ronald C. Fox was the founder of the company (then ZAKRON prosthetics) in 1946.'

Jack closed his laptop and stood up abruptly, swinging round to face the self-portrait that stood unfinished on the easel. It glared back at him with improbably huge eyes. Karin had liked it. 'It's got attitude. Like you.' It made him look older than forty-two but then, Christ, he'd lived more than most forty-two year olds. 'You can't expect to look forty-two, Jack, when you've spent two years of your life chucking spirits down your throat.'

Out of the corner of his eye he noticed one of Karin's cardigans dangling from the back of a chair. He took it in his hands for a moment and held it to his nose, breathing in deeply. Then he flung it into the corner of the room.

He walked back to his desk and picked up his mug, half wishing it was full of Talisker. *Don't go there, Jack. Do not even go there.* Then he went through to the kitchen, switching off the light to his study.

TWO

It was gone seven-thirty in the evening by the time the plane made its final descent into Hanford Airport and almost nine when the cab pulled up outside ZAKRON. Jack paid the driver and stepped out into the night air. Christ it was hot, like a fan-heater on full tilt. He shed his linen jacket.

The ZAKRON building was set back from the highway. It was shaped like a lop-sided dome, not unlike an egg, with the apex sloping away to the back. The shell was burnished metal, or that's how it looked in the darkness. It was reflecting the orange glow of the interstate, spinning the streetlights to a blur.

As he approached the entrance the smoked-glass doors snapped open. He stepped into the chill of the building and instantly recognized the woman standing there in a white lab coat, loosely buttoned, her blond hair tied back and held neatly in place. She was wearing the same retro glasses that Karin had bought just before she left.

'Well,' she said, extending her hand. 'After all the emails. Tammy Fox.'

'Jack Raven,' he said, smiling. 'Jack. Good to meet you at last.'

'Not too exhausted? Sorry to drag you from the airport but I wanted you to see him straight off.'

Jack ran his hand through his hair.

'You got me intrigued. Wouldn't have missed it for the world.'

She led him down a corridor towards the lab, swiping the

door with a smart-card and flicking on the lights. Then she stood back to allow him through.

'Here we are,' she said, pointing to an oblong glass container on the far side of the laboratory. 'Can't wait to get your take on it.'

Jack walked across to the container. Its interior was chilled to minus 10 Fahrenheit, so cold that the outer surface was etched with frost. He pressed his hand to the frozen glass. His skin stuck there for a moment, forming a glue-like bond. But then the warmth of his hand melted the thin veil of ice. He took a cloth from his pocket and wiped away the wetness, creating a porthole through which to get a clearer view.

The corpse was naked, deep-frozen, outstretched on his back. Male. White Caucasian. His feet were iced to steel, arms locked stiffly to his side. He had a yellow rubber tag attached to his left ankle, like one of those locker-key straps you get at public swimming pools.

Three halogen spots shone onto the container, their light reflecting off the frosted glass. A fourth had been positioned at the far end, throwing light onto the head. Jack scrutinized the corpse with care, his eyes shifting from the head to the feet and then back to the head. Mid-thirties, he reckoned. Physically fit. Strong boned. His hair was intact, it was dusky-blond, and the skin was as smooth as a pebble. The genital area, often the first part to deteriorate, was in perfect condition, even after all the years that he'd been in the ice.

The left eyelid, frozen ajar, revealed a pupil that was a sharp blue and beautifully translucent, though veiled in frost. The right eye was sealed with a delicate zip of ice. The way he was lying there, frozen like a rock, he could have been a fallen statue, renaissance, Italianate, marble. Perfect muscles, perfect physique.

Jack lifted his gaze and looked back across the laboratory to Tammy. The light was gilding her hair and tracing her profile into a firm silhouette.

'Just perfect,' he said with a smile.

She flashed her eyes at him in a questioning sort of way.

'The corpse, I mean. Completely perfect. Never seen anything -'

He turned back to the container and looked at the body more closely. Something was strange about the curvature of the back and spine. It was as if he had died in his sleep, relaxed, stretched out on a comfortable mattress.

'Was he like that when he was found?'

'Pretty much,' said Tammy. 'Except he was head down. That's what's so strange. It's like he fell through a hole in the ice. Fell, got stuck and was then unable to get back out. That's not a pretty death.'

'No. But I guess not many deaths are pretty.'

She smiled, embarrassed.

'But surely – '

He glanced up at her but she broke off mid-sentence.

'Normally there'd be fractures in the skin,' he said. 'You'd get ice cracks here and here.' He pointed to the eyes and mouth. 'And I was expecting him to be white. When we found Mallory, he looked like he'd been bleached.'

He paused. 'Do we have any idea what he was up to in Greenland?'

'Tom's been in charge up till now. Tom Lawyer. The boss. Maybe you read about him on the website. You'll meet him tomorrow. He says we've reached the end of the road. Discovered everything we're going to discover.'

'But what *have* you discovered? All I know is the stuff in your last email.'

'There's more,' she said. 'He had an I.D. bracelet. Just initials - F.C. - but enough to set Tom on track. Name's Ferris Clark. American. A serviceman. Died in wartime, that's clear, and Tom's been going through the military records.'

She hesitated. He sensed she had more to say.

'But to be honest, even with all this new stuff it hasn't exactly got us very far. We've no idea how he got there. Not even sure what he was doing in Greenland. And we certainly don't have a clue why he was naked.'

She turned to face him.

'*Naked* for Chrissakes. That's just weird.'

'You're right. It *is* weird.'

'And that's why I had to get you over. Find out how he died. If *you* can't come up with an answer, I guess no one can.'

She went over to the desk at the far side of the room and rummaged through a couple of files, as if she was looking for something.

'Tom pretends it's all solved, of course, but he's not even close to giving us a cause of death. Murder? Suicide? It's like all the balls are in the air.'

She lowered her voice, even though the only other person in the building was the night security guard. 'And then there's the whole question of why he's so well preserved.

'I worked on the George One case. Three Second World War pilots found in the Antarctic. And I can tell you one thing, they looked a million miles different from Ferris Clark.'

Jack went back over to the glass box that was housing the body, nodding slowly as she spoke.

'Why was he brought here?' he asked. 'Why ZAKRON? I checked your website, saw all the stuff you've done. But there's other places that can do this.'

'One or two. But well, I guess it was cos of George One. It was us, right from the outset. They brought him straight from Greenland. Delivered him to the military airport just down the road. You must have passed it on your way here. And then he was brought to us.'

She ran through the events of the evening the corpse had arrived. Twenty-ninth of June. They'd unpacked him, weighed him and measured him, calculated his body mass, etcetera, etcetera. And then they'd transferred him to the vitrification box.

'And this thing,' she said, pointing back to the glass container, 'is real state of the art. Even NASA couldn't do better. Equipped with optic sensors, thermostatic control panels, the works. Keeps him at a constant temperature. Even scans his organs.'

While Jack looked over the equipment, Tammy picked through a bulging file marked *F. Clark*. It was filled with charts, tomographic scans and computer print-outs.

'You'll get a good look through them tomorrow. But, well, we've run through pretty much everything, as you'll see. Body scans, organ scans, internal probes, blood analyses. White and red corpuscles. Dioxides. I'll get you the whole set in the morning, if I can persuade Tom to hand them over.'

'Brain scans? DNA?'

'Yep, brain scans and DNA. Haven't seen those. Tom's got them in his office.'

Another pause.

'Everything points in the same direction. Froze the very second he died. Like he was tipped into liquid nitrogen. You're right about him being perfect. Exactly what I thought the moment we unpacked him. It's like he's too perfect, if you get what I mean.'

She reached for a second file and pulled out a glossy print of the dead man's heart.

'Check this.'

Jack took it from her hands.

'Jeez, Tom'll kill me. Shouldn't be showing you any of this without his say-so.'

Jack put down the high-res scan for a moment while he took out his glasses. Then he held it close to his face and studied it more closely. Frozen corpses had a peculiarity of their own, he knew that more than anyone. The three Austrian soldiers they'd pulled from the Forni glacier - brain, liver, lungs, they'd scanned them six, seven times. Every image revealed those tell-tale whitish spots. Each spot was an ice crystal of shattered blood cells, the inevitable result of death by freezing. Cells explode and fragment as they turn from liquid into ice.

But this scan was flawless.

* * *

'You're all over the internet,' said Tammy brightly. 'Jack Raven, forensic archaeologist. I checked out your website. You make it sound somehow – ' she paused – 'romantic.'

'*Romantic!*' He laughed.

'Jack Raven with that body in a peat bog. Jack Raven on Everest clutching George Mallory. Jack Raven with a human skull. I get this feeling you'd hack through the Amazon if there was a dead body at the end of it.'

'It's a job like any other,' he said.

'Not really,' she said with a smile. 'It's not like you're a trucker. Or an accountant.'

'True. To be honest, most people think it's a totally weird thing to do.'

'And all this stuff with death masks.'

'Ah, that – '

He paused, changed tack. 'And you?'

'I do the labs. Keep them clean. Wash them down. And that's anything but romantic.'

She looked up at him again.

'One thing I didn't tell you. I should have said something before you left England. But I thought you wouldn't come.'

'Oh?'

'Tom and Hunter, they've only just found out about you. It was all my idea, see. I'm the one that got you over from England. Tom was on vacation. And – '

She turned to face him directly. 'Tom's, well, a bit of a hard-ass. Takes no crap, particularly right now, what with his divorce and all that. And with you here -'

Jack laughed again. 'We'll get on, I'm sure of it. After all, I've come to find him some answers.'

'And that's the problem,' said Tammy with a frown. 'Answers are the very last thing Tom wants.'

THREE

Tammy was summoned to Tom Lawyer's office as soon as she arrived at work. She expected trouble.

'Who the fuck is he?' said Tom as she entered the room. 'And why the fuck didn't I know about him?"

'Name's Jack Raven. A Brit. Very smart. And an expert on death. I'm telling you, he's the smartest forensics guy in the business. Made his name on the Mallory case. Pieced it together like a jigsaw puzzle. They even showed it on Discovery. We need him. And you were on vacation, *remember?*'

Tom stabbed his hand through his hair, fingers splayed, as if to express his exasperation.

'But this was meant to be kept in-house. Absolutely in-house. Use only the team. You knew that. This isn't a repeat of George One. And we do *not* want the press all over us. For fuck's sake, I couldn't have made it clearer. What were you thinking of? I just don't get it.'

The July sun thumped at the porthole window, its morning heat broken by the reflective glass. The air con gave a sudden whine as if struggling to keep itself at a constant. Tom's newly acquired tan had a tinge of orange, like it had been sprayed from a can.

'*This was meant to be kept in-house.*' He said it again.

'I know you wanted it kept in-house. You *did* make it clear. But it's just, come on Tom, we're talking about a real person for

Chrissakes. Ferris Clark. Who just happens to have died upside down, naked, in the middle of nowhere in Greenland. In my mind that all adds up to something weird. If you of all people can't see we need to know more, then I don't know what.'

Tom was staring at her hard, listening to what she was saying. 'Yeah, yeah.'

She ignored him. 'Look, when I read about Jack Raven, well, he sounded like just what we need. And it wasn't *all* my doing. Accounts have been just as much involved. You can't stick it all on me.'

There was a long silence. She took off her glasses and placed them decisively on the desk in front of her. And then she edged them forwards with her finger. Tom's eyes contracted slightly. She smiled. Men were so territorial, at least Tom Lawyer was. She was invading his personal space and he didn't like it one bit.

'Jack Raven can help us *Tom*,' she continued, saying his name in a half-pleading fashion, like it might win him over. 'He's the best there is.'

'What does he know? What have you told him?'

'Nothing. Precisely zero.'

'He came here last night.'

She shrugged.

'You brought him here last night.'

'So?' She looked at him. 'How d'you know?'

She knew Kingston wouldn't have said anything.

Tom emitted a sarcastic laugh, like he was playing the gangster. 'Nothing in this sweet little town happens without me knowing.' He chewed on his gum then jabbed his finger towards her, leaning casually back in his chair as he did so.

'D'you know what I'd like more than anything in the world?' he said. 'I'd like this Jack Raven to get himself back on a plane to England and take his British ass away from here. He's not getting involved in Ferris Clark. And you should have known that.'

Silence.

'Listen, you're a lab tech, right? Your job's to keep him cold, keep him constant, nice and steady. If you can only do that, we'll all be happy. We can all get along just fine. Your job's *not* to hire people when I'm away on vacation and nor is it to persuade the accounts people that we need to call up a forensic fucking scientist from England.

'And just cos ZAKRON was founded by your old grandpa, God bless his memory, it doesn't mean you've some special licence to do whatever you want. I take decisions. Hunter takes decisions. We're full members of the board. You're just an honorary member. Thanks Grandpa. Remember that. It's not the same thing.'

Tammy let out a weary sigh.

'Listen,' she said. 'I got Jack Raven here to find answers. That's all. And that's what you should let him do. Find answers and then go home.'

Tom waved his hand nonchalantly through the air. Then he stood up and paced around the room. 'You all signed the confidentiality agreement,' he snapped. 'Doesn't that mean anything? And what about Plaxon? They'll hit the fucking roof if they hear about this. For Chrissakes, what other crap are you going to spring?'

He pointed a finger directly at her. 'If I was in your dainty little ballerina shoes I'd be seriously watching my step.'

'Tom,' she said, ignoring the bluster, 'I honestly thought Greg would clear it with you before he bought the ticket.' She paused. 'Anyway, it's too late now. He's smart and he's on the ball. I told him to come at –' she looked at her watch – 'at ten-thirty, to catch the end of the meeting.'

FOUR

The cab was waiting in the Logan's Corner parking lot, engine growling softly and indicator winking redundantly. Jack opened the door and stepped into the chilled interior. Cold as a morgue.

'ZAKRON, isn't it?'

'Please.'

The driver nodded from the front, swung the car into a giant circle then turned onto the Interstate 50. The indicator stopped ticking as they straightened onto the main highway. *This is Radio KMZQ on six-seventy AM. Nevada's number one news talk.* A sign flashed passed the window. 'Hanford Gap: Oasis of Nevada.' It was an oasis that everyone seemed to be leaving. Homes, bars and grocery stores were strung out along the highway like some sort of disjointed town. Yummies' Ice Cream. Grand-daddy's Bar. Nugget Social. You could eat junk for miles, all the way to the desert.

'You from England?'

'Arrived last night.'

'What brings you to our lonely little town?'

'A corpse.'

The driver looked into the mirror, as if to double-check that he had a passenger in the back and was not hearing voices in his head. Most visitors came for the air base. If they were tourists, they came to see Sand Mountain.

He forced a laugh and shrugged.

'Well, you've come to the right place, I guess. Must have a few at ZAKRON. They did George One you know.'

Jack nodded. 'I saw it on their website. D'you know the place? Tom Lawyer, he's the guy in charge?'

'Everyone knows Tom Lawyer. Been the boss for years. They'll tell you he's the richest guy in Hanford.'

'How so?'

'Must be big money in frozen corpses,' said the driver as he bought the vehicle to a gliding halt. 'Walt Disney and all that. D'you do this cryonics business in England?'

'No.'

It took just a couple of minutes before they were glancing off the highway and into the parking area at the front. Jack paid the driver and stepped out of the cab. It was like walking into the blast of a hairdryer. The air was hot and grainy and smelled of aviation oil.

He looked once again at the ZAKRON building. He hadn't seen it properly in the darkness of the previous evening. Now, its burnished metal skin was screaming sunshine. The windows were tiny, square, like airplane portholes. And behind, stretching into a silver-foil mirage, was the parched wasteland of the desert scrub, baked to bread by the sun. Not quite ten-thirty, yet the sun was already pumping enough heat to soften the tarmac.

He walked to the entrance and the doors snapped open, more aggressive than welcoming. He passed from furnace to fridge. The air temperature was about sixteen degrees.

The visitor reception area had been almost dark when he'd arrived on the previous evening. Now, it was lit by a row of halogen spots and looked like some sort of Philip Zervos creation. Spiked legged chairs and an oval chromium table that had been designed to represent the building itself. There was a water dispenser made of clear blue glass. Every few seconds a bubble emerged from the bottom and shimmied its way to the surface, creating a pond-like ripple.

He walked over to the reception desk and was greeted by the smile of a receptionist with perfect white teeth.

'Hello. Doctor Raven?' She extended a hand. 'Tammy's been telling us all about you.'

He smiled and gave the stock response. 'Good things I hope.'

She laughed. 'Yeah. She's been giving you a big sell.'

She looked up at the clock. 'You can go up straightaway. To the conference room. They're all there. Upstairs, fourth door on the right. And good luck now.'

Jack climbed the stairs and found himself in a long corridor lit with the same white spots. They were humming slightly, emitting a sound that clashed with the buzz of the air con. He made his way along the corridor and stood outside the room for a moment. He could hear Tammy's voice. She was talking about him to the team.

'He's smart. Calls himself an amateur expert. Very British. Guess some of it's self-taught. But a lot of it's just brains.'

He knocked on the open door and entered the room just as Tammy finished speaking. Eight pairs of eyes snapped towards him. He immediately sensed hostility. He'd had it once before, exactly like this, when the Pryce brothers went down for murder.

There was no doubting which one was Tom Lawyer. He was suspiciously tanned, like he spent too many hours under a sun lamp, and balding, though in denial. He was half-heartedly wearing a tie, a flag at half-mast. His suit was cut to look expensive.

'You must be Doctor Jack Raven. We've been hearing all about you.'

Jack sat down in the empty seat next to Tammy and looked around the room. Sterile as a corporate boardroom. An interactive whiteboard hung on one wall, a touch-screen unit on the other. There was a huge framed photograph of what seemed to be an abstract landscape of frosted hills and valleys. But when he looked at it more sharply he realised it was a highly magnified human cheek and eyebrow, dead and frozen to ice.

'I've been telling them how you saw Ferris Clark last night,' said Tammy.

Jack glanced across to the windows. Strange how the thick glass gave the sunlight a greenish hue that fell into the room as a dull block, like it was shining through water.

'Can't we cut the air con?' said Jennifer, the only one who seemed oblivious to Jack's presence. 'It's July, it's a heat-wave and I'm cold.' She folded her arms across her chest, tightening them for warmth.

Jack looked more closely at Tom. There was a contrived menace in the undone tie and the red face suggested high blood pressure. *A bit of a hard-ass.* That's what Tammy had said. He reckoned she'd got him just about right.

'So -' said Tom in more emollient tone. 'I guess you better meet -' He paused, looked round the room. 'Tammy you already know. Doctor Hunter King. He's my number two. Doctor Ryan Lee. Jennifer Jackson. Riley Young. Owen Green. Doctor Luke Gonzales. He's smart. And me -' he pointed to himself - 'Tom Lawyer. Doctor.'

Jack looked at them one by one and nodded. 'Good to meet you all. And great to see Ferris Clark last ni-'

'You bring quite a reputation,' said Tom, interrupting him. 'We've all been looking at your website. Mallory. And that iced up corpse in, where was it? Austria? Italy? Tammy tells us you're the best in the business.'

Jack smiled. 'She's over-selling me.'

Tom's eyes narrowed to a squint. He emitted a brief snort and leaned forwards in his chair, folding his arms on the desk in front of him like he had something important to say.

'Look,' he said, 'I have to tell you this straightaway, before we go any further. There's been a mix up. Worse. You've been brought here under false pretences. You see Tammy here -'

He paused for a moment, as if in search of the right words. And then he changed tack.

'There's nothing more to be discovered about our frozen

corpse. We've been through all the records. FBI too. If there was anything more to know about him we'd know it already. Fact is, we've found everything there is to find.'

There was a moment's silence before he continued. 'Real sorry you've been dragged all this way, but I don't want to waste your time any further.'

Jack looked to Tammy for an explanation, but she'd turned to face Tom and now had her back towards him.

'Hold on, hold on,' he said, not quite believing what Tom had just said. 'Let's get this straight. You're saying I've been asked to come all this way. And now – '

'It's like this,' said Tom, interrupting him again. 'ZAKRON's been tasked with finding out about Ferris Clark, checking the records, doing the tests. That's what we've been doing for the last four weeks. Not many places have got the sort of equipment we've got. And now we've reached the end of the road. We've found everything there is to find and the case will soon be closed, not by us but by the FBI.'

He tapped the desk with his pen. 'I've been away for a few days, see, and – ' he cleared his throat – 'Tammy here took it upon herself to get you over. Fact is, these sorts of decisions can only be taken by the board.'

There was a moment's pause, as if no one was sure what to say next.

'Has it been in the press?' Jack was looking directly at Tom. 'I checked the internet but there was nothing. Why's it not been in the papers? On TV? Twitter?'

Tom looked up sharply.

'Everything's taken place in confidence. No one knows about the discovery of the corpse. No one's been told what happened.'

'Why so secret? Who actually found the body?'

'The natural gas folk,' said Tom. 'Taking some sort of ice-core samples from the Greenland ice. And they were not - how do we put this? - drilling exactly where they were meant to be. And then, bang, they hit upon Ferris Clark. Stuck there in the ice, like he's slipped into a crevasse. Those folk called the FBI, the FBI called us. And then Hunter and I flew out there with Sergeant Perez.'

'What was the procedure? With the corpse, I mean? This sort of thing usually -'

Tom sighed heavily before explaining how Ferris Clark's corpse had come into their possession. The fact that he'd been found in Greenland, which ultimately fell under the jurisdiction of Denmark, had threatened to lead to red tape, bureaucracy, complications and bla, bla, bla, especially as the gas guys were drilling where they shouldn't have been. But Perez smoothed the way and managed to get the body brought to America.

'That's why it's had to be kept quiet,' said Hunter. 'The whole Denmark side of things could've caused problems. Wasn't in anyone's interest for the press to hear of it.'

'And that's also why these folk have all signed a confidentiality agreement,' said Tom. 'It's sensitive'

'I can see it's sensitive. These things always are, especially if they involve two countries. We had similar problems with Utzi. He was found smack on the border. Almost sparked a war between Austria and Italy. But surely in this case -'

Tom smiled, nodded. 'Glad you get it,' he said. 'And before you leave us, you'll have to sign the confidentiality agreement as well.'

'I'll sign. Of course I'll sign it. But -' he thought for a moment - 'Tammy said he was found with some sort of I.D. bracelet?'

'Yep,' said Tom, the impatience sounding in his voice. 'A medical one. Army regulation. Only had his initials, of course - F.C. - but enough to set us on the trail. It's gone to Washington now. FBI are keeping it.'

'And the DNA results? What about them?'

Tom Lawyer stared hard and cold. 'Corrupted. Tried three times. No clean result. Distorted by the ice. We'll try again, of course, but I'm not expecting much.'

'And Ferris Clark himself? *Naked?* In fifteen years in the

business that's got to rank as pretty much the most bizarre death I've come across. Suicide? Murder? Or just some sort of weird accident? What's your take on it?'

Hunter leaned back in his chair and smirked. 'Everyone gets their kicks somehow,' he said. 'A naturist at the ice cap. Takes balls.'

'Ferris Clark -' said Tom, cutting Hunter in mid-sentence. He sounded like he wanted to wrap the meeting up. 'Okay, here's what we know. Only child. Born North Carolina. Parents dead before the war. No family. No siblings. No children. Born in nineteen-seven. October. Makes him thirty-seven in nineteen-forty-four. Drafted in January. On paper, he got lucky. US Army Corps of Engineers, North Atlantic Division. Sent to Greenland in March. But not that lucky. He was dead in nine weeks.'

He let out a heavy sigh.

'Whole story's in the Vegas archives. Clear as day. Six get home alive. One snuffs it. That *one* just happened to be Ferris Clark. Six to one - not a bad ratio for World War Two.'

'I helped Tom put the stuff together,' said Hunter. 'And I've been involved in the searches. There's not much to add. Some people make noise in their life. Some people remain silent. Ferris Clark was probably as boring as fuck.'

'Who was assigned to the case?' asked Jack. 'When he was first found, I mean.'

Tom stared at him. 'What's that got to do with it?'

'Always good to know. Often affects the way things are handled.'

'It's like I said. FBI. Within hours. Special Agent Jon Perez. Washington's finest. Been on it since day one. And so have we.'

Tom sat back in his chair and visibly relaxed. He seemed more expansive.

'We were alerted to what happened within minutes. Speed was important and we'd dealt with Perez before, several times. FBI gets the call in the morning, we're on the case before lunch.'

'I see. And you flew out to -'

'*What* d'you see?' Tom's momentary good humour passed in a flash. He stared at Jack, irritated by all the questions.

'This Perez guy. He's still on the case?'

'Yeah. But it's like I said. The original investigation's all but closed.'

Another silence. Jack looked around the room. All of them except Tammy were staring at him.

'So what happens next?' he asked.

'What happens next?' Tom threw the question back into the room. 'He'll be transferred to Arlington. Military funeral. Big brass band. Stars and stripes on his coffin. That's when it goes public. There'll be some backstage diplomacy with the Danes. And then, hell, Ferris Clark's goin' to get quite a send-off. He'll be well looked after by the Arlington folks.'

Jack nodded. 'And when's all that due to happen?'

'Next week, the week after. Not sure just yet. Still waiting for the nod from Washington.'

He tapped his pencil on the table-top as if to announce that the meeting was at an end.

'Look,' he said, adopting a more sympathetic tone of voice. 'I'm real sorry you were dragged all the way here for nothing. Tammy here – '

He shot a look towards her. Jack also turned his head and saw that she was leaning back in her chair and giving Tom a detached stare. He had to hand it to her, she wasn't fazed by anything.

'We'll get you a new ticket. Sort you out. Reimburse you for expenses and for your time. You won't be out of pocket, that's a promise.'

He gave a smile that seemed to be genuine. 'Anything else we can do for you? I'd be happy to make it up. You've been brought a long way for a whole lot of nothing.'

Jack was silent for a moment, still wrestling with the unexpected turn of events. Of all the possible outcomes, this was the very last thing he'd been expecting.

'One thing,' he said, thinking aloud. 'Since I've been brought all this way.'

'Yep?'

'I'd like to check out the body. Examine it. An external autopsy. Purely professional curiosity, but it would mean the trip wasn't a complete waste of time.'

He caught a reflection of Tammy in the framed photograph on the wall opposite. She had a half-smile on her face.

'Deal,' said Tom. 'We can do that.' He looked across to Hunter. 'Yep. We can do that. Lab two. Can you arrange for Ferris Clark to be taken there? Three o'clock sharp. Luke, you can help.'

He turned back to Jack. 'You staying at Logan's Corner?'

Jack nodded.

'You should get out of Hanford. Nothing of any interest here. Take a day or two in Vegas. Have a little gamble while you're here.'

'Gave up gambling,' said Jack. 'Only gambling I do these days is on dead bodies.'

FIVE

J ack stepped out of the taxi and was blasted by the midday heat. Logan's Corner parking lot smelled of kerosene and a lone palm tree was spreading tyre-tracks of shade across the tarmac. Two vehicles were parked by the entrance, a blue Ford station wagon, all dents and chrome, and a Subaru Cruiser the size of a tank.

He pushed the glass door and stepped into air-freshener coolness. The lobby smelled of pine forest and the floor was drying in smears. A red fire extinguisher hung on the wall like a glazed doughnut. The only sound came from the TPS vending machine, clunking loudly as it automatically refilled itself with Sprite and Cherry Cola.

He made his way through to the dining area. There was a folksy cheerfulness to the decor, all wagon wheels and red-checked tablecloths, and Country music was spilling from the bar. *You've broken the speed of the sound of loneliness.* He knew that song. Nanci Griffiths. Why did country music always sound so melancholy?

'You just sit where you want sir. Any table takes your fancy.'

The cheery voice came from behind him, all rhythm and lilt. He turned round. The waitress wore a name badge, Destinee, and was carrying a large pitcher of iced tea.

'Want something to eat? We've got burgers, pizzas, fries, I'll get you the menu.'

He chose a table by the window that was covered in sunshine. Trucks on the interstate were vibrating through the floor and the tarmac outside was shimmering in the heat. Tom had said the examination of Ferris Clark's body would take place at 3pm. He checked his mobile. Three hours to kill.

'Here's the menu,' said Destinee.

He glanced down quickly. 'A pizza, thanks.'

'Texan Grill? Sicilian? Hot and Spicy? Boston Barbeque?'

'Texan Grill. And a Coke. Regular.'

She nodded, noted it down. 'And what brings you to Hanford?' she said, taking a bottle of Hunt's ketchup from the adjacent table and placing it on his. 'Business?'

She gave a desultory shrug then continued speaking before he had a chance to reply.

'What line of business? The air base? Most folks come for the air base. Or Sand Mountain. Biggest dune in the States, or so they say. But they're tourists of course.'

Jack nodded.

'Or, let me guess. ZAKRON. You're here for ZAKRON?'

He looked up sharply, but she said it with a smile so he took it with a smile.

'ZAKRON. You're right. D'you know the place?'

'Everyone knows ZAKRON. Don't want to be speakin' out of turn,' she said, leaning in towards him, 'but it freaks me somethin'.'

She played with the salt and pepper pots while she stood there, pushing the salt to the far side of the pepper and then the pepper to the far side of the salt.

'I mean why would anyone in sound mind want to be frozen? Freaks me, tellin' the truth.' She laughed. 'I'll be burnin' when I'm dead, and not in the flames of hell neither.'

She wandered back to the kitchen. 'Be right back with that Coke.'

Jack picked up his phone and checked the pictures he'd taken on the previous evening. They were better than he'd expected.

The face of the corpse was clearly in focus and he could even see the clear blue pupil of the left eye. He emailed them to his iPad and heard it ping as he took it from its case.

The events of the last few hours had been so bizarre that he was still trying to get his head round it. Tammy must surely have known the case was almost closed, so why the hell had she got him all the way to Hanford? And why was Tom Lawyer so anxious for him to leave? Every question spawned another two.

What surprised him most was his own reaction. Christ, by rights he ought to be furious at having been dragged all the way here for nothing. Twelve hours on the move, what with the change of planes, and a shed-load of hassle. Yet he couldn't help feeling the story wasn't yet over.

He looked back at the photos of Ferris Clark. Naked. And upside down. It had to be suicide. But, Jesus, what would drive you to take off all your clothes in the middle of Greenland?

Sven Erikson's diaries had shown that men could be tipped into madness by an Arctic winter. Four months in perpetual darkness and even hardened explorers start to crack. He'd also read about that solo yachtsman shipwrecked on Spitzbergen, Larsson, that was his name. They'd found him six months later, eyes glazed like marbles and a mind turned to slush. And he had been used to solitude.

Destinee lumbered back to his table with pizza in one hand and Coke in the other. Then she wandered off to serve a couple that had just sat down in the corner of the dining area.

Jack cut a thick wedge from the pizza and ate it with his fingers. His mobile buzzed into the table. *Welcome to Verizon: Voice-mail is available for collection by dialing 1-877-469-2144.* He saved the Verizon number into his contacts and then clicked onto his messages and read through the ones from Karin. There were seven in total - all more than a week old - and they stopped abruptly on July 17. *If you can't see it for what it was, a stupid mistake, then there's nothing more I can do. How sad to end like this. I'm flying back to Germany tomorrow.*

He hit the delete key and then flicked through her other messages and deleted them one by one. He was on the point of deleting her name from his contacts as well when a voice in his head stopped him. Not yet.

* * *

He cut another triangle of pizza then took out the map Tammy had given him on the previous evening. Greenland, featureless, abstract and blank, terra incognita, an entire country in two colours, blue and white. He glanced down at the scale and made a rough calculation in his head. It was eight hundred miles from coast to coast and a further 800 from north to south. That, at least, was the area covered by the map. That made 640,000 square miles of nothing.

He ran his finger up the coastline, looking at the names of the inlets and harbours. Bredefjord, Soranerbraeen, Skaerfjorden. And Miss Boyd's Land. *Miss Louisa Boyd.* He remembered, years back, reading about the expedition she had led up the north coast of Greenland in search of Amundsen.

He traced a line around a blue inlet of water until his finger had left the sea far behind and was travelling over the smooth expanse of ice-cap, heading south-east across the whiteness. Here, the map was a complete blank. There weren't even any names. His finger reached X, marked in red on the map. It was close to an inlet, three hundred miles from nowhere. Ferris Clark. A lonely place to die.

'Everythin' alright?' Destinee was speaking.

'Just what I needed.'

'Just shout if you want somethin' more.'

He finished the pizza and then drank off the Coke. He glanced at the time on his mobile. A quick power nap and then he'd head back to ZAKRON.

SIX

Carla, the receptionist, looked up from her computer screen as he entered the building.
'Doctor Raven, hello again.'
She started flicking through a pile of envelopes on the desk in front of her.

'Here, this one's for you,' she said as he walked towards her. 'Just printed it off.'

'For me?'

'Real sorry you're leaving us so soon. Thought you'd be here a week or so.'

Jack took the envelope. He immediately saw it was a plane ticket from Las Vegas to London. Departure 27 July, at 14.25. He glanced at his watch. That was in three days.

Carla noticed his frown. 'Anything wrong?'

'Who booked this?'

'I did. Tom - Doctor Lawyer - asked me to. Said I should get the first available flight. It's okay, isn't it?'

'Yes, yes. Just perfect. Did you cancel the old one?'

'Ah, no,' she said. 'D'you want me to?'

'Don't worry. I'll do it later.'

'Take a seat. Tammy said she'd be down in a minute. She's going to give you a quick tour.'

Tammy appeared right on cue, an apologetic expression written across her face. The top two buttons of her lab coat had come undone, revealing a slender neck. She led him to one side. 'Look I'm real sorry about everything,' she said. 'Don't even know what to say. I'm entirely to blame. All my idea. And I had no idea Tom would be so – '

'No problem,' said Jack with a smile. 'Really. Don't worry. I'm not even annoyed. And he's going to reimburse me for it all.'

'On top of everything else you must be wiped,' she said, still in her own train of thought. 'I get terrible jetlag, especially flying west.'

Jack pulled a box of Modafinil from his pocket. 'These help. And dead bodies always sharpen the mind.'

She led him down to the far end of the corridor where a door slid open automatically. It led into in a different laboratory from the one housing Ferris Clark. It was cold, only a few degrees above freezing, and lit with rows of halogen spots. The walls were lined with glass cabinets, all steel and glass, containing specialist medical equipment.

'Least I can do is give you a tour,' she said. 'Explain what we do. You haven't even seen what we're about.'

'I was hoping you'd show me round. I want to know how it works. Who chooses to come here?'

Tammy waved her hand around the lab, pointing to various items of equipment. Three Superheart defibrillators, two ventilators with dedicated anaesthetic machines, a set of pulse oximeters and a cupboard filled with nasogastric pipes. There was a sequential compression device and a biospectral index monitor. One of the cupboards was filled with aspiration tubes and suction pumps. The place was like a state-of-the-art intensive care unit.

Jack walked across to the bank of computers that lined the side wall. They were using the G6OXS system. Not many labs in England could afford that.

'And this, here, is ALP,' said Tammy, laying her hands on another computer the size of a small cupboard. It had a surface of brushed steel and two interactive panels, one at the front and one on the side.

'ALP?' he said.

'Latest acquisition. Only took delivery three weeks ago. It links all the equipment here - dialysis, defibs, sat monitors. Coordinates them all.'

She tapped a code into one of the panels then turned back to face him.

'Say something.'

'What d'you mean, say something? What shall I say?'

A light on the computer blinked and then an automated voice responded. *Voice not recognized. Request permission to start VRR.*

'VRR?'

'Voice Recognition Registration. Soon as he hears a new voice he starts processing it into his memory. Shouldn't do it now. Tom'll throw a fit. In fact -'

She paused.

'You won't tell Tom I've shown you this?'

Jack laughed. 'What's the problem? State secrets?'

Tammy stood in front of the computer, one hand resting on its shiny surface. 'Co-developed with Plaxon in California. Sacramento.'

'The pharmaceutical guys? You work with *them?*'

'Yep. There's a whole research wing there. And they've been working closely with this place. That's Tom's department. He got them on board and also got them helping with finance. The Plaxon guys are dead serious and mind-blowingly rich.'

Jack nodded slowly. The equipment in front of him outclassed anything he'd ever seen in England.

'So how does it work?' he asked. 'With the bodies, I mean?'

'We call them clients.'

'Fine, clients. Whatever. How does it work?'

She paused for a moment before answering. And then she began speaking like an official guide. 'Cryonics has always been more about hope than reality. Hope that technology will develop, solutions found. That's why people choose it. And it's also why they choose ZAKRON.

'Cancer patients, leukaemia, terminal illnesses, they're the ones we usually get. They're desperate, often young. They don't want to die.

'We took a girl just last month. Twenty-six. Terminal cancer. Real sad it was. She didn't want to let go. Died praying that one day we'd bring her back from the deep freeze.'

'They die *here*? In this lab?' Jack's voice betrayed his surprise.

'Yeah. We aim to have them die here, if possible. There's a team on stand-by when they're close to the end. Even the coroner's here. We have to get death certified immediately, see. Sounds crazy, but that's how it is. There's a huge legal side to all of this.

'Once it's all been signed we can start injecting them with the cryo-protectant.'

'That's this?' said Jack, pointing to one of the refrigerated cabinets.

Tammy nodded. 'Yep. It's what stops the cells, tissue, the internal organs being damaged by the liquid nitrogen. And that's –'

She paused for a moment.

'And that's what's so strange about Ferris Clark. He was never injected. Never preserved. Never given anything. Yet his internal organs are just perfect, like you saw from the scans.'

She led him into the lab next door, a larger space that housed four containers made of greenish, low emissivity glass.

'Once they're legally dead, injected, we cool them down to one-hundred-and-thirty below.'

She walked over to a gleaming aluminium tube, eight feet in length and marked with the code A-3491. Her body was reflected in the metal, only elongated into a slim band.

'Soon as they're frozen, bang, they go in one of these. It's sealed and the whole unit gets immersed in liquid nitrogen. Minus one-hundred-and-ninety-six. Their new home. Once they're here they're safe forever. As long as ZAKRON exists, they will too.'

Jack listened carefully to what she was saying. In effect they were putting death on hold, preserving corpses in the final second of life when their heart had just beat its last. If they hadn't elected for the cyro-protectant, the hours that followed would see them tipped into rigor mortis. But they'd been cryonically frozen before that could happen.

Tammy looked sharply at her watch. 'Almost three. Better get back to reception. Remember what I said? You haven't seen any of this. And by the way, Tom told me he's only giving you fifteen minutes with Ferris Clark.'

'Thought it was thirty. Why only fifteen?'

'He's changed his mind. Something he's in a habit of doing. You're lucky he didn't cancel it completely.'

* * *

Tammy led him back to the entrance area. 'Back in a moment,' she said, heading off to the washroom. 'Tom, Hunter, they're just getting the body ready. They'll be out in a moment.'

Jack took a seat by the water machine and watched the slow stream of bubbles rising to the surface. He'd performed more autopsies than he cared to remember yet each time it was different. The only constant was that sense of stepping into the unknown, a benign intruder in the final moments of a person's life.

In his lectures, he always began with the words written above the door of every autopsy theatre. *Hic locus est ubi mors gaudet succerere vitae.* This is the place where death delights in helping the living. They gave dignity to the corpse on the slab, even if it was five or six weeks dead.

He remembered when he'd first tried to explain it to Karin,

but she hadn't got it at all. 'Seriously Jack, it's just morbid,' she'd said. 'You're obsessed with everything morbid.'

Hunter was the first one to appear in the entrance area, speaking loudly into his phone. He was too preoccupied to acknowledge Jack. Next to arrive was Doctor Luke Gonzales, dressed in an immaculately ironed lab-coat.

'Afternoon, Doctor Raven.' His voice had no intonation. He sounded like the computer in the lab.

Tammy stepped back into the entrance area and took a seat next to Jack.

'All prepared?' she said in a low voice. 'I really hope you find something. It'll go some way to making up for me dragging you here. I feel really – '

Tom Lawyer was the last to arrive. He'd left his lab-coat undone, exposing a chest that had been waxed. He avoided eye contact with everyone except Hunter and spoke briskly and sparsely. He wanted to get the whole thing wrapped up as fast as possible.

'So –'

He swept them out of the waiting area in great strides, forcing them all to play catch-up behind him. 'You know the procedure. We'll go straight through to decontamination. We'll be seen by Jackie.'

He turned to face Jack.

'Jackie's the lab nurse.'

Jack nodded.

'I hardly need remind everyone that he's been moved from one sterile environment to another. No bacteria, no viruses. This examination is purely for Doctor Raven's benefit and – ' he turned to address Jack – 'hope you don't mind if we keep it short. We've got a busy day, but at least you'll have seen him before you leave.'

He paused for a second.

'Did Carla get you the plane tickets?'

'Yes, she gave them to me just now.'

'She tried to get you on an earlier plane but that was the first one with seats.'

* * *

The smell was the first thing to hit you. The dense, wet, sweet smell of putrefaction. Or phenol, swilled over surfaces and floors. Or hypochlorite, acrid, ammoniac, that went smack to the eyes. But here, with Ferris Clark, there was nothing. Only a block of freezing air that cut him as he entered the lab. The room was close to zero. The thermometer showed the air temperature to be hovering at a fraction above four degrees. He could feel the sting in his nostrils.

The body had been taken out of the vitrification box and now lay there on a specialist gurney chilled to well below freezing. He was outstretched, naked, a frozen block of a uniform colour that was not quite human flesh. His hair seemed blonder and thicker than when Jack had seen him in the glass container.

Hair can keep growing after death. Elizabeth Siddal came up at every lecture. Coffin full of hair when Rossetti dug her up. But Ferris Clark's hair had not grown at all. In places it had frozen into a tangle, like ice-cold wire wool, but at the sides it was unmistakably the cut of a 1940's soldier. Regulation. Trimmed just days before he died.

Six wires were attached to his chest with blue silicon suction pads. They linked him to one of the computer systems. The other three were wired to a vitrification machine. The computer panel was constantly flashing with readings and information.

Jack took a couple of paces back from the body and did what he always did, pausing to take an overview. This was usually the point when the stench really hit, lurching your breakfast to your throat. But not this time.

His eyes made a complete tour of the body: chest, hips, groin, legs, arms. The knees. Fingers and toes. Then he turned back to the head. It was important to study the form. The muscle structure, the bones. And also the skin. The skin held many clues, if only you knew what you were looking for. Lacerations. Bruises. Had pressure been applied to the throat? Had he been involved in a fight?'

Tom entered the laboratory a few seconds after Jack.

'We'll do two five minute shifts. And five minutes to warm up in between.'

The others entered the lab soon after, Hunter first, then Tammy and Doctor Gonzales.

The most disturbing aspect of Ferris Clark was his left eye. Jack had noticed it before. But now, close up, he could see that the retina was glassy from the cold but very far from dead.

No lesions, no creases in the skin. The ice had smoothed away the body hair, like he'd been put through a full Brazilian. No perfusions, abrasions or grazes. In fact no surface blemish of any kind.

He studied the epidermis of the chest and limbs. Also beautifully smooth. No birthmarks. No moles. Unusual but not uncommon. Slightly enlarged thyroid cartilage, but nothing untoward. His right ear was glued to his head with a small sliver of ice.

He looked at the groin and scrotum. It had tightened in on itself and the testicles had withdrawn inside the body, a natural reaction caused by the shock of the cold. Penis curled and half hidden but clearly uncircumcised.

He examined the feet and hands, ankles and wrists. There was abrasion around the ankles, perhaps surface bruising, but the severe cold had acted like an eraser, wiping away any damage to the epidermis. Light bruises to the upper chest, but neither significant nor serious. The sort of bruising you might get from a fall from skis.

'Need to measure him.'

Doctor Gonzales held the sterile measuring-line fast against

Ferris Clark's head while Jack took the reading at the feet. Six foot, one inch. Chest: 38 inches. Upper leg: 17 inches. Lower leg: 19 inches.

Hunter was bored. He took the smaller ruler and placed it alongside Ferris Clark's penis. The organ was snared with ice and half-tucked into his groin, like a letter stuck in an envelope. 'Seven inches.' He laughed and looked at Tammy. 'What d'you reckon?'

'We're in a lab, Hunter.'

Jack wasn't listening. He moved round to the head, examining it closely. A small patch of right eyebrow was missing, a few eyelashes lost to the ice. A light stubble, like fine sand stuck to the face. He was beautifully intact, like an Albrecht Dürer, the Christ with golden hair.

An experienced eye can read the moment of death. The Simlett murder had been one of the worst. Her jaw had been stuck rigid at the point of death, leaving a twisted grimace on her face. He'd never seen that before. But the only expression on Ferris Clark was a blank. No pain. No suffering. No trace of the acute hypothermia he must have experienced. He gave the appearance of having been in control of every last part of himself until the very last second. Tammy was right about one thing. It was as if he'd been tipped into a vat of liquid nitrogen.

He asked her for some lube, ignoring Hunter's low snigger. He rubbed it onto his surgical gloves to stop them from sticking to Ferris Clark's skin. Then he cupped his hands together and placed them carefully under the back of the skull, feeling for the parietal bone. The cold stabbed through his gloves. He gave himself fifteen seconds to feel his way around the skull.

Frontal bone. Occipital bone. And then the side. Zygomatic arch, frontonasal structure. Beautiful.

Tom glanced at the clock. 'Five's already up. Let's go. Five minute break. Then back in.'

'One minute.' Jack looked up from the corpse. 'I'll join you -'

He moved to the side of Ferris Clark's body as the others

chattered their way out of the lab. He could hear Hunter's distant joking as they warmed themselves up in the adjoining room.

He wanted a clearer look at the ribcage, examine the muscle structure. There were clues to be found in muscle structure. As he bent downwards to take a closer look he was suddenly brought up short. Ferris Clark's left arm was glued to his body with ice and the skin was powdered with frost, but there was a strange skin blemish close to the armpit, almost concealed. So faint he almost missed it.

He rubbed at the flesh and an icy dust fell from the corpse like a shower of dandruff. It settled on the gurney and stuck to its frozen surface. He rubbed again, only harder, in an attempt to expose the pallid skin beneath. Then he wedged his fingers between Ferris Clark's arm and his side. For a second they were glued to the cold flesh. And then he leaned in to enable him to examine it more closely.

It looked like a small birthmark, bluish, oval-shaped, the size of a thumb-print. The pressure of the ice had nipped the muscle into the armpit and rendered it almost invisible. He tried to measure it, but it was hard to get an accurate reading. Approximately four-and-a-half centimeters from the left nipple.

There are two types of birthmark, pigmented and vascular. Pigmented, because there's too much pigment. That's what causes dermal melanocytosis and moles. Vascular, because there's too much blood. That's what causes port-wine stains. All benign and rarely hereditary.

He studied it more closely. It looked like dermal melanocytosis. Certainly that's what the colour suggested. Blue-grey on the outside and darker towards the middle. But it couldn't be. Dermal melanocytosis, Mongolian spots, were rarely found on white Caucasians. And they almost always faded at puberty.

The only other possibility was a port-wine stain. Nevus flammens. He was thinking back through the other cases he had seen. They were extremely rare under the armpit and always irregular.

Ferris Clark's was perfectly rounded at the top. He rubbed the skin once again in the hope of examining it more closely. But the birthmark was faded with cold.

There was the breezy sound of laughter as the others came back into the lab. Tom looked impatient to call it a day.

'Five more minutes and then it's a wrap.'

'Just want to check the leg muscles,' said Jack. 'Then I'm done.'

He looked over the calves and thighs and then examined the knee-caps. Then he stood back from the corpse and made a sign that he'd finished.

'Anything,' said Tom as he snapped off his gloves.

Jack shook his head.

'It's curious. Nothing.'

'Suicide,' said Tom, less as a question than a statement of fact.

SEVEN

Tammy invited Jack back to her office as soon as the autopsy was over.

'Coffee?'

She left the room for a moment in order to get the drinks from the machine at the end of the corridor. He got up and walked over to the window. The view outside was a picture sliced in two. Top half, a slab of bright blue. Bottom half, the first hills of the scrub, filtered greenish-brown by the window. It hadn't rained for ten weeks, or that's what everyone kept saying. It was unlikely to rain for another ten.

He switched his gaze back to Tammy's desk. It was as if she'd turned her handbag upside down and tipped out the entire contents. Bobbi Brown lipstick and a Cartier Diabolo pencil. A packet of cough sweets, a credit card and lip balm. There was an envelope with a letter half-sticking out. He checked she wasn't coming before turning it over. *Tammy Fox, 14 Golden Park Drive, Hanford Gap.* So that's where she lived. With husband? She hadn't mentioned one. He was about to pull the letter from the envelope when he heard her coming back down the corridor. He quickly placed it back on the desk.

'They yours?' He pointed to the photo of a young boy and girl as she re-entered the room. It stood on her desk in a clear plastic frame.

'Yeah.' She looked at the picture and smiled. 'Fran. And Elsie.

Five and three. Sweet. But big trouble.'

He picked up the picture, looked at it more closely. 'They got mum's looks alright. He's got your eyes. And she's got your nose. Unmistakably.'

'Thanks!' she said. 'I'll take it as a compliment. And you? Any little Jack Ravens running around, helping you track down dead bodies?'

He shook his head.

Tammy sat down and placed the two mugs of coffee on laminated mats. Then she picked up a glass of water and poured it very slowly into the flowering orchid on her desk. The flowers were pink, great bell-shaped blooms flecked with yellow stripes.

'So,' she said, 'what did you make of the corpse? Any clues? Didn't want to ask while Tom was still there.'

'Amazing,' he said. 'And strange. Only confirms what I said last night. Really, I've never seen anything like it.'

'But what happened to him? How the hell did he end up like that in the ice?'

Jack shook his head. 'No obvious signs of bruising. No abrasions, no cuts. No sign he was involved in a struggle. Bruises were the first thing I was looking for. Even after years in the ice you'd expect some sort of marks.'

She frowned slightly as he spoke.

'He's got a strange birthmark. Under here – ' He pointed to his armpit. 'Couldn't get close enough to see what it was. Never seen one like that.'

'But that's not what – '

He smiled. 'No. Just my curiosity. It's pretty unusual to see one so regular.'

There was a pause.

'He must have somehow flash-frozen. It's the only possible explanation for the state of his body. But even so – '

He leaned forwards to reach for his coffee. As he did so, the envelope in his jacket pocket slipped out and dropped to the floor. He bent down to pick it up, then pushed it more securely into his pocket.

'My new ticket home,' he explained. 'Carla – is that her name? – she gave it me earlier. Christ, she seems efficient.'

'But you're not going? Not right away?'

Jack shot her a look. *What did she mean?* She'd been at the meeting when Tom had spelled it out. He could hardly have been clearer.

'Of course I'm going.'

'But –'

She turned to face him. 'Can't you stay on a few days? When's your new flight?'

He looked at her again, only this time more sharply. Had he missed something?

'But you were there this morning,' he said. 'You heard everything. I can't do anything more without Tom's go-ahead. I can't get involved unless Tom wants me to. And to be honest, until I got here last night I had no idea it wasn't an official invitation.'

'But –'

She interrupted him for a second time, but broke off before saying anything more.

Jack stared at her.

'Look,' he said. 'Tom's made it pretty clear he's expecting me to leave. And unless he has a dramatic change of mind in the next twenty-four hours I'm not sure what else I can do.'

He paused for a moment, changed his tone. 'I agree with everything you've said. It's one hell of a strange case. I've never seen a body so well-preserved. And I've no idea how he could have frozen without the blood cells getting ruptured. That's the weirdest thing of all.'

'But *how* did he die?'

Jack looked at her and slowly shook his head.

'Beats me. But like I said, there's nothing I can do unless I'm officially employed by Tom Lawyer and the board.'

He glanced at her and saw a change come over her face. She looked deflated.

There was a moment's silence that she filled by pushing back her chair and walking over to the door. She closed it firmly and then turned back towards him.

'Can we meet later?' she said in a low voice. 'At your hotel. I'll come to Logan's Corner. Six o'clock. There's something you urgently need to know.'

EIGHT

J ack went down to the bar in Logan's Corner just before six. There was no one else there apart from the barmaid. She was wearing a name badge, Scarlett.

'Yessir, as in O'Hara.'

He sat at one of the tables in the corner and glanced at the plasma television that was suspended from the ceiling. Boston Red Sox had just scored against the Miami Marlins. He read the text travelling across the bottom of the screen. 'Breaking News - Wal-Mart Stores Inc. pleads not-guilty to dumping hazardous waste in Florida.'

Why was Tammy so keen to see him? *There's something you urgently need to know.* He doubted it. A proper apology before he left, that was it. She felt bad about everything that had happened.

He ordered a Kaliber then picked up his phone and looked at the time. Exactly six o'clock. Tammy appeared right on cue. She looked flustered, as if she had hurried in from the car. She was dressed in jeans, ironed white shirt and cowboy boots. It was the first time he had seen her not in a lab coat.

'Not late, am I?'

Jack shook his head. 'Not at all. I was early, in fact. What d'you want to drink?'

'Should be on me really. What are you drinking?'

'Oh don't have this stuff. It's disgusting.'

'Then why are you drinking it?'

'Alcohol free,' he said. 'Better that way.'

'Ah. I need something a whole lot stronger.'

She ordered a gin and tonic then took off her sunglasses and sat down, looking round to check there was no one else in the bar.

'You've got me intrigued,' he said, filling the silence that followed. 'What's so urgent?'

He was expecting a smile, but she only frowned.

'Tom'll skin me alive if he ever finds out,' she said, glancing behind her to check that the waitress was out of earshot. 'In fact he'll kick me out and make sure I never work again.'

'What the hell is it?' said Jack. 'Don't keep me hanging on too long. The suspense will kill me.'

'Ferris Clark,' she said, speaking so quietly that he had to lean in to hear what she was saying. 'Can't you see? They're using him as a human guinea pig. They've been planning it all along. There's been a breakthrough in technology, a major one, just in the last few weeks. They want to bring him back to life.'

Silence. The only sound was music coming from the bar.

'That's why they're desperate to get rid of you. And it's why they're so mad at me.'

Jack looked at her but didn't say a word. He was struck, most of all, by the fact that he wasn't even surprised by what she'd just said. In a weird sort of way everything suddenly fell into place. He'd never seen such well-equipped labs as those at ZAKRON. And he also remembered noticing the sign hanging outside the autopsy room. It wasn't the usual Latin one. Rather, it was the ZAKRON company logo. *Turning Death Into Life.* And now they were hoping to make it more than a hollow promise.

'Wow.'

He looked directly at her.

'But how? When? They serious?'

'Deadly. Remember how I told you they'd been working with Plaxon? Developing new technology. Undertaking all sorts of research.'

Jack nodded. 'What sort of research?'

'Experiments on mice, blood, transplants, organs, that sort of thing.'

She was still speaking in a low voice, only faster now.

'Began with a kidney. They removed it from a mouse, injected it with cryo-protectant, froze it. And then surgically reinserted it.'

'And it worked?'

'Perfectly. They've done other organs too. Liver. Lungs. Luke's been in charge of it all. Doctor Gonzales. He's the brains, not Tom.'

As Jack listened he was trying to recall his conversation with Professor Reiter in Innsbruck. They'd spoken about transplanting organs, frozen eggs and sperm, about the cutting edge research taking place in America. But Reiter had said it would be another generation, perhaps more, before reverse cryonics would be anything other than science fantasy. Another generation to develop the drugs, the technology, the equipment.

'Remember the cabinets I showed you? The ones filled with phials?'

'In the lab?'

She nodded. 'That's been the breakthrough. They've created this stuff called dioximyde. Plaxon developed it. And it's changed everything. Tom calls it the miracle drug.'

'What does it do?'

'I don't know the science behind it,' she said, 'but it sends vast quantities of oxygen through the blood. At high speed. It's dioximyde that's enabled Luke to do all the transplants. And it's what they're intending to use on Ferris Clark.'

Blood. That was another thing Professor Reiter had said. Until science found the means to get oxygen back into the organs – and fast – then resuscitating a cryonically-preserved body would be biologically impossible.

'*Jack –*'

She spoke sharply, interrupting his thoughts. Then she looked him coldly in the eye.

'They've got to be stopped. They've absolutely got to be stopped. Surely you can see? Ferris Clark may be brain damaged, he may have been murdered. Jesus, the poor guy might even have killed himself. We still don't have any clue as to how he died. In fact we hardly know the first thing about him.'

She stopped talking for a moment and took a gulp of gin and tonic. When Jack failed to respond she carried on talking.

'The clients at ZAKRON, the ones we've got stored on ice, they chose it, they wanted to be frozen. They're hoping one day in the future we might be able to wake them. And they're protected by more laws than the Constitution. There's even laws dictating how they're looked after.

'But Ferris Clark, he didn't choose to be preserved. And he certainly didn't choose to be a guinea pig in some hokey scientific experiment. I hate it.'

She looked at him again, as if to gauge his reaction.

'ZAKRON was founded by grand-daddy. My dad was its president. Back in those days the company slogan was Death with Hope. How times have changed. Now it's in the hands of a gangster. And if any of this becomes public knowledge it'll be the end of ZAKRON. They'll shut it down.'

'*But –* '

Jack held up his hand to stop her. He was thinking through what she'd said.

'But - it's - amazing. Can't you see? Surely you can see? They've got the most perfectly preserved corpse. They've clearly got the technology, Christ, I've never seen such well equipped labs. And now they've got this dioximyde stuff. Tammy, they might actually succeed.'

'I know they might actually succeed. And that's what scares the living shit out of me. It's unethical. It's immoral. It's illegal. And it's just plain wrong. Poor Ferris Clark. Just imagine –'

'Stop, stop, stop. Hold it a minute, Tammy.'

There was excitement in his voice and his hands were trembling as he spoke.

'Think of the bigger picture. Imagine what it would mean if they're successful. Think about all the people who could be saved. All the people who died young, whose lives were cut short. From now on that could all be a thing of the past. Just think of that young girl you were telling me about yesterday. She could have died knowing that as soon as they'd found a cure for her cancer she'd be resurrected and cured. If they succeed with Ferris Clark, Tammy, it changes everything. Absolutely everything. Human life will never be the same again.'

'But – no - - *NO* - - !'

She looked at him aghast.

'But Jack, there's bigger issues at stake. You can't just resurrect someone cos you've decided to.'

'Yes but come on, surely you can see? You've got young kids. What if it was you falling sick? You that was dying? Your children left without their mum. Come on. If you had a chance to come back, you'd take it. Think of all those children left without their mothers. Think of all the young people who died too soon. Alice was only thirty-two – '

'*Alice* - ?'

'My wife. Alice was my wife. Cancer. Diagnosed in May, dead within six months. Have you ever gone through anything like that? Ever lived through such a nightmare? I'd have done anything, Tammy, anything in the world, if there'd been any chance to get her back. She was young. Beautiful. And then she was gone forever.'

He fell silent for a moment, swallowing hard. The emotion had got him in the throat.

Tammy was completely lost for words. This was one outcome she was not expecting at all.

'I got you here to stop it,' she said. 'And now you're saying you're on their side.'

'I agree that Ferris Clark didn't choose to be a guinea pig.

Of course he didn't. But this isn't about Ferris Clark. It's far, far bigger. It's about the future of life and death.'

'So you support them?'

'*Support them*? I wouldn't miss it for the world.'

He turned to face her with intense eyes.

'Look, I agree we need to find out who he is. Urgently. That's the priority. Even if they're successful in reviving him, there's a very real chance he'll have forgotten who he is, how he came to be in the ice. His memory might have been wiped. You're right in one respect. He'll need all the help he can get.'

'*But* - ?' Tammy slowly shook her head. She couldn't quite believe what she was hearing.

'I'm sorry, Tammy, but I'm with them all the way. One hundred per cent. If I'd known what they were doing, Christ, I'd have come weeks ago. It's like I've been waiting all my life for this.'

He paused for a moment.

'Look, I agree we need to tread with care. Tom and the others, they couldn't have said more clearly that they don't want me here. The last thing I want to do is land you in trouble. It's better they don't know I'm staying on. If they find out it'll only get you in even deeper shit.'

He felt inside his jacket pocket and pulled out the airplane ticket. 'And although they've bought me *this*, they didn't cancel my old one.'

Tammy picked up her glass and drained it, then wiped off the lipstick with a tissue and placed it carefully back on the table. She was lost for words.

'One other thing,' said Jack. 'When does it all start? How long have we got?'

Tammy frowned. 'Originally it was set for two weeks. Then it was eight days. But last night I heard they want to kick off in four days.'

'Four days.'

Jack tapped the desk with his pen. He felt suddenly exhilarated.

'When I was on Everest I had less than an hour. And it was minus twenty. And I was dangling off the end of a rope. Yet I still discovered exactly how Mallory died.'

He smiled. 'Four days sounds like luxury.'

PART TWO

NINE

J ack spent much of the following morning at Logan's Corner
working out a plan of action. Tom Lawyer was expecting him
to leave for Las Vegas within the next twenty-four hours.
Remaining in Hanford meant changing hotels and finding
somewhere discreet to stay. He'd ask Tammy for suggestions.

He still couldn't quite get his head around why she was so
against the experiment on Ferris Clark. She'd said it was unethical. So was euthanasia, yet plenty of people did that without any
scruples. And this was the very opposite of euthanasia. It was
about life, not death.

He turned to the file that she'd given him on the previous
evening. It was filled with print-outs, photographs and scans, all
relating to various aspects of Ferris Clark's body. He first looked
through the segment scans of the heart, liver and kidneys, then
re-checked the X-rays of the spine, paying particular attention
to the uppermost vertebrae. If Ferris Clark had fallen headfirst
into a crevasse, he'd have expected to see impact damage to the
neck, the shoulders and the collar-bone. But there was none.

He turned to the X-rays and tomographic scans of the
skull and brain. There were six in the file, yet none revealed any
imperfections whatsoever. The most plausible explanation for
the lack of internal damage was that Ferris Clark had fallen into
water. Tammy had said he'd been found entombed in clear ice.
That suggested water had frozen around him, something that

could only happen in a glacial crevasse.

Minus forty-seven was the lowest temperature ever recorded inside a crevasse, he knew that from the Forni case. Water wells up from the depths of the glacier but is prevented from freezing by the pressurized currents far below. Fall into water that cold and you're in big trouble. Hypothermic shock as your head tips under. Hyperventilation as you resurface, your heart pumping in your throat. A dramatic loss of dexterity and your brain jack-knifing out of control as you're plunged through intense physiological stress. How long would it take to die? Two minutes, maybe three? You'd be unlikely to survive any longer.

During one of their Everest training weekends, Steve had fallen into a glacial crevasse. He'd later told them how he'd been jerked upside down, wedged between the icy jaws. 'Mind-shit cold.' Each time he had tried to extricate himself, he'd slipped deeper inside.

They hadn't heard his cries at first. Ice deadens the sound of screaming. He had been lucky to escape with a broken rib.

Jack reached for the beige envelope inside the file and pulled out the scans of Ferris Clark's lungs. They contained no water. At least, they contained no water that had later frozen. And that strongly suggested that he was dead *before* he hit the water. He had not asphyxiated from drowning.

The Mallory business had shown him it was possible to reconstruct the final moments of someone's life with considerable precision. A dislocated elbow, a frayed rope, a shattered rib: bone by broken bone he had mapped out the 1924 disaster. Mallory had slipped in the darkness and spun into the rock-face. The rope had snapped and he'd fallen on his leg. He'd slid down the scree, shredding his skin. Dead in less than five minutes.

He flicked through the other scans, paying particular attention to the magnified prints of the blood cells. Tammy was right. They were perfect. So perfect, in fact, that they looked like they'd been preserved with cryo-protectant.

He recalled a paper he'd read about the Arctic frog. It had

developed a unique system to protect itself in winter, storing masses of glucose in its liver. When the temperature dipped below freezing it released the stuff back into its body. It stopped breathing, its blood stopped flowing and its legs froze solid. But the core cells were protected by the glucose, like antifreeze in a car. And when spring came round, its organs would kick-start themselves into action.

He sat back in his chair, deep in thought. Even if something similar had happened to Ferris Clark – somehow - his body would still have had to flash-freeze, and that was impossible without liquid nitrogen.

He switched on his iPad and checked through the notes he had made after the autopsy. Clark's body mass was not far short of ninety kilograms. His core temperature at the time of death would have been around thirty-six degrees. And his body would have contained a minimum of fifty-five kilograms of liquid.

He stopped typing for a moment. Fifty-five kilos of liquid doesn't freeze in an instant. In fact – he jotted down some more figures - Ferris Clark would have had to shed 8,500 kilojoules of heat energy for his blood to drop to minus two Celsius, the temperature at which it would start to freeze. It would have taken a minimum of seven hours for him to freeze solid.

* * *

The more he looked through the information, the more he realised that Tom Lawyer had only ever viewed the Ferris Clark case through the eyes of a scientist, as a set of neuro-reports and thermo-optic scans. There was nothing in the file about Ferris Clark's life and very little about his weeks in Greenland.

Tom had said he was a conscript, drafted into the US Army Corps of Engineers. *Drafted in January. Sent to Greenland in March.* That meant he'd received just two months training, very little for someone being sent into such harsh terrain.

Jack opened a new file on his iPad and began noting down possible lines of enquiry.

- Ferris Clark's army conscription record.

- US Army archives.

- Medical certificate
  (unlikely to be in the public domain).

- Birth certificate.

- Local county records.

- The 1940 census.

He felt sure that if he was ever going to discover the truth of how Ferris Clark died, then he needed to know how Ferris Clark lived. Who was Ferris Clark?

'Not exactly the Eastern Front.' That's what Tom had said about the war in the Arctic. Yet it had clearly been important enough to warrant an American base served by a rotating group of conscripts.

Jack turned back to his iPad and clicked onto Google, typing 'greenland, 2ww, american base.' The information appeared on screen immediately. The base had been operational for almost three years and situated at a place called Cape Hvitfeldt.

Cape Hvitfeldt. He searched for it on Google Earth. It was on the exposed south east coast of Greenland, a bullet-shaped peninsula some three miles in length that pointed due east into the ocean. So that was Ferris Clark's home for the final few weeks of his life.

He zoomed closer onto the map. There was a long inlet to the north of the peninsula, not much wider than a football pitch, and another, twice as long, to the south. The base itself, which had been known as Camp Eggen, was situated at the very tip.

Jack changed to an image map and zoomed in so close that the picture was reduced to a blur. He could just about make out an embracing cliff that looked to be some twenty metres in height. That must have been why it was chosen, as a natural buffer against the Arctic wind.

He typed in Camp Eggen and found a few more references. Established by the Americans in early 1943, the year of Soviet victory at Stalingrad. Jack counted up the months. That meant it had been operational for almost a year by the time Ferris Clark pitched up.

> Camp Eggen never served as anything more than a refuelling depot. Planes and sea-going cargo vessels broke their journey here before continuing across the Atlantic. It was at its busiest in the summer of 1943 and the spring of 1944, when as many as twenty planes landed here each day, most of them Douglas Skytrains and Curtiss Commandoes.

The website suggested it was nothing more than a temporary wartime base: a few metal huts and a petrol station in the snow. There were storehouses, living quarters and vast petrol tanks. Camp Eggen was essentially a refuelling stop for planes on route to Iceland, Scotland and the north of England.

Yet the importance of the place was clear simply by looking at its position on the map. And Camp Eggen had started to receive regular visits from destroyers, cargo ships and planes within weeks of being established. This landing strip in the snow was their lifeline.

Not exactly the Eastern Front. But Jack had enough experience of working in sub-zero temperatures to know that it would have been no picnic either. The summer months would have been bearable. Ferris Clark and his comrades would have been able to supplement their supplies by plucking lobsters and shellfish from the rock-pools. Southeast Greenland had a mean June temperature of thirteen degrees. They might even have grown vegetables in the more sheltered spots of land.

But the rest of the year would have tested their endurance to the limit. The climate spoke for itself. Far below freezing, even in spring. The highest precipitation in Greenland. And at that latitude, Camp Eggen must have been in darkness from November to February. Daylight would have been gradually returning by the time Ferris Clark pitched up in March. But even so, acclimatizing to the isolation would have tested the mettle of even the sanest person.

Did they drink? Fight? And who was the group leader? In the Antarctic polar research stations, leadership had always been of paramount importance. Minor grouches could lead to tensions. Tensions could lead to hostility. And hostility could - perhaps - lead to murder.

* * *

There was a knock on the door.

'Come in.'

The door opened slowly with the clatter of a tray against the handle.

'Room service.'

It had taken so long that Jack had forgotten he had ordered it. The waitress entered all smiles. Her red and white apron made her look like she'd just stepped out of a TV soap. She placed the tray on the table by the door.

'Here you go, Club sandwich and Coke.'

The sandwich was cut into a neat triangle and pinned together with a blue-parasol cocktail stick. It sat on a sea of crisps, which gave it the air of a shipwrecked yacht. The bottle of Coke, still frosted, lay on its side next to the plate.

'Stayin' long?' she asked with a friendly smile.

Jack shook his head. 'Nope. Flying visit. I'm off tomorrow.'

'You're from England.' She said it as fact, rather than a question.

'Yes.'

'Don't get many from England. ZAKRON isn't it? I was talking about it with Destinee. She was on shift yesterday, at lunchtime. She doesn't like the idea but I think it's cool. Cryonics, that's what they call it. Just imagine, you get woken up a hundred years from now and find yourself in a whole new world.'

'Could be confusing,' said Jack.

'Yeah, well, cars that fly, robots doin' the cleaning. No sickness. That'd be the best. But you'd have no friends, I guess.'

She smiled, glanced at the tip he'd given her and thanked him.

'Anything else – ?'

She left the room, closing the door behind her.

Jack got up, picked up the tray and placed it on the desk next to the window. Then he looked blankly into the room. It was so functional that there weren't even any pictures on the walls. One double bed, one laminate desk and a TV and DVD player. That's what you got for sixty-two dollars a night in Hanford Gap, Nevada.

Karin would have hated it.

* * *

He snapped the lid off the Coke and took a swig, wincing slightly as the ice-cold liquid hit a nerve on his tooth. He ate one half of the Club sandwich, wiped his hands on the paper napkin and then turned back to his iPad and ran an image search on

Cape Eggen.

A dozen or so photographs of the base flashed onto the screen, along with a dozen more of glamour girl Vicki Eggen from Vegas, topless and with her legs wrapped round a pole. 'Glamour girl Vicki bares all.' She was goofy, permed and looked like she was still at high school.

The photographs of Camp Eggen showed four small huts, probably the men's living quarters, and two oil-tanks that were twice as long as the biggest hut. They had pipes and valves sticking out of one side and oil had leached into the snow, leaving a dirty black stain extending halfway down the slope. Behind the tanks was a cliff of ice, split through the vertical with a giant fissure.

There was one picture that arrested his eye. It showed some of the men from the base, conscripts-turned-soldiers-turned-Arctic-explorers. Woolly hats, pipes fuming like bonfires, cheery faces. Too cheery, in fact. They looked like they were faking it for the camera.

He studied each of them in turn, looking to see if any of them matched Ferris Clark. But none of the men looked remotely like the corpse at ZAKRON.

* * *

He reached for his notebook and started jotting down some facts. 'Camp Eggen. Established June, 1943.' That meant it was fully functioning by the time Ferris Clark arrived. 'Permanent staff: 8 men.' He made a note to track down the others.

'Rotating length of service: 7 months.' If Ferris Clark had arrived in March, 1944, as Tom had suggested, then he wouldn't have been relieved until the beginning of November. He'd have left on the last icebreaker to call at the base before the waters finally froze. Except that by the time the ship pulled into harbour, Ferris Clark had been dead for at least four months.

He changed screen, looked at the map once again. The information about Camp Eggen added nothing. Ferris Clark's body had been found in the middle of nowhere, miles from the American base. Tom Lawyer said it was suicide. Jack was not convinced. An accident also seemed unlikely, given the fact that he was naked.

That left murder. He'd been stripped, killed and dumped in the middle of nowhere. It had happened many times during the war, notably at Stalingrad. Jack remembered reading how the Russians had taken German prisoners from 'the pocket', forced them to strip and watched them die in temperatures as low as minus fifty.

He ate the second half of the Club sandwich and took another swig of Coke. Then, as if playing a game of lucky dip, he typed 'nazi greenland' into his computer. Dozens of entries appeared on the screen, some containing historical information, some not. 'Nazi Leaders Last-Ditch Greenland Escape Plan.' He clicked on it and found himself on a site with links to the Fortean Times. Another click brought him to 'Axis History: Nazi Fighting in Greenland.'

German soldiers first landed on the east coast of Greenland in the summer of 1942. They arrived on the cruiser *Admiral Scheer* and initially made their base at Sabine Island, which lies at latitude 74.

The Germans had established two meteorological stations, Weather Station Edelweiss and Weather Station Linden. Both were operational within days and both were vital to the war effort. The battle for the North Atlantic was dependent on accurate forecasting.

Jack looked at the map to position them. Linden was far beyond the Arctic Circle at fractured Sabine Island. Edelweiss was also on the coast, but further to the south. A few huts, some fuel tanks and an enormous radio transmitter. The on-line photos suggested that it was very much like Camp Eggen. The only difference was the red and black swastika flying from the flag-pole, almost certainly put up for the photograph. It looked like a still from a Leni Riefenstahl movie.

If Camp Eggen was remote then these Nazi outposts were even more desolate. Few supply ships could ever have reached the men living here, making them reliant on hunting and fishing. Jack sat back in his chair for a moment. You'd have to be a diehard Nazi to volunteer for service at such northerly latitude.

The website said that the Greenland Nazis had done work of vital importance. They'd sent weather reports back to Berlin, advance warnings of North Atlantic storms, mappings of the high and low pressure zones that swept eastwards from Greenland.

Nazis in Greenland. Jack felt he was onto something.

TEN

It was almost six o'clock by the time he had finished going through all the information that was available on-line, far later than he had thought. He picked up his phone and called the agency for a hire car, hoping it was not already closed for the evening. He wanted to get himself a Chevy Corvette, sleek, fast and perfect for the four-hour trip to Vegas.

'*Chevy Corvette?*' said the voice at the other end. He could sense the smile in the way she said it. 'Nothing like that here at our Hanford office. You'd need to go to Vegas.'

There was a pause.

'But let me see. What can I offer you - ?'

There was the sound of rummaging in the background, followed by the click-clicking of a keyboard. 'Ah. Hold on. Yeah. We took delivery of a Dodge Viper last night. That's a cool car. Good?'

Jack nodded into the phone. It was very good indeed.

'A Dodge Viper will do just fine.'

He gave his card details and arranged for it to be delivered to Logan's Corner.

'We'll have it by eight,' said the woman. 'I'll get Ricky to drop it off. We can leave the keys at reception if you're not there.'

Jack shaved, took a shower and started packing his clothes. He intended to check out in the morning and set off to Vegas for the day. He scrolled through the news channels on television before noticing the time and realising he needed to head into Hanford for dinner with Tammy. He picked up his mobile from the table and made his way down to the lobby.

'Out for the evening?' asked the receptionist.

He nodded. 'And tomorrow I'm checking out. Early. Six-thirtyish.'

He told her about the delivery of the hire car and then stepped out into the hot evening air, glancing at the sky as he did so. Overhead it was rich satin-blue, like it had spilled off Van Gogh's palette, and the first few stars were starting to shine. The lights of Hanford lent a dull stain to the darkness and the lamps on the highway cut orange gashes into the sky.

Tammy had suggested they meet at Taylor's, a steakhouse on South Taylor Street. 'We need to talk things through.' That's what she'd said. 'Work out a plan. If Tom hears you're staying on, I'm dead meat.'

Jack walked into town, turning left out of the parking lot and onto the highway, following the dusty verge. A few spiked thistles clung precariously to life, their seed-heads crisp and ready to split. There were dented plastic bottles, Styrofoam boxes, a discarded condom. A neon burger did its best to tempt drivers off the highway. Burgers with ketchup. Burgers with cheese. Flame-roasted burgers. There was a queue of cars at the drive-thru.

The taxi-ride of the previous day had contracted the distance from Logan's Corner into Hanford. What seemed like a few hundred yards by car was in fact more than a mile. By the time he got to Taylor's Steak House it was almost eight-thirty.

He pushed the door and looked around, checking the place out. Tammy had yet to arrive. There were wood-panel walls and check curtains, a long bar flanked with red-leather bar stools and a chrome and glass juke-box in the corner. A lone couple sat on the far side under the stuffed head of a buffalo. The place screamed nostalgia for the days when it was rough out there on the scrubland and flies swarmed around in clouds. The sort of place Ferris Clark might have dipped into for a few beers, if only he'd made it through the war.

'*Jack - ?*'

Tammy's voice came from behind him. 'Sorry. I was running late.'

'No problem,' he said. 'Just got here.'

She suggested a table in the corner and called over to the bar, motioning for the menu. The waitress brought it over, along with a tray of condiments.

'Can we get iced water,' said Tammy. 'And a bottle of Switchback red.'

'Not for me,' he said.

'Oh, a glass or two, surely?'

He held out his hands in a vague gesture of refusal, but the waitress had already nodded and was making her way back to the bar.

'Listen,' she said, lowering her voice to a whisper and abruptly changing the subject. 'Bad news. Just heard this evening, before I left work. Luke told me. They're bringing Ferris Clark forwards by a day. We've only got two days left.'

Jack nodded slowly. Two days. It was not long.

'I'm heading for Vegas in the morning,' he said. 'First thing. I need to see the archives. I want to go to the Family Search Center, the one where Tom found the military stuff. He might have missed something. And you never know – '

He paused.

'Never know what?' she said.

He shrugged. 'Just want to see it for myself.'

'But tomorrow's Saturday.'

'It's open. I checked. Closes at two.'

'Can I join you? I mean, only if – '

He smiled. 'Two brains are better than one. We'll go in my car, but we need to start early, soon after six.'

'No problem. Fran and Elsie are at Bill's this weekend. That's their dad. As long as I'm back by evening.'

He nodded. 'I'll need to get a new place to stay. Any ideas? I'm checking out of Logan's Corner in the morning.'

She reeled off a list. 'Plenty of places. I'll call tomorrow when we're on the road.'

Jack reached across for the menu and was about to open it, but she held it shut with her hand and pointed to the blackboard.

'Daily specials,' she said, and started to read them out. 'Pan-Fried Oysters. They're good. Southern Fried Catfish. Not bad. Or an eight-ounce New York Steak. The steak's great.'

'You choose. You know the place.'

Tammy turned to the waitress who'd reappeared with the bottle of wine. 'Steak, fries, salad, times two, please.' She looked back at Jack. 'Sound okay?'

He nodded and took the bottle from the waitress, pouring wine into Tammy's glass and water into his own. Then, when the waitress had gone again, he asked her more about ZAKRON. 'Your granddad really founded it?'

'Yeah. That's why it's like home. And if I'm honest it's how I got my job in the first place. But like I said earlier, it's starting to feel like Tom's taken it over. I'm becoming a stranger there, and a stranger in danger of being fired.'

She told him how her grandfather established the company in the nineteen forties, how he'd spent the war years working at Hanford military base.

'Not even sure what he was doing there. All kept secret. Even gran never knew. Only thing I remember is her telling us how he slept with a gun under his pillow.'

'But where did cryonics come from?' said Jack. 'I don't get the leap from working for the army to freezing human bodies. He was some sort of war scientist?'

She shrugged. 'Guess so. Science was always his thing. But I have no idea how cryonics fits in. He was hooked for years, that's for sure. One of our good old fashioned American pioneers. And Hanford has been cutting edge science since Christ knows when. Before the war, during the war, after the war. And even today. It's not just ZAKRON. There's all the aeronautics stuff on the north side of town. This place is so teched up it makes Silicon Valley look like it's got stuck in the eighties.'

'He worked alone? Granddad, I mean.'

She shook her head. 'No, there was a whole team of them. Colleagues from the base. They stayed on in Hanford after the war, became the founders of ZAKRON. It was a huge success. All medical stuff in those days. They made a lot of money. And then, wind the clock forwards a few years and I get my job.'

'But cryonics in the nineteen-forties - ?'

'Just a dream. But then along comes liquid nitrogen and the whole thing becomes a reality. Money was already trickling in by then. And then, in sixty-eight, ZAKRON gets its first patient. Steve Waller. A multi-millionaire many times over. Died of lymph cancer. We've still got him on ice.'

She paused, smiled. 'But hey, what's this got to do with Ferris Clark?'

'Nothing I guess. Just interesting.'

He abruptly changed subject, telling her everything he'd discovered about Greenland, Camp Eggen, the German weather stations.

'Jesus you've been productive. Can't believe you've done all that from your laptop. I searched for Greenland, Ferris Clark and frozen corpses and all I came up with was you.'

'*Me* - ?'

'Yeah. Frozen corpses led me to Mallory and Mallory led me to you. Mallory's the one to blame for bringing you here.'

'We'll drink to Mallory then,' he said. 'There's few places I rather be right now.'

'Lucky you. I can honestly say, cross my heart, there's few places I'd rather *not* be. I don't mean right now, here in Taylors, with you. I mean the whole Ferris Clark business.'

She paused.

'I sometimes think I'm the only person left in the world with a conscience.'

'*Conscience*! Christ, Tammy, if you got your way we'd still be in the Dark Ages, groping around looking for acorns to eat.'

He looked at her and realised he'd overstepped the mark. He changed subject, running through the various scenarios that could have cost Ferris Clark his life. Suicide. Murder. Or capture by Nazi commandos.

'Only theories,' he said. 'And I hate theories. But this Ferris Clark's so strange –'

'But I still don't get how he fits into it all,' she said. 'You're saying he attacked one of the Nazi weather stations? And then somehow gets himself captured and dumped in a crevasse?'

'I don't know. But why else would his body end up in the middle of Greenland?'

He fell silent for a moment, still thinking it through.

'The Allies must have known about the Nazi weather stations,' he said. 'The radio signals would have been intercepted by Bletchley Park. Enigma, you know, the code-breakers.'

She gave a nod. She'd heard something about code-breakers.

'But they couldn't have attacked the German base from the air. A few cabins, a radio antenna and a snow-field the size of a country – you can't see a small cabin from ten thousand feet up, especially when it's buried under snow. So what do you do? You alert Washington. Washington sends an expedition. And Weather Station Edelweiss is attacked. Cue Ferris Clark.'

He unfolded his map and pointed to the various stations he'd identified. They were marked with red dots. And then he showed her the most direct route to Edelweiss, one that would have taken them straight up the coast. Two hundred miles in a line, due north.

'But I've looked into it,' he said. 'This coast here is choked with glaciers and ice. You can't even get husky dogs up there. When Greenlanders head north for hunting they take this route here.'

He pushed his finger away from Camp Eggen, sweeping inland by more than a hundred miles before tracing a route north-east towards the dot that marked one of the German weather stations.

'They harness their huskies, load their sledges and then they're off. It's bitterly cold. Minus twenty. Thirty, even. Your breath crystallizes in that sort of cold. The hairs in your nose freeze.

'They travel three hundred miles north. Then they turn east, towards Edelweiss. And at this point here -' his finger came to a halt at the spot where Ferris Clark's body was found - 'something went wrong.'

'What -?'

'That's exactly what I want to look for in Vegas. Maybe the Germans picked up some intelligence. They know they're going to be attacked so they go on the offensive. Lead their dog teams out across the ice.'

'You sure spin a good story,' she said.

* * *

The door to Taylors opened and they both looked up.

'Oh shit,' said Tammy under her breath. 'What the hell's he doing here?'

It was Tom Lawyer.

The expression on his face was one of sly surprise as he approached their table. 'Farewell dinner?' he said. He turned to Jack. 'Hope it's on her.'

Jack nodded. 'It really is farewell,' he said. 'I'm off to Vegas tomorrow.'

Tom smiled. 'Good, good, you'll enjoy it. Although there's more point to it all if you gamble. Caesar's Palace and all that.'

'Only got a day,' said Jack. 'And there's a few things I'd like to check out.'

Tom stood with his arms resting on the empty chair at their table.

'Well I won't join you,' he said, waving his arm towards the bar. 'Meeting some folk.' He looked around the place and pulled a disapproving face. 'Haven't been here in years. Hasn't got any better.'

He was about to make some sort of parting jibe when the waitress cut him short by serving them their steak.

'Best get to the bar,' he said. 'There's drinks need drinking.'

'What the hell's he doing here?' said Tammy when he was out of earshot. 'Mighty strange coincidence. I picked this place precisely cos I thought there's no way we'd meet anyone from ZAKRON.'

She picked up the bottle and refilled her glass.

'You've got to try it,' she said, hovering it over his glass. 'Go on. You can't eat steak without wine.'

Jack hesitated.

'And it's from just over the hills. California.'

'Well –'

'And I'm certainly not going to drink an entire bottle by myself. Jeez, you'd have to take me out on a stretcher. Here –'

Jack held the filled glass to his nose and inhaled. Similar to the reds in Tuscany. Montepulciano. Rich, like alcoholic jam. He took a mouthful. It *was* good. And Tammy was right, it was perfect with the steak.

'So –' she said, suddenly hesitant.

He looked up.

'I wanted to ask – your wife – Alice, you said? I love that name. And it's just too goddam tragic. What happened? D'you mind me, like, asking? It's been on my mind ever since last night.'

Jack was silent for a moment. Then he looked up at her.

'She was my muse,' he said. 'Pretentious, I know, but it was for real. We met at evening class. Drawing. She was good. Better than me. And I asked her to model –'

Tammy raised an eyebrow then gave a smile.

'Nothing like that,' said Jack. 'We were both totally into painting. I still am. And it went from there. Married in eight weeks.'

'*Eight weeks!* You don't mess around.'

'Couldn't see any reason why not to. Love at first sight and all that.'

'And then?'

'Four happy years. Didn't realise you could be so happy. We'd have had kids but then –'

He drained off his glass. 'And then it's like I told you.'

'So sudden. It's terrible, Jack. Tragic. I can't even begin to imagine –'

'Yes. Sudden. That's all there is to tell. End of story.'

'But –'

He raised his hand.

'Sorry - I'm always sticking my nose in. One thing you need to know about me is that I'm up-front. Jesus, you have to be if you work at ZAKRON. Only way to survive.'

'It's fine,' he said. 'Really. I don't mind. And it's my fault for bringing it up in the first place.'

He refilled his glass then looked back at Tammy. Her profile was caught in the glimmer of candlelight and her huge eyes looked just like Karin's.

'If I had a pen and paper I'd draw you right now.'

She laughed. 'That's too kind. But why would you want to draw *me*? Besides, I couldn't sit still for long enough. Too impatient. Always have been.'

She got up and went to the washroom. When she returned, she did so with the restaurant owners in tow.

'Dane and Elida, Jack Raven.'

They shook his hand, all smiles, welcomed him to Hanford. 'Tammy's been telling us all about you.'

'Sounds ominous.'

'All good. And it's not always like that with her.'

The steakhouse had filled up in the hour since they'd arrived. Now, most tables were occupied and a group of men were clustered around Tom Lawyer, drinking beer at the bar.

'I recognize some of them,' said Tammy when Dane and

Elida had gone back to the kitchen. 'Bill's mates. Had no idea they also knew Tom.'

'Bill's the ex?'

'Yep. Bill's the ex. And he doesn't come here any more, which is one of the reasons why I still do. Dane told him he wasn't welcome.'

One of the men put money into the jukebox. There was a clunk of a coin and Marvin Gaye burst into play. Jack finished his wine in a single slug and helped himself to some more. Each time he glanced at Tammy he noticed she was already looking at him.

'Problem about having dinner with a forensic archaeologist,' she said with a dry laugh, 'is that I get this feeling I'm under the spotlight.'

'You *are* under the spotlight. It's shining full on you, right now.' He smiled. 'It's like I told you. I like to draw, paint. So I end up imagining how I'd paint people. And places too. And people in places. I mean, in their own environment, if you see what I mean. Like you, here.'

'I think I get it.'

'It feels –' he cast his gaze around the restaurant – 'so exotic. After London, I mean.'

'*Exotic!* That's definitely the wine speaking! It's Taylors for Chrissakes. In Hanford. It's about as exotic as a cheeseburger and fries.'

'No, I mean being here. Getting away. Enjoying life after all the crap.'

'Yeah – getting away's important. Unwinding. Good food and wine.'

'Shall I get another bottle – ?'

'Bad idea. I mean I'd happily stay here all night. But – ' she glanced at her watch – 'if we're really heading to Vegas in the morning, I need my beauty sleep. When I'm tired I snap.'

'Wouldn't want that,' he said. 'You're right. The voice of reason and all that. Something I have in short supply. And tomorrow's going to be a long day.'

He paid the bill and then Tammy offered him a lift back to Logan's Corner. 'Don't worry. I only had two glasses. And I didn't even finish the last one. It's fine.'

Jack settled himself into the passenger seat and gazed idly out of the window. He hadn't felt so mellow in ages. In fact he hadn't felt so good since - ? The last time he'd had a drink seemed to belong to a different planet. And the last ten days of his life, Christ, had been a diet of coffee and sleeping pills.

They passed the ZAKRON building on the other side of the highway. It was in near darkness. The only light came from Kingston's office. A few minutes later they were pulling into Logan's Corner. Tammy put the car into neutral then silenced the engine. Jack looked at her for a moment, her face perfectly illumined by the lamps outside.

'So – ' he said abruptly. 'D'you want to come upstairs - ?'

Her eyes widened.

'Wow. Thought you Brits were meant to be reserved!'

There was an awkward silence and then Jack folded his head into his hands.

'Can't believe I just said that. Forget it completely. Erase it from your mind. It never happened.'

She turned to face him, only this time with a smile on her face. 'But if you're – '

He didn't hear. 'Sorry, sorry, sorry. It was the wine. Two glasses – or was it three? – and I'm inviting you to my room. That's – '

'My fault,' she said, holding up her hands in a gesture of surrender. 'Totally my fault. The wine was all my idea. I didn't realise at all. I'm real sorry. And besides, I need to get home. Really. Another time. We've got an early start.'

ELEVEN

Karin -

Hello. Day 12. So I'm breaking my rules and email-ing you. It's late and I've been out and now I'm back and lying here in my crap hotel room after a long day's work and wondering how your filming's going.

I'm in Nevada – yes, Nevada. Two days after you left I got an email. A corpse found in the Greenland ice. No idea how it got there. And naked. Make of it what you will. Anyway, just what I needed in the circumstances. I've been re-reading your phone messages. Nevada's a long way from Germany, if you stop to think about it. There, that's it.

Keep well,

Jack.

He received a reply almost immediately.

Jack,

What a total surprise (nice) to hear from you! That's one thing I wasn't expecting at all! It's not drink that caused you to email, is it? Tell me it's not.

Great you've got a case to be working on. I've been worried about you, if I'm honest, but didn't think you'd want me to call. Tell me more about your naked man. Probably a German naturist. Is he fat? Maybe there's a documentary in it???

I've got news for you, too, but I'll tell you another time. In fact, I've got something to show you, but only if you're interested...

(love, if allowed) Karin.

* * *

Karin – what news? I want to hear everything. As for me, nothing more to report. The corpse isn't a German naturist. It's a 2WW soldier. Should find out more tomorrow.

BTW - not drink that caused me to email you!

* * *

Well I'm glad you haven't been drinking. Don't!

Truth is I need your advice. We've been filming and I think it went well. We found the woman we were looking for and she agreed to be interviewed and I was the one that did it on camera. I've attached it as a video file.

Will you look at it? All thoughts, comments, advice (& criticism) appreciated. As you know, I always value your help. Text me when you've seen it. And keep well.

* * *

Jack downloaded the attached file, *Interview 1*, and found himself watching an uncut, unedited version of the interview that Karin had done on the previous day.

He pulled the screen towards him, adjusted the brightness. He could see her in the foreground, leaning forwards in a Biedermeier armchair, almond-eyed and fashionably dishevelled. She had the air of a contented cat sitting in a warm pool of sunshine, slim, dark, her long legs accentuated by her skinny jeans. Her face was an almost perfect symmetry, except for the dimple on her left cheek that showed up when she smiled. When he'd first sketched her, he'd kept her smiling to capture the dimple.

She was positioned to the right of a Sony Betacam SP camera and was being test-filmed by one of the crew, probably on her hand-held Canon.

Jack hit the pause button and looked closely at the lady that Karin was about to interview. Late-sixties or thereabouts, although she looked a lot younger. Silver hair neatly coiffed into a bun and lively blue eyes. The sort that wore eau-de-cologne from Kiehl's and took herself off to Café Buchwald each afternoon for coffee and chocolate gateau.

He pressed 'play' again and heard Karin explaining how the film was being made for a production company in London and was to be screened on the History Channel.

'If you could start by saying your full name and date of birth,' she said. 'Talk to me, not the camera, even though I'm just the prompt. I'll ask questions, but I won't be in the final film. So if you can remember to frame your answer so as to include the gist of the question.'

Jack noticed Karin give the woman a reassuring smile. Then she reached out and touched her hand to reassure her further.

'It'll be fine, promise.'

The woman nodded but the nerves were visible in her face.

She had that pained expression that he'd seen in people who were about to identify a corpse.

'Can I stop if I need to?' she asked. She had just the trace of an accent. Her composure broke for a second. 'It's just that, see, I've not done anything like this before. I need time to think.'

Karin gave another smile. 'Of course. Just try to relax. Be yourself. We can stop the camera at any point. And we can shoot and re-shoot. We've got all day. If you need to think about anything, run through it with me first, that's all fine. Just as long as you're comfortable.'

The film switched abruptly from the hand-held Canon to the big Sony Betacam. The quality was better and the angle much wider. Jack could see the wall hangings and shelves of books behind the woman. The room was one of those huge 1920's salons with an improbably high ceiling and plate-glass windows the size of wall mirrors. The sort of place that once hosted soirées for idols of the German silver screen.

'All phones on silent, *please*.'

It was the voice of Viktor, the producer. There was the sound of mobiles being switched off.

'Ready?'

'Camera rolling.'

'*Ready?*' Viktor's voice again.

'And - action.'

The woman began with a confidence that seemed to surprise even herself. 'My name is Katarina Bach and I was born in February, nineteen-forty-five.'

She stopped abruptly, unsure what to say next. Jack heard Karin come to the rescue.

'What was your earliest memory?'

Frau Bach placed one hand on her silvery bun, as if to check it was still tidy.

'Sorry,' she said, pausing once again. 'It's not easy.'

'Don't worry.' Karin's voice again. 'Take your time. We've got as much time as you need.'

'Camera still rolling –'

'It's not really a memory,' she said. 'It's what I learned many years later. It was my first birthday, the seventh of February, the day that Himmler came to visit. He was the Reichsführer, of course, and because it was my birthday he brought me a box of Rapunzel chocolates. Chocolates for a baby! And he also brought a golden candlestick with my name, Katarina, engraved in the old German letters.

'"You are the future, Katarina." That's what he said to me. The future indeed! When defeat was just around the corner.

'It was many years before I learned the truth about my birth, my parents. That my mother had been working for the lebensborn programme, that she'd volunteered to take part in Himmler's project to breed a pure Aryan race.

'No one wanted to speak about it, of course. Not after the war. My adoptive parents wouldn't tell me anything. They were embarrassed, especially in Adenauer's Germany. But I wanted to understand. You see lebensborn was a part of *me*, whether I liked it or not.'

She paused. Jack could hear Karin's voice filling the silence. 'And your mother? Your real mother?'

'My mother had been singled out as 'very good for propagation'. Isn't that a terrible expression? I mean it's like animals. She was blond, the right weight and height. A loyal member of the Bund Deutscher Mädchen. And she was of pure German stock. That was very important.

'My father was an officer in the SS, loyal, fanatical and devoted to Himmler. He was hand picked to be a biological father, yes, hand picked to breed a child with my mother.

'Many years later, when I was seventeen or eighteen, I tried to track down both my mother and father. But it proved impossible. The records were destroyed when the Americans arrived. I never even discovered their names.

She stopped speaking.

'Great, great,' said Karin quietly, adding: 'Can you tell us more about how it felt? It's hard to imagine.'

'Camera still rolling -'

Frau Bach nodded.

'It made me feel, well, inadequate. Lonely. Yes, there was much loneliness. I've often thought children of rape victims must feel the same, uncertain who they are. I was bred – *bred* - as an experiment, a genetic experiment, and it's taken all my life to accept that fact. I live every single day of my life knowing I carry the genes of my father and mother. You can't escape your genes.'

She sighed wearily. 'I'm grateful to the organization Life Sentence with Hope. They've been wonderful in supporting those of us who struggle with this every day of our lives.'

She turned away from the camera for a moment and her eyes seemed to drift towards Karin.

'I wasn't at all sure about agreeing to be filmed. But, well, I think it's important for the younger generation to know about lebensborn and the terrible impact it's had on people's lives. Today's young people often ask how so many Germans could be so stupid to follow Hitler. My father certainly wasn't stupid. I'm told he had a degree and had brilliant prospects.'

She faltered.

'Fantastic.' Karin again. 'It's moving. You were wonderful.'

The camera clicked off but the sound continued.

'Coffee everyone?' A man's voice. 'Thank you very much, Frau Bach. A very eloquent witness. We're going to break here for lunch. D'you want to stay? Can we give you a lift anywhere?'

'No. It's very kind but I can walk. I'm only going to the Tiergarden for some air. It feels quite breathless today. They were saying there'll be a storm later.'

There was the sound of a door closing and then the talking grew more muffled, as if they'd all turned away from the mike.

'But surely, somewhere in Germany there must be a lebensborn mother still alive? *Karin - ?* We really need a mother as a witness. The film would benefit a lot.'

'We've been trying, Viktor.' Karin's voice again. 'But it's not easy. Two of the ones we tracked down have died, a third's got pleurisy. There's only one we haven't yet managed to contact. She's in some nursing home in Murnau. Near Munich, I think. She must be in her nineties.'

'That's the one,' said Viktor. He clicked his fingers. 'Can you get on the case?'

There was a pause in the recording. And then the sound clicked off abruptly.

* * *

Jack turned back to re-read Karin's email.

'Viktor wants a lebensborn mum,' she'd written as a post-script. 'You'll hear him talk about it on the clip. But they're mostly dead. I called the old people's home in Murnau where one woman's supposed to live. Spoke to the matron in charge. A nightmare called Frau Schmidt. She didn't even want to hear what I had to say. And she said Frau Trautwein wouldn't agree to be interviewed. Help! Any ideas?'

Jack looked at his watch. Almost midnight. That meant it was morning in Germany. He picked up his mobile and toyed with the idea of calling Karin. Only when he'd decided against it did he realise that he'd hit the call button and it was ringing. She answered immediately.

'*Jack*? Well that's a surprise. Lovely to hear your voice. You alright?'

'I'm fine,' he lied. 'Just fine. And you were great. In fact you were excellent. One day soon I'm going to turn on the TV and you'll be incredibly famous and I'll be saying to myself, that's the woman I used to share my life with.'

There was a long silence then Karin said with forced jollity: 'Well that's just flattery. And let's not go there. Listen, a question for you. What do I do about this old woman they want me to interview?'

'Go and visit her,' he said. 'Use all your charm. Christ, you could persuade anyone to do anything. Believe me, I know.'

'But they'll never let me into the home. And they're hardly going to let me speak to her.'

'If you can't get in, no one can. Go with your instincts. And your powers of persuasion.'

He heard a sigh. 'I'll try, I'll try. Did you really think it was okay?'

He laughed. 'More than okay. I'd say great.'

'And *you*?' she said, suddenly hesitant. 'Are you okay? You don't sound it.'

'I'm fine. In fact I'm good.'

He told her about everything that had happened. About Tom and Hunter. About ZAKRON. About Ferris Clark. And then he told her about the project to bring him back to life.

'Holy shit,' she said when he'd finished. 'Jack, don't get involved. For Christ's sake don't get involved with these people. Are they crazy or what? You'll get yourself arrested and locked up if you're not careful. I thought all this lebensborn stuff was mad but what you've just told me is a million times madder.'

'You're right.'

'What's the name of the place?'

'ZAKRON. Most high-tech lab I've ever seen. Makes the Innsbruck place look like the Middle Ages. And Tom Lawyer's dodgy but smart. Took against me from the moment I set foot in the building. He does *not* want me here.'

There was a moment's pause before Karen spoke again.

'Then why the hell did he invite you in the first place?'

TWELVE

Jack rubbed his left hand over his unshaven chin and then glanced towards Tammy. She was gazing into the small mirror on the sunshield and applying dark red lipstick. He put the car into drive and swung out of Logan's Corner. It was a few minutes after six in the morning.

'So what d'you think?'

She ran her fingers over the dashboard. 'Not bad. And fast. At least it's fast when you're at the wheel. But -' she threw a glance towards the back seat, where his cases and computer bag were occupying most of the space - 'not great if you've got two kids and three bags of groceries.'

Hanford Gap was a town that ended unsatisfactorily in every direction. The spaces between the houses widened, first into gardens and the occasional kitchen plot and then into dry wasteland. There was the odd bungalow, a petrol station or two. A stray panel advertised chiropody at the end of the world. And then all sign of human life was gone. They were driving across the surface of the moon. Miles and miles of dried-up gravel that stretched all the way to Vegas.

Not until they reached Walker Lake did the landscape start to change. A giant bulldozer had scoured a wide trench across the scrub, pushing up two lines of rock-strewn hills. Tammy called a couple of hotels to see if they had rooms available. She found one on the third attempt.

'Hanford Comfort Inn,' she said. 'On the east side of town. Not exactly the Four Seasons. But it's anonymous at least.'

There was a long silence as they crossed a huge rocky valley, barren and waterless. Jack was the first to speak.

'Tammy I've got to say something. I'm sorry about last night. Christ, what the hell was I thinking of?'

'Don't have to be sorry. To be honest I was flattered. And I like your style. Direct, up front, no messing. Exactly what I want in a guy. Never been the romantic type. Romance went out of my life when I met Bill.'

She paused for a moment and then hastily changed the subject.

'Say you were a gambler,' she said, 'and you were gambling on finding the truth about Ferris Clark, how much would you bet?'

'That's the Vegas girl speaking.'

He thought for a moment. 'But not sure I can answer. It's like I said to Tom. I gave up gambling years ago. Bad for your health.'

'And wealth,' she said. 'Bill's a gambler, nearly ruined us. Hundreds of dollars lost in a single spin of the wheel. Every Friday he'd come home with empty pockets, a black eye and breath like a beer hound.'

'I don't trust chance. Does your head in. I prefer dealing in facts. Probably makes me dull as crap, but that's how it is.' He paused. 'I reckon we'll find Ferris Clark's records. Check everything Tom's said. Least we'll know where we stand. Confirm where he lived. What he was up to in Greenland. Never know, Tom might have overlooked something. Deliberately.'

'Yeah. But none of this is going to tell us how he died.'

'No. But it might tell us why he wasn't conscripted till nineteen-forty-four. Why wait 'til he was thirty-seven? That's weird. And why Greenland? It's not like he came from somewhere like, I don't know, Montana, where they ski before they walk.'

He pulled over to the side of the road and stopped the car for a moment. They put down the roof. Tammy delved into her bag and pulled out her sunglasses, pink retro and Vegas chic. She tied a chiffon headscarf around her neck.

'Like it,' he said. 'Quite the nineteen fifties movie star look.'

She laughed. 'No. Just Tammy Fox in danger of getting fried.'

They stopped once more to buy cold Cokes at a lonely roadside caravan, then set off again across the scrub. She told him about her divorce from Bill, about her kids, about everything. And then she asked him about the corpse he'd pulled from a bog in Lincolnshire.

'Pickled like an onion. Like he'd been dumped in balsamic. One of the best preserved bodies I've ever seen. Skin, internal organs, you'd never have guessed he was medieval. Tortured, garroted and then shoved into a bog. Slow and brutal. Not nice.'

'I saw it on your website. Loved the pictures. The Wragby man, yeah?'

Jack nodded. 'Not his real name. It's actually the village where he was found. Not very original. And not my idea. He didn't even come from there.'

'You found where he came from?'

'Opened his intestines, analyzed the contents. Identified his last meal and when he'd eaten it. Poppy seeds. Flax. Grains of barley. Enabled us to piece it all together, bit by bit. Very south of Lincolnshire, on the border with Cambridgeshire. See what I mean about forensics? If you can do all that for someone who died six hundred years ago -'

They talked some more until Jack put down his foot and the flush of the wind forced them to silence. He was enjoying the drive and the car and having Tammy beside him. He was in a film and they were heading into the unknown and there was the dusty scrubland and the sun just kept beating down. The Viper handled well, especially at speed, snapping at the silver foil mirages that scuttled across the road. In less than three hours the first low-rises of Vegas's outskirts appeared ahead of them. Then the buildings grew in height and the traffic increased until they reached a huge neon sign saying 'Welcome to Fabulous Las Vegas'.

'You can seriously lose here,' said Tammy.

'Only if you gamble.'

She checked the GPS. 'You need to bear right into Las Vegas Freeway then come off at West Charleston Boulevard.'

Ten minutes later they were standing outside the Family Research Center at 509 South 9th Street. Two palm trees, a steep gabled roof and a ferociously blue sky. Inside the building, if Tom was to be believed, was a slim wartime file on Ferris Clark.

The librarian wore a name-tag that read: 'Betsy: Happy to Assist.'

Mid-fifties and big hair.

'Now then,' she said, peering over her green-rimmed glasses. 'How can I help?'

Tammy explained they were seeking information on a wartime conscript named Ferris Clark.

'Ferris Clark - Ferris Clark,' she said slowly, deliberately, as if she'd once known someone named Ferris Clark. 'Why does that sound familiar? Weren't you here a few weeks ago?'

She paused before answering her own question.

'No, no. Wasn't you. There were two of them, it's all coming back, but they were both guys.'

'That's Tom and Hunter alright,' said Tammy to Jack. She turned back to the woman. 'Mid-fifties? Suntanned? Balding head? And the other one taller. Italian looking.'

Betsy searched for their faces.

'Yeah, yeah, that's them.'

Pause.

'Yeah. I remember. Missing in Greenland. That's what they were after. Strange request. First time in years, in fact. Service personnel in Greenland. They ordered up all the files.'

'*All* the files?'

'Yeah. We file the army personnel individually, see. Always have. There were six or seven of them, I think. Maybe more.'

Jack looked at her and smiled. 'Exactly the ones Tom asked

us to look through again. Can we get those same ones?'

'Yeah,' said Tammy, nodding. 'All of them.'

'Of course.'

She told them to find a seat in the reading room then continued speaking, half to herself, half to the room. 'Ferris Clark. Yeah, Ferris Clark's the one that interested them most. But we only had one file.'

She checked the catalogue references for him and his comrades then noted them down on individual request sheets. Then she stamped each one in turn.

'Give me fifteen, twenty minutes. And here, take a look at this. Never know, might be useful.'

She reached up for a slim hardback on the shelf behind the desk. 'I found this after they were gone. Timing's never been my strong point. Knew it was here but didn't think of it 'til it was too late. Even looked through it myself. Things you discover about the war!'

She handed the book to Jack. His eyes went straight to the title. *Wartime Operations in Greenland* by D. G. Wengel.

'We'll be just over there -' He pointed to a bank of unoccupied desks.

She nodded. 'Give me twenty.'

The book fell open at the chapter entitled *Sirius Sledge Patrol*. He placed it between them and they both read.

The unit known as the Sirius Sledge Patrol, also known as the Greenland Army, was formed in the autumn of 1941 with the aim of preventing German landings on the east coast of Greenland. It was notable for being the smallest independent army of the Second World War. There were ten native Greenlanders and two Danish leaders, Captain Knut Emetssen and Captain Ejnar Thorsen.

The chapter recounted how the Germans were anxious to establish weather stations along the coast of Greenland in order to collect meteorological date that would assist their U-boat campaign in the North Atlantic.

'Well that we know already,' said Jack.

> The job of the Sirius Sledge Patrol was to locate these German bases and destroy them. Anyone who has ever visited the eastern seaboard of Greenland will understand that this was no easy task. The entire coastline is extremely gruelling terrain, even for those familiar and experienced with Arctic conditions.

He turned back to the map at the beginning of the book. It was at least 1,000 miles from Camp Eggen to Weather Station Linden, if taken as a straight line. But the coast was contorted into thousands of deserted islands, frozen bays, promontories and inlets, all choked with sea-ice. You could search that coast for years and not find a thing.

'The Sirius Sledge Patrol was joined on a number of occasions by US army officers based at Camp Eggen.'

'*Huh* - !'

Tammy looked at Jack wide-eyed.

'Might just be getting somewhere.'

> In the late summer of 1943, Sirius was alerted to the existence of a weather station on the north-east coast of Greenland at approximately latitude 74. Its discovery is believed to have been a result of deciphered signals from Bletchley Park in England.

Jack tapped his finger on the page.

> Captain Knut Emetssen led a five-man mission
> to Weather Station Linden and successfully
> destroyed the place. Two Wehrmacht officers
> and two German meteorologists were killed.

Summer, 1943. He made a note of the date. It meant that by the time Ferris Clark arrived in Greenland, the only German weather station still operational was Edelweiss, ironically much closer to the Sirius base at Eskimoness.

He read through to the end of the chapter, hoping for some mention of Ferris Clark. But there was nothing except tables listing tonnages of shipping and air-freight that had passed through Greenland.

'Still, starting to make some sort of sense.'

He flicked through the pages until he came to a section on Camp Eggen. There was information on the role of the base, the supplies, the equipment stored there. And then he saw the two words he'd been looking for all along. Ferris Clark.

> In March, 1944, a six-strong relief team arrived
> at the base. Serving under the auspices of the
> US Army Corps of Engineers, North Atlantic
> Division, they were posted there for the so-
> called summer shift, March to November. The
> names of these men were Mike Davison, Sam
> Hucknell, Ferris Clark, Jon B. McGuire, Rob
> Towler and Dick Waller.

Tammy clicked her fingers. 'Found him!' Then she looked up from the page, turned to face Jack.

'Know what, until now I couldn't quite get my head round

the fact that he existed. I've seen his body every day for a month but he never seemed real. There he was in his glass box, a corpse, a name, yet the two never quite added up. But now -'

Jack agreed. He'd had no trouble imagining Camp Eggen. He'd even been able to picture the men at the base. Yet Ferris Clark himself had never seemed real. But now, he and his comrades had names and identities. They were a team. His mates were Mike, Sam, Jon, Rob and Dick.

He flicked through the pages that followed but there was no further mention of the summer shift of 1944. Nor were there any more references to Ferris Clark.

'Strange expression,' he said. 'Don't you think?'

'What?'

'Well it says he was serving *under the auspices* of the US Army Corps of Engineers. That suggests he wasn't working for them directly, but somehow else.'

Tammy looked back at the page. 'Good spot. You're smart. Hadn't seen that. I guess -'

Betsy arrived as she was still speaking, clutching a small armful of folders.

'Now then -'

She stooped slightly as she put them down on the desk then brushed the dust off her sleeve.

'Here we go. These are the ones your friends looked at. And *here* -' she pointed to the file at the top – 'is your Ferris Clark.'

'Fantastic.'

'Give a shout if you need help.'

Jack took the files and laid them out on the table. He glanced towards Tammy, and she at him, as he reached for the Ferris Clark folder. It was made of a dark green card, matt, and had 'Ferris W Clark: 23 CX 571' printed neatly in the top right-hand corner.

'More suspense than Hitchcock,' said Tammy. 'Open it, for Chrissakes.'

Jack unfolded the file and Tammy emitted a groan. There was

a single sheet of paper with no more than six lines of writing. Ferris Walton Clark. Date of Birth: 22 October, 1907. Father: Walton D. Clark. Mother: Madeline Clark, née Kane. Siblings: none recorded. Draft Date: 17 January, 1944. US Army Corps of Engineers, North Atlantic Division (USMOD). Date of Death: 2 June, 1944. Height: 6 foot 1 inch. Weight: 187 pounds. Eye colour: Blue. Distinguishing features: none.

They digested the information in silence then sat back in their chairs.

'That's it?' said Tammy. 'Three hours' drive for *that*. Nothing more than what Tom's already told us.'

But Jack had seen two things of interest.

'What's USMOD?'

She shrugged. 'Beats me.'

He called over to Betsy who came scurrying over, helpful faced.

'What's this?' he said, pointing to USMOD. 'D'you know?'

She laughed. 'And now I really am feeling I've been here before. That's exactly what your friends wanted to know. USMOD. United States Meteorological Observation Department. This Clark person would have been working for them, under the umbrella of the engineering corps.'

'Of course!'

Jack sat back in his chair and folded his arms. It suddenly made sense.

'*What* – ?'

'Ferris Clark wasn't a soldier at all. He was a meteorologist. A weatherman. He was there to do forecasts. For the Americans.'

Betsy nodded and pointed at the single sheet in the file. 'You're not wrong. That's why there's nothing more. Any other information would have gone to USMOD. That's what I told your friends.'

'And where's USMOD?'

'Ah, that's in Washington. We don't keep copies of those files. Not any longer. They were moved in, let me see, the nineteen eighties I guess.'

She left them to look through the other files. Mike Davison, Sam Hucknell, Jon B. McGuire, Rob Towler and Dick Waller. Jack was looking for one thing in particular and he found it in every single file.

Mike Davison: *distinguishing features, scar on right thigh.* Sam Hucknell: *distinguishing features, mole on upper left shoulder.* He put the Hucknell file down and picked up the Dick Waller one. Dick Waller: *distinguishing features, facial scars from childhood chicken pox.*

Then he turned back to Ferris Clark. *Distinguishing features, none.*

He tapped his pen on the desk. Whoever wrote these reports was meticulous in recording every detail. Moles. Scars. The works. Yet when they came to Ferris Clark they had neglected to mention his birthmark.

He cast his mind back to the autopsy. It was small, that was for sure. And yet it was undoubtedly there. Why hadn't they recorded it?

He went back through the files looking at something else. All of Ferris Clark's comrades had families. Mike Davison, Sam Hucknell, Jon B. McGuire, Rob Towler, Dick Waller. They all had brothers, sisters, parents. Sam Hucknell had five brothers. Mike Davison had two sisters and a brother. Rob Towler had a sister. Ferris Clark was the only one with no one.

'What is it?' asked Tammy, looking at him quizzically. 'You look like you've found something.'

Jack shook his head. 'Not really.'

Tammy took the Ferris Clark file from his hands and wrote down the Clark's family address.

'We've got to go there. See if it still exists.'

She paused in thought. 'Isn't it weird?'

'Isn't what weird?'

'He lived in Hanford, Nevada. And he ends up back in Hanford, Nevada.'

Jack thought about this for a moment before turning back to the files. 'Let's finish off here first. D'you think we can photocopy it?'

He went carefully though each file, noting any detail that was relevant to Ferris Clark. One of the files still had the request slip from when Tom and Hunter had ordered it. He took that as well. Then he photocopied all the relevant documents.

When they finally left the Family Search Center an hour or so later, they did so with a small sheaf of copies taken from both the files and the book. They stepped from the cool interior into the pulsing midday heat and made their way slowly towards the car.

* * *

Number 2586 Avery Street, Green Diamond was a large ranch-style building set in scrubland a few miles to the south west of Hanford Gap. It had wooden walls, a low sloping roof and a dirt track that led to the door. What struck them most was how unremarkable it was. It looked like any number of extended cabins from the back-ends of Nevada. The yard was filled with trash and there was a parched square of dust as an excuse for a lawn.

Two pick-ups in the yard, both sunbaked with dust, and the wreck of a rowing boat to the right of the driveway. It looked like it had been left adrift by some improbable tsunami.

'So this little place is where Ferris Walton Clark hung out,' said Tammy. 'Not exactly Caesar's Palace.'

They parked on the road and walked slowly up the driveway. There was no shade. It was scorching. Jack wiped the sweat from his forehead.

'Hello?' He called out as they approached the front door.

'*Yeah - ?*'

They were greeted by a boiler-sized man in dirty blue overalls. He was clutching a heavy ratchet spanner and his face was smeared with oil. He looked Tammy up and down, undressed her and clearly approved of what he saw for he put the spanner down on a gasoline drum and wiped the oily sweat from his face.

'You lost?'

Tammy did the talking, inventing a story on the spot. She told him she was researching her family, trying to find a certain Ferris Clark. She said she believed this was where the Clarks used to live.

The man shook his head, noisily cleared his throat then gruffly called to his wife. 'Ferris Clark,' he said. 'Know the name?'

She appeared at the door, as wide as him and with sandals made from tyre rubber. 'Clark? Why yeah, Larry. I do know that name. But dunno where from.'

'*Please*, if you can try and remember.'

'Didn't we buy this old home of ours from a Clark?' she said, looking at her husband. 'Clark - Clark - or was it - ?'

It was no use. She couldn't remember, even with Tammy's eyes begging for more.

'Well -' She wrote down her number. 'Here's my phone. Call if you remember anything. Anything at all. It's real important.'

'Sure,' said the woman, retreating back into the kitchen. Larry picked up his spanner and banged it on the drum before giving a final glance at Tammy.

'Good luck girl.'

Jack smiled. Not for the first time, he was invisible in Tammy's presence. All eyes naturally turned towards her.

Her phone buzzed and she checked the message.

'Shit.' She looked panicked.

'What?'

'Look,' she said, passing him the phone. 'From Tom. Warm-up's been moved to tomorrow. Shit, shit, shit.'

She cupped her head into her hands. 'Jack, what d'we do now? They're starting in less than twenty-four hours. They're starting everything before we even know who Ferris Clark is.'

THIRTEEN

They were seated in the conference room waiting for Tom to address them. It was eight in the morning, half an hour earlier than usual. It was set to be a long day. One seat was empty, the one next to Tammy.

'You all know what's at stake.' Tom spoke with unusual gravity, lingering over every word. 'We're trying something no one's ever tried before. And we've got technology on our side. Plaxon's developed the best equipment. Best drugs. Best computer system. And there's a big fucking prize dangling at the end of it all. If it works, we'll get very, very rich.'

He stopped for a moment, looked at them each in turn.

'*If.* It's a big if, of course. Not sure we'll be able to wake him. Don't know if he'll survive without life support. Don't even know if he'll have any memory of who he is.'

He looked directly at Doctor Gonzales. You could see the pressure in his eyes.

'It's no secret Luke's had his doubts.'

Luke Gonzales stared back at Tom, not saying a word.

'But we've overcome that now.'

All heads turned towards Gonzales. He was massaging his hands on his brow like he had a migraine.

'Of course there are concerns,' continued Tom. 'It's science, for Chrissakes. Galileo didn't have it easy either. We're heading into uncharted waters. The land of the unknown.'

He clapped his hands together, as if to mark the end of the conversation. Then he abruptly changed subject.

'The policy of absolute secrecy holds until further notice. And unless that's not clear to you all, let me say it in the vernacular. No one breathes a fucking word. Girlfriends, husbands, wives. One hundred per cent silence. I don't want to find myself waking up and seeing ourselves on TV.'

Tammy looked up from her notebook.

'But why now?' she said. 'Why so soon? I just don't get the hurry. He's been in the ice for decades. And we can keep him like that for decades more. A few more days or weeks won't hurt.'

Tom cleared his throat noisily, like he always did when irritated.

'*Why now?* Cos Plaxon wants it now. Plaxon's put up the money. Developed the science. It's only normal they get to call the shots.'

'But you're on the Plaxon board. You could delay it.'

Tom stared at her coldly. 'Why in hell's name would I want to delay it?'

Tammy placed her hands flat on the table for a moment, fingers stretched, then clenched them tightly.

'Cos we don't know who Ferris Clark is. You're the one who said he might not have any memory. That he'll need all the help he can get. And so far, unless I've missed something, we know almost nothing about him. What happens if it all goes wrong? That's what I want to know.'

Tom emitted a heavy sigh.

'Okay, let me explain so we're all clear. It's important that everyone knows. If there's a hitch, if something screws up, if there's serious brain damage, if his memory's shot, that's all been factored in. We've cleared it with Perez, with the FBI. Even Governor Jackson knows about it. Hunter and I will jointly take responsibility. And we'll need to act fast. One, he gets a shot of sodium thiopental. That'll render him numb. Two, he gets a shot of pancuronium bromide. That'll shut down his breathing. And three, he gets the final shot, potassium chloride. Stops the heart in seconds.'

He paused.

'Maybe you now get why secrecy's vital. Wouldn't want some snitching bastard trying to get us for murder.'

'Why not unplug him?' said Jennifer in her usual blank voice. She was toying with a packet of gum.

Tom slammed his hands down on the table. 'He could be conscious, for Chrissakes. He might have movement in his limbs. We need something that will kill him in seconds.'

He tapped his pen on the table, took a deep breath and then looked down at the list in front of him.

'Ah yes, practicalities. Harry Jackson's driving up here tomorrow night. Jon Perez will be flying in. And we'll also have Sam Taylor, Jim and the rest of the board. The only one who can't make it is Roland. He's off in Hawaii with Hannah, lucky dog.'

They all nodded. It wasn't often that the governor and the board came to ZAKRON. In fact it hadn't happened for years.

Tom turned to face Tammy, the trace of a smile on his face.

'One other thing. Our British friend Jack Raven's left us. Headed out of town this morning. Gone back to England. I hope no one else is intending to spring any surprises. I don't like surprises.'

He glanced briefly at Hunter before continuing. 'Now, anything else?'

They all shook their heads.

'Good. Then we meet in two hours. Eleven o'clock sharp. We'll get prepared, then straight into theatre. Step by step. You all know the procedure.'

He'd finished speaking and they slowly filed out of the room, one by one. Tammy was the last to leave.

'Good dinner with your friend?' said Tom. 'You looked quite the couple. But he didn't even come and say adios.'

He loosened his tie and smiled, as if he'd just won at poker. 'Hope that's the last bright idea you're going to inflict on us all.

Stick to playing nurse from now on. You're not bad at that. You might even earn yourself a drink when this whole thing's over.'

* * *

Ferris Clark was winched from the vitrification box at just after eleven. The surgical pulley eased him gently upwards until he was almost a foot above the glass container. It then swung him slowly through ninety degrees and transferred him to the moveable gurney. This was attached to a wheeled trolley that was rolled carefully into the theatre lab next door. Tammy knew they were fast reaching the moment of no return. There could be no going back.

Everyone on the team was present but no one spoke. It was as if the gravity of what they were attempting to do had suddenly struck home. The only noise came from ALP, the mainframe computer. Its glossy brushed steel box was linked wirelessly to the various components in the lab.

Owen went over to the keyboard and typed in a command. ALP responded immediately, ordering manual checks to be run on each individual item of equipment before they were connected to the operating system.

Defibrillator? A computer-generated voice without intonation or inflexion.

'On timer and set,' said Tom.

Dialysis?

'On timer and set.'

Biospectral index monitor. Electro-encephalograph. External cranial pressure monitor?

Tom checked the latter piece of equipment and adjusted its setting before tapping in a code that linked it wirelessly to ALP.

Oximeter. External Brain Tissue Oxygen Monitor. Renal Dialysis Pump.

ALP ran through each item in the room before speaking again.

Tom Lawyer - ?

Tom looked up at the machine. He hated ALP addressing him by name.

Remember, Tom Lawyer, dioximyde pump must link to left carotid, femoral artery, pulmonary vein.

'Yeah.'

Zero-point-eight fluid ounces in each instance, first dose.

'Yeah.'

Back up systems as agreed.

'Yeah.'

Remember, Tom Lawyer, continued ALP, *links to cell phone must be connected and secured.*

'Yeah, ALP, just wait for fuck's sake.'

No, Tom Lawyer. ALP responded in the same blank tone. *Links to cell phone must be connected and secured now. Request check on links to cell phone. Cell phone must be connected and secured. Connect and secure now.*

All six of them performed their allotted tasks in silence. Ferris Clark lay outstretched on the gurney, still deeply chilled. But he wouldn't be ice-frigid for much longer. ALP would soon switch the thermal wrap from 'standby' to 'on', and the warming process would begin. And that would mark the beginning of a whole new phase.

'Get a print-out of the thermal readings,' said Tom, turning to Tammy.

ALP answered immediately. *Thermal readings printing.*

'And, Tammy, make sure the thermal wrap's linked to the correct computer file. Don't want to be hunting for fucking information when it starts coming in.'

ALP blinked and responded. *Thermal-wrap now being linked to correct computer file: file AD-six-three-two-Z.*

'Good,' said Tammy, addressing ALP. She turned back to Tom. 'Just re-checking all the drip attachment files.'

All checked and correct.

It took ninety minutes to get Ferris Clark wired to all the machines, pumps and drips and then another thirty to ensure that all the equipment was 'talking' to ALP. The only machine that stood redundant was the EMO unit, used to pump blood through an oxygenator. If the dioximyde failed, it could be used as an emergency standby.

Tammy stood back for a moment and looked at Ferris Clark. It was strange. Being linked to all the equipment had somehow transformed him. Although the thermal wrap had yet to be activated he already looked more like an intensive care patient than a deep frozen corpse. Deadly cold, deadly white, deadly stiff, yet someone who might yet be kick-started back to life.

When all the equipment had been checked and connected there was a tangible sense of relief in the lab.

'So,' said Hunter, breaking the silence. 'He wakes up, sees all these computers, what's he going to say?'

'Where the fuck am I?' offered Jennifer.

Hunter scoffed. 'What time is it?'

'My alarm didn't go off,' added Owen.

'Okay, shut up all of you,' said Tom. 'Not the time for comedy. And no wisecracks once Governor Jackson's here. He doesn't do humour.'

He looked at his watch then turned to face the room.

'Right. Everything's ready. It's checked and re-checked. All good to go. Everyone happy?'

ALP blinked and answered.

Happy is a value judgment. It is not recognized by my lexicon.

'For fuck's sake.' Tom rephrased the question. 'Are all links live and running?'

Correct.

'Then the thermal wrap can be switched on.'

Correct.

Doctor Gonzales stared at ALP in silence. It was the moment he'd feared for weeks. There was a low click and one of the lights flicked from red to green

Thermal wrap activated.

'Good.' Tom rubbed his hands. He then turned to look at one of the monitors linked to ALP, studying it closely. 'Okay, it's giving us a predictive wake-up time of fifteen-thirty-seven tomorrow afternoon. That's just after three-thirty. Which means it reckons he's going to take around twenty-seven hours to reach the point where all this stuff -' he pointed to the banks of machines - 'will kick into action. Longer than we expected.'

He turned to Tammy. 'I'm expecting you to run hourly checks. Luke, you'll monitor the thermal? Everyone clear on their jobs?'

They all nodded.

'Good. Then we'll leave him to ALP for the time being.'

FOURTEEN

Jack spent the afternoon at the Hanford Comfort Inn, a roadside motel with even less charm than Logan's Corner. Tammy had said it was anonymous. She was right. You could stick Al-Qaeda inside and no one would ever ask any questions.

Several times Jack called the National Archives in Washington to find out more about the USMOD records. There was never any answer. In the end he sent an email instead. He got an instant rely. 'We aim to respond to all email enquiries within 3 to 5 working days.' So that was that, for the time being.

He turned back to his iPad and started making a resumé of everything he had discovered. Ferris Clark had been conscripted in January, 1944. He was 37 years of age. Compulsory conscription of American males had begun on 5 December 1942, when Roosevelt signed an executive order ending voluntary registration. From that date onwards, anyone between the ages of eighteen and thirty-eight years was legally obliged to join the army. Fifty million males at the stroke of a pen.

Ferris Clark fell within the age range: 35 years old in December 1942. But there was good reason why he'd escaped the draft. He had specialist meteorological training, training that was invaluable to the US army, navy and air force. His services were required in Greenland, and never more so than in 1944 when the Atlantic convoys were the lifeline between North America and Europe.

He was sent to Eastern Greenland in March with five comrades, Mike Davison, Sam Hucknell, Jon B. McGuire, Rob Towler and Dick Waller. According to the records in Las Vegas, all these men had families. Some probably had descendants who were still alive. And it was possible that at least one of them might have kept a record of what happened to their old friend Ferris Clark, from Green Diamond, Nevada.

Jack was confident he could trace these descendants, given time. There would be census returns, the electoral roll and probably other records as well. But time was the one thing he didn't have. And tracking a family forwards in time is far more complicated than tracking it backwards.

As to the cause of Ferris Clark's death, Jack was increasingly sure he hadn't committed suicide. Throwing yourself into a crevasse leaves signs on the body. Nor had he drowned. There was no water in his lungs.

An accident was also unlikely. Meteorologists don't drop dead from the cold. Ferris Clark would have known the risks of being outside, of exposure, of hypothermia. Besides, if it was an accident then why was he naked?

That left murder. He'd been stripped and killed, possibly by exposure to the cold. And then he'd been dumped in a glacial crevasse. He was dead by the time he hit the water. Murder was by far the most plausible scenario, except that it didn't explain the pristine state of his internal organs and blood cells.

The phone rang, cutting through his thoughts. It was Tammy.

'It's all started,' she said, the despondency sounding in her voice. 'And I've got to check on him again at six-thirty. Want to join me?'

'*Sure*? It's your quickest route to getting fired.'

'Tom and Hunter won't be there,' she said. 'Tom's linked wirelessly to the lab. Monitors everything from his house. And anyway, we'll know if they're there because their cars will be outside.'

Half an hour later she picked him up from the Comfort Inn

and drove directly to ZAKRON. There was only one car outside. It was Kingston's.

'You haven't met him yet,' said Tammy. 'He's ZAKRON's gentle giant. Only decent guy here. And he'll never breathe a word about anything. He's got a big soft spot for me.'

'What's he do?'

'Officially he's the night watch. But he's far more than that. He keeps an eye on everything. He knows the equipment here like it's his babies. Ferris Clark couldn't be in safer hands.'

She opened the main entrance door with her swipe card and motioned to Jack to follow her into Kingston's ground floor office.

'Why Miss Tammy!' said Kingston, smiling broadly when he saw her. 'And you must be Mister Jack Raven. So you haven't left us after all.'

Tammy gave a brief explanation, telling him that he was staying on in secret for a few more days. 'Some new lines on Ferris Clark. Needs to follow them up.'

'That'll please the boss,' said Kingston, turning toward Jack. 'Heard him the other day saying he wanted to give you a special send off.'

'Who to?' asked Tammy.

'He was talking with Mister Hunter. Talking about it in his office. Heard them laughin' about it.'

He paused for a second.

'Anyway, your secret's safe with me. I won't tell you came here. Mister Tom's hard at times. Hard on me, too. And not always fair, neither.'

They left Kingston and changed into surgical gowns. They then made their way into the lab-theatre. The emergency strip lights were already on, but the overhead spots also flicked into action as they entered the room. The lab was silent, apart from a low hum.

'I feel sorry for him,' said Tammy when the door had closed behind them. 'Kingston, I mean. They pay him a pittance. And yet he's always the first one to see when things go wrong. If he left this place, Tom'd be in deep shit.'

She flicked her eyes towards the mainframe computer. 'Eighteen hundred hours update report on Ferris Clark,' she said. ALP's voice activation light blinked.

Situation normal. All data in conformity with expected norms. No anomalies to report. Stage two de-thaw reached at eighteen hundred hours and fourteen minutes.

Ferris Clark was lying stiffly on the gurney, outstretched on the reflective thermal mat. He had blue suction caps attached to his scalp. They would detect the first signs of electrical energy coming from the brain. Specially adapted ventilation tubes were clamped into each nostril and an inter-cranial pressure monitor was externally attached to the back of his head.

Jack studied each item of equipment with care. Five intravenous infusion pumps had been inserted into his neck and arms. They would allow the swift infusion of dioximyde at the appointed time. A saturation pulse oximeter was strapped to his finger.

'For oxygen levels?'

'Yeah. The readings are fed straight into ALP. He makes instant calculations. He'll be the one instructing the intravenous infusion pump. He's the one taking decisions, not us.'

They turned to look more closely at Ferris Clark. He seemed to have changed since the morning. The thawing process had moved from stage one to stage two somewhat faster than anticipated. ALP had originally given a predictive time of seven hours before the onset of stage two. Only five had passed yet changes were already taking place. Ferris Clark's skin was no longer frosted. In places it was glistening with moisture, like cold sweat, and the suction cushions beneath him were drawing the accumulated water from the heat mat into a small drain-hole below.

They both stood in silence, staring at his face. That, too, had undergone a change. He still looked very far from life but he didn't have the marble pallor that comes with clinical death. His skin was grey rather than white and Jack noticed that his fingernails had a purplish tinge above the cuticle. He pointed it out to Tammy.

'One of the first things you get with patients in intensive care.'

Ferris Clark's left eye had not moved. It was still stuck in the same position, slightly ajar. But tiny droplets of condensation had formed on his eyelashes, like miniature tears. Jack felt the heat mat. Warm to the touch, even through his surgical gloves. It was reflecting heat deep inside the body.

'Jack,' said Tammy, turning to face him. She was speaking in a low voice. 'Listen, I've got to tell you now, before it's too late. I'm not happy with this. I'm not happy at all.'

He looked at her.

'I've got this feeling, right here. Don't know what it is. I can't explain it. I just feel uneasy. I've had it for days, right here in my stomach. Like you get when something's about to go wrong.'

'Nothing's going to go wrong.'

'How can you be so sure? You talk away in this confident tone, like the whole world's under Jack Raven's personal control. How can you be so sure?'

'*How can I be so sure?* Open your eyes, Tammy. Look at him. And look at all the equipment. He's linked to some of the most sophisticated medical machinery in the world.'

'*But Jack -*'

She was more insistent.

'Really, I don't like it. And, you know, it's not too late to stop it. Not too late to cut the link to Tom's phone, pull the plug. I could stop the warm-up right here and now. And then it'd all be over.'

Jack looked at her like she was mad.

'But you'd ruin his body. You'd be destroying his organs. You'd be killing him. Forever.'

'Precisely. And then he'd get the lasting sleep he wanted.'

'How d'you know that's what he wanted?' he snapped back at her. 'And besides, who are you to decide? For all you know, this might be the moment he's been desperate for, craving for, ever since he died. And anyway, it's too late now. There's no way back, Tammy. It's too far down the line.'

'But Jack – '

He held up his hand, silencing her before she could say anything more.

'Look, I agree with you on one thing. Yes, they should have found out more about him. Yes, they should have found out what was going on in Greenland. But it's too late for that now. And it might not even be necessary. You keep saying he won't remember who he is. But there's also a chance he'll remember exactly who he is.'

'Well I want you to know one thing,' she said in a cold voice. He could see real anger in her eyes. 'If you weren't here, I'd have switched off the equipment.'

'You're completely mad. And lose your job, salary, everything. And on top of everything else, you'd have landed Ferris Clark in a coffin. Your problem, Tammy, is that you don't understand death. And I can tell you this, if you'd unplugged the equipment, I'd have plugged it straight back in again.'

'Then it falls on your shoulders.'

He nodded. 'I don't have a problem with that. I'm a scientist. This is science. It's what I do.'

She went back to checking all the various leads and wires that fed the dialysis, defibrillator and oximeters. She also checked the wireless connections with ALP. Then she made a check on ALP himself, ensuring all the systems were connected to Tom's phone. ALP gave an indignant blink. *System checked. All systems functioning normally.*

Any change in Ferris Clark's status, any problems or irregularities, would be flashed to Tom.

'ALP, I need an update on the brief data report.'

Data processing underway. Information will be sent to monitor in less than three seconds.

She switched her gaze to the principal monitor. It flashed the required information instantaneously.

'17.47hrs. Patient constant. All readings normal. Surface body temperature, 76F. Inner core reading (heart), 71F. Inner core (brain), 70F. Heat mat (surface), 102F. Deflective heat source, optimized. Scan layers, all normal.'

'Tom'll access all this tonight,' said Tammy with a sigh. 'He'll check the new stats and readings once ALP's calibrated it. And Kingston will be doing the same thing, only he'll be doing it from here of course.'

Jack moved round to the far side of Ferris Clark's body. He wanted to see if the birthmark was any clearer. The surface frost had melted slightly and the skin was now almost translucent but it remained frustratingly folded into itself.

He reached for the magnifying glass that stood in a rack next to one of the monitors. A Buxton triplet 30X. Best magnifying glass ever made. And British too. He shifted the surgical spotlight a fraction in order to shine a beam directly onto the armpit. Then he held the glass close to the skin so that he could study the mark more closely.

'Still too cold. Another two hours and it'll be visible.'

He turned to face Tammy, asked if ALP could estimate the time at which his core temperature would reach the point at which everything would switch from standby to action.

'He can do that in seconds,' said Tammy. 'ALP, what's the current projection for Operation Pump?'

Current estimation was 15.24 on the following day. Jack glanced at the time now, 18.52, and did a quick calculation. If all went according to plan, the process of kick-starting Ferris Clark's heart, organs, blood circulation and brain would begin in twenty-one hours.

They turned to leave the room and the spots clicked off automatically behind them, leaving only the emergency strip lights. Ferris Clark's body was bathed in a bluish-green glow.

Jack removed his surgical gear and washed his hands. Then he waited for Tammy to do the same before the two of them made their way down the corridor to the entrance hall. They paused for a moment to say goodnight to Kingston.

'How's patient Miss Tammy?' he said. 'The equipment's tellin' me everything's okay. That your take on it?'

She gave a nod of her head and sighed. 'Seems that tomorrow's the day. Mid-afternoon. And maybe not till evening.'

A low rumble of thunder could be heard coming from outside. It sounded like a lorry on the highway. It sent a vibration through the floor and walls.

'You hurry yourselves home now,' said Kingston. 'They've announced a monster rolling in from Carson way. Just saw it on CNN. We'll get rain at last.'

'Rain,' said Tammy. 'That's what we need.'

She turned to face Kingston. 'You won't mention anything to Tom? About Jack being here.'

Kingston put his finger to his lips. 'Secret's safe with me, Miss Tammy. Won't breathe a word. Wouldn't tell Mister Lawyer nothin', even if it was my last day on earth.'

Jack and Tammy stepped outside. They were stopped in their tracks for a second. The air was thicker than usual and a hot wind was driving hard from the west. It was like opening an oven door. The distant sky was split in two by a fork of lightening.

Tammy turned to Jack. 'Look, you know I disagree with you. You know I think you're wrong. Let's agree to disagree. And, well, I'd have invited you back for something to eat if only I didn't have to get the kids to bed and there's no food in the house and the place is a complete dump and – '

'I'd love to come another time,' said Jack, briefly holding her arm. 'If the invitation still stands, that is. Maybe we'll even be able to celebrate.'

'That'd be nice. Dinners are a whole lot better when you're celebrating.'

FIFTEEN

The storm rolled in towards Hanford shortly after 2am. It arrived as a dirty stain in the night sky, spreading outwards like ink on blotting paper. It swallowed the moon then snatched away the stars. In the hills to the west of Reno, it spat sky-length bolts of lightening that fizzed into the trees like Old Sparky.

Jack listened to the rain steaming down outside, a power shower gone mad. He hadn't heard rain driving down so hard since he was in Nepal. It sluiced down the gutters then washed itself out into the parking lot.

He slept in fits and starts, dreaming of Karin and that it had all been a misunderstanding and that she was still living at his place. But then the doorbell rang in his dream and he opened the door and his entire world slid into catastrophe. And the next moment there was a rumble of thunder that encroached into his dream, a drum roll that grew constantly louder. And then there was one tremendous crash that seemed to wrench the sky in two. Abruptly woken, he switched on the bedside light. Almost five. Daylight in an hour, if ever daylight would break through the storm clouds.

He abandoned sleep and tried to recall his dream. But the images had already faded and so he reached for his book and skimmed the blurb on the back cover. *Operation Eichmann: The True Story of how Mossad Agents Captured Adolf Eichmann*. It was the very last thing Karin had given him.

He glanced through the chapters, reading passages at random. It told the story of Hitler's right-hand man, how he'd been living undercover in Argentina ever since escaping from Germany. He was one of several dozen SS commanders who had built new lives in South America. But unlike the others, Adolf Eichmann had severed all links with his German past. He'd given himself a new identity, new papers, new persona. He knew that Israel's secret agents were seeking out all the senior Nazis who'd fled from the disintegrating Third Reich.

Mossad's biggest challenge was the question of identity. It was imperative not to seize the wrong man. Eichmann was rumored to be living under the assumed persona of Ricardo Klement, but this was only a rumor. The man leading the Mossad operation, Natan Pazy, had investigated Ricardo Klement and also researched the private life of Eichmann. He was convinced that they were one and the same man.

The dates were crucial. According to official records, Ricardo Klement had married later in life, in the autumn of 1952. But Eichmann was known to have married on 21 March, 1935. It was a key difference, one that Pazy exploited to the full.

> The Mossad operation began at the beginning of March, 1960. The team was aware that in less than two weeks it would be Adolf Eichmann's silver wedding anniversary. A twenty-four hour watch was therefore placed on the house in which he was believed to be living as Ricardo Klement.

At a few minutes after six-thirty on the evening of 21 March, 1960, the man who described himself as Ricardo Klement could be seen walking down the street towards his apartment. Pazy and two fellow agents were installed in a building opposite his home. They exchanged glances. Klement-Eichmann was carrying an enormous bouquet of flowers.

'When his wife opened the front door he handed them over as a wedding anniversary gift,' wrote Pazy. 'It confirmed that Ricardo Klement was not Ricardo Klement at all. He was Adolf Eichmann.'

Jack set down the book on the bed. Lateral thinking. And a brilliant piece of detective work. Mossad swooped, seized Eichmann, whisked him to a safe house. He protested, of course. Said he'd never heard of this Eichmann fellow. Insisted he was Ricardo Klement.

Mossad had to be absolutely certain they'd got the right man before flying him to Israel. There was going to be international publicity and a big show trial. And they already knew there was one further means of identifying Eichmann.

Mossad had been informed that during the latter years of the Third Reich, there was a select inner elite of SS officers who had been singled out for their unflinching loyalty to the Führer. Among this elite was Adolf Eichmann. He, in common with the other officers, had been granted the privilege of wearing a badge of honour unlike any other. It was a small tattoo in blue ink, not much larger than a thumb-print, that depicted a human skull. It was etched into the skin under the left armpit.

Brilliant, thought Jack. The incontrovertible piece of evidence, and tattooed onto his own skin.

His eyes flicked back to the beginning of the sentence. '*It was a small tattoo in blue-ink, not much larger than a thumb-print, that depicted a human skull. It was etched into the skin under the left armpit.*'

As he read it for a second time, his right eyebrow trembled slightly.

A small tattoo under the left armpit.

A badge of honor.

An inner elite of SS officers.

He lay back on his bed. Then, almost immediately, he sat upright.

A badge of honor.

Ferris Clark! He'd known it wasn't a birthmark. He'd known it wasn't dermal melanocytosis. He'd known it wasn't Nevus flammens. It was too regular. Too neat.

A small tattoo in blue ink.

It wasn't a birthmark. It wasn't a mole. It was a goddam fucking tattoo. He recalled the shape of it, its neatness, its rounded top. And the colour. It was the tattoo of a human skull. Ferris Clark had the tattoo of a human skull etched into his armpit.

He slowly closed the book and placed it on the table next to the bed. Then he reached for the phone and tapped in Tammy's home number. It rang four times before she answered.

'*Tammy - ?*'

Silence. And then a sleepy sounding voice. 'Hello - ? Who's this - ?'

'Tammy. It's Jack. Are you awake?'

A long pause.

'Yeah. But - Jack – Christ - it's not yet six.'

'Tammy, listen. The body - Ferris Clark -'

'*What - ? Who - ?*' She was still half asleep.

'Just listen. The body –'

'Yeah - Ferris Clark –'

'That's exactly the point. I'm not sure it is. The birthmark's a tattoo. A symbol of the SS. Hitler's inner circle.'

'*What - ?* What d'you mean, inner circle?'

'They were mad. Crazy. Fanatics.'

Another pause. He could hear his words jolting Tammy awake.

And then she was suddenly alert.

'What? *What* - ? Jesus! But how - ? Shit. What've you found?'

'Can you come? Right now. We need to get to ZAKRON.'

* * *

7.05am: Tammy's car pulled up outside the Comfort Inn. Jack made his way downstairs and climbed in.

'How the hell did you find out?' She looked pale, like she hadn't slept. It was the first time he'd seen her without make-up.

'I'll go through everything,' he said. 'But all you need to know right now is that the corpse isn't Ferris Clark. I'm sure of it. In fact it quite possibly belongs to a member of the SS.'

'But – shit. *Shit*. Jack. I just knew – '

'Yes, well - least there's still time to do something about it.'

She swung the car out onto the highway. Jack sighed heavily and then held up his hands in a gesture of surrender.

'I was wrong, Tammy, and you were right. They've shouldn't have rushed it. And I should have listened to you.'

In less than five minutes they were pulling into ZAKRON. Tammy cut the engine. They got out of the car and walked around the puddles left behind by the storm. Jack glanced at the sky. It had taken a bruising and the air was like a steam bath. The storm wasn't over yet.

Tammy opened the main door to the building with her swipe card.

'Need to tell Kingston we're here,' she said. 'He might think we're intruders.'

It was quiet inside the building and unnaturally hot. It was hard to breath. It felt like the air conditioning had been switched off. The lights hummed.

Jack followed Tammy as she walked across the entrance area towards Kingston's office. His door was closed. She pushed it.

There was something blocking it. She pushed a little harder. It inched opened, but just a fraction. And it was then, at that precise moment, she let out a piercing scream.

Jack stepped forwards just in time to catch her. She collapsed into his arms, shaking violently.

Jack looked through the gap in the door.

Kingston was lying on the floor in a deep pool of congealed blood. There was an arc of blood that covered the walls. He was almost naked, apart from his underwear, and had a deep slash in his neck. His eyes were wide open and he was staring blankly at the ceiling. His tongue was lolling out of his mouth.

Jack had seen death many times and in many guises, but this was certainly one of the more violent. Kingston had been killed with a single swipe of a surgical scalpel that had cut deep into his carotid artery. A professional killing. A deep thrust into his neck, a twist of the blade and an uncontrollable torrent of blood. Dead in less than two minutes.

'But who - ?' said Tammy lamely, still sobbing and gasping for air.

Jack pulled her away from him for a second, shook her hard. '*Tammy -*'

She looked up, pale, her blue eyes smudged and bloodshot.

'Tammy. We need to check the lab. Come. Now. Follow me.'

He pulled her by the arm and they ran down the corridor that led to the laboratory. Jack grasped at the door. The lights flicked on. And they both looked towards the gurney. It was empty.

Alert, system malfunction. Alert, system malfunction. ALP was talking to the room. *Alert, system malfunction.*

'He's gone.'

Tammy turned and glared at Jack with accusing eyes. 'I told you it was wrong. Shit. Shit.' She tore at her hair. 'I was right all along. Should have trusted my instincts.'

'Jesus,' said Jack, only half listening to what she was saying. 'What monster have we unleashed?'

SIXTEEN

Tammy folded her head into her hands.

'*Shit - shit- shit* - It can't be for real. *Jack?* Tell me it's not real.'

Her voice was hoarse and hollow. 'Why Kingston? Of all people, why poor, poor Kingston?'

She leaned heavily against the side wall of the lab, trying to get it straight in her head. Smiley friendly Kingston. Kingston with the big, white teeth. *Why, it's Miss Tammy! Hello Miss Tammy!* Kingston had always been Dooley Wilson playing Sam in Casablanca. Kingston with the cheery laugh that erupted from his belly. And now he was lying in eight pints of blood, viscous and sticky like strawberry jam.

Alert, system malfunction. Alert, system malfunction. ALP was still announcing disaster to the room.

Tammy stared blankly across the chaos of the laboratory.

'*Jack* – I knew it'd end like this. I knew it.'

She bit her lip. 'Oh God – Kingston - what d'we do? We can't just leave him.'

She reached for a plastic beaker. 'I need water.' She hadn't drunk anything since getting up.

Jack took a step backwards, as if to physically remove himself from his surroundings. He picked his way around the gurney towards ALP, kicking away the tubes and wires. They littered the floor like discarded intestines. He twisted a couple of dials.

Alert, system malfunction. Then he found the key that controlled the voice activation and pressed it with his thumb. The lab at last fell silent. Now, the only sound came from the nasal whine of the florescent strips.

He took a closer look at the lab, surveying the wreckage of the equipment. The floor was soaking wet. Pipes and wires were strewn across the floor, lying where they'd fallen when the ice man had ripped them from his body. He must have dislodged the draining valve from the gurney for that also lay discarded.

Swabs, a set of unopened needles, even a thermometer lay broken on the vinyl floor-tiles. Jack pushed his shoes through the stuff and uncovered the magnifying glass he'd used during the autopsy. It also lay on the floor, its convex lens shattered from within. It looked like a bubble of water was trapped inside.

The dialysis machine was dripping fluid and the intravenous bags hung empty and deflated, like party balloons gone pop. One of the lights on the defibrillator was winking like crazy.

'Kingston's been dead four hours or more,' he said abruptly. 'Need to get moving.'

'But what can we do?'

'Call Tom. That's the first thing. Do it. Now.'

Tammy nodded and reached for her phone. She punched in Tom's number. 'What the hell do I say?'

It rang six times before he answered.

'Tom?'

Silence.

'Tom?'

'Who is this?' The voice was dry and filled with sleep. '*Tammy?*'

'Yeah. It's Tammy.'

There was a fumbling sound in the background as Tom reached for his watch.

'Tammy. Jesus. What the fuck's up?'

Tammy paused for a second, wondering how to put it into words. 'Tom, it's Kingston. It's -'

She swallowed hard but her throat choked up.

'Tammy - *Tammy* - ?' There was the first detectable sound of alarm in Tom's voice. He'd realised something was wrong.

'*Tammy?*'

Jack took the cell phone from her hand.

'Tom?'

'What the fuck's going on? Who's this?'

'Jack. Jack Raven. You need to -'

'*Jack Raven!* What the - I thought you'd gone. I thought -'

'Listen. Forget that. Just get in your car and drive over here. Now. To ZAKRON. Fast as possible.'

He paused.

'Kingston's dead.'

'*What!*'

'Kingston's dead.' He said it again, slowly. Slow enough to ensure it would sink in.

'Kingston's dead. Killed. Murdered. And *Ferris Clark* is gone.' He put emphasis on the words Ferris Clark.

There was a long silence, a splutter, the sound of Tom pulling himself up in bed and fumbling with his alarm clock.

'Jesus. This isn't some sort of mind-fuck?'

'Just get over here. And prepare yourself. It's not pretty.'

Another long pause. Jack could hear Tom's brain cranking through what he'd just been told, trying to make it make sense. Suddenly his voice broke back through the silence.

'Don't call the police. Do NOT call the police. Wait until I'm there. I'll be there right now. Give me twenty.'

Jack switched off the phone and handed it back to Tammy. She looked at him, her face framed with questions.

'But where's it gone? *Jack* - ? The corpse? *Jack* - ? What if it's still here?'

Jack shook his head, only half aware of what she was saying.

'He's professional,' he said. 'Not many can kill with a slash of a scalpel. Requires medical know-how and -' he searched for the right words - 'mental preparation.'

The killing of Kingston *was* professional. The ice man knew exactly what he was doing. Jack had worked on dozens of murder cases: what always surprised him was how the average person didn't have a clue how to kill someone. Nor how easily it could go wrong. Three blows of a spanner instead of one. A knife-wound that misses all the major organs. He'd seen that on several occasions. And DNA writ large over the crime scene.

'Murder's a two-fold process,' he said. 'If you want to succeed.'

Tammy looked at him. 'Oh?'

'Preparation. And skill.'

He drummed his fingers on the gurney then wiped them on a paper towel.

'Most murders are sudden, spontaneous, unplanned. Police see them all the time. Domestic row turns violent, an argument turns murderous. They're the easy ones to solve.'

He paused, still thinking it through. This one was different. The ice man knew exactly what he was doing, even after almost seven decades in a deep-freeze.

'He's been trained to kill.'

There was a long pause. Tammy pulled at her hair. Her hands were shaking.

'Where will he go?'

Jack shrugged.

'And what's his next move? *Jack*? Surely he won't last five minutes out there. *Surely*?'

'Maybe not. But -'

'But - ?'

'Like I said, we're dealing with an expert.'

'But Christ, Jack, you're supposed to be the fucking expert. Why d'you think I got you here in the first place.'

Her voice had an agitated tremor. She was close to breaking point. The sight of Kingston's corpse, the blood, it was all punching home.

'One thing -'

She looked up, expectant.

'He's not holding too many cards right now. He's woken into

a world that must be totally alien to him. Think about it. He must feel like he's landed on another planet. Even the lab here -' he swept his arm around the room – 'no machines like these in his day. No computers. And the last phone he'd have used would have been a chunk of Bakelite with some German fräulein at the other end. The world's moved on since he last blinked. He must be very lost.'

Tammy rocked backwards and forwards on her heels. She was listening to what he had to say.

'He left home in, what, forty-four? It was still the blackout. Photos of Hitler in all the shop windows. Swastikas flying from the lamp-posts. *Heil Hitler. Heil Hitler.* Goose-stepping soldiers marching down the Unter der Linden. And suddenly he wakes up, finds himself wandering along Interstate Fifty with cars, trucks, unlike anything he's ever seen. The road outside isn't Hermann Göringstrasse, Tammy. There's no banners telling him how marvelous the Führer is. Instead, there's adverts for Hollister and grilled flame-burgers and the latest four-by-four.'

There was a moment of silence.

'But Jack, shit.'

She clenched her fist, banged it so hard on the shelf next to her that a dish of syringes clattered to the floor. 'We need to catch him now, before he kills anyone else.'

'Yes.'

Jack dropped his voice.

'Fact is, we've no idea what's been brought back to life. All we know is it's not Ferris Clark.'

'Sure?'

'Sure.'

'D'you think Tom and Hunter knew?'

'Dunno, but possibly. You know they visited the Vegas archives *before* they even got on the plane to Greenland. I reckon they were looking for an identity to go with the corpse.'

Tammy threw a puzzled look.

'They left ZAKRON knowing only that a mystery body

had been found in Greenland. A mystery body in an unusually perfect state. And that was on the afternoon of June twenty-seventh.'

'So - ?'

'But by the time they've boarded that plane to Greenland, they've visited the archives, done some research, and decided it'd be extremely useful if the corpse belonged to Ferris Clark of Nevada.'

'Cos he's got no family?'

'No family, no ties, no one to cause problems. Tom's desperate to test out his dioximyde. A huge amount's riding on it, both for Tom personally and for Plaxon. And suddenly he finds himself with an unidentified corpse. He needs an identity if he's to persuade the board, Sergeant Perez, and everyone else involved that it's a body without complications.

'You saw the stuff in the archives. You couldn't get a more perfect candidate than Ferris Clark. Childless, parentless. He's got no siblings. Christ, they could send him into outer space and no one would give a shit. It's identity theft, pure and simple. Happens all the time. Fake credit cards. Stolen bank accounts. The only difference here is that they've stolen the identity of someone who's dead.'

'But what about the ID bracelet. F.C.?'

Jack scoffed.

'Did *you* see it? Are there photos of it? Does it even exist? Yes, ID bracelets were issued by the US army. I checked that one out right away. But only medical ones. And only for soldiers with diabetes. You saw the blood tests. The corpse, the ex-corpse, did not have diabetes.'

There was a low rumble of thunder from outside, the last vestige of the previous night's storm.

Tammy walked over to one of the sinks and turned on the cold tap. The water spurted in a freezing gush. She let it run over her hands then splashed it onto her face and hair.

'Feel like I've been up a week.'

She kicked at one of the tubes that had fallen under the sink, still thinking through what Jack had just said. It suddenly made sense. So much sense that it made her wonder why she hadn't seen through it earlier. And then she realised that she *had* seen it earlier. She'd seen it right from the beginning. And that's why she'd emailed Jack.

* * *

Jack made his way to the room that adjoined the lab and helped himself to a sterile gown. Then he unwrapped a pair of surgical gloves and pulled them onto his fingers one by one, allowing the latex to snap itself firmly around his wrists.

'Need to examine Kingston's body. I want to do it before the others get here. There's certain to be clues.'

He pointed to a CCTV, high in the corner of the room close to the ceiling.

'This thing recording?'

'Yeah. Always on at night. Works on a constant roll.'

'In Kingston's office as well?'

'Should be.'

He thought for a moment.

'Then half our work's done for us. It'll all be on the loop-tape. The ice man's made his first mistake. Caught out by technology.'

'You mean Kingston's murder will be on film?'

He nodded then made his way out of the lab, heading down the corridor towards the entrance area.

'I'm guessing you don't want to watch me examining him?'

Tammy shook her head.

'I'll wait here.'

She shuffled her feet.

'You're sure he's not still here?'

Jack nodded. 'There's bloodstains on the door. He'll have

got the hell out of here just as soon as he'd got into Kingston's clothes.'

He pushed his body against the door to Kingston's office in order to shift the leg that was jamming it closed. Then he squeezed himself through the gap.

Tammy put her foot against the door for a moment, holding it ajar, then relinquished the pressure and allowed Kingston's leg to push it closed again.

Jack swung his eyes downwards to the body. It was an extraordinarily precise killing. The carotid artery had been opened with a single cut.

He knelt down, avoiding the pool of congealed blood on the floor. Kingston lay twisted half sideways, as if he'd been trying to turn his head. His eyes were open but glassy and so far from life they looked like marbles. The tongue hung out of his mouth at a weird angle, like it was trapped between his teeth. It was a dull pink-grey. The pose in which he lay, contorted, made Jack think that he'd been caught off guard. The ice man had managed to enter the room in silence, not easy to do with a door that was on squeaking hinges.

He felt the muscles of the neck then positioned his fingers either side of the slash. The cut was so clean he could hardly feel it through the latex gloves. He pushed his second finger inside the wound. It just slotted. There was still a faint hint of warmth. He felt the depth of the cut. The flesh-tear was sloping, angled deeper at the front of the neck where the blade had initially been plunged in. It had then been jerked through the artery, like cutting soft cheese, and swiftly pulled out. Left–handed. And Kingston had been attacked from behind.

Why hadn't he turned? He must have heard the door open. Or perhaps he was watching his computer screen, listening to music, lost in another world.

The scalpel cut had been devastating. The walls, computer screen, paperwork, everything had been showered in a fountain of warm red blood. It had sprayed the floor, even reached the ceiling. Jack looked at the pattern of the blood, trying to calculate how Kingston had fallen. It splattered downwards towards the computer, suggesting that he'd slumped forwards, slid from his chair then landed with his face twisted upwards. And then, within seconds of his death, the ice man had stripped him of his clothes and dropped him back into his death pose.

Jack cupped his hands underneath Kingston's right shoulder and lifted the stiffened body slightly. He was always surprised how much a corpse weighed. Dead weight. How true were those words.

He twisted Kingston's torso upwards, towards him, flipping him onto his back. Winced. That was something he hadn't expected. A human skull had been crudely gouged into his chest. The ice man had found time to leave his signature.

He had a sudden thought and looked round the room for Kingston's holster and gun.

It was gone.

* * *

Jack pushed his way out through the door and into the entrance area. He removed his surgical gloves and dropped them into a bin. Tammy was about to ask a question when she was interrupted by a noise outside. Both of them looked up. Tom Lawyer's dark blue Buick was drawing up outside. The tyres coughed at the gravel and two doors opened and slammed. Tammy met them at the main door, pointing at the smear of blood on the glass.

'What's goin' on?'

Tom pushed his way into the entrance area, unshaven, disheveled, his shirt not ironed. The same one he'd been wearing the previous day.

Hunter pointed towards Kingston's door. 'You serious?'

Jack looked at them both.

'It's not pretty.'

He escorted them across the entrance area, like he was showing round new tenants. Then he pushed his weight heavily against the door to Kingston's office. It was still partially jammed by his left leg. Tom was the first to peer through the gap.

'Holy shit.'

He reeled backwards. As he did so, the door was pushed shut again by Kingston's leg.

Hunter was the next to look.

'Jeez -'

Jack watched the blood drain from his face. He was fumbling with his neck-tie.

Tom cleared his throat noisily.

'And the lab?'

He set off down the corridor, brushing passed the trash and knocking it over. Hunter picked it up then followed. The two of them entered the laboratory with Jack and Tammy close behind. Tom scanned the room. His eyes flicked from the gurney to the computer and then to the detritus on the floor.

'Shit.'

He turned to Tammy. Glared.

'My cell phone never rang. Why the hell didn't ALP - ?'

Tammy threw up her hands.

'The storm. Must have interfered with the signal. Must have short-circuited something. Caused it to overheat.'

'But there's back-up. What happened to back-up?' Tom paced around the lab, thinking hard. He kicked at the tubes and wires on the floor. Then he laid his hands on the gurney. It was still pumping heat, far hotter than it should have been.

'Turn this off.'

It was as if he needed to do something, take a decision. Turning off the gurney seemed the first step in solving the crisis.

'ALP predicted no earlier than four o'clock. The projected time for Operation Pump was late afternoon. How in hell could he get it so wrong?'

Jack filled the silence that followed. 'You realise it's not Ferris Clark?'

Tom glanced at Hunter but said nothing.

'Tammy and I came here at six last night,' said Jack. 'He was warming faster than expected. But nothing alarming. Tammy's right. The storm short-circuited something.'

He told them he'd examined Kingston's body.

'I'd put the time of death at between one and two in the morning, judging by the blood. And that means – '

He paused to look at his watch.

'And that means the ice man's already had five hours to get himself into hiding.'

SEVENTEEN

The picture was grainy and scratched. Slightly pixelated. It had the greenish tinge of CCTV footage. The camera was positioned close to the ceiling and covered a wide perspective of the lab. The gurney formed the centre of the picture, slightly distorted and skewed by the angle. The still-frozen corpse could be seen lying flat, stiff and immobile, its feet closest to the camera, toes curled inwards.

ALP was to the left of the shot. Nearby there was a low cupboard and the dialysis machine. A long tube linked the machine to the corpse. On the right side of the picture you could see the other equipment. Ventilator, defibrillator, the sequential compression device and three intravenous drips. Along the bottom of the screen a band of letters and numerals that recorded the location, date, time: LAB 2. 11.47:07.

Five of them were watching the footage. Jack, Tammy, Tom, Hunter and Jon Perez. Perez had arrived in Hanford late on the previous evening, having caught the last flight from Washington. He'd not intended to visit ZAKRON till the afternoon, when the rest of the board were also due to arrive. But Tom's phone message had abruptly changed his plans.

Perez was just as Jack had imagined him. Hispanic, dark-skinned, receding hair-line. A thin black moustache traced the contour of his upper lip. It could have been applied with a felt tip. Oval face, businesslike eyes. His handshake tightened into a vice.

'Heard about you. Hope we can do business.'

Do business. He made death sound like a transaction.

Jack flexed the muscles in his hand and felt Perez relax his grip.

Hunter had been busy trying to link the CCTV to his laptop. He'd finally been successful and now all five of them turned to face the picture in front of them. It was momentarily held on pause.

Tom swiveled his chair towards Hunter. 'Can you fast-forward this thing?'

'Yeah. Give me a minute.'

Hunter played with the keyboard, adjusting the speed of the fast-forward.

'Okay. Shout when you want to pause.'

The picture puckered and distorted as the image shot forwards. But the lab remained unchanged and the position of the corpse didn't move. Without the flashing dots and numerals at the bottom of the screen, it would have been impossible to know it was on fast-forward.

'Stop. Stop there.'

Tom shot his eyes towards Hunter.

'Can you rewind a bit?'

'What is it?'

Hunter hit the keyboard.

'Rewind sixty seconds or so.'

'Yeah?'

'And now play.'

They all stared at the screen.

'There –'

'What?' Hunter looked puzzled. 'What is it?'

Jack had also seen it.

'It's ALP. Rewind again.'

At exactly 11.56:22 ALP's warning lights flashed three times.

Perez turned to Tom. 'Why did it do that?'

Tammy supplied the answer. 'It's running a check on the

equipment. Does it routinely on the half hour. And if anything's wrong it alerts Tom's cell phone. Strange thing is, it shouldn't have done it at eleven-fifty-six. It's too early.'

'Now move it forwards slowly,' said Tom. 'Frame by frame.'

At 11.57:07 one of the lights on the control panel flashed and switched itself off. It was replaced by what looked like a different coloured light just above.

'Another warning light,' said Tammy. 'Look there. At the screen.'

She pointed to ALP's left hand monitor.

'Move it frame by frame again.'

It could be seen flashing a warning. 101. 102. 103. The numbers were coming faster now and the gap between each new one was shortening with every flash. 104. 105.

'No volume on this thing?' Tom smacked his hand on the table-top. 'Thought our CCTV had volume.'

'It does. But it's CCTV. Quality sucks.'

Hunter adjusted the volume control, turning it to maximum. The sound remained muffled. They could just make out a faint blip and a message flashing across ALP's left hand monitor. *Signal failure. Unknown recipient. Undelivered mail. Attachment failed.*

'Stop.'

Jack looked at the time on the screen. 00.03:44.

'ALP tried to send you an email, Tom,' said Tammy. 'Look. He's trying to tell you something's wrong.'

'Just after midnight.' Jack was trying to remember when he'd first been woken by the storm. 'Exactly when it was at its worst.'

ALP's system programme could be heard switching to the next stage of alert, transferring to voice mode and speaking to the room. *Alert, system malfunction. Alert, system malfunction. Alert, system malfunction.* Six warning lights were now flashing and the mainframe continued to issue verbal warnings to the room. The blank computer-generated voice gave no hint of panic, but the constant repetition revealed that something was urgently wrong. The lab looked like the control panel of a plane whose engines have just shut down. There were more than a dozen flashing lights.

'See that?'

Jack pointed a finger towards the pulsing and fading of the electric strip lights. You could see them clearly on the screen.

'Something seriously wrong with the current. Don't you have back-up power?'

00.04:06. The thin green line of the defibrillator could be seen starting to move. The dialysis machine gave a low clunk as it switched itself to standby. They watched frame by frame as the automated oximeter arm squeaked slightly and gave a mechanical shudder as it ratcheted through ninety degrees. Everything seemed to be taking place in slow motion.

'Shit.'

Jack saw alarm on Tom's face.

'Whole lab's swinging into action.'

The mechanized frame supporting the dioximyde grip dropped a fraction and let out a low hiss. It, too, had switched itself to standby.

Alert, system malfunction. Alert, system malfunction.

No one spoke. All five were watching intently, focused entirely on the laptop screen in front of them.

'It's happening.' Tom was talking to the room. 'Any moment. Keep it moving, frame by frame.'

00.04:12

00.04:15

00.04:17

Alert, system malfunction. Alert, system malfunction. Surface body temperature - malfunction. Inner core reading - malfunction. Inner brain reading - malfunction. Deflective heat source - malfunction. System override. All systems to manual.

Another warning light flashed up on ALP's screen. *Current 93.2F. Current 94.1F. Current 94.5F. Current 94.6F. Current 94.8F. Patient approaching optimum temperature.*

Danger.

Danger.

System override. All systems switch from standby to high alert.

A slamming noise. Then a clunk. Twenty or more lights were blinking on ALP's control panel. The thermostatic warning light flashed to 95F - DANGER - and all hell broke loose.

The defibrillator, the ventilator, the massive shots of dioximyde, the entire laboratory sprung violently into action, each machine focused on injecting life into the long dead body.

Jack kept his eyes focused on the face of the corpse. This was more exhilarating than any of his experiments with the death masks. As the light flashed 95F the face was transformed. The pain was tangible. Before, it had been rigid, immobile, locked up like a statue. But in the space of a second the mouth and eyes were lifted into a mechanical wince. It was scarcely noticeable at first, but then it was suddenly much sharper, as a piercing thump slammed into his chest.

You could see the acute discomfort, even though he was still a corpse. It was as if molten steel was spilling through his body, an explosion jolting his innards, wrenching his bones and stretching his ribcage. His chest was jerking uncontrollably, as if two invisible fists were pumping it up and down.

'Stop. Stop it right there.'

They'd all noticed it. The left eyelid of the corpse had dropped open. It was 00.06:34.

'Almost there -' There was nervous excitement in Tom's voice. 'Moving towards lift-off.'

The quality of the footage was still poor, but if you looked closely you could just make out the liquid being siphoned through the various tubes and pumps. And then, without any prior warning, the corpse gave a series of violent twitches and its second eyelid flipped itself out of the glue.

A gut-wrenching spasm pushed him downwards, deep into the gurney. And then his entire body shuddered.

'Jesus -'

Tom looked at Perez. His fists were clenched so tight that his knuckles gleamed white.

Slowly and with great effort the left arm of the corpse raised itself from death. It rose to just above the level of his chest, then fell heavily across his face. As it did so it knocked the tubes from his nose. They clattered noisily to the floor.

Manual removal of ventilator tubes. Cut oxygen feed.

'He's breathing -' Tammy whispered into the room.

They watched his face as he gasped in reflex. He was clutching at the air, just as he would if he'd burst upwards from deep under water. There was panic, but only for a second. Then he let out a long exhalation. Soon after, his chest could be seen rising and falling.

And now his right arm was moving, but also in slow motion. It was half-numb. It also swung across his chest and knocked away more of the drips.

Manual removal of dioximyde feed. Cut flow from feeder.

'*Huh -*'

Tammy let out a gasp.

'Look - look -'

His fingers twisted slightly, as if in a cramp, then clutched at the pads on his scalp. In one motion he ripped them violently away.

Manual removal of electro-encephalograph.

The five of them watched the screen in silence. The footage was moving frame by frame, jolting forwards at quicker speed.

'*Huh -*'

The corpse was starting to move. It was coming to life.

It was mechanical at first, a machine that was cranking into action. But when they watched it for a second time later that day, they realised it was the slow-frame mode of the play-back that made his movements look mechanical. He was actually moving more smoothly and naturally than they could ever have expected.

He struggled to lift his head from the gurney, like it was a block of concrete. Slowly he drew his elbows towards his chest. He pulled in his arms, clenched his fists.

Alert, system malfunction. Alert, system malfunction.

His mouth twitched then extended itself into a yawn. A second or so later, in another shudder, his body pushed itself into a prolonged stretch, more natural than the first.

'Holy shit.' Tom was whispering under his breath. 'The resurrection of the dead.'

When he finally started to lift himself up, he did so in a single fluid movement. He used his arms to raise his body from the gurney. He lifted his legs a fraction. Then, growing in confidence, he swung them towards the floor. He sat upright but unsteady, his head uncomfortably lolling on his neck. He looked dizzy. Drunk. Jack noticed one hand clutch at the edge of the gurney to steady himself.

'Left handed.'

His head swung like a heavy ball, lopsided, as he looked around the lab. He lifted his hands to his eyes, rubbed them. It was as if he was wiping away the disbelief. He clutched at his neck, his chest, his groin. He tugged briefly at his penis, like a toddler in the bath. And then, with a shove from both arms, he propelled himself onto his two feet. He was unstable at first. Even on the CCTV footage you could see the unsteadiness.

Tammy gasped.

'He's going to fall.'

But he didn't. He clasped at the dialysis machine, eyeing it suspiciously. He shook his head. A cloud seemed to fall from his eyes. And then he turned so that the left side of his body was facing the camera.

Jack turned to Hunter.

'Pause.'

Hunter stopped the shot in mid-frame.

'What - ?'

'Can you enlarge the image?'

'Yes.'

Hunter played with the keyboard.

'Can you focus?'

He pointed to the ice man's chest.

'Focus there. Closer. Closer.'

The more Hunter enlarged the image, the less distinct it became.

'What is it?'

Tom was frustrated. He couldn't see anything.

'*That*,' said Jack, pointing to the dark patch under the ice man's arm, 'is the tattoo of a human skull.'

Tom looked at the tattoo on screen. He glanced at Perez. Then he told Hunter to put the laptop back to full screen mode.

Hunter hit the play button again and the ice man turned to face the camera, just for a moment. He was unaware his face was framed centre screen. The quality was poor but you could see steel in his eyes. He looked down across the lab, lifted his arm. Then he swept files, syringes and boxes of swabs to the floor. A half smile as he surveyed the destruction he'd wrought. And then he suddenly stopped. His eyes had sighted on something.

'What's he seen?'

Tom stared hard at the screen.

'What is it?'

Hunter paused the film.

'*Tammy* - ? What's in that box?'

She moved closer to the screen, peered through her glasses.

'That's the sodium thiopental.'

Perez turned to her.

'What's sodium thiopental?'

Tom answered. 'Numbing agent.'

The ice man could be seen picking up the carton, examining it carefully, then putting it down for a second. He did the same thing twice. Then he looked round at the other items in the lab, inspecting the machines and twisting the dials.

He caught sight of himself in the mirror on the far wall and seemed to notice he was naked. Then he looked around for a second time before disappearing into the adjoining room.

Tom sighed. 'Shit. Out of shot.'

But after a pause of a few seconds he reappeared in the picture, now dressed in a white lab coat.

'Not so stupid.'

Perez turned to face Tom. 'Brain's most definitely not shot to shreds. You said his brain would be shot to shreds.'

Jack was thinking the same. 'He's behaving as any sane, rational person would do. He's naked. He wants to cover up -'

Tom raised his hand. 'Look. He's noticed the door. He's going out.'

They watched the ice man walk out of camera shot. It was 00.12:56. It had taken just six minutes for the machines to bring him back to life.

The click of the latch and he was gone. The picture on screen was of the empty lab, littered with detritus, lights winking and the voice of ALP talking blankly to the room.

Alert, system malfunction.

* * *

They sat in silence for a moment.

It was as if they needed to digest the miracle they'd just been watching. Jack was struck by how natural it all seemed. There had been no moment of crisis, as there so often was in intensive care. No moment when it looked like everything was tipping towards emergency. The perfect corpse had been brought back to life in perfect fashion. It had worked like clockwork.

Tom addressed them in a hushed tone. There was muted excitement in the trembling of his voice.

'This footage, d'you realise? It's priceless. It'll earn us millions. Imagine the syndication. Every goddam channel in every country in the world is going to want this.'

Hunter nodded in agreement.

'Can it be cleaned up? Sharpened?'

Perez jabbed his finger at the laptop.

'You can edit the fuzz. We do it all the time. But you need a professional and it takes –'

'For Chrissakes,' cried Tammy, turning to him accusingly. 'Kingston's dead. Murdered. Slashed to pieces. And all you give a shit about is your fucking TV footage.'

Tom swung round to face her, ignoring what she'd just said. 'What's the time?'

She checked her cell phone. 'Eight twenty-two.'

'Can you call Carla? Right away. Tell her not to come in till later. We need to remove Kingston's body. Need to get his room cleaned up.'

'What do I say?'

Tom shook his head. 'Dunno. Think of something. But not what's happened. Do *not* tell her about Kingston.'

Hunter was fiddling with the laptop, trying to link it wirelessly to the looped CCTV in Kingston's office.

Jack looked at Tammy. 'Sure you want to see this?'

'Can't be much worse than what I've already seen this morning.'

'True.'

The single camera in Kingston's office was set high above the door. It was focused on the electricity control panel and the cupboard that housed all the codes giving access to various areas of the building. But Kingston's back was clearly visible, along with the screen of his computer.

Tom shifted his chair nearer to the laptop.

'Let's start it a few minutes after midnight.'

Hunter forwarded the footage at double speed until he reached 00.04:00. And then he hit play. Kingston was seated in front of the computer, back to the camera. He was watching what looked like Fox TV. The sound was loud – there was the noise of canned laughter – and Kingston was dipping into a bag of Natchos. A bottle of Dr Pepper, half drunk, sat on the desk next to him.

Perez watched impatiently. 'Let's fast forwards. Move to twelve after midnight.'

At exactly fourteen minutes after the hour a slight shadow fell across the footage.

'Stop the film.'

Jack pointed to the screen.

Kingston was still seated in the same position and appeared not to have noticed anything.

'What is it?' asked Hunter.

'See that shadow. That's *him* opening the door a fraction.'

It lasted only a few seconds. And then the lighting returned to how it had been before.

'What's going on?' Tom's voice was hoarse. It sounded as if he'd just woken up. 'What's he up to?'

Jack told Hunter to switch back to the lab camera. 'He's going back to the lab. Just you watch.'

Hunter changed screens. According to the numbers at the bottom it was 00.14:59.

'Play -'

The lab was empty, silent, strewn with equipment. And then, at 00.15:08 you could hear the door open on its hinges. The ice man intruded back into the picture, still in his white surgical gown.

You could see him quite distinctly. He walked over to the low table next to ALP.

'My God.'

Jack whispered under his breath.

'This guy's smarter than we thought.'

'*What - ?*'

The ice man could be seen picking up the box of sodium thio-pental, opening it slowly. He withdrew a capsule and held it up to the light, like a doctor examining its contents. Then he placed it carefully back on the table and looked around the lab once more.

Tammy stared at the screen, perplexed.

'What's he doing?'

'Just wait.'

Jack watched, appalled. He'd seen Hitchcock. He'd seen all his movies. But this was altogether more disturbing. The ice man crossed the room, picked up a hypodermic syringe. He carefully removed its plastic cap and dropped it unwanted to the floor. Then he stuck the needle into the phial of sodium thiopental and sucked up its contents.

Tom glanced at Perez. Both of them were unsure as to what he was doing.

The ice man moved back towards the door, helping himself to a scalpel. He slipped it into his pocket. Then he moved out of shot.

Perez murmured under his breath. 'See him take the scalpel? That's your murder weapon.'

Jack looked at Hunter. 'Okay. Can we switch back to Kingston's office?'

Hunter connected to the other footage.

The scene was just as before. Kingston, back to the camera. Natchos. Dr Pepper. Still watching TV, although no longer Fox channel. It looked like he'd switched to TMZ. And at exactly 00.17:47 that same slight shadow fell across the footage.

'It's him,' said Jack. 'Look. He's entering.'

There was no noise of the door opening, no squeak of the hinges. You could hear Kingston chuckling to himself. Something on screen was making him laugh. He clutched the bag of Nachos, helped himself to a handful. Some of them dropped on the floor. And then his arm extended outwards as he reached for the Dr Pepper. He undid the plastic capsule. Fizz.

The darkish shadow hung over the room. Kingston had not yet noticed it.

Tammy was gripping her seat.

'Turn around,' she said out loud. 'For Chrissakes turn around.'

She felt as if she was watching it live, as if Kingston was

in the next room, as if he would hear her speaking, if only she spoke loud enough.

'*Turn around.*'

Kingston was shaking with laughter. Something he was watching was funny. You could hear his deep throaty laugh.

'What's he watching?'

'Springer.'

The screen blurred slightly. Kingston leaned forwards in his chair. As he did so the shadow darkened. Tammy placed her fingers over her eyes. She couldn't bring herself to watch.

But it didn't turn out at all how they were expecting. Jack alone had seen it coming.

An arm flashed into view, the arm of the ice man. He plunged the needle deep into Kingston's back, squeezed hard on the syringe. Kingston flexed slightly, backbone arching upwards. Then he jerked himself forwards, an involuntary jerk, as if in reaction to the sharp bite on an insect. He slumped forwards onto his desk, knocking the computer keyboard to the floor.

Tammy uncovered her eyes.

'What's happened?'

Jack turned to her.

'He's cleverer than we thought. He's injected him with the sodium thiopental. Knocked him out. And now -'

But even as he spoke, the ice man could be seen looming back into view. He stood over Kingston, pushed his limp body to the floor. Then he began removing his clothes. First he pulled off his shoes. Then his trousers. And then, moving round to the other side of his body, he raised Kingston upwards slightly in order to pull his arms from the sleeves of his jacket. He worked fast. By the time the on-screen clock reached 00.18:00 Kingston was naked, apart from his underwear.

They watched the ice man walk over to the door, once again out of shot.

'He's putting the clothes in the entrance area so they won't get covered in blood.'

And then he reappeared once again, large against the camera. He knelt down next to the unconscious Kingston, took out the scalpel from his pocket. He carefully unwrapped the blade from its metallic pouch.

It was appalling to watch. Kingston was unconscious, unaware of what was about to take place. The ice man seized Kingston's head and twisted his neck to one side. It was facing away from him. Then he took the scalpel in his left hand.

'*No -*' Tammy cried.

One deft movement of the wrist. A fountain of blood traversed the room. It sprayed in an arc across the walls, tracing a thick red line. A drop hit the camera lens, leaving a dark blob on the screen. It was 00.19:38, the moment of death. Seconds later the ice man could be seen turning the body over and gouging a crude human skull into the skin on Kingston's chest. It took him less than a minute. And then he was gone. The camera was locked onto a scene of horror. It was rendered all the more surreal by the picture's greenish hue.

* * *

Perez checked the time on his phone. Almost nine o'clock. The ice man had already been on the loose for more than eight and a half hours.

'Need to catch him. And soon. Before he does any more damage.'

He paused for a moment, still thinking about what Jack had said about the tattoo. Then he brushed his hand through the air, as if to dismiss the very idea.

'Don't give a damn *who* he is,' he said abruptly. 'All I care is *where* he is.'

Jack shook his head. He was thinking exactly the opposite.

EIGHTEEN

They moved Kingston's body into a vitrification box and set the thermostat to just below freezing. It gave them time to decide what to do with him.

'Sure he's got no family?' asked Perez.

Tom nodded.

'Sure. Only an old mother. Lives in some home in Reno. And she's halfway to the clouds. Kingston isn't our problem right now.'

They went back to the lab to settle on a plan of action. Perez shifted Hunter's laptop towards him and clicked on the keyboard, staccato-fingered.

'We've got a killer on the loose,' he said, stating the obvious. 'Priority number one, find him. And fast.'

'We'll go down for this,' said Tammy quietly. 'Each of us, individually, will go down for this. You've brought back to life a killing machine. And we'll be charged with murder.'

She glared at Jack accusingly. 'And I've got two young kids.'

Tom also looked at Jack, a cynical smile written across his face. 'Starting to regret staying on?' he said, rubbing his hands together. 'Kingston, *aagh* - we can get away with Kingston. You're all missing the bigger picture. Zero imagination. We've raised a corpse from the fucking dead, that's what we've done.'

Perez opened a street map of Hanford. He ran his finger across the screen, dividing the town into three equal sections.

'Nine out of ten fugitives are caught in the first three hours. Did you know that? Nail them early, that's what you need to do.'

Tom emitted a sarcastic laugh as he looked at his watch.

'He's been gone six hours, Jon. FBI up to their usual speed, then.'

Perez shot him a warning. 'Want us to mop up your mess or not?'

He placed his hands on his thighs then slid them down towards his knees. 'We need to get out there. And soon. He must be lost as hell. Wouldn't be surprised if he shakes out within half a mile of here.'

He pointed back at the screen. 'Okay, Tom and I'll take the Buick. We'll cover here, north of Oats Park. We'll do Lovelock Highway, East Williams Avenue, this area here, right up to the perimeter of the military airport. He can't have got further than that.'

'And me?' Hunter's eyes flicked from the screen to Perez.

'You take Kingston's car. Cover this part here. South Maine Street. Wildes Road. Beeghly Park. Drive every street. Keep your eyes focused.'

Hunter nodded.

'You two -' he glanced at Jack and Tammy. 'You do Sheckler. West Williams and up to the Skate Park.'

He pointed to a blank area at the top of the screen. 'Isn't this waste ground?'

Tammy nodded.

'Check that out too. Fugitives always end up in waste ground.'

He shut the laptop firmly, as if the case was almost solved.

'Any sighting. Anything dodgy. Call my cell phone. We'll be right with you. Any questions?'

Jack looked up. 'What about the police? Local radio? TV? Twitter? We're hunting a killer, for Christ's sake. He might strike again.'

Perez glanced at Tom then shook his head firmly. 'Not involving anyone for the time being. This could rebound big time. Tammy's right, we could find ourselves in the deepest pos-sible shit. Accomplices to the crime. And up to our necks. But we can still salvage everything, if we play it right.'

'Can't salvage Kingston,' said Tammy sourly.

Perez stood up and the others followed suit. Then he swept them out of the lab and into the entrance area, pausing for a moment as he caught sight of the bloodstain on the glass of the main door. He hadn't noticed it on the way in.

'Can we get this cleaned?'

Tammy nodded.

'And lock Kingston's office. And keep it locked. From now on, no one goes in there without my say-so.'

Jack made his way outside and waited while Tammy wiped the blood from the door. The sun was pumping hard and the puddles had shrunk to dark stains on the tarmac. He glanced up at the sky. A lone goshawk was tracing a spiral high above the ZAKRON rooftop, wheeling in a vent of warm air. The dark storm clouds of the previous night had been bleached clean. Now, they hung weightless like candy floss in the watercolour sky.

Jack clicked his keys to unlock the car then opened the door for Tammy.

'I could have saved Kingston,' she said despondently. 'If only I'd listened to myself for once.'

Jack pretended not to hear. He put the key in the ignition, started the engine. The air con blew hot for a moment before changing register and pumping coolness onto their faces. He felt the sweat dry tight on his skin.

'What planet's Perez on?' he said. 'Does he really think we're going to catch him strolling along the side of the road? Christ.'

Tammy folded her hands across her lap. 'At least we're getting out. Had enough CCTV for one morning.'

They took the eastbound Interstate 50 towards downtown Hanford, the sharp glare of the morning sun piercing the windscreen. The traffic was light and moving fast and they were soon on West Williams Avenue. The truck in front braked hard, forcing Jack to slam down his foot. Tammy kept her eyes fixed on the side streets, looking at everyone out and about.

'What happens if we see him?'

'We call Perez.'

'And then what? What's Perez going to do?'

'You didn't see?'

Jack tapped his hip, where Perez kept his gun. 'They'll shoot him if they catch him.'

'Jesus. The nightmare gets worse.'

It was cool in the car but the heat outside was visible as a shimmer on the tarmac. The brilliant yellow ginkgoes that fringed North Bailey Street hung limp in the sunshine. A hot breeze was sweeping dried husks and leaves through the gutters.

Jack turned on the local radio as they drove down West Bailey Street. Mrs Robinson was playing. They both scanned the sideways and alleys that led between the low bungalows. Few people were outside. They passed a sports car draped in thick tarpaulin. The top end of West Bailey Street was deserted and littered with trash. It might have been the end of the world.

'Turn, here –'

Tammy pointed right.

'Head up North Russell.'

Jack swung the wheel and they passed another row of identikit bungalows. A mechanic in blue overalls was messing with a car on the sidewalk, sweat shining on his face. Further on, a mother with a pushchair was struggling to open a parasol. Jack turned onto South Drive, passing CVS, the drive-thru Macdonalds, the Morris and Luvine drugstore. A giant red publicity cube stuck into the sky on the end of a tall pole. 'TAMGO'S BOX: seniors' morning Wednesdays.'

Jack slowed the car as they passed a garage. A pump attendant was filling a rust-coloured Subaru Forester, its owner watching on idly, hands on hips in full cowboy pose. They passed Econo Lodge. Three businessman stood in the porch, shiny suits and shiny shoes.

Tammy's cell phone rang. It was Tom.

'Anything - ?'

'No.'

'Then keep driving. Drive, drive, drive. All day if you have to. Find him.'

There was a pause. She could hear him muttering something to Perez.

'*Yeah, yeah* – if you need us we'll be at ZAKRON. Call if there's anything. Call if there's nothing. I want to know what's going on.'

Tammy cut the conversation and Jack stopped the car for a moment, tapping his finger on the steering wheel.

'They've gone back to ZAKRON?'

She nodded.

'First sensible thing they've done. Finding him in Hanford's going to be harder than finding him in Greenland.'

He started the car again, put it into drive.

'I'm going back to the hotel, Tammy. Get to work. Need to sharpen our act if we're going to have any chance of catching him.'

* * *

Jack dropped Tammy back at ZAKRON before returning to the Comfort Inn. He got a black coffee from the vending machine and took it up to his room. There were things he urgently wanted to check on the internet.

He logged onto the site of NARA, the National Archives and Records Administration in Maryland and clicked onto the section relating to Nazi war records.

When United States troops entered Germany at the end of World War II, they seized tons of Nazi party

and SS records. These are now housed at NARA and most are available on microfilm. The collection contains approximately 240,000 dossiers for individual SS personnel and their spouses. In addition there are incomplete records of the organizational structure of the SS, with some 135 files on the various units and commands.

The site had a keyword search engine designed for those who knew the name of the person they were searching for. It was less useful for general queries. Jack toyed with the keyboard, typing 'ss tattoo'. No results. He tried 'eichmann tattoo' but it produced just two entries, both about the Far East. He typed 'hitler inner circle' and 'eichmann inner circle'. These added little to what he already knew about the Mossad operation.

He had more success when he searched for 'ss inner circle'. He was directed to a page that listed the elite command units of the SS, along with an historical outline of the various Death's Head Battalions.

These were the units responsible for administering the Nazi concentration camps. But one of them, the 2nd SS Division Totenkopf, had been tasked with spearheading undercover missions, in advance of the regular army.

Jack paused for a moment, his thoughts turning momentarily to Greenland. Then he clicked on the link.

The most elite specialist unit of the Waffen-SS was the Totenkopf, formed shortly after the outbreak of war. It soon developed a reputation for ferocity and fanaticism, instigating and participating in a number of massacres on the Eastern Front, notably the 1943 Dyatkova killings, in which 163 Russian civilians were murdered by exposure to the extreme winter conditions. The Totenkopf undertook similar massacres at Vyazma and Narva. At least five of the unit's commanders are known to have been awarded the Ritterkreuz (Knight's Cross) for their participation in what would later be classified as war crimes.

He returned to the 'Search the Collections' page and typed in Totenkopf. There was only one entry and it reiterated what he already knew, that American forces had failed to seize the SS-unit files. 'Surviving records of the Death's Head Battalions (Totenkopfverbände) are housed in the Bundesarchiv in Germany.'

He stood up from his desk and went into the bathroom, tipping the residue of his coffee into the sink. Then he went back to his iPad and clicked onto the Bundesarchiv site. None of the documents were available on-line, but there was a lot more information about the 2nd SS-Division Totenkopf.

It had been formed in the autumn of 1939 with half a dozen recruits, hand-picked from the famed Thüringen regiments. These men led sabotage missions in the Low Countries. They also orchestrated the Blagny-sur-Ternoise Massacre, in which ninety-seven British soldiers of the 7th Battalion West Yorkshire Regiment, were machine-gunned to death.

In the spring of 1941, the Totenkopf played a key role in Operation Barbarossa. It was tasked with breaching the Stalin Line and establishing advance communications systems deep inside Russia. In this it was entirely successful. It then turned south, to the Demjansk Pocket, where it was encircled for several months before breaking through Russian lines in an operation that involved ferocious fighting.

In November 1943, the Totenkopf, reduced to just six men, was recalled to command headquarters in Hohenstein Castle in Bavaria. Henceforth and until the end of the war, it was engaged in highly secretive overseas operations.

Totenkopf. He looked up the word on Google. The death's head had been used as a military insignia ever since the reign of Frederick the Great, whose fifth hussars wore a black uniform adorned with the symbol. It was adopted by the Third Reich and used by a number of the SS-Death's Head Battalions. But Hitler personally intervened to ensure that it became the exclusive preserve of the 2nd Division Totenkopf.

'Those who served in this elite division were granted the unique honour of sporting a death's head tattoo on the left side of their chest. This came to public attention during the 1961 trial of Adolf Eichmann, although it was already known to the Mossad agents involved in the operation to snatch him from Argentina.'

Eichmann himself revealed that fewer than two dozen men were ever granted the privilege of wearing this badge of honour.

Fewer than two dozen men. If Jack was correct about the tattoo, then the ice man was one of those twenty-four. If he excluded Adolf Eichmann, that left twenty-three. But he felt sure he could narrow it still further. The Totenkopf unit couldn't have landed in Greenland until the end of 1943 because they were busy fighting in Russia. That meant the ice man must have been one of the six men who was sent to Hohenstein Castle in November 1943. And if that was the case, the net was closing faster than Jack had dared imagine.

He checked the time. Still only midday. Midday in Nevada meant it was evening in Berlin. He sat back in his chair for a moment, deep in thought.

Karin. He needed her help, there was no other way. Reluctantly, he connected to Skype and called her, catching her just as she was about to go out.

'Holy fucking shit, Jack,' she said when he'd finished telling her what had happened. 'Holy shit. I told you not to get involved. And now –'

'Never mind that. It's happened and now I'm coming begging for help. Any chance of you going to the archives? Tomorrow? It's on – ' he checked his notes – 'Finckensteinalle.'

There was a moment's silence. He could hear Karin leafing though her notebook.

'It's hardly ideal, Jack. We're shooting in the afternoon. Three-ish. But I guess there's the morning.'

'I didn't want to ask you but –'

'It's okay. I'm free in the morning. And well – ' she emitted a sour laugh – 'I'm used to digging you out of your own holes.'

'Anything about the Totenkopf,' he said. 'Anything about Greenland. And more than anything else, any names.'

* * *

Jack returned to ZAKRON shortly after lunchtime. He found everyone in sober mood. Carla had been crying. Her eyes were bloodshot, her cheeks blotched and flushed.

Tammy had already said she'd take Kingston's death the hardest. She used to arrive at work just as his night shift came to an end and the two of them would take themselves to Mabel's for a coffee and a muffin. Kingston was Carla's agony uncle, listening to her problems with a sympathetic smile. 'Why Miss Carla,' he'd say, 'you just trust your pretty instinct and it'll all end like it does in those fairy stories.'

Jack looked up just as Tammy appeared in the entrance area. She looked pale and agitated.

'Any news?' he said.

'Nothing. Been looking on Twitter. I'm following the local news sites. Thought there might be some mention by now. Some sort of sighting. But nothing. He's vanished.'

Jack glanced across to Kingston's door and noticed it was ajar. He was surprised. Perez had ordered it locked. He walked over and pushed it open, his eyes anticipating the scene of carnage. But all trace of the murder had been wiped clean. Kingston's chair, desk, computer, even the walls, were spotless. The only hint of what had taken place was the smell of phenox.

Ryan sauntered into the entrance area and saw Jack peering into Kingston's office.

'Took two hours,' he said. 'Needed to get it done before the directors arrive.'

One by one the team began to drift into the entrance area. Ryan, Luke, Hunter and the others. It was as if they needed to be together for a moment. Tom appeared from upstairs, his permatan skin a dullish grey, his brow etched with stress. You could see tiredness in his eyes, but also a glint of defiance. Jennifer alone retained her expression of blank indifference. You had to hand it to her, she didn't give a shit about anything.

Tom turned to face Gonzales, eyes like spotlights. Jack could sense that the blame-game was about to start.

'How, for fuck's sake, how?'

He spoke slowly and in a low voice.

'What went so spectacularly fucking wrong, Luke? I need explanations. And fast. We'll have the directors here in fifteen. Sam. Jim. Jordan. Todd. What d'you expect me to tell them? That he's taken himself off for a picnic?'

Doctor Gonzales's mouth twitched slightly before lifting into a curious half-smile. He was washing his hands of the whole affair.

'Don't even go there,' he said to Tom, brushing down his spotless white lab-coat. 'I warned you. Right from the outset. I told you that corruption of the brain was not just a possibility, but a probability. You chose not to listen.'

Ryan nodded in agreement. Doctor G had indeed warned them of the danger. In fact he'd spelled out the risks on several occasions. But he'd always been overruled by Tom and Hunter.

'I warned you we were entering uncharted waters. Those were my very words. I warned you we were testing a compound that was still in trial stage, But you – '

Tom cut him in mid-sentence.

'You said his brain might not function. You said he might be brain dead. But you never said he might be deranged.'

There was a long pause. Everyone was staring at Tom, expecting his rant to continue. But it was Jack who cut through the silence.

'That's precisely the problem,' he said. 'He's *not* deranged. A deranged person does not coolly, carefully take a capsule of sodium thiopental and inject it into their victim before surgically slashing their throat open. If he was deranged, we'd have caught him by now. We'd have found him staggering along the highway. Or lost in town. If he was deranged he'd be a push-over.'

'*So?*' Ryan wanted more.

'Your problem is this. He's done what any professional killer would do. He's gone into hiding.'

* * *

The ZAKRON directors arrived in two cars, Sam Taylor and Jordan Carreras in the first, Todd Roland and Jim Bartholomew in the second. Carla greeted them at the main entrance and then led them upstairs to the conference room. She kept the conversation to small talk.

'*Hey-hey-hey-* !' Tom overdid the welcome as they entered the room. He shook their hands in turn, slapped their backs. 'Long time.'

The four of them worked their way around the table, all handshakes and grins. Jack introduced himself. In the general enthusiasm, none of them thought to ask who he was and what he was doing there.

'Sit down, sit down everyone,' said Tom. Jack could see he was thinking on his feet.

'So -' Jordan leered at the room. 'How's the patient?'

Jim Bartholomew slapped the palms of his hands noisily on the table. His outsized forehead was beaded with sweat and his draping jowls looked greasy. 'We'd been hoping you'd text us. But then again, as I was saying to Todd in the car back there, no news is better than bad news. Isn't that what Nixon used to say?'

Tom shifted uncomfortably. It was the first time Jack had seen him on the defensive.

'I'm afraid to say that in this case no news is bad news.

Silence. All eyes snapped towards him.

'We've got a problem.'

The smiles vanished.

'*What - ?*'

He explained it all: the storm, the warm-up, the CCTV footage, the killing of Kingston. When he was finally finished the room remained in shocked silence. Sam Taylor cleared his throat as if it was full of mud.

'So what you're saying is this. We have a killer out there and it's not even Ferris Clark.'

Tom nodded. It was the first time he'd admitted it wasn't Ferris Clark. But before he could say anything more, Hunter pushed everyone's thoughts into a U-turn.

'Wait a minute. Aren't we running ahead of ourselves?'

'How so?'

'Let's not give up on Ferris Clark quite so quick. Let's just have a little think. Ferris Clark went missing in eastern Greenland in the summer of nineteen-forty-four. *Fact.* We take delivery of a body from eastern Greenland. *Fact.* The body matches the date. *Fact.*'

Todd, Sam, Jim Bartholomew, all were anxious to hear what he had to say.

'It's only our friend from London -' he speared a finger towards Jack - 'who's saying we've resurrected a Nazi.'

Jack watch all the heads swivel towards him. It was his turn to speak.

'Yes,' he said, scratching at his unshaven chin. 'And it's only guesswork.'

'*Guesswork*?' Jim Bartholomew snorted into the room. 'We've got a killer on the loose and all you're giving us is guesswork.' He looked at Jack more sharply. 'Who are you?'

He was interrupted by Carla, who appeared at the door with a tray of coffee. She handed the cups round, putting the only mug in front of Tom.

'Keeping this within these walls is our absolute priority,' said Perez in a low voice. 'We're in a hard place right now. In fact we're in deep shit. And Hunter's got a point. Whatever happens, and I mean *whatever*, we need to keep running with the story of Ferris Clark.'

Tom drummed his fingers on the table, like it might yet work out okay.

'Ferris Clark. Ferris Clark,' he said. 'Keep his name in your head. The living corpse that's hiding out in Hanford is to remain Ferris Clark until we decide otherwise.'

Jim Bartholomew reluctantly agreed. So did Jordan and the others.

'Gives us cover,' said Todd Roland. 'Room to manoeuvre. But Christ, Tom, what were you thinking?'

NINETEEN

The Bundesarchiv in Lichterfelde was all glass and concrete, a four-storey building that looked like it dated from the seventies. It could have been the extension block of a secondary school.

Karin followed the paved path around the outside, pausing for a moment at the front and turning her face to the sun. She felt its warmth on her skin and took off her sunglasses for a moment. Another beautiful day.

She'd been intending to spend the morning at her favourite café on Blumenstrasse, the boutique one with the garden that spilled onto the pavement. Croissant, cappuccino and cigarette in that order, with the latest German *Vogue*. But Jack's phone-call changed everything.

Jack. She could sense the old demons rising to the surface. One drink would lead to two, and then the bottle. She'd seen it all before. That's why he'd emailed her in the first place.

The porter at the Bundesarchiv information desk directed her to the second floor, where she was told to speak to Nikolaus, one of the archivists. She found him seated in front of a pile of documents that he was indexing. He had the earnest, anxious-to-help look of a student on work experience.

The way she was standing there, skinny jeans, almond eyes, hands on hips, she knew she'd provoke a reaction. Nikolaus flushed slightly. Spent too much time with white-haired history professors.

'Problem is,' she said, scraping her long hair back into a pile, 'I don't know *exactly* what I'm looking for.'

He fiddled with his collar for a moment then offered a librarian's smile.

'You're not the first,' he said. 'It's SS Totenkopf, you say?'

She nodded.

'We've got quite a lot on them. Let me see -'

He went over to one of the computers.

'Yes, it has its own section. Totenkopf, of course, is quite well known. Here we go. 'Totenkopf was the smallest of the Death's Head Divisions. It saw service on both the Western Front and Eastern Front before being directed into special operations.'

He paused for a moment. 'One, two, three - looks like we've got six individual files. But they're not complete. Never are.'

He looked up at Karin, his fringe of dark hair falling across his face. 'D'you want me to get everything?' And then his eyes switched back to the screen. 'Anyway, it all seems to be in the one box.'

'Please. Everything.'

'It'll take half an hour or so. I should warn you, they might be written in the old Gothic script. The Nazis brought it back. Revived it. Even I find it hard to read and I used it for my thesis.'

She nodded and asked if there were any other files that were relevant to the Totenkopf. 'D'you have lists of personnel? Men who served in that division? Anything.'

He frowned. 'Yes and no. And more no than yes. A lot were taken by the Americans after the war. Others were destroyed, some deliberately, some not. What we've got here are the files about individual units. What they did. Where they were sent. That sort of thing.'

'No problem. I'm sure I'll find something.'

'What exactly are you researching?'

'Trying to track someone. But like I said, I'm not exactly sure who.'

He gave a weak smile, as if to suggest that he knew what she was trying to say. 'A grandfather? Great uncle? We get people all the time looking for family information. They're often embarrassed. And not always happy with what they find.'

The phone on his desk rang. He left it unanswered.

'I'll go and get those files. I'll bring them to you.'

Karin crossed the reception area and entered the reading room. There were twenty or so desks, some computer terminals and three researchers, heads bowed. The scene took her straight back to university except that there, she'd spent her time checking out the boys. Now, she was checking out a killer.

She chose desk 22 and read the notice on the desk. No biros. No felt pens. No chewing gum. She gave a guilty glance at her bag. She had all three.

She pulled out *Vogue* and turned to the section on German fashion week. But before she could start reading, one of the security guys came over and told her that magazines weren't allowed in the reading room. She pulled out her mobile phone instead and skimmed through her messages.

The files arrived in less than twenty minutes. They were housed in a large grey carton with the words 'acid free' embossed on the cardboard. There was a single label on the spine: **SS Totenkopf**.

Karin opened the box with care, unpicking the thick black ribbon that held the lid in place. It had been tied with a double knot and took her some time to work it free. Inside were six flimsy envelopes. Each bore a name and date inscribed in pencil. 'Nord-Frankreich, 1940' was written on the envelope at the top of the box.

She unlooped the string fastener and lifted the front flap. There were a dozen or so sheets of yellowing paper, closely typed in German wartime script, along with several maps of Northern France. They were marked with red battle-lines and crosses. There were also two black-and-white photographs. One showed a brick farmhouse with dark window frames and shutters. The other was of a barn. She turned them over. Blagny-sur-Ternoise was written on the back of each.

She put the photos to one side and turned back to the printed papers. One set of sheets was stapled together and looked like an official report. It was stamped with an SS seal. When she turned to the last page she saw it bore the signature of someone named Balthasar Kraas. As soon as she started reading she realised it was an eyewitness account of a massacre.

```
I was able to look into the field
from the lane at the back of the farm.
The corpses were in British military
uniform and were lying in the long
grass, close to the barn. They lay in
such a position that I could only assume
they were killed by a prolonged burst
from machine guns. The dead men were
not wearing helmets and nor did they
have any military equipment with them.
I took photographs of the corpses. At
Reiter's request, these photographs
have been forwarded to Berlin. Reiter
himself told me that he had come to the
conclusion that a summary execution
had taken place. It had been carried
out by the SS Totenkopf.
```

Karin read through the report until she understood more or less what had happened. A hundred soldiers of the West Yorkshire Regiment had got trapped at a village called Blagny-sur-Ternoise, unable to make it to Dunkirk. They'd surrendered under the flag of truce, expecting to become prisoners of war.

Unbeknown to them, they had given themselves up to Oskar Weitzel, one of the most feared SS commanders. He had only recently replaced Adolf Eichmann as head of the Totenkopf. He had no time for conventions on the treatment of prisoners of war. He ordered his team to machine-gun the British soldiers.

There were other names mentioned in the text. Rochus Günsche had operated one of the guns. The second had been fired by Hans Dietrich. Joachim Schrieber and Heinz Piess had marched the men into the field. Hermann Eicke had bayoneted the fallen men to ensure they were dead.

According to one of the papers, two English soldiers had miraculously escaped death and fled from the scene. Their eyewitness testimony of the atrocity ensured the eventual trial and execution of Oskar Weitzel.

Karin chewed on her pencil, pleased to have eliminated one member of the SS Totenkopf. The ice man was not Oskar Weitzel.

She pulled a sheet of notepaper from her bag and made a list of the names mentioned in the account. Rochus Gunsche, Hans Dietrich, Joachim Schrieber, Heinz Priess, Hermann Eicke.

Jack had said that the ice man was probably a late recruit to the SS Totenkopf, since most of the early ones had been killed on the Eastern Front. But she decided to make a list of all the names mentioned in the various reports and then start the process of eliminating them one by one.

The second envelope was marked *Dyatkova und Vyazma*. This was even more shocking than the first. It contained a report of two massacres of civilians undertaken by the SS Totenkopf in the Soviet villages of Dyatkova and Vyazma.

A map was glued to the last page. From what she could tell, it showed villages in land already occupied by the German army. The report was stamped *Streng Geheim* (top secret). As with the previous one, it was embossed with the official seal of the SS Totenkopf.

The author of the report was Reinhard Kamptz, one of the men involved in the killings.

9.42am, 24 January, 1942: two miles south-east of Dyatkova village. Temperature minus twenty-seven.

At shortly before 9am, it being still dark, we entered the village of Dyatkova. This is a squalid place of twenty-three homesteads, built of wood, typical of this part of West European Russia. The villagers were known to have been hiding partisans who had inflicted two serious ambush attacks on the 88th Infantry Division of the Wehrmacht. More attacks were anticipated and were believed to be being planned and orchestrated from the 'safe houses' of Dyatkova.

We therefore ordered all the inhabitants from their beds at gunpoint. The majority obeyed, though reluctantly. Three remonstrated and refused to leave their homes. They were shot *pour encourager les autres*. After this, everyone came outside and, upon instruction, formed two orderly lines.

The operation thus far consisted of seven of us: myself (Reinhard Kamptz), Joachim Schrieber, Heinz Priess, Hermann Eicke, Hans Dietrich, Rochus Gunsche and Paul Loeper.

The mercury was hovering at twenty-seven below. The wind, easterly, was sharp. It felt more like the minus forty we had experienced in Minsk.

At this juncture we were joined by Wilhelm Wunsche and Georg Augsberger, to help in the next stage of the operation. The villagers were led towards the thick woodland to the north of the village. Most were dressed in their nightclothes. They were shaking with cold. A few jogged up and down in an attempt to get warm. Captain Schrieber ordered them to form themselves into a square. They were then addressed by Georg Augsberger, who speaks good Russian. He informed them that they had been sheltering resistance fighters. He then ordered them to strip.

There was general confusion at this point. No one obeyed. Augsberger ordered them again to remove their clothes. When still no one acted, Hans Dietrich and Hermann Eicke seized one of the older men and forcibly tore off his garments. Hans Dietrich then shot him in the forehead. When the villagers saw this they removed their clothes.

Hans Dietrich ordered them to lie in the snow. There was once again reluctance (the wind, blowing from the east, was biting cold) but the sight of Captain Wunsche walking across to the machine gun helped them obey.

As you are aware, Herr-Professor Theodor Keppler of the Kaiser Wilhelm Institute for Anthropology and Eugenics in Berlin-Dahlem had requested information on the efficacy of acute hypothermia as a means to exterminate large numbers of people in the shortest possible time. We were using the villagers of Dyatkova as guinea pigs.

Hans Dietrich informed the men, women and children (the latter numbered twelve) they would be free to return to their homes after fifteen minutes exposure to the cold. I, Reinhard Kamptz, vouch for the fact that this vow was made in earnest.

Hans Dietrich walked between the bodies as they lay in the snow, watching their reaction to the extreme cold. He has written a full report for Professor Keppler. It has been sent directly to Berlin-Dahlem. He timed the process on his stopwatch. Captain Schrieber also filmed the event for Professor Keppler: the film will also be sent directly to Berlin. The results of this experiment were remarkable. Within twelve minutes every single villager was dead. Acute hypothermia proved itself a highly effective method of disposing of large numbers of people with little or no expenditure.

This being a true account of what occurred in Dyatkova village on 24 January, 1942, I, Reinhard Kamptz, commend the following to be awarded the Ritterkreuz: Hermann Eicke, Hans Dietrich, Otto Streckenbach, Joachim Schrieber.

Karin felt sick. The report was so meticulous in its details and its tone so matter-of-fact, that it made even more disturbing reading than the Blagny-sur-Ternoise account. The Dyatkova massacre had been undertaken as a chilling experiment into hypothermia: clinical, ruthless, efficient.

She looked through the rest of the papers. There was another report on the Dyatkova massacre and a much longer one on 'hypothermic killing'. After photographing each document in turn she made a note of all the names mentioned in the text.

She then turned back to the box-file. The next envelope was marked 'Demjansk Pocket'. As with the previous folders, it contained military reports and diary entries that gave a summary of the various SS Totenkopf operations. The envelope also contained a letter written by one of the men to his mother.

'Our work is not without hardship but also with rewards. You will be proud to learn that I have been cited for the Ritterkreuz with oak leaves and swords.' It was signed 'your ever affectionate Otto' and gave a poetic description of the landscape, villages and people of Western Russia. It omitted any direct mention of the massacres.

The fighting in the Demjansk Pocket had been ferocious and deadly. One assault on Soviet positions had left three Totenkopf men dead and a further two injured. Karin was able to rule out Hermann Eicke, Wilhelm Wunsche and Heinz Priess as candidates for the ice man.

A counter-attack by the Russians had killed a further two: Rochus Gunsche and Reinhard Kamptz. Karin put a pencil line through their names as well. But she still had a list of five possible candidates and had not yet come to the ones recruited after the spring of 1942.

'Everything okay?' said Nikolaus, the archivist. His persistent helpfulness was starting to annoy her.

He picked up the envelope marked Demjansk Pocket and tapped it with his finger. 'One of the great untold stories of the war,' he said. 'Everyone wants to know about Stalingrad and the siege of Leningrad. But this –'

He opened it and leafed through the contents. 'Haven't seen this file before,' he said. 'But we've got many documents on the Demjansk Pocket. And they fought in mid-winter, too. You've heard of Otto Ohlendorf?'

Karin shook her head.

'At his trial he was asked if he had anything to say. He told the judge his greatest concern was for his men, because they had to kill such large numbers of civilians each day without any break.'

He put the file back on the desk. 'Just ask if you need help.'

Karin thanked him and then took out the fourth envelope. It bore the title 'Restructuring' and contained many more sheets of paper, most of them handwritten.

Jack had already told her that the SS Totenkopf had undergone a complete restructuring in the aftermath of its break out from Demjansk. The break out itself had left eight men dead (she noted their names), leaving only four of the original band still alive: Otto Streckenbach, Emil Lorenz, Hans Dietrich and Gunther Rauter.

These survivors were now joined by two highly decorated recruits named Ludolf Gebhardt and Kurt Becker. These were the ones that Jack considered to be the most likely candidates for the ice man. But Karin now knew that any of the six men serving in 1942 was a possible contender.

Otto Streckenbach.
Emil Lorenz.
Hans Dietrich.
Gunther Rauter.
Ludolf Gebhardt.
Kurt Becker.

She was hoping that the fifth envelope, *Grönland, 1944*, would reveal everything. But on opening it she found there was just one sheet of paper. 'The records of the SS Totenkopf's 1944 mission to Greenland and all sequential papers are currently held in Schloss Hohenstein, Bayern, 85447.' The paper was signed Bruno Wachter, Archivist, 28 March, 1963.

'Shit.'

She pushed back her chair and stood up slowly, tying up her hair with an elastic band and glancing momentarily in the reflective glass. Then she wandered over to Nikolaus, still clutching the sheet of paper. She showed him what it said.

'Yes, this is quite possible. Our records here are far from complete.'

'But what's the likelihood they'll still be there? At the castle, I mean. This was written in – ' she looked again at the date – 'in sixty-three.'

He swung his chair around to the computer, as if it held the answer to everything. 'After the war most of the Nazi records were moved to local archives,' he said. 'In this case -' he typed Schloss Hohenstein in order to check where it was situated – 'yes, they'd almost certainly have gone to Murnau. Some of the records came to us in the nineteen-fifties, but by no means all. We still have many missing gaps. One day it'll all be on line. But it's money, money.'

He paused, thinking for a moment.

'You should contact the castle. And also the Murnau archives.'

He punched at his keyboard and then wrote an email address on a scrap of paper. 'Here,' he said, handing it to her. 'That's for Murnau.'

Karin returned to her desk and untied the string that sealed the final envelope, half-expecting it to be empty. But no, there were more than a dozen photographs inside, tied into two batches. She laid the first lot out on the table. Two of them depicted the farmhouse and barn in Blagny-sur-Ternoise. There was also an out-of-focus picture of a group of homesteads, built of wood and almost certainly Russian. The ground was covered in thick snow.

The second batch was more promising: portraits of the men serving in the SS Totenkopf. One of the head-shots depicted a commander in full SS regalia: clipped cap, death's head badge and eyes that pierced, even in black-and-white. She turned it over. *Obergruppenführer Oskar Weitzel*, the one executed for war crimes.

There was a group picture of six men standing in sunshine, naked from the waist up. One was holding a leather football above his head. Karin looked more closely and instinctively clicked her fingers. Here was something for Jack. The man had a small tattoo, clearly visible, under his left arm.

All six men were remarkably good looking: blond or blondish, physically fit, well-toned. In another life they'd have made body-perfect male models. But in Nazi Germany, they'd chosen to become murderers.

She looked at their faces. They had that well brought up look that's hard to fake: good schooling, good manners. But which one was the ice man? From Jack's description of the frozen corpse, any one of them could have been him.

She flipped the photo over. 'SS Totenkopf, Schloss Hohenstein, Bayern, 1942.' There was a list of their names: Emil Lorenz, Ludolf Gebhardt, Kurt Becker, Hans Dietrich, Joachim Ulrich, Otto Streckenbach. Unfortunately, there was no clue as to who was who.

Two pictures showed soldiers in deep snow. Another depicted them sitting astride a captured Soviet tank. Karin searched through the rest of the photographs until she found what she'd been hoping to find all along: individual portraits of the soldiers. They were from the 1942 intake, head-shots and formal poses, almost certainly copies of the ones used for their identity papers. When she turned them over, she found their names written on the back.

She studied each one in turn. Emil Lorenz had straw-blond

hair and languid eyes. He was giving a strange half smile to the camera and didn't look like a killer. In fact, he looked the sort of diligent young lad who played the organ in his local church.

Ludolf Gebhardt was also fair-haired, but he had lips so curiously thin that it was as if he didn't have any at all. He had obviously blue eyes, even in black-and-white, and looked every inch the Nazified Aryan.

Kurt Becker was darker and had a dimple on his right cheek. His expression was a mix of jollity and bemusement, as if he was suppressing a laugh.

Hans Dietrich was the best looking of the group, roman nosed, well chiseled. He had the air of having hailed from a long dynasty of landowners. Strange how some people could look effortlessly distinguished.

At first glance, the last two, Joachim Ulrich and Otto Streckenbach, resembled each other so closely that Karin wondered if they were related. But when she studied their faces more closely she realised their physiognomy was actually quite different. Joachim had high cheek-bones, Otto's eyes were slightly misaligned.

She laid each picture out on the desk and photographed them in turn. If Jack's assumptions were correct, one of these six had been brought back to life and was now wandering around Hanford with blood on his hands.

She checked the images on her camera to make sure they were all in focus. Then she put all the papers and photos back into their envelopes.

'All good?' Nikolaus looked concerned as she handed everything back to him. 'Find what you wanted?'

'Think so.'

'Not a good band of men, those.'

'Not at all. Any idea what happened to them? At the end of the war, I mean?'

Nikolaus shook his head. 'So many simply disappeared. Some went to South America. Others managed to cover up what they'd done. And quite a few had no shame at all. Have you heard of Fritz Simon? He joined the Berlin Philharmonic in the fifties and played the violin till his death. The only one who paid the price was Weitzel.'

'I saw that in the file.'

'Still, they're all dead now. Or if they're still alive they must be in their nineties.'

Karin thanked him for his help.

'You're welcome. Any time.'

She made her way downstairs, pausing for a moment at the main door before stepping outside into the hot sunshine. She looked at the time on her phone. 12.16. She was surprised it was so late. She'd been in the archives more than two hours. Just enough time to get changed and call Jack before heading off for the shoot.

* * *

Jack answered his phone immediately. She knew she'd woken him.

'Find anything?' he said in a sleepy voice.

'You haven't checked your emails?'

He looked at his watch. 'No. Jesus, it's not yet five. Hold on.'

She could hear him opening his laptop, waiting for it to connect to the internet.

'Here we go. Here's your message. Seven attachments. Downloading them right now.'

While he waited, he asked about the archives.

'I've got you names. And photos. They all look like they work for Models One. But I don't know which one's your ice man.'

He opened the files individually, hoping that one of them would match the ice man. It wasn't Emil Lorenz, he could tell that immediately. The eyes were far too big. Nor was it Kurt Becker. His nose was bulbous at the tip and completely the wrong shape.

'*So – ?*'

'Hang on.'

He looked at Joachim Ulrich and Otto Streckenbach. Neither of them fitted his face. But when the fifth picture came up on screen, yes, when the fifth picture came up on screen –

'*That's him. That – is – him. Unmistakably. That's the ice man.*'

'Which one? Which are you looking at?'

He looked down at the caption.

'Hans Dietrich. The ice man is Hans bloody Dietrich. Without any doubt.'

He clapped his hands together then switched on the bedside light.

'Shit – shit –' He could hear the alarm in Karin's voice.

'*What? What is it?*'

'Hans Dietrich –' she said, speaking very deliberately. 'He's the only one to have been in Totenkopf from the beginning.'

'*Oh* – ? What d'you know?'

'Only this. He was at the massacre in France. He was at Dyatkova and that other place. And he was one of the few who survived the Demjansk Pocket.'

Jack was listening carefully.

'Ninety-seven killed in Blagny-sur-Ternoise. Two-hundred-and-fourteen killed in Russia. Christ, Jack, he's already been involved in the deaths of –' she counted it up in her head – 'of more than three hundred people. And they're only the ones we know about. And now there's Kingston, of course.'

Jack nodded to himself. He was wondering how long it would be before he killed again.

TWENTY

W hat am I supposed to say?' said Jack, throwing his hands into the air. 'What the hell d'you want me to say?'

He was seated in Tammy's office on the first afternoon after the murder. 'That I'm sorry about Kingston? Of course I'm fucking sorry.'

'*Sorry* - !' she scoffed. 'Too late to be sorry. Kingston's dead, butchered, murdered, and nothing's ever going to bring him back.'

Jack leaned backwards in his chair. The way she was speaking, Christ, she sounded like Karin on her last night.

'Kingston was the kindest person on earth. He was my friend. He was the only honest person in this place. And now he's dead.'

'Tammy,' he said, looking directly at her. 'I could not be more sorry. I was wrong. I admit it. Wrong about everything. But I had my reasons. And it wasn't exactly all my doing. You're dumping it all on me. What about Tom, Hunter, Gonzales? This would have happened even if I hadn't been here.'

'I blame myself,' she said with a sigh. Her expression was caught somewhere between anger and sorrow. 'Should have listened to the voice in my own head.'

* * *

The weather had once again turned stormy, with a battalion of thunder clouds stacked up on the western flank of the sky. When Jack had driven into Hanford at lunchtime, a few splats of rain had hit the windscreen like flak then vaporized into the heat. The rolling hills of the scrubland had taken on a tinge of diluted green, like they'd been washed with watercolour.

It was just after five o'clock when they gathered once again in the conference room. Tom Lawyer addressed them first: he had very little to say. There had been no sightings, no one in Hanford Gap had noticed anything untoward. The ice man had simply disappeared.

'Jon and I agree that Jack should stay on.'

Jack smiled to himself. In the hours since Kingston's murder he'd seen a subtle change in Tom's behaviour. Outright hostility had turned to grudging acceptance. All talk of plane tickets to London had been dropped. And now he was being invited to join the team. Tom was no longer working from a position of strength.

Jack had noticed another change, one he'd first detected on his first full day at ZAKRON. Tom's new target was Gonzales. He'd been selected as the one to carry the can.

'Jack, anything to add?'

Jim Bartholomew was nodding, as if in agreement with Tom's question.

'Yes,' said Jack. 'Brace yourself. We're dealing with someone who's committed dozens of atrocities, summary executions, that sort of thing. He fought in northern France and Soviet Russia. Served in special operations. And I've got a name for you.'

Their heads turned sharply towards him.

'Hans Dietrich.'

He handed round the photo that he had printed off his laptop. The quality was not great, but good enough for everyone to see the striking resemblance. The ice man and SS-Hauptsturmführer Hans Dietrich were visibly one and the same.

Jack watched their reaction with interest. They all flinched when he said the name, as an abstract was suddenly turned to concrete. *Hans Dietrich*. The name transformed him into a real person.

'What more?'

'It seems as if six men went on a mission to Greenland. Emil Lorenz, Ludolf Gebhardt, Kurt Becker, Joachim Ulrich, Otto Streckenbach and, of course, Hans Dietrich.'

Sergeant Perez was nodding to himself.

'I don't know what they were doing there. I can't tell you why these six were chosen. But you don't send your most elite soldiers to Greenland unless they have something pretty important to accomplish.'

He paused for a moment, then told them about the information he had received from USMOD, Ferris Clark's organization.

'*Ferris Clark!*' Tom snapped out his name as if he was an intruder in the room. 'What in hell's name has he got to do with it?'

Jack swung his chair round towards Hunter.

'It's you, Hunter, I should thank. You got me back on the trail of Ferris Clark.'

Hunter looked at him blankly.

'Remember what you said? Yesterday. Ferris Clark, Ferris Clark, Ferris Clark. You told us not to give up on Ferris Clark. Well I haven't.'

There was a long silence. Jack could see from their faces that they didn't get it at all.

'Could you enlighten us?' said Tom, his voice leaden with sarcasm. 'Is the ice man Hans Dietrich or is he Ferris Clark?'

Jack tapped his pen on the table.

'It's just as I've told you, the ice man is Hans Dietrich of the SS Totenkopf. But Ferris Clark – here - look -'

He clicked on his iPad, brought up a picture on screen.

'Take a look at this -'

He held it up and showed it round. 'Can you all see?'

They nodded.

'This is Ferris Clark. Always good to put a name to a face.'

The picture looked as if it had been taken when Ferris was still a student, eighteen or nineteen. Round glasses, baby face and a neatly combed fringe, like mum had spruced him up for the camera. He was wearing a suit, tie, collared shirt, and appeared to be seated in a laboratory, hands folded neatly under the table. The pose said it all. A diligent student, one who knew the chemical elements by heart. Shy with college boys, blushed with college girls. The air of a loner.

Ferris Clark was probably boring as fuck. That's what Hunter had said. But Jack now knew that this was very wide of the mark. The USMOD information suggested that Ferris Clark was brilliantly gifted and possessed of a formidable intellect. Perhaps even a genius.

'Hold on - hold on -'

Tom raised his hands into the air, not understanding a thing. His face had taken on a peculiar hue, grey with tiredness yet also flushed with stress. Jack noticed that his eyes were bloodshot; he hadn't found time to change his contact lenses.

'Can we hit rewind? One minute you're telling us it's not Ferris Clark, the next you're showing us shots of Ferris Clark.' He looked round the room. 'Is it just me or is everyone lost? I'm somewhere down on the Mexican border.'

Jack began to explain.

'Ferris Clark. Studied here in Hanford till twelfth grade. We don't know much about his time at high school, except that he seems to have been exceptionally gifted. Aged seventeen or thereabouts he's snapped up by North Carolina State University. It's in Raleigh, as I'm sure you know. Best place for meteorology, least it was in those days. And he was their most brilliant student.'

Jim Bartholomew reached out across the table and clutched his hand around the neck of a bottle of carbonated water. He pulled it towards him and unscrewed the cap with his plump fingers, breaking the metal fastening with a clack and letting it drop onto the table. The water fizzed and sent a fine spray across the table. He wiped it with his handkerchief then turned back to listen to Jack.

'Ferris Clark was a brilliant student. One of the best. And before long he was in correspondence with all the great weathermen of the time. Bergeron, Douglas, Pettersen, Harding. Seems to have known them personally. He wrote several key papers on the development of showers and thunderstorms. And also wrote key papers on -'

He turned his iPad round so that he could read from the screen.

'Wrote key papers on the creation and movement of weather fronts. He believed these could be found in the horizontal movements of air that are associated with large depressions and anticyclones.'

Ryan gave a deliberate yawn. 'Is this relevant?'

Jack stared hard.

'Absolutely crucial. Doesn't matter if you don't understand the detail. Just listen.'

He told them how Ferris Clark had pioneered the use of aneroid balloons, getting data from higher in the atmosphere than ever before. He'd noticed a discrepancy between the surface winds and upper winds and realised you could produce highly accurate forecasts if you had accurate readings of these different sets of winds.

Tom drummed his fingers on the table.

'And then he developed a system of prognostic charting. In laymen's terms, he was using previous weather patterns to predict future ones. All very primitive compared to today's forecasting, but a work of genius for the nineteen forties.'

He paused.

'One other thing I learned from the Washington stuff. Ferris Clark had a photographic memory. Had more than a decade's forecasts stored in his head. Memory. Prodigious skill. And brilliance.'

Jack ticked them off like they were on a list.

Jim B swept his hand around the room.

'Please. I'm lost.'

'Remember,' said Jack. 'The Nazi weather stations in Greenland have been destroyed by this point in the war. And not knowing the North Atlantic weather forecast spells potential disaster for Hitler. So he sends a team of his most brilliant SS officers, including Hans Dietrich, to rectify this.'

Tom butted in, shaking his head from side to side.

'Nope. Still don't get it.' You could hear the frustration in his voice. 'You're saying Hans Dietrich killed Ferris Clark? Or Ferris Clark killed Hans Dietrich?'

Jack shrugged.

'A lot doesn't add up.'

All the while he'd been talking, Tammy had been toying with her cell phone, flicking from Twitter to Facebook and then back to Twitter. Now, as she scrolled down the screen, she gulped loudly.

'*No!*'

She froze.

'What - ? What is it - ?'

'What's happened - ?'

'Oh my God. Breaking news. On Twitter. There's been a murder.'

TWENTY-ONE

Tom drove at speed through the commercial district of Hanford, swinging the Buick left into Sapphire Way, then left again into Rio Vista Drive. The huge sun hung like a ball on the horizon, so close you could reach out and snatch it away. The surrounding sky was slicked pinkish-blue.

'What number?' It's one hell of a long street.'

Tammy checked the twitter feed.

'Just says Rio Vista Drive. Doesn't give a number.'

Tom squeezed his foot gently on the accelerator. The car snapped up the empty street.

'Look, up there. They've thrown up a cordon. Across the driveway.'

As their Buick approached, two cops, one male, one female, emerged from the front yard. Jack looked them up and down, checking their badges and guns.

Officer Aaron Don. Twenty-six years or thereabouts, eager face, intelligent eyes. Faint smear of acne on his forehead, shoulders that sloped into his chest. Too young to handle a homicide.

Officer Shannon Cass, even younger, wavelet hair like it was still the nineteen eighties and a thick wedge of gum in her mouth. Strangely small feet. They were the small town American cops he'd seen in too many movies.

Jon Perez slid down the passenger window and greeted them with his FBI pass. Officer Don took it, scrutinized it then looked back at Perez.

'Weren't expecting you guys. No one told us nothin'. We've had Rayno here, that's all.'

Perez pulled a puzzled face.

'Lem Rayno, Churchill County sheriff. The serious guys are on their way from Vegas. We're just here to keep watch. Make sure no one comes pokin'.'

Perez nodded like it all made sense then explained how they'd seen it on Twitter. 'Thought I should swing by. Take a look.' He forced a laugh. 'Telling you, you're never on vacation in the FBI.'

Officer Don smiled (it was a line he could re-cycle) then peered inside the car.

'Who's your friends?'

'This is Tom Lawyer. Tammy Fox.'

'Doctor Jack Raven,' said Jack, extending his hand through the open window. 'From London, England.'

He produced an out-of-date Metropolitan Police pass, wondering if it would wash. Officer Don took it, examined it and then showed it to his colleague.

'Hey Cass. Check this out. Haven't seen one of these.'

Officer Cass studied the royal crest and gave a nonchalant shrug of her shoulders. Then she chewed hard on her gum and handed the pass back to Officer Don.

'Dunno,' she said. 'Rayno said no one crosses the cordon. *And no one means no one.* That was his words.'

There was a moment of indecision. Officer Don scratched at his head, like it might help him find an answer. FB-fucking-I. It just got better and better.

And no one means no one.

He couldn't say no to the FBI. He could already picture them back at the station, a shedload of laughter. *Hey everyone! Officer Aaron Don refused the FBI into a murder scene.*

Officer Cass was nodding her head, like she'd made up her mind.

'You - and you -' Officer Don pointed a finger at Perez and Jack.

'But you guys –' He gestured towards Tom and Tammy. 'Fraid you'll have to wait here. Otherwise Rayno'll eat us alive. And he's one hungry son-of-a-bitch.'

Tom nodded. 'We'll wait. We'll wait here.'

Perez and Jack got out of the car and shook hands with the two officers, establishing a bond of trust. From the way they were shifting on their feet Jack could tell it was their first murder.

'London, you said?'

Jack nodded.

'What brings you here?'

'This.' He pointed towards the house.

Officer Don laughed. 'Welcome to the centre of the universe. I can tell you one thing, we don't get this crap every day.'

Jack glanced back down the empty street. The bungalows were widely spaced out, front yards scrawny and littered with junk. Trailers and tarpaulins. A few dusty cars parked along the sidewalk, hot from the day's sunshine. He swung his gaze around to the murder house. It was very different from all the other homes – clapperboard, white paintwork, wooden porch and two sets of six steps that met as a triangle outside the front door.

There were two sash windows on the ground floor, black as slate in the shadow of early evening. Three more on the first floor. And there were two smaller windows that protruded a touch from the tiled roof. They were catching the evening sunshine and making it glint like shots of gold. It could have been a dolls house, with the façade hanging on hinges that swung open to reveal the rooms inside.

Officer Don watched Jack carefully as he eyed the house, keen to note what professionals did.

'Neat, eh? No change from half a million. Not so many like this left in Hanford.'

He waved his arm down the street.

'See. Bungalows. All modern. But this one –'

Jack agreed it was old.

'Not so old for you I guess. Buckingham Palace and all that.

But this is President Lincoln for us. When this was built -' he jerked his finger back towards the house - 'Hanford was ten shacks and a county sheriff.'

He paused for a moment. 'Wanna step inside? You oughta go inside.'

Officer Cass turned to Perez. 'Guess you see this all the time.'

He nodded. 'Business.'

They picked their way across the front garden, its grass scorched to baking parchment by the heat. A pink climbing rose was making a half-hearted attempt to mount the white balustrade that provided a handrail to the front door. Its leaves were gleaming in the sunshine.

'What d'you know so far?' asked Perez.

Officer Don stood on the third step and turned to face him and Jack.

'Chilling. Worst thing I've ever seen. Car crashes, petty theft, break-ins, that's our daily fare. But this -'

He let out a low whistle.

'Single cut to here -'

He pointed at his neck.

'Prepare yourselves. Been raining blood in there.'

Jack caught Perez's expression.

'Not suicide?' he asked, disingenuous.

Officer Cass looked toward him, twisted smile, gum caught in her front teeth.

'First suicide in history where the person doing themselves in cuts a skull into their chest. Like I said, not pretty. Skull gouged with a knife. And neck sliced open. You'll see -'

He continued up the steps then opened the front door.

'Any idea of his identity?' asked Perez. 'The victim, I mean?'

'Yup. Name's Ashton Brookner. But that's not public yet. Family not been informed.'

Officer Don ushered them into the hallway, pausing for a moment to give them the chance to look around.

'He's in the back room. Guess in the old days it'd have been some sort of parlour.'

Jack paused for a moment in the hall, eyes focusing through the gloom. There was a long woven runner that lined the floor, leading from the front door to the staircase. A pair of stout rubber boots on the mat, covered in a thin film of dust, a galvanized wall-clock stuck at 3.32. And there were three hand-coloured engravings of New York that looked like they dated from the turn of the century. A man's house. Middle aged, prosperous. Liked his comforts. The stairs were painted white, like the walls. There was a scent of baked cinnamon.

Officer Don stopped again, hovering in the doorway to the back room. 'Hardly need tell you guys not to touch. We've checked him out, of course, poor bastard. Works for - sorry, worked - for Vortec Aerospace. D'you know the place? Out beyond the airport.'

Perez looked up. 'Green Valley Way?'

'That's the one. Spoke to the manager. Rayno got me and Officer Cass here to do the calls. Friendly guy, the manager. Shocked out of his mind. Known Ashton Brookner for six years three months and wouldn't hurt a cockroach. Exact words. Wouldn't hurt a cockroach. Funny what folk say.'

Perez raised his hand a fraction, signalling a question.

'Did he have issues with anyone? Business deal gone wrong? Relationship problems? Family? What you found out?'

Officer Don shook his head. 'Nothin' like that.'

'You see -' Perez continued - 'of the last twenty, thirty homicides I've dealt with, I reckon two thirds have been family.'

Officer Don stood silent and let Officer Cass pitch in the stuff she'd found out.

'Not this one. Not married. No lady in his life. But not gay, neither. And from what the manager-guy said, it was all happy families. Rayno's checking it all out. Going through his contacts. Should know more later.'

They filed into the back room one by one.

'*Jesus fucking Christ -*'

Perez was used to violent death but he was still caught unprepared. He hadn't seen Kingston's body, only been told about it. And now this.

A gently rising arc of blood in russet brown, splattered all over the walls and ceiling as if someone had lifted a can of spray paint and ran their arm through the air.

'*Holy shit –*'

For Jack it was like Kingston in duplicate. His eyes shifted straight to the corpse. It lay in an ungainly position, fully clothed, unlike Kingston, and with the neck twisted backward a fraction. The head was lying heavily on the right ear.

He moved closer, looked at the contorted face. Leaden white, drained, the blood sucked away. The chest was exposed. As Officer Don had said, it was carved with a crude skull. A professional hit. And he'd had time to leave his signature.

'Said it weren't pretty and it's not. And now there's flics comin'.'

'Time of death?' asked Perez, gulping. 'Any steer?'.

Officer Don told them that Rayno thought he'd been killed in the early hours. Two o'clock. Perhaps three.

Jack looked at the body again and then counted back the hours. He agreed. Dead for at least sixteen hours, maybe longer.

'Who found him?'

'Cleaner. Opened up. Came in. Screamed. And made the call.'

Jon Perez looked back down at the corpse and shook his head. 'The work of one violent psycho.'

Officer Cass agreed. 'Psycho and sicko. Why'd anyone do this? And why *him*?' She pointed at the body. 'Worked hard. Didn't harm no one. A regular guy who keeps himself to himself. And then he's jumped.'

'Anyone see anything?' asked Perez. 'Hear anything? Neighbours?'

'Away on both sides,' said Officer Cass. 'Spoken with pretty much everyone in the street. Most of them away on vacation. August. But those who *are* around heard nothing. No scream.

Not even a car.'

'Any sign of a struggle?' asked Jack, though he already knew the answer.

Officer Don shook his head.

'Nope. Like he was caught completely unawares. Rayno reckons he might not even have heard the murderer. That's what freaks me, honestly. Been tryin to get my head round the idea of gettin yerself killed without even seein your killer. Slash, stab and the show's over. Lights out.'

Perez asked if they'd found the weapon. Officer Don shook his head.

'Nope. Nothin. But Rayno says it was a hunting knife. Or razor. Scalpel. That sort of thing. And real sharp.'

Jack examined the wound more carefully. It was exactly the cut that had killed Kingston.

'Carotid artery,' he said, addressing them all. 'One cut and it's done. Dead in two minutes. If you have to be murdered, it's painless at least.'

He asked if anything had been stolen. Officer Cass shook her head.

'Hard to see. We've had a poke. Rayno too. Maybe some cash. Valuables. And the upstairs wardrobe was open. Clothes scattered all across the floor. But that could be nothin'.'

Jack's eyes caught Perez's for a second time.

Perez forced a laugh. 'Not many people kill for a new wardrobe.'

Officer Don turned to face Jack and Perez, concern suddenly written across his face. Jack could see he was regretting letting them in.

'You'll keep this quiet? *No one crosses the cordon.* We gave our word to Rayno.'

Cass nodded. 'Our jobs on the line.'

Perez clapped his hands together.

'We'll clear off your patch. Leave you to it.' He put a finger to his lips, a signal that their secret was safe with him. 'Had to see it, though. Saw it on Twitter and thought to myself, well how's that? You go off on vacation and five minutes later there's a murder on your doorstep.'

He paused, changed tack. 'You said the Vegas folk are on their way?'

Officer Don nodded. 'Yeah. Sendin' two detectives. Guess they'll take it all off our hands. But sure hope they hurry up. Can't leave him much longer in this heat. Smells already. Goin' to stink by morning.'

Perez nodded. 'If they've got any sense they'll keep you guys on board. You know the ground. Know the local people. That kind of stuff. Local knowledge counts.'

Officer Cass shook her head.

'I know local and this ain't local. An outsider did this, that's for sure. One mother-of-a-screwed-up-outsider.'

Jon Perez handed them his business card; they responded by giving him theirs.

'Mind if we keep in touch?' he said.

'Sure. When we catch him, you'll be the first to know who's danglin' on our line.'

* * *

'So? It was him?'

Tom wanted every detail.

'Him alright,' said Jack. 'Couldn't have left a clearer signature.'

'Skull?'

He nodded. 'A skull. Clear as day. And same cut to the neck.'

Tom winced. 'Fuck. So ice man's got a brain alright. And the shit's just got deeper.'

Perez turned to Tammy.

'The victim, can you Google him. Name's Ashton Brookner. Works for Vortec Aerospace. See what there is. Maybe the company website has something.'

Tammy typed his name into her phone then looked at the results.

'Three mentions. And yeah, he's on the Vortec website.'

She scrolled down. 'Been there six years or so. Technical advisor, whatever that means. Not much else.'

She returned to the search page.

'He's on Linked-in. *Ashton Brookner, Ashton Brookner.* Here we go - "Ashton Brookner works at Vortec Aerospace." Previous employers, all engineering stuff. One job in Virginia, one in Florida. Likes the novels of John Steinbeck and Ernest Hemingway. Likes Bach, Wagner. Sixty-three connections. And that's it.'

A moment's silence as they thought it through. *Wagner.*

'And he's mentioned in some local news story. Something about an aircraft museum.'

Tom banged hard on the steering wheel.

'Why kill Ashton Brookner, of all people? Why *him* for fuck's sake?'

He started the engine, put the car into drive, moved off slowly down the length of Rio Vista Drive. Then he swung back into Sapphire Way and continued until they reached downtown. He pulled the car up outside the Slanted Pine Bar and Resto.

'Let's get a beer. We need thinking time. We're heading top speed to the deepest possible shit. Need to outsmart him.'

They made their way through the swing door, Tom first, then Perez and Tammy. Jack paused outside for a moment, thinking it through. *Hans Dietrich.* It would soon be his second night in hiding. Two nights. Two murders. Not a bad ratio, even for a seasoned killer.

He made his way inside and joined the others at their table by the window.

'Four Millers,' said Tom to the bar-girl. 'Cold as you can.'

'Three,' said Jack. 'I'll have a Coke.'

She brought them right away. Tom wiped the frost off the

bottle then slugged it, like he needed to hydrate fast. Perez drank more cautiously, twisting the bottle round and round.

Jack asked for a glass.

'You don't like beer?' said Perez.

'Coke's fine.'

'Went to Britain once. Two-thousand-and-one. London. Nice place. But you don't know how to drink beer.' He turned to Tom. 'They drink it warm and flat.'

Tom was thinking hard, clicking his finger joints as he did so. 'He's killing cos he likes killing.' He turned to face Jack. '*He likes killing*. Simple as that. You told us about France and Russia and all that. You told us about the massacres. He gets his kicks from death. Period.'

Tammy was nodding as he spoke. 'Yeah, exactly my thoughts. Remember what you said? He goes to Russia, pulls some guy out of a crowd, shoots him in the head. It's all about power over someone else. He gets his kicks from killing. He's an addict, like he's doing coke. He's woken up, wants to kill. And he doesn't care who.'

Perez looked up from the table. 'Kingston was different. *He* was nailed for his clothes. But this one, it was sport. And a scalpel, too. Violent son-of-a-bitch. Tells you something.'

Jack slowly turned his glass in a circle and watched the bubbles rising through the dark liquid.

'No.'

They all looked at him.

'The killings in France, in Russia, they weren't random. The very last thing they were is random. There was always a reason for them, even if it was a chilling one. Yes, they picked on individuals, just like you said. And yes they singled them out from the crowd. But never random. They shot the ones who didn't obey orders and then killed the rest. It was preordained, premeditated and planned.'

Tom looked at Jack. 'What you trying to say?'

'Only that it's not random. I don't believe that Hans Dietrich broke into the house of a complete stranger and murdered him for kicks. He's chosen his victim with care. Selected him. For some weird reason, and I don't know what, he wanted Ashton Brookner dead.'

Perez tutted, shook his head.

'Nah. How can he have *chosen* to kill Ashton Brookner?'

He took another sip of beer.

'Nothing adds up,' he said, putting the bottle back down. 'Number one, what makes him want to kill some guy at Vortec Aerospace? And number two, *why?*'

He drained his beer in a decisive fashion. 'No. He killed cos he likes killing.'

Still Jack disagreed. He reminded them that the SS Totenkopf were soldiers. Elite. Highly trained. Professionals.

'Agreed, they liked killing. Their business was death. Murder. Extermination. Call it what you will. But however evil their work it always had some sort of weird logic.'

He stopped talking, looked at each of them in turn. He wasn't getting through.

'Why did they kill the villagers of Dyakova? Random? No. It was because they were sheltering partisans. Same goes for the inhabitants of Vyazma. And why did they kill Jews? Not random at all. They killed them because they were Jews. It was all part of a chillingly rational plan. They killed gypsies because they were gypsies. And handicapped people cos they were handicapped. I can tell you one thing for sure, there's a reason why he killed Ashton Brookner.'

He drained his glass.

'I just don't know what it is.'

TWENTY-TWO

Karen took the overnight train from Berlin to Munich, then hired a car and headed for Murnau. The road south was busy. Trucks, vans, holidaymakers, all tail-gaiting out of Munich and heading for the Bavarian Alps. The truck in front was Romanian.

She stared blankly at the baked landscape. Bleached corn stubble and sunflower fields. It was flat, monotonous, hot. But once she'd passed Penzburg, the land started to fold in on itself. Slopes contoured into hills, woods darkened to forest. It was fairy tale land, all bears and wolves. Even the houses were story-book. Gables and thatch with painted pink facades.

She stopped for a coffee and pretzel at Obersöchering. The air was spiked with freshness, like breathing through mint. It was the first clue that somewhere to the south, beyond the Zugspitze, lay glaciers and high altitude snow.

It took her another hour to reach Murnau, baroque, folksy and quaint. It was market day and the main street was filled with shoppers and stalls. Striped awnings sliced shadows across the heaps of onions, potatoes and tubs of picked gherkins.

The nursing home, Sonnenhof, stood on the eastern edge of town. It had the air of having been dumped in the wrong town, in the wrong century. Nineteen seventies, with two storeys of concrete and sheets of glass in between. The garden was filled with hydrangeas, all blue and pink. Old people's plants.

She pushed the main glass door and stepped into an entrance area lit with sunshine. A janitor was polishing the dark melamine floor to a high sheen. Hanging over the reception desk was a plastic sign in red and gold. *Herzlich Wilkommen.*

Karin strolled up to the desk, thinking about what to say. The duty nurse, Frau Götte, contrived a smile.

'You've come to see - ?'

Karin explained who she was, what she was doing. She said she was hoping to have a few words with Frau Trautwein.

'Ah, you're the one that phoned? From Berlin, wasn't it? Sigrid was telling us last night.'

Karin made an apologetic face, like, sorry, she shouldn't have come. Then she hesitated for a second, unsure how to continue.

'Sigrid's rather strict about visitors,' said Frau Götte. 'More than the rest of us, I have to say. And when she heard the word *lebensborn* -'

She emitted a peculiar sound, half-way between a sigh and a groan. Then her voice dipped to a conspiratorial whisper.

'I must say it surprised us all. Set us chattering all evening. We only know what they tell us. First time we knew Frau Trautwein had anything to do with lebensborn.'

There was a pause before she continued.

'Sigrid was very much against you coming. But -'

She rubbed her hand across the spotless surface of the counter in front of her, as if wiping away imaginary dust.

'I'll share something with you. She's not working this morning, it's my shift, see, and my personal view is that these things don't do any harm.'

These things. Karin smiled.

'They love talking about the past. Stimulates the mind. And if I'm honest it's got me intrigued. But you'll have to go gently, gently.'

She paused again.

'That's her. Over there.'

She pointed to a day room, all glass and plants. Sunshine was pumping hard from outside, the light falling across the floor in sharp triangles.

'Sitting in the corner.'

Karin looked. Frau Trautwein was in a high-backed arm-chair, nineteen-fifties style, the caricature of an old lady. Fragile as china and hair like snow.

'Eighty-nine. Our second oldest.'

Karin hesitated.

'And you'll introduce us?'

Frau Götte nodded.

'But -' pause - 'you need to know the problem. She was taken ill last spring. Thought we were going to lose her. Stroke. Diabetes. My word, everything. And ever since her mind's been wandering. Gets mixed up. Very confused at times. My fear is, she won't understand who you are. Or why you've come.'

She wiped the counter again.

'I don't mind introducing you. But you must be careful not to upset her. Sigrid will explode if she finds out and then we'll never hear the end of it.'

She called to a colleague and asked her to cover the front desk.

'Come. Follow me.'

The day room was oven-hot and when Karin breathed in she smelled the biscuit-like smell of old people. Two lady residents were watching a quiz show on television, maximum volume. Frau Trautwein was looking through a glossy garden magazine. Karin glanced at the cover. *Bayern in Blüte.*

'Frau Trautwein - ?'

Frau Götte tapped her shoulder lightly then spoke into her ear. 'You've got a visitor.'

She looked up, smiled. Her face was radiant.

'For me?'

'Yes. From Berlin.'

Frau Trautwein extended her hand to Karin, smiled again. A frail hand, all bones and blue veins, yet the tips of the fingers were beautifully tapered, like those of a young woman. Karin looked closely at her face. She must been beautiful in her youth. 'Hello my dear.' She spoke softly, with a pronounced lilt. 'Lovely of you to come again.'

Frau Götte looked towards Karin, frowning. 'She's confused, see. I'll do my best to explain who you are.'

Karin kept her eyes on the old lady's face, seeking any hint of understanding.

'This lady, Karin, is hoping to ask you some questions.'

'Good, good -'

Frau Trautwein turned once again to Karin, smiled.

'How are the children? Of course I know it's hard for them to come. They all lead such busy lives these days. But they do try and come at least once a week. I had Sabine here only the other day. She brought cake and chocolates. And some flowers. Such lovely flowers.'

Frau Götte turned back to Karin and spoke in a confiding sort of voice. 'See the problem? She's getting you mixed up with I don't know who.'

'Let me talk to her,' said Karin. 'Give me one minute.'

She positioned herself very close to Frau Trautwein and kept silent for a moment as she thought how to begin. Then she started to speak in loud, clear German.

'I'm making a film about the war. About what life was like back then. I was wanting to try and wind back the clock. Go back to your childhood.'

She paused for a second. Frau Trautwein was nodding and seemed to understand.

'It's nineteen-forty-three. You're eighteen. Eighteen years of age. The war's going badly, of course, but the Führer still speaks of victory. Even after Stalingrad he speaks of victory. And you - a beautiful young fräulein - you wanted to do something, play your part.

'Remember how you loved to dress in the blue and white uniform of the Bund Deutscher Mädel? The white blouse and the navy skirt. The neckerchief that you all wore like a badge of honour.

'And then there were the vows, the slogans. "Hitler is Germany and Germany is Hitler." Wasn't that one of them? "To be one nation is the religion of our time." You all used to shout it at the meetings you went to. "Anything that undermines our unity must go on the pyre."

'And the songs. The theatricals. The bonfires to celebrate the summer solstice. "Young nation step forwards, for your hour has come." The future belonged to you. It really did.'

She paused.

'And there was Lebensborn.'

Lebensborn.

The word had a dramatic effect on Frau Trautwein. It was as if the fog had been burned away by the sun, revealing a whole new landscape underneath. Thoughts of non-existent children, of the visit of Sabine, of cake and chocolate, all fell away like scales. Frau Trautwein was eighteen again, a fresh-faced maiden with the Bund Deutscher Mädel, dressed proudly in white and blue. She was back in a schoolroom packed with her girlfriends and they were all being addressed by a stern looking lady in her late forties.

'Yes, yes.' Her voice was weak. 'Yes. Nineteen-forty-three.'

She paused for a moment as the scene turned vividly real, almost seven decades after the original. And then she started to speak.

'Yes, we thought it funny at first, and why shouldn't we? We were only girls. And innocent ones at that. Not like today's ones clad in their trousers and what-not. And then this lady came. Rather ferocious we thought her. Addressed us and started telling us we should consider giving a child to the Führer.

'Of course we didn't know what she meant at first. *Give a child to the Führer!* It didn't make any sense at all. But then she explained. Told us we'd be taken to a place of luxury, like a smart hotel. Given the best food. Fancy rooms. And then we'd meet the men. Good looking men, too. Men who looked like Heinrich Schroth. We all laughed when she told us they'd be the best looking men we'd ever seen. I think we were all a little embarrassed.'

There was a pause and then Karin encouraged her to continue.

'We all chatted about it afterwards. It was *all* we talked about. Some of us rather liked the idea. But most thought it was immoral. It seemed so very strange. You see for the previous three years, more, we'd been taught how to be good hausfrau. Dutiful wives. Running the household and bringing up the little ones. And now we were being told to have a relationship with men before we were married. We were being told to have a child for the Führer.'

'So what happened next?'

'Sorry dear - ?'

Karin kicked herself. She mustn't interrupt. Frau Trautwein needed to relive her thoughts by herself.

'Yes, a child for the Führer. I couldn't help thinking it all sounded terribly exciting. You do at that age, of course. Eighteen and never been kissed. So we made a pact, three of us. Eva, Anna and me. We decided to say yes. We contacted the woman by telephone, I think it was, and then one day a car came to pick us up.

'I only had my father at that time because Mutti was dead. Horrified by the whole thing he was. He didn't even like me being part of the Bund Deutsche Mädel. But what could he say? They'd have taken *him* away if he'd tried to say no.'

Frau Götte glanced at Karin. Their eyes met briefly.

'They came for us in a car. Big black shiny thing it was. Oh, they had lovely cars in those days. I'd never been in anything quite like it. Chauffeur with cap. All leather and walnut inside. I can smell it even now. Leather and walnuts. And we were given tangerines. It was close to Christmas, see. They liked to give us tangerines.

'My goodness dear it was quite a drive. And there was a gate-house. Soldiers on guard. Of course there were soldiers every-where in those days. All very smart. Good looking young ones. They had the finest uniforms. Very well turned out. And lots of snow. Yes, there was so much snow that year. It did nothing but snow and snow.

'We were ushered inside. It was -'

She paused as she searched out the memories.

'Yes, we had forms to fill out. That was it. They bought us forms. Medical ones. They wanted to know so many things. Oh my dear it was such silly things. Did we have illnesses in the family? Tuberculosis? Syphilis? Well you can imagine we all had a good laugh at that. Syphilis! *I mean*, I'd never even been kissed. And our families, that was it. Parents. Grandparents. Great grandparents. They wanted to know everything about us.

'And d'you know the lady was quite right about the food. Here it was, wartime, and not much meat to be had. Yet we were given schnitzel and great bowls of soup. It never seemed to end. Syrup made from elderberries. It was lovely that syrup. I like elderberries, see. I've always liked elderberries ever since I was tiny and we picked them by the Walchensee. And then one day they called us all together and told us that the results had come back and that they were all very good and that we must now begin our work.

'We were all a little nervous. Eva, Anna and I. I mean, I'd never even been kissed. We had the best rooms. Clean linen sheets. A bed so big. I'd never slept in such a bed. My bed at home was no wider than a door. And so much food, of course. Great bowls of soup. And it was strange. I remember lying in that bed and there was the Führer hung on the wall and he was staring down at me. He looked rather stern. He *was* stern, of course. We'd listen to his speeches on our old Empfänger and he always sounded angry. And I was lying there thinking to myself, "I'm doing all of this just for you."'

She paused for a moment, placed her magazine on the table

in front of her.

Karin looked at her. *Please don't stop.*

'The first one they sent to my room was tremendously good looking. Just like the lady had said. Bit stupid, I think. Didn't say much. But a fine face. He was a rough one and I had to keep my eyes firmly on the Führer. Still wasn't sure if what I was doing was right. We all chatted together later that evening. Eva and Anna came into my room. Eva still thought it was wonderful but Anna had doubts like me.'

She paused as the door to the day room opened. One of the helpers wheeled in a trolley piled high with cups of coffee. She served the two ladies watching television then wheeled the trolley over to Frau Trautwein's armchair. It clinked and clattered as it approached.

Not now. Please not now.

'Frau Trautwein. Coffee? Biscuit?'

Frau Trautwein looked at the lady, pointed a bony finger at the coffee jug. The helper poured it into the cup then offered some to Karin. She shook her head.

'And then?' asked Karin when the trolley woman had left. She was anxious to resume the story.

'What's that, my dear?' said Frau Trautwein, her eyes cloudy and confused. She held out her hand and clasped Karin. 'It's so good of you to come again. Sabine makes it so rarely these days you see.'

* * *

She drove south for half an hour, through valleys scooped from the landscape like deep green bowls. Giant cow parsley fringed the steeply climbing road and the trees were charged with purple plums. The ripest had already fallen and were squashed into the road like road-kill. Meadows, baroque domes and spires. Hansel and Gretel traipsing through the forest.

The mountains, foreshortened by perspective, had become a single mass of rock that brought the green landscape to an abrupt halt. The Zugspitze, Schneefemerkopf and the others whose names she didn't know. They rose like a wall from the steeply rolling pastures.

She continued for another five miles until she came to a sign pointing up a sharp incline. *Schloss Hohenstein: 3km.*

Karin shifted down to second gear and swung right into a single track lane. There was grit under the tyres. The lane lurched upwards in a coil of switchback bends until it was swallowed by the purple-grey shadow of the mountains. She hoped there was nothing on its way down.

There was a sudden chill to the air and the clean sky was now under threat from a billow of clouds. She shivered, wound up the window. The high pastures roughened and faltered as the slopes grew steeper then disappeared completely and were replaced by near vertical cascades of mountain scree.

Each bend in the road seemed to close the vista rather than open it. She'd left the sunshine down in the valleys below. Now she was dodging through cold shadow. Another steep corner, this time hacked from the bedrock and then she swung through one-hundred-and-eighty degrees. A giant cinematic screen unfurled before her, all cliffs and overhangs.

'*Wow!*'

She braked hard as she looked towards a near-vertical pinnacle of rock. From its fractured summit, a sheer retaining wall rose some thirty metres into the sky. Its top spouted chimneys, towers and spires. Hohenstein Castle.

At first glance there seemed to be no way up, unless by rope and basket. But when she looked more carefully she could see a faint dark line scoured into the rock. Another five minutes brought her to the beginning of the steepest section of track. It wound around the pinnacle like a corkscrew and eventually led underneath a high stone arch. She found herself entering an enclosed square courtyard that doubled as a car park. On three sides it was encircled by thick stone walls, the remains of a medieval redoubt. The fourth wall had two small windows and a vast double door. The visitor entrance.

Karin cut the engine and opened the car door. She inhaled deeply, savouring the pure air. It was fresher than in the valleys below.

She paused for a moment at the information panel by the entrance and read what it said.

'The first mention of Schloss Hohenstein is in 1180, when the surrounding land came under the control of the fiefdom of the Wittelsbach family, Counts Palatinate of Schyrein. Count Rupert Wittelsbach built the white tower, the oldest surviving part of the castle, in order to control the mountain pass.'

The castle had played its role in the War of Succession, supporting the Duke of Bavaria-Landshut. It had been involved in the Thirty Years War, under the Auenbrugger dynasty.

The twentieth century was glossed in a single sentence. 'Schloss Hohenstein served as a garrison training centre during the Third Reich. In 1948 it was restored to the Auenbrugger family, in whose possession the castle has been since the early seventeenth century.'

Karin's eyes switched to a smaller panel giving practical information about the place.

Visitor Hours: May-September, 9.30-16.30.

October-April, by appointment only.

Admission: Adults, 8 euros, children, 3 euros.

Family ticket, 20 euros.

Guided tours at 10.30, 13.30 and 15.00.

She walked over to the entrance door, pushed it hard and stepped inside the hall. The medieval gloom smelled of wood smoke. A shaft of light pierced through one of the high windows, dissecting the dust in a faint golden beam. The only other light came from a desk lamp at the ticket desk.

Karin walked over to the desk. A lady, greying, fiftyish, looked up from her book, smiled warmly.

'*One?*'

Karin explained how she'd called on the previous day and was hoping to see the castle library and archives.

'Ah yes, yes,' said the woman, responding in German. 'Herr Fischer's got it all prepared, I think. It should be up there waiting for you. Schloss Hohenstein during the war, wasn't it?'

Karin nodded.

'But first you should take the little tour we have. Won't take you long. Fifteen, twenty minutes at the most. Gives you an overview of the history. And you'll pass the library close to the end. Herr Fischer should be there, unless he's off on his break.'

She nodded and made her way towards a circular stairway in the corner. Enclosed in stone, it was dimly lit by a couple of weak light bulbs. At the top it opened into a small antechamber.

There was a mullioned window, its diamonds of leaded glass beaded with fresh raindrops. She walked over to it and looked out. The rock dropped away into shadow. To the left, towering above the castle, was the misty peak of the Zugspitze, clinging to its cape of dirty snow. In the other direction, north, she could see the pewter surface of the Alpsee.

She made her way through the exhibition at speed. Hatchets, halbards, pikes, axes, muskets. The castle's history was a litany of violent death. Six centuries of bloodshed. One cabinet contained six human skulls, all fractured.

'This is more like it,' she said to herself, pausing at one of the display cases. 'Schloss Hohenstein during the Third Reich.'

A series of black-and-white photographs told the story of the Nazi period more eloquently than the accompanying text. A polished Mercedes Benz was drawn up in the courtyard. Military figures saluting and goose-stepping. Schloss Hohenstein under deep snow. And a shot of the castle from afar, swastikas billowing from every pinnacle and turret.

'In May 1943, Schloss Hohenstein became the permanent headquarters of the SS Totenkopf, along with several other elite divisions of the Waffen SS. The surrounding mountains provided the ideal training ground for endurance exercises and extreme winter training. The schloss was visited on a number of occasions by Adolf Hitler, and both Hermann Goring and Josef Goebbels are also known to have stayed here.'

Karin took several photographs of the display panel then took a careful look at each of the individual pictures to see if she could spot the face of Hans Dietrich. Several of the men could have been him, but without removing them from the cabinet it was hard to tell with any certainty.

The library was housed in the cavernous great hall, a barrel roofed room like an upturned ship with a forest of antlers at the far end. Desks in neat rows and a smell that didn't quite ring true. Wood-polish masquerading as beeswax.

Herr Fischer was seated at the far end, comfortably rotund. He'd sunk into the chair's embrace, contented, and looked as if he never intended to get up. The desk lamp gave him a faint aureole.

He beamed as she approached. 'Frau Braun just called to say you were on your way up. You must be -'

Karin returned the smile, her eyes alighting on a stack of files. 'The Totenkopf, isn't it?'

She nodded.

He shook his head in desultory fashion. 'A mix of material. Some personnel files. A few mission documents, I believe. But a lot's been lost, probably in the final days of the war.'

He lowered his voice to a whisper, as if to confide a secret.

'Probably deliberate. Cover the tracks. They knew it was all over.'

Karin took the files from his hands and scanned through them to see what there was. Far more than at Lichterfelde. The thickest was marked *Belegschaft* (Personnel) and looked to contain papers on the soldiers in Hans Dietrich's squad, including Hans Dietrich himself. Another was marked *Vermischt* (Miscellaneous). It was crammed with letters. The third had a label, *Grönland*. Several more had nothing written on them.

'Sit yourself down at a desk. I'll let you crack on.'

She opened the personnel file about Hans Dietrich and sorted through the items that mentioned him. There were his SS Totenkopf identity papers, a couple of bills, a letter from his mother saying how happy she was to know he was safely returned from Russia. More promising was an account written by Hans Dietrich himself. Eight pages of foolscap.

She scanned the first page. It was an account of his early years in the SA and the SS.

In June 1932, two local SA men were murdered by the Freiburg Reds. It was what made me determined to join the SA. I got a reference from Otto Strecken-bach, who was already a member, and was accepted. Our job was to maintain order at Party meetings and we were delighted to at last have something to fight for.

The first time I saw action was at a large Communist rally. We disguised ourselves as 'civilians' and joined the throng in the hall. When the meeting was underway, I lit a stick of cordite and hurled it towards the rostrum. There was a loud explosion that shattered all the windows. The room was filled with dust and smoke.

We stood up, seized chairs and began smashing them into the faces of the Reds. They squealed in terror and tried to rush the doors, but we had already blocked the way. We beat them to a pulp. We were not allowed to

carry guns in those days, so we had to
learn to fight with our fists and with
knuckle-dusters. Afterwards we sang
the usual victory songs: 'Throw out
all the Yiddish gang' and 'When on the
knife the Jew blood spurts'. But it
was the Horst Wessel song that became
our battle hymn.

Karin put down the diary for a second, thinking hard. Jack had
described Hans Dietrich as a clinical killer, fastidious, choos-
ing the carotid artery with care. But here he came across as a
common thug.

After the Röhm business the SA was
demoralized. I applied for member-
ship of the SS and was immediately
accepted. My past record spoke for
itself. It was like joining an elite
club, just like the old Germany. We
swaggered about in our smart black
breeches and polished jackboots and
cracked jokes about the simple brown-
shirts.

We trained hard, both physically and
mentally. We were an institution, an
order that was dedicated to controlled
violence. We did not much care for the
Regular Army who were snobbish and
old fashioned. Besides, it was us who
had done all the fighting against the
enemy and we all knew that fighting
counts more than medals and uniforms.

Once I had sworn the oath, the Führer
became my life. His genius had brought

light and renewed life to millions of
people. I vowed to devote my lifeblood
to the task of translating his decrees
into practice. I was promoted in 1936
and again in 1939. Then, one morning
we were listening to the wireless when
we heard the words: 'It is now no
longer the Poles alone who shoot.'

I was selected to be among the first
group sent to Poland and I worked sys-
tematically and with diligence, performing many acts of daring. The hard
training now paid its dividends. The
work I undertook in the sector to the
south of Warsaw ensured my entry into
SS Totenkopf.

In the spring of 1942 we were

Karin turned the sheet. Nothing. The account stopped in mid
sentence.

'Bugger.'

She made her way over to Herr Fischer and pointed to where
the account broke off.

He shrugged.

'Afraid they're all like that. The castle was in a terrible state
after the war, see. Everything jumbled up. The archivist at the
time tried to piece it together as best he could but -' He threw
up his hands. 'What can you do?'

Karin went back to the desk and sorted through the rest of
the Dietrich papers. Then she looked at the letters and notes
belonging to the other men, Emil Lorenz, Ludolf Gebhardt,
Kurt Becker, Joachim Ulrich, Otto Streckenbach. A pattern
started to emerge. The men in the SS Totenkopf had been
singled out for their physical prowess and their intellect. All had

degrees. All spoke several languages. And all shared a passion for the business of death.

There was also more about life at Schloss Hohenstein. Mountaineering, rock-climbing, abseiling, chess and logic puzzles: every aspect of life was designed to fine-tune the skills of the men stationed here.

She was in the process of putting the Hans Dietrich papers back into the file when she saw a sheet she hadn't noticed before. 'Huh!'

She looked again, puzzled by the name and address that was staring out from the sheet. Ferris Clark. Number 2586 Avery Street, Green Diamond.

She sat up sharp and looked at it again. It was written in black and white. Ferris Clark. Number 2586 Avery Street, Green Diamond.

She thought for a moment, trying to make sense of it. *Ferris Clark*. If they'd been sent to Greenland to kill him, then it was no surprise that his name should be in the file. But why his home address?

She looked at the paper underneath. It was some sort of architectural drawing. She turned it over, still thinking hard. Written on the back were those same words: *Number 2586 Avery Street, Green Diamond*.

It was a floor plan of Ferris Clark's house.

* * *

She photographed everything then packed up the files and took them back to Herr Fischer.

'Find what you wanted? Sorry about those missing papers. It's always the way.'

Karin smiled. 'More than I was expecting.'

'Good, good. And if you ever need to come back, well, you'll know where to find us.'

'Thank you. I might well do so.'

She headed back through the display rooms then made her way downstairs to where Frau Braun was still seated at the ticket desk. The place was deserted. There were no other visitors.

'All good?' she asked with a quizzical smile. 'Find what you needed?'

'Yes.'

'Not a bad little display,' said Frau Braun. 'They try to keep changing it. Each year they put new things in the cases.'

She paused, picked up her pen.

'Of course there's one thing you ought to know, if you're interested in the war.'

'*Oh?*'

Karin looked up expectantly.

'They never include it in the display. Say it taints the place, although I'd have thought the SS being here already taints it.'

'Yes.'

'Nineteen-forty-three. Summer, I think. That's when the castle was first used by the lebensborn people.'

Karin swallowed hard.

'Perhaps you don't know what I'm talking about? Lebensborn, I mean?'

Karin gave a vigorous nod.

'*Lebensborn.* This was a *lebensborn* castle - ?'

'That's what they say. You can only imagine what went on inside these walls.'

'*Frau Trautwein -*' murmured Karen. 'I need get back to Murnau.'

TWENTY-THREE

Awoken by the sun, Jack turned on the television to catch the news. It was just before eight. Adverts, jingles, adverts, then a spinning planet earth that slowly focused on Nevada. Cut to the studio.

'KVTV good morning. My name's Jenna Newman. This morning's top story. A truly *gruesome* murder in Churchill County, Hanford Gap, has led to a huge manhunt as police attempt to track down the killer. The victim has been identified as forty-seven year old Ashton Brookner, a technical advisor working for Vortec Aerospace. He was found dead in his house at shortly after ten yesterday morning, one of the most shocking killings that Nevada has seen in decades.'

Jack sat up in bed, propped pillows behind his back. He felt a tingle of alarm. Everything was sliding out of control. Where was it going to end?

The scene shifted to Rio Vista Drive. A group of reporters were standing in front of the house that he had visited on the previous evening. He saw Officer Don standing on the front lawn, mouth caught in an awkward half-smile, as if he knew this was the biggest day of his life. One to tell the grandchildren in years to come.

The house looked different in daylight, more modern, and the cameras, journalists and police had transformed it into a regular crime scene. The property would never again be admired as the finest piece of real estate on Rio Vista Drive. Henceforth, and until it was condemned and knocked down, it would be linked with a particularly brutal murder.

The camera closed in on the KVTV news reporter, Marty Beck, metal-blond hair and a slick of make-up. A frown on her brow, contrived, as if a serious news story deserved a serious expression.

Studio: 'Marty, you're there on the scene for us. Do we have any more details about the murder and the victim, Ashton Brookner?'

Marty: 'Yes, and good morning from Rio Vista Drive, Hanford Gap. And I have to say first of all, Jenna, that the murder's left this normally quiet neighbourhood in deep shock. It was an extremely violent attack with the victim, Ashton Brookner, as you said in your introduction, killed by a single cut to the carotid artery. What makes it particularly distressing is the fact that, well, the police have just told us that when they found the body it was mutilated.'

Studio: '*Mutilated* - ? Can you give us more on that?'

Marty: 'Yes. And I should warn you that some viewers will find this disturbing. But I'm told that some sort of *human skull* -' she put additional emphasis on the words human skull - 'was roughly cut into the victim's chest.'

Pause.

Studio: 'Do we - do we have any idea as to a motive? The identity of the killer? Can you give us any more information on this?'

Marty: 'I've been talking to detectives on the scene here this morning, Jenna. No clues so far. In fact I was told just before coming on air that the murderer appears to have entered and left the house without leaving any trace whatsoever. Of course the situation on the ground is changing fast and forensics will certainly provide more answers.'

Studio: 'And Ashton Brookner. What do we know about him? He worked at Vortec Aerospace. But did he have family?

Any enemies? What's the sheriff, the police, saying on this?'

Marty: 'No family, Jenna, and, as far as we know, no one who might want to commit this -'

Studio: 'And what's the -?'

Marty: 'But - but - sorry to interrupt, Jenna. I'm joined here in Rio Vista Drive by Sheriff Lem Rayno, who was the first to arrive at the crime scene. I'm hoping he'll be able to fill us in on a few more details.'

The camera panned outwards slightly, into a wider shot. Sheriff Rayno loomed large into the picture, belly like a punch bag and a neck pumped up pink. Sheriff's badge. Gun. And mirror sunglasses, which he removed for the camera. He was James Best playing Rosco Coltrane, only playing it harder.

Marty: 'Sheriff Rayno, you've been in charge of the case so far. What can you tell us? Any leads? Any ideas?'

Sheriff Rayno shifted uneasily, looked down at his polished boots. Then he turned to half-face the camera.

'Nothing so far, Marty. We're looking at a high level of brutality. In all my seventeen years as sheriff of Churchill County -' he swallowed hard - 'in all my seventeen years I've never seen nothin' like this. Detectives from Vegas are currently inside -'

Marty: 'The victim. We know he was Ashton Brookner and he worked at Vortec. Of course Vortec's an important business here in Hanford. You got any leads from the folks there?'

Sheriff Rayno: 'Obviously we're checkin' that out. And the fact he worked for Vortec - well, as you well know -'

He paused, half-wondering how much he should say. He shrugged at the camera, raised his hands. Then flung them downwards through the air.

'I dunno. We're checkin' all angles. It's a bad one, a real bad one, this is. Never seen nothin' like it.'

Marty (turning to face the camera): 'So, Jenna, that's where we are at the moment. Not too much to go on. But police are warning people that if they see anyone suspicious, anyone acting strangely, or have any information about the murder of Ashton

Brookner, then they should call the special hotline that should appear at the bottom of the screen.'

Studio: 'Yes, Marty, we have it now. It's seven-seven-five. Four-two-three. Five-zero-five-zero. That's seven-seven-five. Four-two-three. Five-zero-five-zero.'

* * *

Jack spent the first part of the morning at the hotel looking through the information he had received from Karin. *Frau Trautwein.* Karin needed to get back to her. And Schloss Hohenstein. There was still a lot to be discovered. He set down a list of questions he needed answered.

He had a quick coffee then drove over to ZAKRON and made his way up to Tammy's office. She was on the phone but made a circular motion with her hands, signaling that he should enter.

'Any news?' she said, cutting the call and snapping shut her phone.

'You haven't seen? It's wall to wall. Local channels at the moment. But it'll go national. Got just the sensational details they love.'

'Exactly my thoughts.'

She paused.

'You know we'll go down for this,' she said solemnly. 'It'll all come out and we'll go down for it.'

He shook his head.

'Glad you're so confident.' She looked at him. 'Don't you feel any guilt?'

'No. Not for this one. I'm through with guilt.'

She pushed back her chair and stood up, asking if he'd had news from Germany.

'Yes. Take a look at this. It came overnight.'

He handed her a print-out of the floor plan that purported to show Ferris Clark's house. She examined it, puzzled.

'What is it?'

'That's one side of the paper. And this -' he gave her a second print-out - 'is what she found written on the other side.'

Ferris Clark, Number 2586 Avery Street, Green Diamond.

'She found Ferris Clark's address in the archives in Germany!'

Jack nodded and told her about Frau Trautwein, the lebensborn programme, the castle. 'Hoping to get more tomorrow. She's going back to the old people's home.'

Tammy glanced at the clock on the wall. It was 11.42. 'Better get to the conference room. Tom's called a meeting. He wants to plan things out. He wants you there too. You're suddenly in favour. He called you "one of the team" earlier.'

They made their way down the corridor and entered the room just as the others were taking their seats. Jack looked at the faces. Twelve of them. One was missing.

'Okay - okay -'

Tom silenced the room with his hands.

'Let's begin.'

The room fell quiet. All eyes on Tom.

'First things first -'

There was a long pause, filled by Tammy.

'Where's Jim?'

It was exactly what Jack was thinking. Jim Bartholomew was the missing face.

'As I said, first things first. Sorry to announce that Jim Bartholomew's no longer with us. Quit from ZAKRON. Resigned last night. And -'

He threw up his hands in an empty gesture.

'Hell, he was never fully switched onto all of this. And he wanted out of it right away. Said we're all on a one-way track to prison. Hunter and I had a hell of a time of it last evening and -'

He stopped himself mid-sentence and started to choose his words with care.

'There's always one that wants out. And Jim's that one. Told us he didn't support what we'd done. And was all for blabbing. Took us half the night to talk him out of it.'

Jennifer half-raised her hand.

'How can you be so sure he won't blab? Only need one to blab and it's all over. We're all shafted. Jim's right. We'll get hung out to dry.'

Tom's lips pursed into a cold smile.

'Jim said he'd keep quiet on one condition.'

'Oh - ?' All eyes were on him.

'That we back-date his departure. On the paperwork I mean. Told us to date it before any of this took place. Hunter and I drew up a document there and then.'

He held it up.

'And here it is. You'll see the date when I pass it round. June. You'll all need to sign it. Once that's done, Jim's out. Official. He's no longer anything to do with us.'

Tom passed the document to Perez, seated to his right. Perez took a pen from his jacket pocket, signed it. Then he handed it to Luke Gonzalez, who was next to him. Gonzalez also signed it.

'It's a little reminder of the importance of secrecy,' said Tom, dropping his voice. 'There's a possibility, of course, that Jim's right in what he said. It's possible, in fact it's probable, that we could all, individually, be held responsible for Kingston's death. And for this new one, if news ever leaks out that is.'

Pause.

'What I guess I'm trying to say is the importance of keeping your mouths shut. Zipped tight. Keep them zipped and we'll swing through all of this just fine.'

'What if he kills again?' Ryan jabbed his pen towards Tom. There was panic in his voice. 'Holy shit, Tom, What d'we do then?'

Tom leaned forwards, elbows out, but dodged the question by looking at his watch. He turned to Tammy.

'Fire up the TV can you? Let's catch the midday bulletin.

Carla just told me it's hit the nationals. Fox. CNN. Unfortunately it's gone big time.'

Tammy hit the remote control and tuned to CNN. The midday news was just beginning.

Ashton Brookner. Third item, after the Davos summit and the stolen uranium business. Gruesome murder. Mutilated corpse. No obvious suspect.

The introduction lasted a minute or so then Sheriff Rayno appeared on screen. He'd aged ten years since the morning and his thinning hair was slicked with sweat. He was being questioned by the news anchor.

'Sheriff Lem Rayno, I've just been handed a note, right as we came on air, saying there's been an important development in the case. Can you shed any light on this?'

Sheriff Rayno nodded at the camera, blinked.

'Yeah. We've been running checks on the victim. And there's some interesting leads coming in.'

'What sort of leads? Can you give us more?'

'What we've got so far is that the deceased, Ashton Brookner, he was involved in developing the new generation of drone. Local folks will know all about it. Called the Zephyr Eagle. Being designed and built here in Hanford. At Vortec.'

'That indeed sounds like a significant development. You're thinking - ?'

'Not jumpin' to any conclusions,' said Rayno, scratching at his armpit, stained dark with sweat.

'Can you give us more on Ashton Brookner? What did he do at Vortec? Was he actively involved on the Zephyr Eagle?'

'One hell of a smart guy from what folk say. Started out with General Atomics over San Diego way, developing the Predator and that. Then afterwards he takes off to Ryan Aeronautical, works on the Global Hawk. After that he comes here to Hanford. Working just up there at Vortec.'

'And doing what exactly?' Do we know?'

'Like I said, Zephyr Eagle. The autonomy tech stuff.'

'*Autonomy tech - ?*'

'Stuff that makes the drone think for itself, or that's what the Vortec folks are tellin me. Artificial intelligence if you like.' He shook his head, like he didn't really get it.

'Sounds like you're focusing on the victim rather than the killer?'

'Yes, ma'am, for the moment.'

Tom lowered the volume on the television and then turned to face the room.

'So there we have it. Something. But not much.'

He paused.

'This drone stuff changes nothing of course. It's phoney-baloney. Our job remains the same, to find him before they do.'

He noticed a smirk on Perez's face.

'What's up - ?'

'You don't see?'

Blank faces in the room.

'Drones. Zephyr Eagle. It changes everything.'

Tom stared at him like he was mad. 'Hans Dietrich can't possibly know anything about drones. He's stuck in the nineteen forties.'

Perez nodded. 'Agreed. But this stuff about drones will bring in the FBI. Dead sure. And that means I can get myself officially latched onto the case.'

* * *

Jack was down in the ZAKRON entrance hall when Jon Perez emerged from the office.

'Any news?'

'That was Rayno,' he said, slipping his phone back into his jacket pocket. 'Asking for help. *Too big for little me.* That's what he said. Need the FBI.'

'He called you direct?'

'Yeah. Those officers we met, Don, Cass, wasn't it? They fessed up to letting me in the house. And Rayno gets my number from the card. And now he wants me on the case.'

'But how does it all work? The process, I mean? You can't just take it on like that?'

Perez lifted his cell phone from his pocket and waved it through the air.

'All sorted. Just spoke with the boss. Reminded him I was here on leave. And now it's official. I'm charged with investigating the murder of Ashton Brookner. This drone stuff's freaking them.'

'But it's nonsense,' said Jack.

'Agreed. They're heading up the wrong avenue and they're heading up it way too fast. But that's all good. It's gotten me on the inside of the investigation. And the big guys want a report from me ASAP. Off to see Rayno right now. Coming for the ride?'

Jack arched an eyebrow. 'If they'll let me in.'

'We'll say you're on secondment. From Britain, something like that. He won't know any better. He's just a small town troll with a fat gut and no brain.'

They took Jack's car, drove over to the sheriff's office on South Street. It was a low, single storey building, basked in sunshine, with a flat roof and cylindrical water tank anchored to the top. 'Churchill County Sheriff's Office' was written in huge letters over the door. Underneath, *Lem D. Rayno, Sheriff*.

Jack pushed the door. It jingled like an old-style candy store. The secretary was talking on the phone. She motioned to them with her left hand, signalling that she wouldn't be long.

'*Yeah - - nuh - - yeah - -* you'll have to talk that through with Sheriff Rayno. *Nuh - -* you'll appreciate he's pretty slammed right now.'

She put down the phone, a signal for Perez to introduce himself.

'Sergeant Jon Perez. FBI And this is Jack Raven.'

'Ah yes. Sheriff said you'd be coming.'

She picked up the phone again.

'Lem, they're here.'

She stood up, pointed to a door at the end of the corridor.

'No need to knock. He said to let yourselves in.'

They entered the room just as Rayno was swinging his feet down off his heavy wooden desk. He greeted them with a punch-bowl smile. He didn't ask what Jack was doing there.

'Haven't slept in twenty-four hours.'

He shook his head then held it for a moment in his hands, like it weighed a ton.

'Flat out since yesterday noon. Haven't showered. Only shaved for the TV. When it's all done and over I'm sleepin' for a week.'

They both nodded in sympathy.

'Was anything stolen?' asked Jack.

'*You're a Brit.*' Sheriff Rayno said it more as a statement than a question.

Jack nodded. 'On secondment. Partnered with Jon here.'

It was Rayno's turn to nod. Then he repeated Jack's question back to himself.

'Anything stolen? Hard to say if things were stolen. Wallet empty. No cash in it. And clothes all over the floor.'

He turned to Perez. 'Cass and Don told me you called at the scene. Said they didn't know whether to let you in or not.'

'Sorry. Shouldn't have. But I was in town. And it was a murder.'

Rayno swept his hand through the air, a sign that it didn't matter. 'They're just kids. Cass and Don. Do their best, but they're still kids. Never even seen a stiff before.'

'Any more leads?' asked Perez. 'Other than what you told the cameras.'

Rayno shook his head.

'Whoever did this knew what he was doin'. One violent,

professional bastard. No fingerprints. Not a trace of hair, blood. No fibres. Nothin', nothin'. Forensics say he floated in, slit the poor bastard's throat, then floated back out.'

'What news on the search?'

'You've seen the announcements? Reckon I've got most of Hanford picking over their sheds, garages, outbuildings.'

'Nothing?'

'A few leads. But nothing that adds up. So far we've turned up one stray dog.'

He rapped his desk hard.

'What's got me, what's got all of us, is the skull. It's a death's head. And that's the freakiest thing of all.'

Perez agreed. 'Apart from the drones it's the only real steer. My guys in Washington already on the case.'

'Yeah,' said Rayno. 'Me too. What's the first thing I do? Type it in Google. And what comes up?'

Jack, Perez, both shook their heads.

'Here -'

Rayno tapped into his laptop then swung it round to show them the screen.

'First item. "Death's head is a fictional comic-book character." Well thanks, Google, don't need *you* to tell me that.

'But look here, second item. *Totenkopf.* See? It's German.'

He read from the screen. '*The German word for the skull and crossbones. An old international symbol for death.*' What d'you make of that? Second hit on Google. Used by Hitler, it says down here. Symbol of some goddam division of the SS. Makes me think we're dealin' with some sort of neo-Nazi. And there's a good number of *them* next door in Utah.'

Perez pulled a face, a mirror to Rayno's doubts.

'Was Brookner Jewish?'

'Nope.'

A long pause.

'Find anything else?'

'Death's Head gets hundreds of entries. Comics. Books.

YouTube videos. But nothing that brings us closer.'

Perez leaned back in his chair and stretched his shoulders outwards.

'Like I said, that and the drones, it's the first line our guys in Washington have set to work on. They're profiling him right now. Trying to build a picture. But there's not much to go on.'

'Nah.'

Rayno shook his head.

'Know something, I've been in this job for what, seventeen years, give or take a few days. Shop-lifting. A stabbing or two. One homicide. *One.* In seventeen years. And never nothin like this. Those folk at Vortec are real cut up. Said Ashton Brookner was the kindest in town. Makes me feel I'm too old for this sort of shit. When it gets you here -' he pointed to his heart - '*really* gets you, maybe it's time to quit.'

Jack gave a sympathetic nod.

'We'll find the killer. Always get them in the end.'

'Yeah, maybe. But in between times I've got a whole town that's going to be shakin' in their beds tonight.'

* * *

It was just after four thirty when Jack and Tammy turned into Avery Drive, Green Diamond. The sun was passed its height but still shining hard. Jack squinted through his sunglasses.

'Seems odd,' said Tammy, trying hard to place herself in the normal world. 'Ferris Clark. Can't imagine him walking down this dusty old street, going home to mom each night. Good college boy with his smart suit and little round glasses.'

They passed a disused trailer, a dented pick-up, a worn tractor tyre coated in yellow dust.

'Maybe it was different back then,' she said, filling the silence. 'Proper ranches, well kept, not this junk-yard.'

Jack stopped the car at the end of the drive, stepped out. Tammy followed suit, closing the car door quietly. She pulled out the small notepad she had in her pocket, flicked through it.

'What were these guys called?' Thought I'd written it down.'

'Larry, wasn't it?' said Jack. 'The guy with the spanner. But doesn't look like they're home.'

They made their way up the dusty path that led to the front door. Rang the bell. Silence.

'No one here.'

Tammy rang it for a second time. She half expected to hear a dog bark, some sign of life within.

'It was all open last time.'

A voice came from behind them, from the far side of the fence.

'*Yeah – ? Hello – ?*'

Jack spun round.

'*Can I help? You lookin' for –*'

'Come to see Larry,' said Jack. 'We came last week.'

The neighbour shook his head.

'Not here. Gone to Indianapolis. Goes every year to see Des and Su. That's his daughter. And the kids too. Not back till, oh, next Tuesday I think they said.'

'Ah.'

'Anything that can't wait?'

Jack shook his head.

'No.'

The neighbour brushed his hand through the air, as if to suggest that everything in the world could wait a week. Then he paused, rooted to the ground for a second, before shifting closer to the fence.

'Did you come last night?'

'Why?'

'Dogs started barking, that's all. Ten-ish or thereabouts. So I take myself outside. Go round with the flashlight. Take a tour of the yard. Could've sworn there's someone.'

A hawkish, grey-haired woman emerged from behind him.
'Who's it, Bob?'
'Some folks come lookin' for Larry.'
The woman stared at Tammy then at Jack.
'Just tellin''em how the dogs barked last night.'
She nodded, looked at them more sharply.
'Ten wasn't it? You went out with the flashlight.'
'And - ?'
'*Nah*, nothin. Coyote maybe. Had a few here recent times. Go for the trash. But strange. Dogs never bark at night. Not less someone's there.'
He scratched his head again.
'Took a walk, just in case. Larry'd do the same for me. But it was all quiet. If it was a coyote it just scampered.'

* * *

Jack was thinking it through as they made their way back to the car. *Ferris Clark.* With Sergeant Perez on the investigation they could get access to the house and check it out, even with the owners away. But they needed to do it without alerting the neighbour. And the dogs would be a problem.
He turned the key in the ignition, put the car into drive. Then he swung left out of Avery Street and into Mountain View Drive. He was about to ask Tammy something when her phone rang.
'*No - No - No –*'
'What is it,' said Jack.
'Shit, shit -'
She pointed sharp left. 'Head this way. And fast. We're going to Douglas Street.'
'Why? What's up?'
'Two more murders.'

TWENTY-FOUR

J ack and Tammy arrived at the house just minutes after Perez. Sheriff Rayno was pacing the front lawn, looking as if he was searching for clues in the grass. He glanced up, gave a vague half wave toward Jack. He looked curiously deflated, his life-blood steadily seeping away. The blue-grey bags under his eyes hung heavy and low, giving him the air of a tired bulldog.

Perez was standing in the porch of the house. Seeing Jack and Tammy, he walked across to them.

'This is the very last thing we need,' he said, stating the obvious.

'You been inside yet?'

Perez nodded gravely.

'Three guesses as to how they died.'

Jack turned to face the house, taking it all in. Detached building, stone walls, six windows on the front façade.

'Any clues how he got in?'

Perez shook his head. 'No trace.'

A small balcony on the first floor jutted out from the front wall. There were French double doors that led outwards from the bedroom.

'Could have got in at the front or back. There's windows at the side, too. But no trace. Your guess is as good as mine. For my money I'd say he got in through the balcony windows. Wide open when the neighbour found the bodies.'

Jack looked at the flowering shrub that was climbing chaotically up the outside of the house, all branches and tendrils. It needed cutting back. A single chimney crowned the top of the roof.

He walked across to Rayno and gave a sympathetic smile.

'How're you bearing up?'

Rayno looked at him, arms folded tightly. He drew them into his chest like he was trying to keep warm. The armpits of his shirt had dark stain of sweat.

'Beats me. What sort of freak would be doing this? And here in Hanford too.'

He let out a long sigh, like it was all too much. 'I'm out of my depth, I'm tellin' you. Out of my depth.'

'Mind if I go in? Take a look?'

'Be my guest. Only it's not pretty.'

'I'll wait by the car,' said Tammy in a quiet voice. 'Don't think I can take any more of this.'

Jack looked carefully at the blue front door. It had two glazed panels and was freshly painted in gloss. No sign of it having been forced. He turned his gaze to the ground floor windows. They had their original locks, sturdy, made of heavy brass, not unlike the ones he had at home. Screwed tightly into the wood and no visible sign of damage.

'See,' said Rayno, ambling back towards Jack, hands shoved into his pockets. 'Just like the last one. No sign of nothin'. It's like he just flits in, does his dirty business, then flits back out again. A ghost with a knife.'

'I'll take a look.'

Jack pushed open the front door. Officer Don was standing aimlessly in the hallway, the watchman of the bodies. He grinned when he saw Jack, half-nervous, half-stupid.

'We told the boss in the end,' he said. 'About your visit last time round. Told him we'd let you in.'

Jack nodded. 'We're in this together now.'

Officer Don removed his cap and ran his hands through his

sweaty hair.

'Yeah. True enough. Better catch this son-of-a-bitch before he strikes again.'

He jammed his cap back onto his head and leaned heavily against the wall, one boot bent backwards against the panelling.

'Boss thinks it's some Nazi weirdo. It's the skull thing. Says its some Nazi stuff. Boss, Rayno, reckons he's from Utah. They're overrun with Nazi shit.'

Jack gave a half nod and looked further down the hallway.

'Mind if I pass - ?'

'Sure thing.'

He made his way down the long hall, rubbing his hand over his chin. He hadn't shaved for two days. The layout of the house was not unlike Ashton Brookner's, except it was bigger and a great deal more homey. Five coats hung on the wall pegs, along with a woollen picnic rug, all red and yellow squares. Trinkets from various holidays stood on the shelves. A gilded metal Eiffel tower, a small doll in native American costume. There was also a postcard of the Reichstag in Berlin. He picked it up and turned it over. Blank. Nothing written on the other side.

'Upstairs,' said Officer Don, coming over towards him. 'First door on the left. Must have been in bed when it happened. Boss reckons they were asleep.'

Jack climbed the wooden staircase and reached the top. He stood on the landing for a second, looking round, before pushing the bedroom door. It squeaked on its hinges. If he'd come through the door, the squeak would surely have woken them. He looked at the French doors, still wide open. Maybe Perez was right. That's how he'd got inside.

The room smelt of death, thick, like out-of-date meat that's just been opened from its packaging. The murdered couple lay on the bed in a bloody tangle, as if they were figures from a grotesque painting. Lucian Freud with blood and entrails. The man was in blue and green pyjamas, the woman in a pink nightdress torn open at the front. Blood, blood, blood. So much blood they could have been ripped apart by dogs. Blood coated the ceiling and walls; it had dribbled down to the floor in long thin streams. And it had leached into the sheets and eiderdown.

It was hot in the room. The blood had dried quickly.

Jack looked more carefully at the corpses. The man lay on his side, his left leg splayed awkwardly outwards, like he was trying to kick the sheet away. Both arms were twisted behind his back, unnaturally, and his neck was slumped into a dip in the mattress.

He examined the chest. As expected it was gouged with a human skull, only less crude than it had been with Kingston and Ashton Brookner. Hans Dietrich seemed to have taken his time over this one, getting the shape of the skull just right.

The woman lay on her back, legs straight, her arms twisted like those bodies from Pompeii, one hand pointing at the ceiling. Her head was on its side, turned onto its left ear, concealing the scalpel wound. The grey hair was caked with blood and blood was smeared on her forehead as well. Her midriff was still covered with her pink nightdress, but her breasts were exposed, hanging down on either side of her ribcage, pendulous but stiff like plastic.

Jack took a step backwards, kicking one foot against the other. He felt an inner panic. Why was his brain working so slowly? How much longer could Hans Dietrich stay one step ahead? Murders three and four. It would only be a matter of time before the story of ZAKRON, Kingston, everything, would break in the press. And then what? The day of reckoning for everyone. And that included him.

He glanced out of the window. In the few minutes since he'd entered the house a media circus had assembled out front. Three vans. A bank of TV cameras. Six, seven reporters, all deep in discussion with their crews. And a forest of microphones poking in the direction of the house, like giant grey hornets.

For a brief moment he toyed with the idea of leaving. He could buy a ticket. Jump on a plane. Head back to London. Yes, unlike the rest of them he could wash his hands of everything.

But then he thought of Tammy. In truth, his hands were tied. He couldn't jump on a plane.

Weldon and Rose Pereira. That was their names. A nice, comfortably off, hardworking middle-class couple. No enemies. No criminal records. No past actions that offered any clues as to why he might have wanted them dead.

Jack looked around their bedroom. It was exactly the sort of place you might have expected Weldon and Rose Pereira of Hanford Gap to have made their home. Pink wall-paper. Satin curtains, all tassels and flowers. She'd chosen the decor and he'd pulled out his credit card and paid for it all.

The stucco rose in the centre of the ceiling was just about the only original feature left. Jack looked back to the French doors. They were also original. And at some point, the corner of the room had been boxed off to create a bathroom.

He took a final look at the bodies then made his way back downstairs, bumping into Sergeant Rayno in the hallway. He looked agitated, excited.

'We might at last be onto somethin',' he said, taking Jack by the arm. 'Come, let's go into the kitchen.'

Perez was already seated at the table and tapping furiously into his laptop. He looked up when the two of them entered the room.

'What you got then?' said Rayno, all anticipation. 'Tell us everything.'

'Weldon and Rose Pereira. Owners of Sunshine Bar on North Park Driveway.'

Rayno pushed his thumbs down on the table.

'Yeah. But we knew that already. Everyone in Hanford knows the Sunshine Bar.'

Perez nodded slowly. 'Okay, okay. But who was a regular drinker at the Sunshine Bar?'

Jack's eyes flickered towards Perez. 'Ashton Brookner - ?'

'Exactly.'

He snapped shut his laptop and looked at them both sharply.

'Listen. I just zipped down there. It's only at the far end of the road. Scummy little place. Not what I was expecting at all. Got chatting to one of the bar girls. And spoke to a couple of regulars.'

'You didn't tell them what's happened?'

'Christ no. But I asked if they knew Ashton Brookner. If he ever drank there. And what does the bar girl say to me? "Why yeah", she says. "He came in here pretty much most nights. Best buddies with Rose and Weldon, he is."'

Rayno sat down at the table, trying to think what it could mean. He'd been to the Sunshine Bar, though not for many years. It was a kids' sort of place. They went for milkshakes and Cokes. He couldn't get his head round why Ashton Brookner would go there.

'That's what she tells me,' said Perez. 'And get this. Brookner used to see the Pereiras all the time. Used to tell them everything, like they were some sort of confidantes. From what I can gather, Brookner seems to have been something of a loner. He'd come to rely on the Pereiras. Used to spend two hours with them *every single night*, even more on Fridays and the weekend.'

Rayno jabbed his hand into the air. He suddenly understood.

'Got it. Sorry, brain's running low on gas. You're saying he went there, blabbed with them, told them about the drones. He's been whispering military secrets. And that's why they got themselves murdered. Cos they knew too much, just like him.'

Perez thought for a moment. 'Yeah, guess that's exactly what I'm saying.'

Rayno stood up, paced around the room then stepped into the corridor.

'Back in two secs,' he said. 'Need to get my head round all this.'

When he'd left the room Jack sat down next to Perez. He noticed Perez smiling.

'Shouldn't have,' he said. 'But I needed to throw the scent elsewhere. Toss them a few clues to get them working. Gives us more time to find Hans Dietrich.'

'Can't you throw some scent to *them*?' said Jack, pointing to the cameras outside. 'You seen?'

Perez nodded.

'Uhuh. Every minute another one arrives. CNN, two vans. Fox. PBS. It's going viral. And we need a result. Before he strikes again.'

Jack made his way to the front porch of the house and watched the commotion outside. Rayno was trying to put up a second cordon, pushing the crews further back into the road. One of the CNN team was setting up lights. Other technicians were hanging around and drinking mugs of coffee. Dozens of black cables were strewn across the pavement. They could have been thick streams of licorice.

'*Sheriff Rayno, Sheriff Rayno*, can you do the six o'clock - ?'

'Sheriff Rayno, Lem - ?'

Jack watched Rayno wave his hand through the air, a sign that he was through with appearing on television.

'*Sheriff Rayno*, CNN here – '

Perez joined Jack at the door.

'We need to get back to ZAKRON. Touch base with Tom, Hunter. But – '

He looked towards the street. 'Not going to be easy getting through that crowd. They know me, cos I've been talking to them. But they're going to be mighty confused to see you.'

The two of them walked down the front steps then strode purposefully across the lawn. Marty Beck took a step forwards and shoved her mike in front of Perez's face.

'Sergeant Perez, what more can you give us?'

She stopped, smiled, added: 'Don't worry, we're not live.'

Perez said nothing. He was unsure whether or not to speak. He stared at the ground for a moment, thinking hard, then turned to face the camera.

'As you know, Marty, there's been two more victims. I'm not yet able to formally inform you of the identities of the victims but – '

'We're standing outside the house of Mister Pereira and his wife?'

'Yeah. This is indeed the house of Mister Pereira and his wife. The crime took place in their home.'

'Then we can assume –'

Perez shot a warning glance at Marty and she backed off. She knew he'd break off the interview if she didn't change tack.

'I'm not able right now to reveal the victims' identities. All I *can* say is they were close friends of Ashton Brookner. Indeed Mister Brookner used to see the deceased every day.'

Marty nodded, paused, then threw an anxious glance towards the cameraman. He nodded in return, a sign that everything was recording just fine.

'So that's the line you're following? That Brookner and the –' She stopped herself naming the Pereiras once again. 'That Mister Brookner and the deceased knew each other and that Mister Brookner –'

She paused in mid-sentence. Perez filled the gap.

'Look, it's no secret Ashton Brookner was working on the development of a new drone. He knew every detail of its spec. He was the technical genius behind it. And, yes, it seems he may have shared some information with the newly deceased. That's one of the lines we're working on. But I can't say too much right now.'

Marty nodded.

'But does it bring us any closer to the killer? We've got half of Hanford quaking in their beds, wondering who's going to be next. When's he going to strike again? That's what half the world wants to know.'

Perez stared hard into the camera.

'All I can do is assure your viewers and the inhabitants of this town that we're doing everything possible to catch this monster and bring him full speed to justice.'

Marty looked back towards the sound guy. Then to the cameraman. 'Anything else?' she mouthed.

They shook their heads.

'Thank you Sergeant Perez.'Then, turning back to the camera, she said: 'That was Sergeant Perez of the FBI, who's heading the team here in Hanford Gap.'

Jack had remained in the background while Perez had been speaking. Now, he walked across to him and pointed towards his car. As he did so, he felt a hand on his shoulder.

'One minute if I may?'

It was Marty Beck. 'You are - ?'

Jack gave her a broad smile, held out his hand.

'Jack Raven.'

Marty pulled a surprised face.

'And a Brit. How come?'

Jack played it cool.

'Working with Sergeant Perez here.'

'Oh? How so?'

'On secondment. We do exchanges. Every year a few of us guys come here and a few of his team go to London.'

Marty nodded. 'Uhuh. I see. So what can you add? From a British viewpoint? We'd love to have you on the six o'clock. A Brit investigating here in Hanford Gap! That'll surprise our viewers.'

Jack shook his head. 'Sergeant Perez told you everything there is to tell.'

He sauntered back towards the car, surprised to see it had been moved much further down the street. Tammy gave a wave.

'Sorry. I moved it. Didn't want them to see you here with me.'

Jack nodded and opened the driver's door. But before he got inside he paused for a moment, turned round, looked back towards the murder house. He'd been struck by a thought.

* * *

They drove back to ZAKRON and met in the conference room. Stress was written across everyone's faces. Tom looked like he'd been punched in both eyes, Hunter had quit playing the smug bastard. Even Perez had taken on an air of weariness. Doctor Gonzalez was the only one who sat upright and alert, mightily supercilious. He seemed to be enjoying the ride.

Riley, Owen and Jennifer, they all sat in glum silence, waiting for someone else to be the first to speak.

'Fuck,' said Tom at length.

'Fuck,' said Hunter. 'Seems like there's nothing to do but wait for him to strike again. Who's next? Does he have some sort of shopping list? Any ideas what we do?'

Jennifer half raised her hand.

'This drones stuff. Is it serious?'

Perez sat back in his chair and slowly shook his head. He looked unnaturally cool, like he was used to being trapped in a hard place.

'Let's call it buying time. We've set Rayno and his team off on the drones. They're looking into it right now. Guess it'll take them a day or two.'

'And that's all you can tell us?'

Jack leaned forwards in his chair and as he did so all eyes looked towards him. He told them about Karin in Germany, how she'd found Ferris Clark's address in Hans Dietrich's papers, along with a plan of Ferris Clark's house.

'There's only one place in Nevada that Hans Dietrich might conceivably know about and that's number two-five-eight-six Avery Street, Green Diamond.'

He paused. The room was absolutely silent. Even the Interstate had fallen quiet. A faint click came from the clock.

'Here's my theory. He's woken up with a degree of brain damage. He can function physically, that's clear. We saw it on the CCTV. And he can work with a certain amount of logic. Like I said before, he's not acting as a mad person and nor is he a psychopath. He's behaving as an elite soldier of an elite division of the SS. He clearly remembers *some* things. He seems to remember who he is. And he perhaps remembers that seventy odd years ago he had an address in his head. Number Two-Five-Eight-Six Avery Street, Green Diamond.'

Tom gave a slight smile. Already he was reaching into his pocket for his car keys. He held them up for everyone to see, then jingled them together.

'So let's go. Now. What's stopping us? Christ, let's go right now.'

It was Jack's turn to raise his hand.

'Not so fast. Tammy and I have already been.'

'And - ?'

'The owners are away.'

'That's not a problem,' said Perez. 'I can get inside, no sweat.'

Jack nodded.

'Of course. But we need to be discreet. Need to do it without attracting any attention.'

He paused.

'Someone was there last night. The neighbours' dogs woke in the night. And he said they never normally wake.'

Perez looked at Tom.

'You thinking what I'm thinking?'

Tom nodded back.

'Sodium thiopental and dog food. It'll knock them out in seconds.'

'You'll kill them?' Tammy gasped.

'No need to kill them,' said Jack. 'Just put them to sleep.'

Tom nodded again.

'And when the dogs are done for we'll give ourselves a little tour of Ferris Clark's old house.'

* * *

They set off shortly after eleven, driving out of town under a sky that was sprinkled with stars. The moon hung low over the distant hills, a silver halo, casting a milky sheen into the darkness.

They went in two cars. Jack and Tammy in the Dodge Viper, Tom and Perez in the Buick. It took less than ten minutes to reach Green Diamond. Jack turned into Avery Street and stopped the car at the far end. Tom drew up the Buick right behind, got out, walked up to Jack's open window.

'Wait here. I'll see to the dogs. Give me five.'

They watched his silhouette shrink as he made his way silently down the street. In his left hand he held a small container with the laced dog food.

'He knows where the cages are?'

Jack nodded.

They waited five minutes, then another five. The street was deserted. No one was out and about. Even the house lights were extinguished. Finally they saw Tom's silhouette coming back towards them. He jerked a thumbs-up sign.

'Not a bark,' he said. 'And the house is all dark. They're still away, that's for sure. We'll make our way round the outside. Check it out. Then Jon, you can crack the lock.'

He handed Jack one of the flashlights. 'Just be careful where you shine it. We'll take the other one.'

Perez felt for his gun then slipped his hand into his pocket.

They left the car door unlocked and made their way down the street in silence. At the far end, two lamps cast a half-hearted glow onto the pavement. The rest of the street was pitch black.

'You can get in round the back,' said Jack in a low voice, pointing to the far side of the yard. 'Let's go through the hedge.'

They pushed through a hole in the fence then made their way towards the house. It stood in a deep block of shadow.

'You go round that way,' whispered Perez, motioning with his arm. 'We'll take this side. Check the windows and doors.'

Jack and Tammy made their way slowly around the eastern

side of the house, taking care to tread on the grass rather than the gravel. There were four windows at raised ground level, all closed and bolted.

'Mind – there's some cables here – '

They stepped over the loops of ropes then turned the corner so they could check the north side of the house. Some sort of climbing shrub was growing outwards from the base of the wall, its huge flowers half-dissolved. Petals lay on the ground - thick flakes of confetti - and there was a heavy scent of perfume.

Two more windows, rectangular and horizontal, almost at the level of the ground. They gleamed black in the darkness.

'Windows for the cellar,' said Jack in a low whisper.

He got down on his knees and pushed at the first one.

'Bolted.'

Tammy was also on her knees, examining the second window.

'Hey, come – '

Jack got up, made his way over to where she was crouched on the ground. He shone his flashlight very briefly onto the lock inside and then gave the window a gentle push. It opened slightly.

Tom and Perez appeared around the corner at that very moment.

Perez spoke in a low whisper. 'Nothing. *You?*'

'Look -' Tammy pointed to the window. 'Open.'

Jack was lying flat on the ground, trying to squeeze his hand inside and release the catch. Finally it clicked and the window opened. The gap was just large enough to clamber inside.

'Looks like there's a two, three foot drop. I'll go first. You, Jon, follow me. You two keep watch.'

Jack sat down on the gravel and swung his legs inside the open window. Then he swiveled his body downwards until he could feel his feet touching the floor. He arched his spine backwards, allowing him to crank his head inside. When he was finally free of the window he pulled at the handle in order to keep it open.

He took a step backwards as Perez's boots swung through the window. There was the clatter of his gun against the wooden frame and he swore as he banged his head. But after performing the same contortions he was also inside.

It was completely dark in the cellar. The only trace of light came from the moon. Jack placed his hand over the lens of the flashlight and snapped it on. Then he gradually spread his fingers in order to control the output of light.

They found themselves in a low corridor piled high with cardboard boxes. A workbench was scattered with tools, a drill, two hammers and what looked like the working parts of an outboard motor. Jack waved Perez towards him.

'Get away from the windows then I can let out more light.'

He inched down the corridor, moving slowly towards the far end. Perez took out his gun, held it in his hand.

'Keep to the side,' he said. 'Just in case.'

Jack hugged the wall as he made his way to the corner. He stopped, peered around. Nothing. Again he waved his hand towards Perez, instructing him to come. As soon as he had turned the corner and was out of view of the window he released more light.

The corridor on the north side of the house opened up into a square room with a concrete staircase in one corner. The cellar was only half-underground, for the house itself was raised four or five feet above the garden.

Jack scanned the room. Boxes and cartons, bottles of turpentine, tins of polish. On the shelves there were loose nails, bolts, old junk. He shone his flashlight all around the room, its gleam sending shadows across the walls and catching on the glass jars and metal boxes. And then –

'*Look –*'

He swung the beam down to the floor.

'*Look –*'

In the corner of the room, lying in a crumpled heap, was a bundle of clothes.

'*Jesus –* '

Perez paced towards it, stooped down. Jack shone light on it.

'You realise what it is - ?'

Perez nodded.

'Kingston's uniform.'

TWENTY-FIVE

It was late morning on the following day by the time Karin was able to return to Sonnenhof. Lunch was already being prepared, the aroma of boiled meat and cabbage hanging stagnant in the airless reception. Karin was pleased to see Frau Götte on the welcome desk. A good start.

She gave a bright smile when she saw Karin.

'D'you know what,' she said, putting down the diary she was holding. 'In the last twenty-four hours Frau Trautwein's spoken of little else except your visit. She was talking about it last night. And again at breakfast this morning. I do believe everyone here knows she's had a visitor.'

Karin smiled. 'She was wonderful. And amazing for her age.'

'Well I don't know what magic potion you put in her coffee but we've rarely seen her on such good form. The way all those old memories came flooding back and the way she talked about them, I must say I had the feeling it had all happened yesterday.'

She moved closer and dropped her voice to a whisper.

'And I have to tell you that we never knew any of this. To fancy she was involved in the whole lebensborn thing. We've all been talking about it. The only one that doesn't know is Sigrid. And that's how we intend to keep it. Otherwise we'll never hear the end.'

Karin smiled again. 'And that's why I've come back,' she confided. 'You see – ' she paused for a moment. 'Frau Trautwein represents gold dust for the programme I'm making. I'd love to talk to her more. And – '

She looked up and saw Frau Götte peering over her glasses, as if she was preparing to disapprove of what she was about to hear.

Karin was undeterred. 'The thing is, I'd love to jog her memory a bit more. And, well, I was wondering if I could take her for a drive. Take her back to Schloss Hohenstein. Maybe if she saw it again, visited inside, everything might come back.'

Frau Götte was silent for a moment, thinking it through. She turned her head and peered into the office, as if to check no one else had heard.

'Sigrid's not on duty today,' she said, carefully tidying the pile of papers on the counter in front of her. 'And we'd have to ask Frau Trautwein herself if she'd like to go for a drive.'

She let out a little laugh.

'Although I have to say, the way she's been talking about you, I have a feeling she will.'

She paused, still thinking.

'You'd have to take one of the staff with you. She needs looking after. And she'll need to have her lunch. And then after lunch she always has a nap. But after that – '

She looked at her watch, checked the time.

'D'you know what?' She clicked the computer keyboard. 'My shift finishes at two. Why don't I accompany you?'

Karin nodded.

'And look who's coming right now – '

Frau Trautwein appeared from the corridor while they were still standing at the welcome desk. She didn't recognize Karin at first, but when she did her eyes visibly brightened.

'Frau Trautwein?'

Frau Götte explained what Karin had proposed and said that if she was interested in going, then she, Frau Götte, would come along too.

'I'd like that very much, dear,' said Frau Trautwein, smiling again at Karin. 'I get out so little, see. It's not easy at my age. I'm nearly ninety, you know.'

'What I suggest,' said Frau Götte in her most matronly voice, 'is that you take a little walk around the gardens. I know, I know, it's all a little tired at the moment. It's because we've had no rain. Although looking at the sky today –' She pointed outside before turning back to them both. 'What was I saying? Oh yes, what I suggest is you go down to the little shop, it's just down the end of the corridor, and you can buy bread and cheese and ham. And then we'll all meet back here at two.'

* * *

Frau Trautwein sat in the front seat while Karin drove. Frau Götte was in the back.

The sky had been threatening rain all morning. Now it started to pour down, large drops at first that splattered onto the windscreen. But soon the wind picked up and they were hitting hard and by the time they swung onto the steep track that led to Schloss Hohenstein it was sluicing torrents. Water cascaded off the black rock, swilling grit and stones onto the track.

Frau Trautwein had hardly spoken since they set out from Sonnenhof. Karin kept glancing at her to check she was still awake. But as they turned a corner and sighted Schloss Hohenstein she suddenly started talking.

'Of course it was nothing like this when we first came. It was winter, see. We had snow. Oh gracious, we thought we were never going to make it. I mean, this part of the country always gets a lot of snow but that year was one of the worst.'

The castle vanished into drifting mist. For more than a minute it remained obscured. And then the grey-black walls loomed slowly back into view.

'Nineteen-forty-four. Seems so clear. We were in this car, see, all polished wood and leather and the driver was terribly smart and he had a peaked cap with a badge on the front. And, gracious, the snow. It must have been on this very road, somewhere round here, that he stopped and pulled the car over and put these chains onto the tyres.'

Karin pressed lightly on the brake and brought the car to a halt. She wanted it to be exactly as Frau Trautwein remembered it.

'And we were so cold. Cars in those days, they didn't have heating like they do now. We had travelling blankets and they looked after us well but by the time we reached the castle we were in need of hot drinks.'

Karin had started driving again as Frau Trautwein was talking and they soon reached the base of the final corkscrew that led to the castle entrance. The rain was sheeting the side of the car, flinging water against the windows. Karin was wondering how they'd get Frau Trautwein from the car to the entrance.

'Ah – yes -' Frau Trautwein lifted her hands from her lap as they swung underneath the archway and into the castle courtyard.

'Look, my goodness! It hasn't changed at all. You know I haven't been back in all these years.'

Karin drew the car to a halt by the main door, pulled on the handbrake and opened the door. It was noticeably colder and the peaks above were lost to the mist. Frau Trautwein was peering out through the windscreen and emitting a little girl's laugh.

'How funny to be back. Thought I never would. And after so many years. Of course I was last here in nineteen-forty-four.'

They succeeded in getting her inside without getting wet, Karen shielding her with the umbrella. The entrance hall was warm and smelled thickly of wood smoke. A bright fire was burning in the grate. The same woman as yesterday was seated at the ticket desk. She smiled when she saw Karin, recognizing her, then raised her eyes in surprise when she noticed Frau Trautwein.

'Back again,' she said, 'and with visitors, I see.'

'Yes.'

'Well I can't very well charge for you again,' she said. 'Not when you came here yesterday. So it's just for your guests. But will –'

Her eyes landed on Frau Trautwein – 'will she be able to manage the stairs. You saw how many –'

Karin nodded and paid for the two new tickets. As she took the change, Herr Fischer appeared.

'Ah –' he said. And then, more significantly: '*Ah –*'

Karin decided to introduce Frau Trautwein to them both. She explained who she was and why they'd brought her here.

'And yesterday, when you mentioned lebensborn, I just knew this was where Frau Trautwein had been. It's the only place in Bavaria they used.'

Herr Fischer's head turned from Karin to Frau Trautwein then back to Karin.

'We can take it nice and slow. And if Frau –'

'Trautwein –'

'If Frau Trautwein is up to it, I'll lead you to parts not usually open to the public.'

Frau Trautwein didn't seem to hear. She was looking around the entrance hall, remembering how it had been back then.

'A guard was stood right here,' she said, pointing to the door. 'And one on either side of the fire place. Ever so good looking, they were. Good Bayrisch types. And the fire was burning, just like today. We were ever so cold, see, and there was so much snow all around. They took us into the kitchens for hot drinks.'

Herr Fischer looked at Karin. 'Shall we go there now?'

He led them through a double door and down a poorly-lit corridor. The floor was partly tiled, partly flagstones.

'Do watch your step. It's rather uneven, I'm afraid.'

In Sonnenhof, Frau Trautwein had walked slowly and clung to the arm that was invariably by her side. But here she held Frau Götte's arm only lightly and gave the impression of floating along.

'I don't remember this part at all.'

There was the faint aroma of soup, onions and fresh lovage. It grew stronger as they made their way down the corridor. The passageway opened onto an internal courtyard all dismal with wet moss. The gutter was spilling water and in one corner a large puddle was submerging the cobbles.

'Drains,' said Herr Fischer.

There was a further twist in the passage and then they found themselves in the castle kitchens.

'And just look –' said Frau Trautwein, looking all around her as she caught her breath. 'Exactly as it was. A fire was burning, of course, and pots hanging from these –

'And, yes, I remember Eva, or was it Anna? No, Eva. She nudged me when she saw the pans boiling away. Must have been game, venison, something like that. And you know we ate so well in those weeks and months. Three times a day, ever so punctual. They'd sound a gong. Boing. Every mealtime. They wanted us in the healthiest way, see.'

Herr Fischer turned to Karin and whispered under his breath. 'This'll make a wonderful addition to our display. Don't think we'll be able to ignore lebensborn any longer, not after this.'

'And then we were taken up to the library. Yes, I remember that much quite clearly. This was all on our first day, you understand.'

Karin looked at Herr Fischer. 'Can we go there?'

Herr Fischer turned to face Frau Trautwein.

'It'll mean climbing some stairs,' he said in a loud voice.

'I know, I know.' She sounded irritated by the way he was speaking to her. 'You pass through that door there – ' She pointed to the far wall – and then you come to a staircase that leads directly to the library.'

Herr Fischer threw a wink at Karin.

'Of course there were always huge numbers of people. Wasn't like now. Cars constantly coming and going. Men in uniform. Generals, even. Marching boots, orders being shouted. So noisy.'

'How many where you?' Karin felt sure that now they were here, inside the castle, Frau Trautwein wouldn't lose her memory again.

'What's that dear?'

'How many girls?'

Frau Trautwein thought for a moment.

'Oh, we were, let's see, there was me and Eva. And Anna of course. And then there was Hannah and Gertrud. Good looking girl, Gertrud. And then the two from Pomerania. And, well, we were a dozen or so in all. But it kept changing of course.'

She looked around the library but didn't seem to take it in.

'After dinner we'd be brought here. We ate well and there was so much food. And then we'd come here for herb tea. They made it from wild flowers up on the mountains. And we'd play cards and then one of the officers came up to me and presented me with a silver charm bracelet. All on the first evening.'

She nodded to herself as she remembered it all happening.

'Of course we were all nervous about everything. We were only young girls you see. I was just eighteen. And Eva was even younger. Only sixteen. I remember we kept having to pinch ourselves to make it all seem real.'

She paused as she sifted through her memories.

'I wonder if it's still here?' she mused aloud.

'What?'

'Yes. It must be through here.' She began walking to the far end of the hall, towards the corridor that led to the exhibition area. 'We'd walk down this corridor and then – '

She pulled herself free from Frau Götte's arm and made her way towards the door.

'And then, here, you turn right. Down a few steps – and – '

Herr Fischer looked at the others and gave a shrug of his shoulders. He didn't know what she was talking about. He moved ahead, pushed the door. Frau Trautwein stopped abruptly as she entered the empty room, puzzled by something. She looked up at the vaulted ceiling, the conical pillars, the polished oak floor.

'This was it.'

'What?'

'Where they did all the medical stuff.'

'*Medical stuff?*'

'The tests. On us girls. To check we were fit, healthy, free from disease. We came here every day. They even tested us for syphilis, you know. That made us laugh. They tested the men, too.

'Only the very finest were brought to Schloss Hohenstein. A real elite. Like one of those shooting clubs you got in the old Germany. Officers. And all highly trained. Every day they would train. One day running. The next climbing. There was hill walking and shooting, They were ever so sportive. And the castle doctor –'

She stopped for a moment, trying to remember his name.

'Doctor – Doctor - Fiedler. That was his name. Doctor Fiedler. You see he'd be injecting them with all manner of things. We called it his wonder drugs, that's what we called it. Wonder drugs.' She smiled as the memories flooded back. 'That was it. It made us laugh and we said it meant we'd produce wonder children.'

Karin broke the pause with a question. 'What were these drugs. Can you remember?'

Frau Trautwein didn't seem to hear, so Frau Götte repeated the question in her ear. She, too, was intrigued.

'Oh, lord, couldn't tell you now. Don't know if I ever knew. What's that thing they all take nowadays. The cyclists I mean.'

'Steroids.'

'Steroids? Well it was probably something like that. And a different one the next day. Pervitin. That was one of them. That was for the men. And glucose. We were given this glucose syrup. Tasted of apricots. But I don't think we ever knew exactly what it was. The men came every day for their injections and what-not.'

She turned to Herr Fischer.

'I'd like to see my room. It was a beautiful room. Up in the turret. It had these curved round walls and a view as far as you could see, or that's how it seemed at the time.'

Herr Fischer thought for a moment. 'That'll be the south turret. The round one. Yes, yes, we can certainly go. But – '

He was thinking of the stairs.

'If we take it slowly,' said Karin.

'It snowed for so many weeks.' Frau Trautwein continued talking, even as they climbed the winding stairs of the south turret. 'Weeks and weeks. It was magical, really. We thought it would never stop. Each time we looked out of the windows there was more snow. At one point even the road leading to the castle was blocked.'

She paused, catching her breath on one of the stone landings.

'I used to run up these. Eighty-two steps to my room. I should have counted them now, make sure they're all still here.'

She tapped at her chest. 'I'm nearly ninety, you know. And they used to go out every day in the snow. Climbing and mountaineering and they'd even camp out, in winter too. All part of the training. They were the elite, see, like an old German club. They were sent off to all sorts of places. You couldn't imagine.'

Karin was about to prompt her for more when she started climbing again.

'Ninety,' said Frau Trautwein before correcting herself. 'No, no, I mean eighty-two.'

At last they reached the top landing. It had three doors leading off it, all of them closed.

'Eva,' said Frau Trautwein, stopping abruptly and pointing at the door opposite the stairwell. 'Me.' She pointed at another door. 'And the third was already being lived in by this girl from Darmstadt I think it was.'

Herr Fischer turned the handle to Frau Fischer's old room and slowly opened the door. It looked like the nineteen forties. An old double bed with a monumental wooden head-board. A dressing table with large porcelain washstand patterned with yellow flowers. There was a smaller table with a lamp and a few books. Hanging on the wall was a large painting of some rural

Bavarian scene.

'Are all the rooms kept as they were?' asked Frau Götte.

Herr Fischer nodded. 'Not all. But most. There are plans to open up the whole place to the public. But as ever – ' He pushed his hand into his pocket. 'Money.'

Frau Trautwein seemed tired by the climb. She rested against a chair in order to catch her breath.

'Would you like to sit down?'

'No, dear, I'm fine. I want to – '

She made her way over to the window.

'On a clear day there's a wonderful view from here. You could see the Zugspitze and the Schneefemerkopf and they'd be covered in snow until late spring. May, even June. And further away, right over there, is the Alpsee. And sometimes on a clear day you could see the spires of Oberammergau.'

They gathered at the window, staring into the rain. Drops of water had stuck to the glass, dribbling like tears. For a few seconds the cliff-face behind the castle loomed dark through the mist. Then it faded back to a grey blur.

'And the men?' Karin dared venture the question.

'Yes of course. That's why we were here. They'd send us one every night. They'd prepared us in advance. Told us what we were expected to do.'

She fell suddenly silent, as if the past was catching up with her. Her mood had changed. Karen looked at her and wondered for a moment if she was going to cry. But after emitting a heavy sigh, she continued talking.

'The first night, I remember it like it was yesterday. Otto Streckenbach. That was his name. From Saxony. Sturdy as a farm-hand with this shock of blond hair. I didn't think he was very bright, but he must have been or he wouldn't have been in the Totenkopf.'

Karin flinched on hearing the word.

'They were rough, some of them. And we could understand why. They'd seen everything. Been in Poland. Russia too. They'd been through the Russian winter. Oh they'd had the airs and graces knocked out of them alright.'

She moved over to the bed and sat down, stroking the blanket.

'Eva became Otto's favourite. I do believe she was hoping to marry him, if ever the infernal war would be over.

'And then there was Hans. He was a kindly type. A real old fashioned gentleman.'

Karin gulped. 'Hans Dietrich?'

'No, no. Hans Metelmann. But you're right. There was Hans Dietrich, too. Could never forget him. He was their leader of course. Came into all our rooms. He was exactly the sort they wanted to give us babies for the Führer.'

'D'you remember him?'

'Hans Dietrich? Of course my dear. How could you forget. Tall. Blond. But then they were all blond in those days. Bright as a button. But cruel. You can see cruelty in the eyes. Never said much, kept himself to himself. But there were lots of stories about Hans.'

Herr Fischer and Frau Götte were listening intently, puzzled as to why Karin was so interested in Hans Dietrich.

'Is he in your film?' whispered Frau Götte.

'No,' said Karin. 'But he might well be.'

Frau Trautwein stood up for a moment but then thought better of it and sat back down on the bed, sighing gently.

'Of course after the war, when it was all over, I regretted everything. Wished I'd never been a part of it. But I was only eighteen. Too young to know better. And I'd lost my mother when I was little. And – ' she looked at Karin – 'we all believed in what we were doing.'

She turned her gaze to the painting on the wall.

'Hitler used to be right there. His portrait. And every time I doubted anything or when it got too much I'd look at the Führer. His face seemed to reassure us all. It was like having a wise uncle always there with you.'

'Who else was there? The men I mean.'

'I can't remember all their names. There were so many of them, all Otto and Hans and I don't know what.'

'But Hans – ' said Karin. 'Hans Dietrich.'

'Yes, yes, bright as a button. But they all said he was cruelest of the lot. He'd won the Knights Cross, you know. Cruel eyes.'

'He was their leader?'

'They were a small group. The elite of the elite if you like. That's what they said. And didn't they just know it. Lord they swaggered round like nobody's business and used us girls like we were their special treat. Eva was the first to see it was wrong. It was after she'd spent the night with Hans. I don't know what he did to her because she'd never breathe a word, but she was in tears for much of the next day. It made us suddenly nervous. It didn't seem such a good thing after all.

'With me he was – '

She stopped speaking for a moment as she replayed the memory. Karin noticed the expression on her face change. She was no longer smiling.

'He came over to me, here in this room. He put his fingers around my neck and squeezed, ever so gently. Then he tightened his grip. He wanted to scare me I think. That's the only explanation I can think of. He wanted to scare me. I don't know what they'd injected him with on that day but there was a glint in his eye and I was very scared. And that's when I learned that you did what Hans Dietrich said.'

'*But* - ?' Karin was trying to think what to ask next. 'What happened to him? Where did he go?'

'They were here for five weeks. Maybe six. What does it matter after all this time? They were the elite, you know. And then one day we were told they were going. Not all of them, only the Totenkopf ones. All very secret, it was. No one was allowed to know. It was always like that here, you see. You never quite knew – '

All four of them were looking intently at Frau Trautwein, anxious to know more.

'You never quite knew *what?*' The urgency was betrayed by Karin's voice.

Frau Trautwein's face creased back to a smile. 'Hans let me play a little game with him. His way of showing he could be kind. I'd seen them training on the high slopes, training with dogs, sleds. Climbing in the worst of the snowstorms. He said I could guess where they were going.

'"Somewhere cold?" That's what I said. And he nodded. "Somewhere *very* cold?" Another nod. "Norway?" No. "Sweden?" No. "Back to Russia?" No. No. And then he said: "Colder."

'Well, I had to think at that. Where's colder than Russia? 'The North Pole? The Arctic? Greenland?' I threw up my hands and gave up.'

He smiled.

'*Greenland! You're going to Greenland?* He looked at me. "You said it."'

'But why?' asked Karin. 'Why Greenland?'

'That, my dear, I can't tell you. I never found out. You see I already knew more than I should.'

'Did he say anything else? Anything?'

She shook her head. Then she looked at Karin, her face suddenly bright.

'He did. He said the strangest thing of all. I thought about it for years afterwards.'

'What?'

'He said to me: 'What would you like as a present?'

'Well I laughed at that. I said to him, 'A present from Greenland?' And he said, 'No, a present from America.' I remember a long silence when he'd spoken, as if he'd said something he shouldn't have. And then he added with a laugh, 'from Las Vegas.' And to this day I never knew what he meant.'

* * *

They drove back to Sonnenhof and Frau Götte helped Frau Trautwein to her room.

'Now all she wants to do is sleep,' she said when she returned. 'You've exhausted her. Don't think she's had quite such an adventure in years.'

Karin thanked her for everything. 'An extraordinary day.'

'For me too. A window on the past. And a mighty strange past at that.'

Karin paused for a moment before turning to leave. 'One thing I wanted to ask but didn't get the right moment. All these men, the lebensborn programme, everything. Did she never have children?'

Frau Götte shook her head.

'I just asked her. Wasn't sure whether I should. But she didn't answer. Just closed her eyes and sighed. And yet – '

She paused for a moment, deep in thought.

'*And yet* – ?' said Karin.

'It's funny. She often speaks about a Katarina.'

PART THREE

TWENTY-SIX

Sergeant Perez sent Riley and Owen Green to keep watch on Ferris Clark's old house. 'Any sign. Any movement. Anything, for Chrissakes get on the phone. We'll be over in a flash.'

He then drove back into town to join Sheriff Rayno. He wanted to keep close touch on any leads that his team might have uncovered.

Jack spent the afternoon with Tammy in her office, running through everything that Karin had sent over by email.

'I'm scared, Jack,' said Tammy when he'd finished. 'How's it all going to end? When's he going to stop? Who's next? It freaks me out.'

Jack looked at her but said nothing.

'Four people killed for nothing. It's just horrible.'

He nodded.

Tammy switched subject.

'This Karin woman, how come you're so mysterious about her?'

'Like I said, she's German. Works in TV.'

'*Hmm –*'

She glanced towards him, hoping for more. When none was forthcoming she changed tack.

'Just thinking about it does my head in. To think there's someone alive, Frau what's-her-name, who actually knew Hans

Dietrich. And slept with him, for Chrissakes. It's crazy. In fact it's more than crazy. It's sinister. Breeding children. Never even heard of it until two days ago. It's too creepy for words.'

'Hitler wanted a Third Reich filled with men like the Totenkopf. Ruthless, fanatical, prepared to kill at the flick of a switch. Hans Dietrich was your model Aryan Nazi. He even looked the part, if you're into blond thugs.'

'What became of the others? What's their names? Otto Streckenbach and the other one.'

'Karin's not had time to check them out. She'll do it tomorrow. But we need to find out more about Hans Dietrich. Who was he? What was he up to?'

Tammy got up and made her way to the door. 'I need coffee. Want some?'

'Black.'

Jack went over to the window. The rain of two nights earlier had transformed the landscape. One more storm and the whole scrubland would burst into life.

'It's so beautiful in spring,' said Tammy as she came back into the room. 'Hope you'll come back and see it then. Come and see it in happier times. There, that's an invitation. It's one giant great carpet of flowers. We drive into the hills and have picnics.'

She paused.

'But that's another world.'

Jack looked at her blankly. 'Sorry, I was miles away.'

'Doesn't matter.'

'It's just that – '

He was trying to get it straight in his head.

'Hans Dietrich was coming to Las Vegas, right? And he was carrying Ferris Clark's address. D'you think Ferris Clark was involved in the military base here?'

Tammy shrugged.

Jack turned to face her. 'Your grandfather. You said he worked there. At the base.'

'Yep. But that's all I know. Got a ton of his papers at home, dating back to God knows when. But I've never gone through them. It's all ZAKRON stuff I think.'

She thought for a moment. 'It'd be better to head back to Vegas.'

'But there's no time. Fact is, Tammy, he's going to strike again. He's absolutely going to strike again.'

* * *

Jack drove down Golden Park Drive later that evening looking for 14. The numbers were still in the hundreds. He headed to the far end where the plots were bigger and the gaps between the houses widened into large gardens.

He'd had a picture of her house in his head – modern bungalow, single storey, like most of the houses in Hanford Gap. But it wasn't like that at all. As he drew up alongside 14 he was surprised to find a large single house with a brick and stone first floor and wood paneling on the upper level. There was a garage adjoining the house on the left hand side. The front lawn was green, well watered, neatly cut. A plastic mechanical digger lay on its side.

The front door opened as he parked up the car.

'*Jack* – boy, am I glad you're here. Hate being on my own with the kids. Scares me.'

He strolled across the lawn towards her. 'This place,' he said, pointing to the house. 'It's fantastic. I had no idea.'

'I should explain, before you think I've got millions hidden away. Could never have afforded to buy a place like this. It's a piece of Hanford history. This was grand-daddy's place. He gave it to my dad who died young. And that's how it came to me. And eventually, if I can afford the costs and bills and what-not, it'll go to these two here.'

She placed her hands onto the heads of Fran and Elsie, who'd run up beside her. They stared at Jack.

'Say hello to Jack.'

Both buried their heads into her legs.

'They'll be shy for less than two minutes. Then they'll be all over you. Be warned!'

He followed her up the steps and into the little porch.

'Quick tour before we set to work?'

The house dated from 1906, one of the first to be built in Hanford Gap. It had originally belonged to Jim Swain Junior, a cowboy with attitude. 'Red-necked gangster turned respectable,' she said. 'Built it in five weeks. Hanford in those days was a one dime coach stop.'

The hallway was wide but the air was still and hot. It felt as if the windows had been closed for days.

'Usually keep everything open,' said Tammy, reading his thoughts. 'It's what's so great about this place. Don't need air con. Even on the hottest days there's always a breeze if you open up back and front. But I'm keeping it all locked until – well, you know what -'

Fran came up and pulled at Jack's leg. 'You're that man from England?' He said it half as question and half as statement. 'Mum's told us about you.'

'Oh yes?' Jack smiled then stooped down to look him in the eye. 'What's mum been saying then?'

'Says you're smart. But you don't look that smart.'

'*Fran - !*'

Jack laughed. 'You're right. Your mum's the smart one. Way smarter than me.'

Elsie whispered something in Fran's ear. He turned to look at Jack.

'She says you've got a cool car.'

'That's true. Always drive a cool car. It's an important lesson in life.'

'Now you two go off and play,' said Tammy. 'I've got a ton of things to show Jack. And I don't want you bothering us.'

She led him into the family room, a spacious area with sliding double doors. Outside there was another spread of lawn. The room had scrubbed wooden floorboards of bleached oak and two large rugs with abstract designs of birds. A piano stood on the far side of the room with a row of framed pictures in a neat line on the top. Tammy took one of them down and handed it to him.

'Here's grand-daddy. Taken somewhere downtown, near the courthouse I guess.'

Jack studied it closely. Grandpa Fox looked more like a successful businessman than a scientist. Sharp suit and expanding girth. The propeller plane in the background hinted at foreign travel.

She picked up another photo. 'And that's mom and dad. Both dead, too, but at least mom lived long enough to see the kids.'

Jack lifted the lid of the piano and ran his finger along the keyboard.

'Can I?'

'You *play* - ? Is there no end to your talents?'

'Only to de-stress.'

He launched into a Bach sonata, but broke off just before he reached the second movement. If he'd been at home, Karin would have come into the room right at that moment. She said the second movement was the best thing Bach ever wrote.

'Don't stop. It's great. Good to hear the thing played for once. No one round here plays it.'

He started the piece from the beginning again and by the time he'd finished, Fran and Elsie had come downstairs and were standing next to him, wide-eyed.

'Play more,' said Fran, sliding between Jack and the piano. 'What else d'you know?'

Tammy looked at Jack, shaking her head. 'You're going to make yourself one popular guy with these two if you're not careful.'

She sent them both back upstairs and then pointed to the

boxes behind the sofa. There were eight or ten of them, some open, some still closed.

'I got them down earlier. Felt like I needed to be doing something. Stupid, probably. But he's out there on the loose and he's killing people and Jesus, Jack, who's going to be next? Another couple who've never hurt a fly? When's he going to stop? It's on my mind every second of the day.' She sighed heavily. 'We're going backwards rather than forwards.'

Jack walked over to the opened boxes. Papers, letters and notebooks were scattered across the floor. Photos, too, and a few unopened files.

'There's hours of work here,' she said. 'D'you want a drink? I'm having a vodka tonic. But I guess you'll – '

'Without the vodka,' he said. 'And lots of ice.'

He picked up one of the files and looked through. It was stuffed with papers and receipts, mostly from the late sixties. There was a photograph of ZAKRON taken on an instamatic, over-exposed, tinged with orange. A huge Chevrolet was parked up outside the main entrance.

Tammy reappeared with the drinks. 'Instant relax. Haven't slept since Monday. And I won't 'til he's caught. Feel kind of sick inside, like someone's twisting my guts.'

Jack took the glass from her hand. 'I should have let you pull the plug. It was your call. And I'm a stubborn bastard. But I'll tell you one thing, even though you won't believe it. Each new murder gets me here – '

He held his finger to his chest.

'I know you don't think I feel like shit. But I do.'

He turned back to the boxes. 'Confession over. What've you found so far?'

She put down her glass and swept her arm over the papers on the floor.

'Useless,' she said. 'All ZAKRON stuff. And all from the late-forties, when it was first set up. Prosthetics, reconstructive surgery, that was their business then. Guess it makes sense.

You've got thousands of soldiers returning from the war and half of them have got legs and arms blown off.'

'And cryonics?'

'Much later. Didn't start till the sixties. That's when the company changed from ZAKRON Prosthetics to ZAKRON Cryonics. But cryonics was only a tiny part of it. Wasn't until quite recently that it started making money. And that's how it's been for twenty odd years. Tom, for all I hate him, is successful. Businessman first, gangster second. Or is it the other way round?'

She pulled more items from the boxes.

'ZAKRON in nineteen-forty-six.'

Jack took the papers from her hands. The building in those days was a tunnel-shaped prefab built of corrugated metal. It looked like an airport hangar. A large sign hung over the entrance: *ZAKRON Prosthetics.*

'And some of their patients.'

She handed him a picture of six men, all war-wounded, forced smiles. 'That's grand-daddy again, only this time with the team.'

'They're so young. The scientists, I mean. Like they're still in their thirties.'

She nodded. 'They were young.'

'And they all worked at the base?'

'Think so,' she said. 'But what's that got to do with it?'

Jack looked at her and shrugged.

'Clutching at straws.'

TWENTY-SEVEN

Their half-drunk glasses were on the table, ice cubes melting. Tammy looked at her watch. It was already seven-thirty.

'A suggestion –'

Jack glanced up from one of the files.

'I cook for these two here.' She squeezed Fran and Elsie protectively towards her. 'I'll cook for us as well. You get the rest of the stuff down from upstairs. It's all in the spare room. If there's anything about the military base, it'll be in the boxes at the bottom. But first –'

He looked at her.

'This is going to sound real weird.'

She checked to see that the children weren't listening. 'Everything that's happened, Jack, it's making me jumpy. Nervous. Would you mind going round the house? Double-checking it's all locked. Doors, windows. I'm sure they are. But you know how it is?'

'Sure. No problem. If it makes you feel better.'

'*Mom, Mom*, what's Jack doing? Mom, can we help Jack?'

'No. But you can go upstairs with him. Get ready for bed. No food 'til you're ready.'

Jack went upstairs with Fran and Elsie trailing behind him. They clutched onto his arms and tried to hang off him, two dead weights.

'Carry us, carry us.'
'You weigh a ton.'

* * *

Tammy made her way into the kitchen. With the children upstairs the house fell silent. She inched open the kitchen door then pushed it hard with her foot. It banged against the wall. The freakiest thing was the way he'd managed to get into their houses without them knowing.

She was used to being alone. Ever since Bill walked out, she'd spent dozens of nights on her own, the children at sleep-overs, school trips and what-not. Tonight it felt different. 'Serial killer' was all over the TV, the newspapers, the internet. It was impossible to avoid it. 'Who's Next?' screamed the headline on the Hanford Courier. Twitter was full of the latest on the Pereira couple. Rayno was the target of public anger.

Tammy went over to the walk-in cupboard and eased it open, checking inside. *He could be hiding.* She looked up at the clock. And then she glanced out of the window at the darkening sky. The sun had sunk in the last ten minutes. Now, the sky was a dull sheet of steel. Night in half an hour, then seven hours of darkness.

He struck at night. That was one consistency. Always killed with the same weapon. Another. And always the skull. He was methodical, that's what Jack had said to Perez. Trained to kill.

She heard Jack coming back downstairs. Reassured, she put the children's pasta in the microwave.

'We'll feed the kids first and then we can eat once they're in bed. I'm making a spaghetti sauce. At least a sort of sauce. A sauce without onions, cos I haven't got any.'

She gave it a stir and then held up the spoon and pointed towards the bottle of vodka. 'Feel like I need it just to keep going.

263

Every evening I get these nerves, like I'm sick inside. Christ, it's like being pregnant again. It's fine in the day. Life goes back to normal. And then the evening comes round and I feel like I'm playing some sort of crazy waiting game. I mean, who's next on his list? He could strike anywhere. Could be me. Or you. It freaks me out, Jack.'

When the children had finished their pasta she sent them off to brush their teeth in the first floor bathroom.

'Right, bed.' She turned to Jack. 'Down in a minute.'

'I'll get those other boxes.'

* * *

Jack followed them upstairs and switched on the light in the spare room. It was full of clutter. Two large wardrobes. Old chairs. A single bed. And a pile of boxes and cartons. He opened one of them to look inside, but then closed it again and started taking them all down to the family room.

Tammy came down soon after he'd finished.

'Jeez, you've found tons. Been meaning to go through it for years. When Bill walked out I'd told myself I'd do it. Break from the past. It's good to do that sometimes. But, hell, you know how it is. Work. Children. Life gets in the way.'

'What happened with Bill then?' ventured Jack when they sat down to eat. 'He walked out?'

'I guess he did. Or rather, well, I kind of threw him out. Just had enough. Fact is, it never really worked. He gets the kids every other weekend.'

There was a pause.

'And you? Mystery Man. Maybe that's what you want.'

Jack was silent for a moment. Then he picked up his knife and tapped it against his plate. 'You sure know how to make a pasta sauce.'

They went through to the family room when they'd finished eating. Jack sat on the sofa and drew one of the larger cartons towards him. It was filled with box-files marked with stickers. One contained account books dating back to the nineteen fifties. Another had medical records from 1963.

'Not sure I should even have these,' said Tammy. 'How long d'you have to keep them?'

'Ten years. In the UK that is.'

There were deeds for the purchase of the ZAKRON plot and legal papers about the construction of the first structure.

'If there's anything about the war it'll be in the ones down there.'

Jack edged out the carton at the bottom of the pile and removed one of the folders. Inside there were five envelopes tied together with black string. Four of them contained papers about ZAKRON's first year. But the fifth, coloured pink-beige, was marked in faint pencil: *Station H G.*

'Eureka! Maybe.'

Tammy got up from her chair, picking up her wine glass. She sat down next to him on the sofa and watched him extract the papers. Three typewritten memos, letters, some cuttings from scientific magazines.

He handed Tammy her grandfather's identity pass. 'That's how he looked during wartime.'

'I like a man in uniform.'

'*Oh?*'

She smiled. 'It's just one of those things you say.'

He looked through the rest of the papers, pulling out photos from an envelope.

'This must be the base.'

There was a row of six corrugated iron warehouses and two smaller buildings of concrete. In the far background were the low pale hills that marked the boundary between Nevada and California.

'That was taken close to the Fifty,' said Tammy. 'Right by the highway. Near Jazzy Joe's. There's still a dirt track.'

Jack pulled a typewritten letter from its envelope. Printed across the top in faded red ink was a single word: *secret*.

'Not for much longer.'

He straightened the paper and held it up between him and Tammy. It was typed on thin foolscap, like tracing paper. He had to put it in front of a blank sheet to be able to read it.

Dear Captain Fox,

The Combined Chiefs of Staff have now had the chance to consider the results of your latest tests (18 March, 1944). The ability to produce endospore anthrax in such quantity - and to be able to trigger its activation in this fashion - is indeed a major breakthrough. General Vincent Caldwell is calling it the greatest biological innovation since the outbreak of war.

The Combined Chiefs of Staff have taken the decision to place an initial order of 200,000 anthracakes, subject to joint approval by President Roosevelt and Prime Minister Churchill. (For your information, their approval is seen as a formality, as they have already signalled their agreement to the Combined Chiefs of Staff.)

As you are aware, the greatest concern remains the means by which the anthrax is to be dispersed over Germany. General Caldwall wishes to have further information before any final decision is taken on this front. To this end, a gifted young meteorologist named Sergeant Ferris Clark will be joining you at Station Hanford Gap in order to discuss the effects of wind patterns on the dispersal of anthrax.

Sergeant Clark is an expert on wind patterns and turbulence and it seems opportune for you and your team to have the benefit of his expertise before he takes up his post in Greenland.

It is hoped that he will be with you at Station Hanford Gap on Thursday morning at the latest. I will be arriving on the following Monday, along with Major Caldwall, when we can discuss these matters more fully.

Colonel Ray D. Smithson.

'Shit.'

Tammy looked at Jack. 'Anthrax. That's what they were up to.'

'Yes.'

He thought for a moment then turned back to the letter.

'What's it called? Endospore anthrax. And they were going to dump two hundred thousand of them on the Nazis.'

He put down the letter for a moment, thinking it through. 'It's no secret Churchill wanted to drop anthrax on Germany. All came out a few years ago. His idea was to wipe out every cow, pig and sheep in the land. Operation Vegetarian.'

'British black humour.'

'Very. They even tested it on some island in Scotland. Dropped tons of the stuff.'

'And?'

'Wiped everything out in minutes. And that was just regular anthrax.'

There was a moment's silence.

'At least one thing makes sense,' he said. 'We now know why

Hitler was so keen to send Hans Dietrich here. He wanted to kill the scientists before they wiped Germany off the map.'

He tapped his fingers on his knee. 'Also explains why Hitler wanted Ferris Clark dead. Christ, he was the lynch-pin to absolutely bloody everything. Churchill needed his expertise for the anthrax drop. Roosevelt needed his forecasts for the Atlantic convoys.'

'And it all happened here,' said Tammy slowly. 'Seems crazy. I mean, just think about it. Ferris Clark must have known granddaddy. They must have met. Even worked together.' She paused. 'I mean, Christ, Jack, there's every chance Ferris Clark came here. Sat in this room.'

'Guess there is.'

He picked up the folder again and handed half of the papers to Tammy.

'We need to go through the lot.'

He sifted through the files at speed, checking for any that might be relevant. There were some newspaper cuttings, more photographs and a long report about anthrax testing in Scotland.

'What's the date on the letter?' asked Tammy.

'Twenty-first of March.'

'Then here's the reply. Or sort of reply.'

She pointed her finger to the last line. 'And look who it's from.'

To Colonel Smithson,

I feel moved to protest in the strongest possible terms about the proposed endospore anthrax drop on Nazi Germany. Were this operation to be undertaken, and in optimum conditions, the effects would be devastating for the civilian population.

Further, it would only take a slight shift in the wind speed and the atmospheric pressure to bring about catastrophic and wholly unforeseen consequences.

I have already briefed Captain Fox and his team at Station Hanford Gap, but I feel I must see you and Major Caldwall in person before I take up my post in Greenland next week. Could you be kind enough to let me know when would be a convenient time for me to drop by your office?

Sergeant Ferris Clark.

Jack looked at the letter, thinking it through.

'Anything else?'

They looked through the rest of the papers but there was nothing more about anthrax and no other mention of Ferris Clark.

* * *

Tammy yawned and looked at her watch. Almost one.

'It's late.'

'Very.'

Jack looked at all the unopened boxes they'd yet to go through. 'We'll never do all this tonight.'

'We've made progress at least,' said Tammy. She thought for a moment.

'Look, I've got a guest room. Not the spare one. Another. Why don't you stay over. Save you going back to the Comfort Inn.'

She paused and looked at him, gauging his response. 'And if I'm completely honest, I'd feel happier having a guy in the house, what with everything that's going on.'

She gave an embarrassed laugh.

'I mean - well - you're a guy. And you're in my house.'

Jack laughed.

'Course I'll stay. Willingly. The Comfort Inn's not exactly – '

'*Comfortable?* Can't promise you five star. And the kids'll almost certainly wake you in the night. And you'll probably hear me talking crap in my sleep but – '

'Couldn't have sold it better.'

They both got up then Tammy ran through the nightly checklist. 'Front door locked. Back door locked. Windows locked. Alarm on. Windows all closed.'

She suddenly turned to face him.

'D'you think I'm crazy?'

'No. I think you're –' he searched for the right word - '*exotic.*'

'Exotic! Again! Next you'll be saying I should live in a zoo.'

'It's a compliment.'

'I'll take it as one.'

TWENTY-EIGHT

It was gone nine when Jack awoke, later than he intended. He had dreamed of Karin during the night and woke up thinking he was back in London.

He threw on some clothes and followed the smell of warm cinnamon down to the kitchen. Fran and Elsie were sitting at the table eating bowls of cereal. Tammy was loading the dishwasher. She had showered and washed her hair. She'd been up for some time.

'Can't believe you slept so well,' she said. 'I was awake half the night. Only got about two hours. That's why I look so crap. *You*, meanwhile – '

He helped himself to coffee from the glass jug and sat down at the kitchen table, running his hands through his hair.

'D'you like Honey Nut Cheerios?' asked Fran.

He forced a smile. 'Love 'em. Know what, they're my favourite.'

'Told you so, mom. Told you he'd like Honey Nut Cheerios. And you said he wouldn't.'

Smiling, Tammy walked across to the table and handed him a bowl.

'Well if Jack Raven's so keen on Honey Nut Cheerios then Jack Raven can eat as many as he wants.'

'Maybe later.'

'Will you play piano again?' asked Elsie.

'Later. If your mum lets me.'

'She said you're staying longer,' said Fran.

'Let's see.'

'You going to marry mom?'

He laughed, then looked up at Tammy.

'Your mum would not marry *me*!'

As soon as the children were distracted he asked her if there was any news. 'Spoken to Tom? Perez?'

She shook her head. 'Guess no news is good news. I checked Twitter. Local TV. All quiet. He didn't strike last night. For once.'

Jack got up from the table and looked out into the yard. It had rained again in the night, but only lightly, and the storm that had threatened all evening had blown itself elsewhere. The garden path was damp and the two acacias were glistening in the morning sunshine. They looked like they'd woken up covered in sweat.

'Thought Nevada's meant to be the driest state.'

'Was until you arrived.'

He drained his coffee and put the cup in the dishwasher.

'Christ,' she said. 'Bill wouldn't have done that.'

'*And* I cook,' he said, 'but only on request.'

'Always said guys must have their uses. Boy, the kids are certainly happy to have you in the house. Just wish the circumstances were different. In every sense.'

Jack went upstairs to take a shower, then came back down to check if there were any replies to the emails he'd sent on the previous evening.

'They promised they'd get back to me before they close.' He looked at his watch. 'And with the time difference, that's in half an hour.'

'Who?'

'The Met Office. Exeter. I sent an email yesterday.'

* * *

The doorbell rang. Tammy went to answer.

'It'll be Perez and the others,' she said. 'They said they were coming round.'

She paused for a moment. Jack sensed she had something to add.

'D'you mind not saying you stayed here? It's just that Tom and Hunter – '

'Course not. If they ask, I had another swell night at the Comfort Inn.'

The others came into the house and went straight into the family room. 'Holy-moley' said Hunter. 'You moving house?'

The papers from the previous night were scattered across the floor and their empty glasses were still perched on the piano.

Tammy appeared with coffee. 'Want some?'

Perez nodded. 'Thanks.'

Tom also took a cup.

Jack told them everything he'd discovered about Hanford military station, the anthrax and Ferris Clark. And then he read out the two letters. Perez frowned as he finished the second.

'Grant you one thing,' he said. 'It explains why Hitler wanted the scientists killed. And why he wanted Ferris Clark killed. I'm guessing Hans Dietrich went to Greenland to kill Ferris Clark. And if he hadn't somehow snuffed it, his next stop would have been Nevada.'

Jack nodded. 'Exactly.'

'By why did he have Ferris Clark's address?' asked Tammy. 'Don't get it.'

'Perfect place to hide out,' said Jack. 'Ferris Clark's dead. The house is empty. They know he hasn't got family. Ferris's house was to be their base in Nevada.'

Perez stood up and paced around the room. 'Yeah, yeah.' He sounded irritated. 'But it still doesn't bring us a rat's ass closer to catching the fucker.'

Hunter slurped his coffee.

'He's left the house in Green Diamond. No sign at all.'

'Really?' Jack looked up.

'Yeah. Owen and Riley went over last night. Doesn't look like he's been back. Nothing's been moved. Nothing touched.'

'Uniform still there?'

'Yep. Least it was. They've taken it away. And rearranged things in the basement. But – '

Perez interrupted him, speaking slowly.

'Where the fuck can he be?'

There was a long silence, as if everyone was searching for an answer.

'And Rayno?' asked Jack. 'What's he up to?'

Perez explained how Rayno had instigated a mass search of sheds and outbuildings. Factories, warehouses and storage buildings, all had been combed for clues. Wasteland, the skate park, Dexter's Wood, they'd been searched by the police.

Nothing.

'Washington's doing profiling,' said Perez. 'Each killing gives them more to go on. But I spoke to Bill last night, Bill Catchpole. Head of profiling. Know what he said? Strangest serial killer they've ever dealt with. They even had a bust-up over it. Half of them say he's killing at random, other half say it's all planned. And Bill, d'you know what he says to me? He says, "And I'm sitting on the fence like a fucking squirrel."'

* * *

Tom, Hunter and Perez left soon afterwards, having agreed to touch base later that afternoon. Tammy went into the kitchen to make an early lunch.

'*Fran? Elsie?* You stay with me here in the kitchen. Jack's busy with work.'

'But why, mom? Can't we play with Jack.'

'You can play later.'

Jack went back to his laptop and checked his in-box. There was a reply from the Met Office. Subject: Ferris Clark.

He scrolled down. Two pages of information, sent as a pdf.

'*Anything?*'

He could hear Tammy calling from the kitchen.

'Bring your laptop in here if you can cope with these two.'

Jack skim-read the email and saw he'd struck gold. The first part of the email gave a historical framework for the D Day forecasts. It had been lifted and pasted from the internal catalogue.

'The Meteorological Office, which was in those days known as the Central Forecast Office, moved out of London in early 1940.'

That much he knew. It had been re-established in Dunstable, thirty miles to the north, and given a codename. The government had quickly realised the importance of forecasting. And as the war progressed and the planned landings in northern France became a reality, accurate forecasting became essential.

'*Jack – ?*'

The specialists working at Dunstable were among the best in the world. Billingham, Jones and Smethwick were brilliant climatologists. CKM Douglas was top of his game. But the accuracy of their forecasts was dependent on data gleaned by meteorologists on the ground. Neave in Spitsbergen, Sam Forsyth in Jan Mayen Land and Ferris Clark in Eastern Greenland. Of all these outpost stations, Ferris Clark's was the most important, because North Atlantic weather patterns move from west to east.

Jack rolled up his sleeves. The family room was hot and airless. Tammy had kept the windows closed for the last twenty-four hours.

He scrolled down the screen, nodding to himself as he digested the information. It was as he suspected. Greenland was the key to everything. Ferris Clark's work had been important through the spring of 1944, but it became vital at the beginning of June. Operation Overlord was planned for the first week of that month and the landings could only go ahead if the weather was good. If they missed June, the next weather-window (with moon and tides) wouldn't be for weeks.

The Dunstable weathermen thought the unseasonable storms were set to continue for the whole week. So did their American counterparts.

But Ferris Clark disagreed.

F. Clark had been meticulously gathering data on air and sea temperature in Eastern Greenland, as well as on atmospheric pressure and humidity. He had produced a series of charts of the counter-clockwise spring storms and he had also produced a ground-breaking study of the Azores High, a semi-permanent high pressure zone that drifts across the North Atlantic.

Jack lifted his eyes for a moment. He could see where it was leading.

Ferris Clark recorded a consistently rising barometer throughout the morning of 4 June. He was the first person to realise that the Azores High was drifting northwards. From the data he gathered, he predicted a weather window on the 6 June that would be just long enough for the Normandy landings to take place.

The American weather team rejected Ferris Clark's data. They urged Eisenhower to launch Overlord on 5 June. But the British team placed their trust in Ferris Clark. In the weeks since he had arrived in Greenland, every daily forecast had been correct. There was no reason not to trust him now.

In the event, General Eisenhower decided to rely on Ferris Clark. It was a huge gamble, for it involved placing at stake the lives of 160,000 men. Not only that, failure would have meant the post-ponement of the landings in northern Europe for at least a year, if not indefinitely.

Eisenhower's trust in Ferris Clark was not mis-placed. The 5 June (the preferred date of the American team) proved to be extremely stormy, with a Force 5 gale that caused a heavy swell in the English Channel. Cloud cover was so low that bombing raids would have been impossible. But as midnight approached, the area of high pres-sure shifted considerably to the east, just as Ferris Clark had predicted. This caused the wind to drop and the swell to calm.

Jack sat back in his chair. So he was vindicated in keeping faith in Ferris Clark. He'd been key to it all. He had accurately fore-cast the weather for D Day. Without him there'd have been no landings. Or worse still, landings that failed. And all done from a lonely cabin on the east coast of Greenland.

There is a sad footnote to this remarkable piece of weather history. Ferris Clark was killed in an enemy ambush on the night of 4 June. He therefore went to his death unaware of the glorious role he played in the greatest sea-borne landing in history.

The email ended with a note informing Jack that any additional information would necessitate a visit in person to the archives held at the Meteorological Office Library in Exeter.

'*Jack – lunch –* '

Tammy was calling from the kitchen. He got up and went through. 'We'll eat with the kids. It's not gourmet, I'm afraid.'

They ate salad and rice and chicken wings in barbeque sauce. Then Tammy sent Fran and Elsie to watch a DVD in the family room.

'So?' she said. 'What news?'

Jack told her what the email had said.

'Shit, Jack! It was Ferris Clark that made D Day a success?'

'Looks like it.'

'And that was the last thing he did?'

'Seems so.'

'And then he was killed?'

'Yep. And then he was killed.'

TWENTY-NINE

They were still sitting at the kitchen table when Tammy's phone rang.

'Yeah?'

Silence.

'No. *NO!*'

Jack looked at her, knowing exactly what had happened.

'Shit, shit – who – where - ?'

She turned to look at him, drew a grim face as she listened to the voice on the other end. It was Jon Perez.

'He's struck again – ' she whispered, cupping her hand over the phone. And then, talking back to Perez, 'D'we know who? And where?'

Jack put down the papers he was holding and waited while Perez gave Tammy the details.

'Another couple,' she said, clicking off the phone. Her face was white. 'Only these ones are young, in their twenties. Shit, shit. It's one big fucking nightmare. Perez wants you over. Now. It's Lovedock Way.'

'Where's that?'

'Downtown. In the one-way system. First you have to – oh, hell, it's not easy to explain -'

She thought for a moment then picked up her keys from the table by the door. 'I'll drive you there.'

She called up to the children. 'Fran, Elsie, come down. Quick.'

She led them out through the kitchen and into the garage that adjoined the house.

'Can you turn the light on?' She then fumbled with her keys, searching for the right one to lock the door behind her.

'Get in the car,' she said to Fran and Elsie, pushing them gently into the back. Jack got into the front seat.

'Mom, I'm hungry,' moaned Fran.

'Me too, Mom. Where's the cookies. We want cookies.'

Tammy sighed heavily and glanced at Jack.

'Sorry. Give me two secs.'

She found the key again, unlocked the door and dashed back into the kitchen. *Cookies, cookies.* She opened the cupboard, pulled out the packet at the front. Then she dashed back to the garage and got into the car.

'Cookies!' shouted both kids triumphantly.

'Yeah, well don't eat them all or you'll be sick,' said Tammy, getting into the front seat and starting the engine. 'Did you hear?'

'Yep mom.'

The garage door swung open automatically and Tammy pulled out into Golden Park Drive, turning right into Manor Street.

'Won't take us more than a few minutes,' she said. 'But it's complicated cos of this one-way system.'

'Where we going?' said Fran from the back.

'Jack needs to see someone. We'll wait in the car. He won't be long. It's something important.'

'Who's he seeing?'

'Doesn't matter. He needs to see someone. Won't be long and then we'll go back home and I'll cook you – '

She paused.

'What d'you want tonight?'

'Pasta.'

'Then I'll make pasta.'

'*Mom,*' asked Elsie, 'is Jack coming for pasta?' Both their faces brightened at the thought. '*Jack! Jack!*'

Tammy looked at him. 'You will stay? I feel safer with you in the house.'

Jack nodded and then turned to Fran and Elsie with a smile. 'Thanks for the invite.'

Tammy parked the car at the far end of Lovedock Way. Jack got out.

'Can we come?' asked Fran from the back seat. 'Can we go with Jack, mom?'

'Not okay for you two. Jack's got business.'

'Give me five,' he said. 'Won't take any longer. I kind of know what to expect.'

He walked to the far end of the street where there was the now familiar gathering of TV vans, cameras and police cars. He noticed the same faces that he'd seen earlier in the day, only now they'd been joined by new ones. Sky hadn't been there before, nor had World. There was even the guy from the BBC. So the story had made it to England. Everyone likes a serial killer.

The scene that greeted him at 416 Lovedock Way was much as he expected. A house dating from the late twenties, no sign of damage to the doors or windows. Sheriff Rayno was looking even more downcast. Officers Cass and Don were standing like security guards on either side of the front door, happy to have made it onto the news bulletins. Something to show to the children and grandchildren. A temporary generator had been erected on the small patch of grass and the TV lights were on, even though it was broad daylight. They bathed the front of the house in a curious white glow, turning it into a film set.

Jack scooped the plastic cordon and passed underneath. Then he walked over to the door, raising his arm into a wave as Rayno looked round. When he entered the house he glimpsed Sergeant Perez in the back room. He walked through and Perez looked up.

'Ed and Hayley Mann,' he said. 'Twenty-five and twenty-two. No kids.'

Jack nodded. 'The same, I guess?'

'Yeah.'

Perez thumped his fist on the desk. 'Why, why, why? It makes no fucking sense. For fuck's sake, why?'

Jack looked at him. It made sense to Hans Dietrich.

'Wanna see them?' said Perez.

'Ought to.'

'Upstairs. Front room.'

Jack made his way up the carpeted stairs, pushed the door. It was exactly as he was expecting. A drop of congealed blood dangled from the lampshade, caught in a strand of hair.

'No links to the others,' said Perez, who joined him inside the room. 'We've got folks working on it right now. Checking it out. These two, the Manns, they don't seem to have known Ashton Brookner. No links with the Pereira couple, at least we haven't established any. It's completely random.'

He paced purposefully around the room, stepping carefully over the carnage.

'And you guessed it, no signs of how he entered. No finger-prints. No fucking trace of anything at all. Jesus, it's like we're dealing with a ghost.'

He paused at the rear window and Jack joined him there. They stared into the back garden. The sun was sinking fast and the sky was an unclean blue. Another storm brewing.

'Shit.'

Perez kicked at the carpet. He was thinking on his feet.

'No link to the others.' He said it to the room, then turned to face Jack. 'At least Brookner and the Pereira couple knew each other. They were friends. We had something to go on. But these guys had never even met.'

'You sure?'

'Yup. We've run checks on their calls. Rayno's been through their contacts, diaries. He's checked out their emails.'

'What did they do?' He pointed down at the corpses. 'Ed and Hayley, was it?'

'*He* worked for that logistics place out on the ring. Exton

Solutions. And *she* – ' He glanced down – 'was a teacher. A classroom help.'

He looked at Jack. 'So what the fuck do we do now?'

* * *

'Look, look. He's coming. Mom –'

Jack could hear them long before he reached the car. Fran had clambered into the front seat and was waving excitedly. Elsie was all legs and feet.

'Sorry it took so long.'

Tammy brushed her hand through the air.

'So,' she said when he was back in the passenger seat. She shot a glance towards the kids, warning him not to say too much.

'Same as ever,' he said, taking the hint. 'All fits the same pattern.'

'So what the hell do we do now? How long's it going to take to catch him for Chrissakes? Jack, I can't take much more of this. I just want to wake up in my bed and find it's all been a nightmare and it didn't really happen at all.'

THIRTY

Karin looked at her watch. Nearly nine o'clock. She reached for the remote control and switched on the TV, flicking through the German channels and then going through the English language ones. Sky's headline news was just starting.

'Good morning. And today's top story. Another couple found murdered in the town of Hanford Gap, Nevada. This now brings the total to five and police are still no closer to finding the identity of the killer.'

'Six,' said Karin under her breath. 'If you include Kingston.'

'One of America's largest manhunts is now underway, with hundreds of police drafted in from neighbouring states.'

The camera turned from the reporter to the house where the couple had been murdered. Karin's heart skipped a beat. There was Jack! In the background and standing in shadow. But it was Jack.

She turned up the volume on the television but her phone rang right at that moment so she turned it down again. Unknown number.

'Hello – am I speaking to Karin Hofmann?'

She recognized the voice immediately.

'Herr Fischer here. From Schloss Hohenstein.'

'Good to hear you.'

He explained how her unexpected visit had sent him back

to the archives. He'd been sorting through all the miscellaneous papers.

'To be honest I was hoping to find more about lebensborn. I'd like to put up a display. Maybe even record an interview. But -'

'*But -* ?' She could almost hear him shrug.

'Nothing more on lebensborn. I'm guessing all the records have been destroyed. Or moved to Berlin.'

Karin told him it was possible. There were files in Berlin she hadn't had time to look at.

'But that's not why you called?'

'No. You see I started to look through the unsorted files. Should have done it years ago to be honest. But there's dozens of them, all the stuff that's never been given a proper home. And I found a little more about the Totenkopf. Not a lot, mind. Don't want to get you excited. But it might just.'

Karin looked at her watch.

'I could come right away. I can be there within the hour. Is that okay?'

She showered, dressed quickly then set off in the hire car, tracing the now-familiar road through the high alpine valleys.

It was her third visit in forty-eight hours but the scenery unfolded differently each time. Yesterday's rain had cleared but the road was still awash with scree and shingle. She gazed upwards, to the high peaks above the castle. Her eyes did a double take. The curved top of the Zugspitz was dusted with snow, blown into the gulleys and dips in the dark rock. It gave a dappled effect of black and white.

Snow. She wanted to come back in winter, just her and Jack.

* * *

The castle library was caught in a twilight gloom, as if daylight was fading before it had even got started. The sky had darkened with cloud. When Karin looked up to the high windows she noticed that it was starting to rain.

Herr Fischer was seated at the far end, as before, and lit by the warm glow of the anglepoise. She wondered if he ever left his desk. He looked up when he heard the creak of the parquet, smiled briefly, and then began to frown.

'Hope I haven't brought you here under false pretences. There's really not very much and it's all a jumble. But you seemed interested in the Totenkopf.'

'Very,' said Karin. 'Anything's better than nothing.'

Herr Fischer picked up a slender folder perched atop a pile of envelopes. All were marked 'Miscellaneous.'

'Here, this is all I've found so far. But I have to confess it's got me intrigued. It seems quite – ' He searched for the right word, then articulated it very deliberately. '*Curious.*'

Karin opened the folder. The first sheet was covered in a jumble of letters and numbers, interspersed with miscellaneous words that didn't add up to anything. The only recognizable feature was the seal of the Totenkopf, stamped in red at the top of the paper. A black swastika was printed on both sides.

'What is it?'

'My thought exactly,' he said. 'Couldn't work it out at first. *Un mystère*, as they say in France.'

'So?'

'Spent the better part of an hour trying to fathom it. And it's still not completely clear. But these numbers here – '

He pointed towards the top of the page.

'They're coordinates. Grid references. Latitude and longitude.'

Karin studied them more closely.

'You're never going to believe this,' he said with a chuckle. 'Couldn't think where they'd lead me to. So I looked them up on a map. And they took me to – hold on a moment – '

He reached across to the shelf on his right, still sniggering, and took hold of a large atlas bound in stiff maroon card. He flicked through the pages until he reached Greenland.

'Your Totenkopf seem to have gone *here* -'

He slid his finger across the map until it came to a halt on a little headland that jutted out into the Greenland Sea.

'And this is the middle of nowhere. This isn't remote, it's the end of the world.'

He peered more closely at the map, as if in hope of finding a clue in the whiteness.

'What they were doing there is anybody's guess. But – '

He looked at her with an expression of genuine amusement. 'I mean, what a place to be sent.'

Karin's eyes switched back to the map of Greenland. Then she turned to the sheet of paper that lay there in the glow of the lamplight. She leaned forwards and took it in her hands.

'But what does it mean?'

There was another row of figures and a corresponding row of letters.

'It's most interesting,' said Herr Fischer, 'though it only tells half a story. It's that very man you kept mentioning when Frau What's-her-name was here.'

'Hans Dietrich?'

'Exactly. Look, here. SS-Hauptsturmführer Hans Dietrich.'

He laid the sheet on the table and drew up a chair, patting it lightly as if to encourage a cat to sit down.

'I've worked out most of it. At least I think I have. These – ' He pointed back to the numbers – 'these indicate the location. Greenland. And this here is the date.'

Karin looked to where his finger was pointing. 05.06.44

'The fifth of June.'

'Exactly.'

'This is the time.'

'Six minutes past four in the morning.'

'Exactly. And all this business here – ' he pointed to the bottom of the page – 'is the message.'

Karin looked at the words. There were no sentences. It was

a series of individual words. Pressure low. *Stop.* Falling. *Stop.* Predicted Channel wind speed, Force Six. *Stop.* Visibility, poor. *Stop.* Cloud level: 100m or less. *Stop.* Storm conditions expected. *Stop.*

'It's a forecast.'

'Exactly,' said Herr Fischer, nodding vigorously. 'It's a forecast.'

'And it was sent to - ?'

'That bit's down here.'

He pointed to the lines at the very bottom.

'It was sent from Greenland, from the spot I showed you on the map. It was sent by wireless. This is a wireless transmission sent from Greenland to the Tirpitz.'

'A ship?'

'Yes. Tirpitz was a ship. German. Operating in the North Atlantic.'

Here was something for Jack.

'Look at the final line. Forward to Third Army High Command. *Stop.* Forward to Field-Marshal Rommel. *Stop.* Forward to station command, Normandy. *Stop.*'

She looked up and her eyes caught the forest of antlers at the farthest end of the library. Hans Dietrich had sent the wireless transmission from exactly the spot where Ferris Clark was living on the night between the fourth and fifth of June.

A loud flapping sound came from one of the high windows.

'*Aach*, pigeons, pigeons,' said Herr Fischer, glancing up. 'The hawks get them in the end.'

'Is here anything else?'

'Not a great deal.' He leaned back in his chair, sending a creak through the back and arms. Then he shifted himself forwards again and adjusted the angle of his lamp.

'The only other thing is this.'

He handed her another sheet of paper. There were a few lines of writing, punctuated with the words Blohm and Voss P900.'

'Blohm and Voss?'

'Aircraft manufacturers. During the war. Still exist of course.'
He lifted himself out of the chair and walked over to a huge computer terminal that stood on a heavy table. Karin followed him and watched as he typed on the keyboard, noisy and inaccurate. She could see his mistakes before they appeared on screen.
'Blohm and Voss. P900. Here we go. Some sort of miniature flying boat. Prototype. Designed to land on ice and water. But it was never developed. According to this, only three were ever built.'
'Land on ice and water?'
'Yes. It had these strange inflatable skis.'
Karin looked over Herr Fischer's shoulder. Then she leaned inwards and rested her elbows on the desk.
'May I?' she said, pointing to the keyboard.
'All yours.'
He pushed back his chair, scraping the legs on the wooden floor. Then he struggled up with fake effort and moved back to his desk.
'She's slow this morning,' he said, pointing to the computer. 'But she gets there in the end.'
'Just one thing to check,' said Karin, half-talking to herself.
She pulled the keyboard towards her, typed Hanford Gap and then clicked on Google maps. The screen filled with a plan of the downtown area. She zoomed out, once, twice, and then a third time. Now, she had a picture of the countryside around Hanford. And there it was.
Less than six miles from Hanford was a lake, four miles long and two-and-a-half miles wide. Big enough to land a Blohm and Voss P900.
She strummed her fingers on the worktop. It was beginning to make sense. Hans Dietrich had landed in Greenland and killed Ferris Clark. Then he'd got ready for stage two of his mission, a trip to Nevada. But somehow, before he'd set off, he'd managed to get himself killed and frozen.
Herr Fischer glanced up from his desk. 'Finding what you want?'

Karin nodded vaguely. 'Sort of. To be honest I need Jack.'

'*Jack*?' he said. 'Who's Jack?'

THIRTY-ONE

Tammy left the children in the kitchen and went through to the family room.

'Another day playing the waiting game,' she said when Fran and Elsie were out of earshot. 'Shit Jack, we're just waiting for him to strike. Who's next on his list? Another one like Ashton Brookner, who never hurt a fly? Maybe he hasn't even decided yet? That's what's so freaky. He's running rings round us. Why can't Perez, Rayno, come up with answers? They're the goddam detectives. That's what they're paid to do.'

Jack glanced at the boxes they'd not yet sorted through. 'There's got to be something.'

'You will stay again, won't you? Just being on my own in the kitchen scares the shit out of me. I've got this feeling he's going to spring out.'

'Course I'll stay.'

He clicked onto his laptop and checked his emails. At last there was one from Karin. He read down to the bottom then sat back in his chair. And then he read it a second time. He couldn't believe it. Yet it was true and it changed everything.

'*Tammy?*'

'Yeah?' She looked up. 'What?'

'Here –'

He was still staring at the screen when she came into the room.

'What is it?'

'The email I got from Exeter. From the Met Office.'

'What about it?'

'Remember what it said?'

'Course. Won't forget that in a hurry. It said Ferris Clark forecast the weather for D Day.'

'Yes. But it's not that simple.'

She sat down with a puzzled expression. 'What've you discovered now?'

'Ferris Clark,' he said, looking at her. 'His last contact with the weathermen in England was at eight o'clock in the evening.'

'That's what you said.'

'Yes. At eight o'clock on the fourth of June, Ferris Clark sent his final report to England. He told them the weather was set to improve. The storms would pass.'

'Yep.'

'And on that basis, Eisenhower launched D Day two days later.'

'Yep.'

'And that was the last contact they ever had with Ferris Clark.'

'So?' She was tapping one of her cowboy boots on the carpet. 'I don't get where this is leading?'

'According to what Karin's just sent me, that was not the last time his wireless transmitter was used.'

'How so?'

'Fully eight hours later, which would have made it about four in the morning, a second message was transmitted.'

'To England?'

'No.' He looked at her, eyes flashing. 'That's precisely the point. Not to England. To the Tirpitz. A German battleship in the mid-Atlantic.'

Tammy was silent for a moment.

'Sorry for being dumb but I'm not sure I get it.'

'The Tirpitz picks up a weather forecast that comes from Ferris Clark's transmitter. But it wasn't sent by him. It was sent by Hans Dietrich.'

'What did it say? The same forecast that was sent to Dunstable?'

'No. That's exactly the point. It predicted storms. A Force Eight gale. Low cloud. And five days of extreme low pressure. And it was sent from the Tirpitz to German Army Command.'

Tammy looked blank. 'Still don't get it.'

Jack stared at her.

'How much d'you know about D Day?'

She threw up her hands. 'Only the stuff everyone knows. The stuff you learn at high school.'

Jack began speaking slowly, as if he was still clarifying it in his head.

'On the day before the Allied landings Field Marshal Rommel was handed a weather forecast. *This* weather forecast, to be precise. He read it, saw the warnings of gales and knew for certain that the Allies couldn't land for at least a week. And because of that, he flew off to Germany for his wife's birthday.'

'The six generals on the ground, the ones in charge of coastal defence, they also received this forecast. They'd been on high alert for weeks. They were exhausted. And when they read this – ' he tapped his laptop – 'they all left their posts. Took themselves off to a party at some chateau, miles from the landing beaches.'

He paused for a second. 'Don't you see? It meant that when Allied forces landed on the sixth of June there was no Rommel, no German generals, no one who was able to lead the counter-attack.'

Silence.

'You're saying that Ferris Clark tricked Hans Dietrich.'

'Exactly.'

'Gave him the wrong forecast?'

'Yes.'

'And – '

They both began smiling at exactly the same moment. 'And managed to fool the entire German army,' said Jack. 'The last thing he did before he died was to play the biggest bloody trick in history. And they fell for it.'

THIRTY-TWO

It's mine – '
'No, it's *mine*,' said Fran, tugging the book from Elsie's hands.

'Oh please, can't you two just shut up,' said Tammy. She turned to Jack. 'It's cos they've been inside so much.'

She went over the kitchen cupboard. 'I'll cook something in a sec, but first I need to get these two doing something.'

'Know what - ?' said Jack suddenly. 'Why don't I cook? Why don't I cook with these two?'

Tammy looked at him in astonishment. Then she turned her gaze to Fran and Elsie.

'Well that's an offer I find hard to refuse. Fran – Elsie – want to cook with Jack?'

They rushed over and playfully beat his legs.

'Okay,' he said, laughing. 'I need eggs, flour, milk – if you've got enough – and salt and pepper.'

'What are we making?' asked Fran.

'We're going to make spätzle. Noodles. It's German. And delicious.'

'But how d'you know it?' he said. 'Are you making it up?'

'No, I was taught.'

'By who?'

'By Karin.'

'Who's Karin?'

'A friend. She's German. It's a German dish. She taught me how to make it. And it's the best thing you'll ever eat.'

Karin. Tammy went upstairs to take a shower.

Jack got Elsie stirring the flour and Fran beating the eggs. 'It's like batter, really.'

He put water to boil then helped them mix everything together.

'This is the fun bit,' he said when the water was hot. 'You have to squeeze it through the colander into the water. Then you wait for the bits to float to the surface. When they're done you scoop them out and they go in the oven to dry off.'

'Can I do some?' asked Elsie.

'You can. You're a born chef, you are.'

Tammy reappeared with her hair still wet. Jack glanced at her. She looked a million dollars.

'Jeez,' she said, surveying the mess. 'Five minutes to destroy a kitchen. It's like a bomb went off. But I guess it stopped world war three.'

Fran and Elsie ate straightaway, finishing off two helpings. Then Tammy told them to get into pyjamas.

'You'd better thank Jack,' she said as she led them off to bed.

* * *

'Well that was a triumph,' said Tammy when she came back down. 'And now it's our turn. Can we have it with the left-over sauce?'

'Perfect.'

She set the table while the sauce was heating up. Jack meanwhile got the spätzle from the oven.

'Here goes,' he said, tasting a forkful.

'Jack, you're a genius! These are great. What're they called again?'

'Spätzle. German. You normally eat them with venison or stew or something like that. In Germany, that is.'

'You've had them in Germany?'

'Yes. In Munich. There's this fabulous restaurant.'

He couldn't stop looking at her. Her eyes were catching the light and her hair was still slightly wet. She'd put on dangly silver earrings.

'We should go.'

'Go where?'

'To Munich. Fly to Germany. Go and have spätzle. And venison. In winter, that's when it's best. There's snow. I'll take you. And the kids. On me, of course. We could all go.'

There was a pause. Tammy put down her fork and looked at him hard.

'What's wrong?' he said.

'I'm confused, Jack. Real confused. I mean maybe it's because I'm stressed and tired and drained. But −' she sighed - 'I don't quite know how to put this -'

'*What?*'

'It's as if − look, maybe you don't even like me and I've got it all upside down in my head and I'm about to make a prize fool of myself. But I can't help feeling that you do like being here and you like me but something's not quite right.'

She sat forwards in her chair.

'Can I ask you something?'

'Sure.'

'Who's Karin? I mean, who − is − she? You keep mentioning her, she seems to be with us every second of the day, but you refuse to talk about her.'

There was a long silence.

'Yes,' he said at last. 'You're right to be confused.'

He got up from his chair and sat down next to hers. But before he had the chance to say anything more she interrupted him.

'I wouldn't mind, Jack, I wouldn't mind about anything.

But there's Fran and Elsie. You've seen them with you. They just adore you. They want to adopt you. And I don't even know where you stand. And -

There was another long pause.

'Okay,' he said, taking a deep breath. 'It's like this -

'It was after Alice died. It was bad. I fell apart. And that's when I started to drink. Heavily. Out of control. For two years, Tammy, I did very little else than drink myself into oblivion. Morning. Lunch. Evening. Evenings were the worst. That's when it really hurts.'

He paused for a moment.

'And then?'

'And then I met Karin.'

'Then I was right. Women are great mind-readers, you know.'

'She was German. And she was in London, working on a documentary. She's a TV journalist. A presenter, in fact. And she came to the rescue. Became my guardian angel. She pulled me from the chaos, stopped me drinking. She taught me that you *can* put things behind you. What's the point in living if you spend your life in complete bloody misery?

'She was beautiful. I mean she *is* beautiful. Ten years younger than me but a hundred years wiser. And things happened fast. She was going back to Germany but I persuaded her not to. She meant the world to me, Tammy.'

'*And –*'

'And then, just a couple of weeks ago, I'm at home on my own. I'd come back early from a trip and there's a ring on the bell. I answer and there's this guy standing there, a stranger, and he looks surprised when it's me opening the door. He's expecting Karin, see. Anyway, it transpired she'd had a fling while I'd been away. She'd slept with him. And I felt like I'd been shot in the head. So I told her to leave.'

'And she left?'

'Yes. Went straight back to Germany. I was mad at her, crazy, and she didn't have anywhere else to go. And you know what, the weirdest thing of all? It happened less than two weeks ago. Less than two weeks!'

'You're still mad at her?'

'Yes. I'm still mad at her.'

'But you miss her?'

Silence.

'How much were you away?'

'A lot.'

'And you've never got up to anything while you're away?'

'Well -'

'You know what, I think you're nuts. You're off travelling most of the time. Karin's on her own. She makes one mistake – a mistake that she almost certainly regrets. And then back comes Jack Raven, having got up to god knows what while he's been away on his own, and he throws a fit and kicks out the woman of his dreams.'

She paused for a moment.

'That's madness. She saved you from yourself, dragged you back to the real world. And what d'you do? You kick her out.'

Jack looked at her. She was glaring at him.

'But –'

'One mistake. And that's enough to kick someone out, in the logic of Jack Raven. What the hell were you thinking of?'

She sighed heavily.

'Look, since it's an evening of confessions, I'll come clean with you. I like you, Jack. I like you very much. In fact I haven't liked anyone quite so much for years. I've loved having you here, even though the circumstances are not exactly the best. Getting to know someone while there's a serial killer on your doorstep is not exactly great for romance. But I've loved watching you with the kids. You're a great guy. And intelligent too. There's not so many of those in Hanford, I can tell you. In fact you're a rare breed. But all along, I've had this suspicion that you were looking at the woman behind me.

'Lucky, lucky Karin. And although I'll probably regret what

I'm about to say forever, I'll at least say it from my heart. Get her back in your life, before you miss the chance.'

She kicked at the floor and sighed.

'Sometimes I feel like putting my whole life in the trash,' she said. 'That way you can start afresh.'

There was a long pause before Jack finally spoke.

'Tammy,' he said. 'I appreciate what you said. I really do. And I hate myself sometimes. Look, I'll tell you the truth right now, so you know it. You're amazing. You're fantastic. You're gorgeous. Look at you, you're completely bloody gorgeous. Christ, I love being here with you, despite the circumstances. Your kids are great. You're the best mother. But you're right, of course, you're totally bloody right. I see Karin wherever I look. I miss her. And that's the problem.'

* * *

It was late by the time they'd finished talking. Tammy stifled a yawn and looked at her watch.

'Past midnight,' she said. 'And it's been an evening I don't think I'll forget in a while. High emotional drama. Christ, talk about roller coaster. And now the nightly terror is about to begin. This is called living on the edge. It'll kill me. D'you mind if I disappear? I'm dead beat.'

Jack nodded. 'I'm going to do the same soon.'

He took her hand in his for a moment. 'Listen, Tammy, I want to apologize. And thank you, as well. I appreciate it more than you'll ever know.'

When she'd gone upstairs he walked slowly over to the window. The garden outside was bathed in yellow glow from the patio lamps. The storm that threatened earlier had failed to materialize. The dampness in the garden came from the humidity.

There were only two boxes that he hadn't yet looked through. Although it was late he didn't feel tired. He decided to go through the last of the papers before heading off to bed.

The contents of the first were the most recent. Architectural drawings of the remodeled ZAKRON building. He pushed them back into the file and pulled the second box towards him. He was hoping there'd be more about the military base during the war but was quickly disappointed. It was filled with correspondence from the three scientists working alongside Tammy's grandfather.

He idly looked through the papers, only half concentrating on their contents. There was a letter from Tammy's grandfather to Gerald Harley, one of the scientists, proposing the acquisition of land for the ZAKRON building. The next was from Walter Boyce, another member of the team. And there was a card from Ralph Proctor and his wife, Beverley, inviting all of them –Walter and Virginia, Gerald Harley, Ronald C. Fox and Hannah – to a celebratory dinner. And it was as Jack read through the invitation that his brain suddenly flashed onto red alert.

'Shit.'

He looked again, flicking back through the letters.

'Holy shit.'

And then again.

'Holy shit. Holy shit.'

He stood bolt upright, headed for the stairs.

'Tammy,' he called.'

* * *

Tammy was half asleep when Jack burst into her room. He pushed the door open with his foot, switched on the light. She woke in an instant and sat upright in panic.

'*What's happening?*'

'Got to get out. Now. Immediately. Throw on some clothes. He's coming. We're next.'

'What? *What?*'

Tammy jumped out of bed, still confused. 'What d'you mean?'

Jack took her arm and showed her the letters in his hand.

'Look -' He unfolded them one by one. 'Look at the addresses. Rio Vista Drive. Douglas Street. Lovedock Way. The three scientists who worked with your grand-dad all lived in the houses where the murders have taken place.'

He stopped for a moment. 'You do get it?'

She looked at him, awake but not yet fully functioning. Jack spelled it out bluntly.

'Hans Dietrich thinks he's killing the scientists. As far as he's concerned, he's still living in the nineteen forties. He thought he'd killed Gerald Harley when in fact it was Ashton Brookner. He thought he'd killed Walter and Virginia Boyce, when in fact it was Weldon and Rose Pereira. He thought he'd killed Ralph and Beverly Proctor, when in fact it was Ed and Hayley Mann. And now, as far as he's concerned, there's only your grandfather left. And *he* lived here.'

She stared at him. He could see her mind working it through.

'It means that when he comes, he'll kill whoever happens to be inside this house. You. Fran and Elsie. Me too. He's a killing machine. He doesn't care who we are. He just wants us dead.'

A moment's silence. She was still half asleep.

'Tom, Hunter –' he said. 'You see what they've done? In bringing Hans Dietrich to Hanford, they've inadvertently brought him to the very place he wanted to be.'

'But Tom brought him here cos of the lab,' said Tammy in a half-protesting sort of voice. 'Tom brought him here cos of ZAKRON.'

'Yes, Tom brought him to ZAKRON. But Hans Dietrich doesn't know about ZAKRON or cryonics or anything. All he knows is that he's somehow woken up in Hanford, which is where he wanted to be all along, and that he's on a mission to kill the scientists. If this was still the nineteen forties, he'd be coming after your grandfather. But now it's the present and he's coming after you.'

He saw her nodding slowly. And then suddenly, her eyes were wide with fright.

'Shit, shit, shit. Two secs. I'll get dressed.'

'And I'll check the kids,' he said, running up the flight of stairs to the top floor.

Tammy threw on jeans and a T-shirt then followed Jack up to the top floor. He was standing outside the children's bedroom, looking in.

'Thank God,' he said. 'They're asleep.'

Tammy stepped into the room and double-checked they were okay. Then she turned back to Jack.

'But where do we go? What do we do?'

'We get out fast. Now. He could come anytime. Maybe tonight. In fact, quite possibly tonight. He hasn't struck for two nights. We'll go anywhere. The Comfort Inn. It doesn't matter, just as long as it's not here.'

'I'll get them dressed,' she said.

'No. No time. We'll take them like that. You take Elsie. I'll take Fran. Let's go.'

She nodded, trying to think straight. 'We'll take my car,' she said. 'There's more room. We can all fit in.'

Jack went over to one of the beds and scooped Fran into his arms, the blanket still half-wrapped around him. He sniffed, buried his head into his shoulders and said sleepily: 'What's happening?'

Tammy took Elsie, carrying her with the blanket wrapped over her shoulders. She was clutching her furry rabbit close to her cheek. She didn't even wake up.

'Got everything?' said Jack in a whisper.

She nodded. 'Let's go.'

They made their way down from the top floor and onto the landing below. Elsie was still fast asleep in Tammy's arms, but Fran stirred slightly and rubbed his eyes in the light.

'You okay?' said Jack.

They made their way down to the ground floor as fast as possible, taking care not to trip on the trailing blankets. As they reached the kitchen, Jack felt Fran waking and struggling in his arms.

'What's happening?' he said. Then he slipped himself out of Jack's embrace and jumped indignantly to the floor.

Jack turned to Tammy. 'Get them in the car,' he said. 'I'll get my stuff. And then we'll get out of here.'

Tammy looked at him anxiously. 'You're not going back inside?' she said. 'What if he's here already? What if he's hiding out? What if he got in earlier, when we were looking through all the stuff?'

Jack shook his head. 'No. He's not here yet. We had the alarm on. We'd have heard him. I was downstairs the whole time, right till the moment I woke you.'

He gave Fran a friendly nudge towards the door that led from the kitchen to the garage. Then he turned back to Tammy. 'Get in the car and lock the doors. I'll be back in a sec.'

'But Jack – '

She pleaded with him. 'He's a killer, for Chrissakes. He's armed. He's got Kingston's gun, remember.'

'Just need to get my stuff. And – ' He glanced around the garage. A crowbar was leaning against the wall. He picked it up, gripped it tightly.

'Get in the car and lock it,' he said. 'Lock it and you'll be fine. I'll be right back down.'

Tammy stooped inside the car as she struggled to place Elsie in the child seat. 'Here we go honey,' she said, stretching over to fasten the seatbelt. She tucked the blanket all around her and kissed her gently on her forehead. Then she went round to the other side and strapped Fran in as well.

'Okay, done.'

She climbed into the driving seat and fastened her seat belt. And then she put the keys in the ignition and gave them a quarter turn. The dashboard lights flicked on and she hit the central locking control. There was a loud clunk as all four doors automatically locked. She suddenly felt safer.

'What's going on?' asked Fran, his head still swimming with sleep.

'Nothing sweetie. Jack's coming in a minute. And then we've got a short drive. That's all.'

'But where, mom?' said Elsie. She'd half-woken as she was being strapped into her seat. She rubbed her eyes. 'Where we going?'

'Just try to sleep,' said Tammy, glancing down at her watch. Why was Jack taking so long? What was he doing?

She felt a wave of panic. What if Hans Dietrich was already inside? *He's not here yet. We had the alarm on. We'd have heard him.* But what if he was? What if he was inside a cupboard right now, watching Jack, waiting to strike?

Fran's voice cut through her thoughts. 'There's a man killing people,' he said. 'It's true, isn't it mom. I heard you talking about it. I heard you downstairs with Jack. There's a man killing people.'

'No honey,' said Tammy. 'No one's killing anyone. Jack and I were talking about something – '

It was as she said these words, in mid-sentence, that something caused her to glance upwards. She looked into the rear view mirror. A drop of fear chilled her spine. She looked in the mirror a second time, only more sharply. The heap of blankets in the trunk of the car had moved.

No –

She froze.

No –

There was a hollow feeling in the pit of her stomach.

It can't be. Please God, no. Not this.

Instinctively she reached for the automatic unlock button, hit it hard, then turned to face the rear of the car. As she did so, a figure burst from the blankets.

She screamed, flung her arms towards Fran and Elsie. They screamed as well, struggling in their seats.

Hans Dietrich lifted his gun. Said nothing. Pointed it directly at Tammy's head.

* * *

Jack made his way through to the living room, clutching the crowbar in his right hand. The house felt eerily silent. Boxes and papers were still scattered across the floor of the living room. He put down the crowbar for a second and picked up his iPad. He pushed it into his bag. Then he took his phone, which was lying on the sofa, and slipped it into his trouser pocket. He seized the crowbar once again and started making a search of the house.

He went back into the hall (nowhere to hide) then made his way through to the front room. A quick glance round. Here, too, there was nowhere to hide.

He made his way back to the hall, then went upstairs and searched the wardrobes in Tammy's room. Nothing. The cupboards in the junk room. Nothing.

He made his way to the top of the house, to the children's room. Two beds, two chests of drawers and an entire wall of walk-in wardrobes. It was as he began searching through the clothes and toys that he suddenly had a feeling that something was seriously wrong.

* * *

Tammy had been staring in horror at Hans Dietrich, unable to make sense of what was happening. At first she screamed. Then she sobbed and beat at the car seat. And then her sobbing diminished to a whimper. Her arms were outstretched towards her children.

'What d'you want?' she cried. 'What have I done? I beg you.

Why are you here? For God's sake stop. Stop.'

Her hands were shaking. She could feel them shaking. Her face was drained. *Where's Jack? Oh God, where the hell's Jack?*

Fran and Elsie were crying, shaking uncontrollably. They were too terrified to scream. Hans Dietrich was staring at Tammy without any flicker of emotion. Then, coldly, deliberately, he raised the gun and pointed it directly at her head. She was four feet from the barrel.

'Where is he?'

He spoke in English, with only the trace of an accent.

Tammy said nothing.

He said it again. 'Where is he?'

'Who?' she said at length, her eyes switching from him to the children and back to him. 'Where's *who*, for Chrissakes?'

Hans Dietrich allowed his gun to sweep nonchalantly through the car and then let it settle back in line with her head.

'Where's *who*?' she repeated, only this time more urgently.

'You know who,' he said. 'Ronald Fox.'

Tammy stared hard.

'*Ronald Fox*? Grandpa?'

As she said it, she realised. She saw it all. It was just as Jack had said.

Her eyes flicked towards Fran and Elsie. Both were still sobbing. Fran had turned his head slightly and was looking half behind him, staring in panic at the gun. Elsie had drawn the blanket tightly around her neck, as if it would save her.

For Chrissakes, Tammy, think, think, think. Think on your feet. Ronald Fox. He's come for grandpa, just as Jack said. Hans Dietrich is still in the nineteen-forties.

She could see the gaping black hole of the open barrel. It was staring at her. She looking into his eyes. Metallic and sharp blue, even in the darkness. And filled with malice.

'At the base.'

She said it without thinking. 'He's at the base. Ronald Fox. Works night shift.'

Hans Dietrich shifted position slightly, moved onto his knees. He did it without changing the angle of the gun.

'Drive,' he said. 'Drive there. Now.'

Where's Jack? Why hasn't Jack come down? Where the fuck's Jack?

'Drive,' he said. 'To the base. Now.'

She saw his finger on the trigger. He lifted the gun a fraction. But then, as if having second thoughts, he shifted it downwards, towards Elsie.

'No,' she shrieked.

'Drive.'

She had no option. She pressed on the automatic control that opened the garage door. Hans Dietrich watched intently, as if he'd never seen such a thing in his life. She glanced in the mirror, noticed his eyes widen as the door began to slide itself open.

Jack. Come down now. Now. Before it's too late.

She was thinking fast, thinking on her feet, trying to work out what to do. Even if she got to the base – or rather, the site of the base - what then? He'd quickly see there was no base, no buildings, no grand-daddy. And then what?

'Drive.'

The garage doors had swung fully open. The paved driveway was lit by the dim glow of the patio lights. It glistened in the night. She slowly shifted the car into drive.

* * *

It took Jack less than a second to realise what was going on. He heard the engine, saw the vehicle emerge from the garage. And then he saw everything. In the rear of the car, visible as a dark shadow, was the figure of Hans Dietrich.

Holy shit.

He rushed downstairs to the landing, paused for a second,

then tore down the next flight as well. He grabbed his keys from the kitchen table, rushed to the front door. His car was out on the street, facing the right direction. He fired the engine, hit the accelerator. He could see the red glow of her tail-lights already at the far end of the street.

He saw her indicate left out of Golden Park Drive, then turn right into Avery Street. Where were they heading? He thought through the possible options. ZAKRON? No. Ferris Clark's place? Unlikely.

He reached for his phone, dialed Perez. No answer. He dialed Tom. No answer either.

He watched her swing into the right lane of the Bluetown Interchange and then second left onto the highway. *Of course.* The base. He wants to go to the base.

He followed them up onto the highway, slowing his speed a fraction in order to put a gap between them. *Mustn't let him see I'm following.* The night was dark but the sky overhead was tin-selled with stars. The moon hung heavy and dim, like it was on energy-save. They passed Flame-Burgers, Yummies Ice Cream, all shut up in the darkness. And then they passed ZAKRON. It, too, was all dark. Tom had yet to find a replacement for Kingston.

The base. The base. He was trying to remember the photo they'd found in one of the boxes. *That's been taken close to the Fifty. Right by the highway. Near Jazzy Joe's. There's still a dirt track.* That's what Tammy had said.

The gaps between the buildings widened. They were reaching the far edge of town. He braked slightly in order to widen the distance between himself and Tammy. He could just about make out the figure of Hans Dietrich crouched in the rear.

He was thinking of Fran and Elsie. Christ, the bastard better not touch them. They passed Jazzy Joe's. The lights inside were still on, casting a curdled glow into the night. And then there were no more buildings. They had reached the deserted end of town.

He noticed Tammy slowing down. She was looking for the

turning. And it was there, exactly where she'd said it would be, two hundred yards beyond the parking lot for Jazzy Joe's. She indicated right and then swung off the highway onto a dirt track.

Jack pulled onto the edge of the road, cut the engine. He'd follow on foot.

* * *

Tammy glanced in the mirror for a second time. It was Jack. She knew the car. It was Jack. She saw him slow, pull onto the side of the highway. Then she saw his lights go out. *Jack*. Thank God.

Hans Dietrich sat up sharply as they swung off the main road and bounced slowly along the dirt track.

'Where's the base?'

Tammy turned, saw him clutch the gun more tightly.

'Here,' she said. 'Need to go on foot from here. They don't allow cars.'

She cut the engine, opened the door.

'I'll take you there,' she said, trying to keep her voice in control. 'But on one condition.'

Hans Dietrich motioned to the children with the gun.

'No conditions.'

'One condition,' she said sharply. She'd once read a magazine article on what to do if you're taken hostage. Act like they wouldn't expect you to act. Surprise them. It either works or gets you shot.

'One condition,' she repeated. 'The kids stay here.'

He swung round the gun to her. No time to argue. He nodded.

Tammy glanced backwards, just for a second. She saw Jack creeping up the path towards them, his shadow visible against the light of the sand.

'Where's the base?' Hans Dietrich was casting around,

looking for buildings. 'Where is it?'

He said it again. 'Where's the base?'

'It's – '

She looked behind her once again. Jack was closing the gap. He was getting nearer. And she was unable to control herself any longer. She let out a piercing scream.

Jaaaack!

Hans Dietrich swung around in an instant, turned the gun from her to the figure approaching through the darkness. Jack. He stopped breathless by her side. She clutched at his arm.

Jack!

Hans Dietrich's eyes flicked from Tammy to Jack, then back to Tammy. And then he looked at Jack for a second time.

'Who are you? Who are you?'

Jack ignored him and turned to Tammy. 'You okay? The kids?'

She nodded. Even in the moonlight he could see her shaking.

'*Who are you?*' repeated Hans Dietrich. '*Are you Ronald Fox?*'

Jack shook his head, stared at him hard. The barrel of the revolver was pointing directly at him.

'Put down the gun.'

'Where's the base? Where's Ronald Fox?' he said. And then he asked another question. 'Where am I?'

He looked around in search of buildings. 'Where are we?'

Jack heard the first note of uncertainty in his voice.

'Put down the gun.'

'What's happening? Where am I?'

He took a step towards Jack. 'What's going on?'

'Put down the gun.'

Hans Dietrich looked at him blankly, his eyes full of clouds. Then he glanced backwards, towards the highway. There was a giant billboard for *Yummies Ice Cream. Strawberry, Raspberry, Chocolate, Whipped for your Delight.*

'Where am I?'

Now he was looking downwards, staring at the ground, trying to make sense of it all.

'Where's the base? The scientists, where are they? Where's Ronald Fox?'

He took a step backwards, tripped slightly in the loose sand.

'This is the future,' said Jack calmly, looking him directly in the eye. 'The base doesn't exist any more. The war ended years ago. Churchill's dead. Stalin's dead. Ronald Fox is dead. All the scientists are dead. They've all been dead for years. The people you've killed are the wrong ones. They were innocent people.'

Hans Dietrich lifted his hands to his eyes and held them there for a moment, as if to shield himself from a bright light.

'You were found in the ice,' said Jack. 'You've been brought back to life. Look at us. Look at our clothes. Look at the car. Look at the signs, the road, everything. You're in the future. Otto Streckenbach's dead. Joachim Ulrich's dead. They died years ago. The only one still alive is Magda Trautwein. Remember the pretty one in Schloss Hohenstein? She's still alive, but she's eighty-nine.'

Silence.

'Germany lost the war. Hitler's dead. He shot himself in the head.'

As Jack spoke, Hans Dietrich lifted the gun slightly, fingered it lightly, then pointed it first at Tammy and then at Jack. It came to rest at the level of his chest. Suddenly he had the eyes of a killer again, coldly, clinically detached.

Tammy looked at him, pleaded with him.

'*No, no. Please.*'

Jack raised his hands, as if in self-defence.

'You've woken into the future,' he said. 'Look at us. Everything's different.'

Hans Dietrich took another step backwards, adjusted the angle of the gun, fumbled with the trigger. He seemed uncertain which one of them to shoot first. And then -

Bang.

When it happened, it happened in a flash. The world spun upside down. A shot rang out. Jack reeled backwards. It cracked like a firework, reported off the rocks.

Boom.

Jack swung round to Tammy, to see where she'd been hit.

B-boom.

But she hadn't been hit.

'*Look –*' she screamed. '*Look –*'

He turned just in time to see Hans Dietrich fall backwards, twisted, slumped downwards into the sand. A single bullet had punctured his forehead.

They rushed over to where he had fallen. There was a clean hole in the front of his head. Right through the centre. And underneath him, in the cool night sand, was a growing stain of blood.

Jack walked across to the body, pushed it with his foot. Blood was still spurting from the wound in uneven pulses and soaking away into the sand. But all life was gone. Already, all life was gone.

Tammy stood unsteady for a second, unsure if what she was seeing was for real. Then she slumped into Jack's arms.

'Jesus,' he said. And then: 'Thank God.'

* * *

They took the body to ZAKRON later that morning and placed it in one of the large refrigeration boxes. Then Tom summoned everyone to a meeting in the conference room.

He was the last to arrive and when he did eventually enter the room he blustered in without even looking around. He'd regained his bravado, his swagger, his arrogant sneer. Jack had to hand it to him, it was remarkable how quickly he bounced back.

'We did it,' he said. 'We got the bastard in the end, just as I said we would.'

He flashed his eyes towards Jack. 'Would have preferred him alive but –'

Tammy shot him a look that warned him to stop right there. Tom took the hint.

'And now he stays here with us,' he said. 'He stays in the deep freeze. He's not going anywhere. And no one will ever know.'

He paused for a moment, as if wondering how to continue.

'One other thing,' he said.

They all looked at him expectantly. A sly grin was wiped across his face.

'You might like to know that I've just received an email. This very morning. Carla, can you get this thing running?'

Carla switched on the interactive wall-screen and brought up Tom's inbox.

'That's the one,' he said, pointing to the top of the list. 'It's from the guys drilling in Greenland.'

Carla opened the email and they all read in silence.

Tom - Dale and I have been trying to get you on your cell-phone. We've been doing extensive drills some 3 miles to the S.E. of where we found the frozen corpse. We've turned up two more bodies, both in good shape. Also, what looks like the wreckage of a plane. We've hacked the corpses from the ice and packed them in Styrofoam. They're yours if you want them.

Tammy groaned. Gonzalez kicked at the floor. Sergeant Perez looked at Tom. Jack immediately started scrolling down his iPad, in search of the names. Otto Streckenbach and Joachim Ulrich. The other two members of Hans Dietrich's Totenkopf team. He read them out to the room.

'Yeah,' said Tom. 'You got it. Otto Streckenbach and Joachim Ulrich. They'll be on their way to us tomorrow. And this time – ' he sneered at the room – 'we won't let the bastards get away. They'll be our little guinea pigs. We can experiment on them until there's nothing left to experiment. Give 'em a dose of their own medicine. And then, when we're done, we'll announce our breakthrough to the world.'

THIRTY-THREE

'This Tammy woman –'
Karin was sitting cross-legged on the sofa, scrunching her hair backwards into a pony-tail. 'She wasn't *too* attractive?'

The London sunlight was filtering through the huge bay window, already autumnal, and falling onto the rug in an abstract triangle. Jack smiled. It was the one question he knew she'd ask.

'A southern cowgirl,' he said. 'All boots and jeans. And the sweetest kids.'

'Oh - ?' Karin looked at him, all surprised. The sweetest kids. She'd never heard that before.

He leaned forwards and scooped a handful of pistachios.

'She's desperate to meet you.'

'*Me*? Why me?'

'I guess you were with us all the time, even though you weren't. Even Tammy felt it.'

'If I was there, it's because I was jealous.'

She got up, walked over to the window. In the garden square opposite there was a couple sitting on the grass drinking from a bottle of champagne. Champagne. It's what she felt like drinking right now.

'Have you contacted the woman in your film?' asked Jack suddenly. 'Katarina Bach. To tell her you've found her mother.'

'I can't be certain Frau Trautwein's her mother.'

'But it's likely.'

'Yes, it's likely. The dates fit and so does the place. They even had the same eyes.'

'Will you? Tell her, I mean.'

She shrugged. 'Maybe. I feel bad about knowing when she doesn't. But I certainly won't be telling her that her father – her *possible* father - is lying in a freezer-box in Nevada.'

'No, perhaps that's for the best.'

There was a long silence before she changed the subject.

'So how did he get into the garage?' she said. 'Hans Dietrich. How come you didn't hear him?'

'That's exactly what we tried to work out. The alarm was on constantly, except for an hour or so when the fuses blew. The windows were closed and bolted and the doors double-locked. Christ, the place was Fort Knox.'

'So?'

'We went back through the whole sequence of events. And we came to the conclusion that it can only have been when we left for the murder at Lovedock Way. We went to the garage, got in the car and then Tammy went back into the house to get biscuits for the kids. When we finally left, she thinks she forgot to re-lock both the kitchen door and the door to the garage.'

'So he was inside the house, lying in wait.'

'Seems so. Must have been there for hours, biding his time. And when we returned, he decided to hide himself in the car. Probably did something similar for the other murders as well.'

'That's freaky as hell. And that's how no one ever heard him coming?'

Jack nodded. 'Exactly.'

'And what about Ferris Clark? You never finished telling me about him. His body's never been found, but he died in Greenland?'

'Yes,' said Jack. 'I'm one hundred per cent certain that Ferris Clark was killed by Hans Dietrich. It must have been on the night of the fourth of June. And it must have been after eight o'clock in the evening, because that's when Ferris Clark sent his forecast to England. I reckon he was already dead by four o'clock the next morning, when Hans Dietrich sent his wireless forecast to the Tirpitz. He was almost certainly killed in the early hours.'

'At Camp Eggen?'

'No. Not at Camp Eggen. That map reference you got from Herr Fischer is some distance to the north of Camp Eggen. That seems to have been where the American weather station was situated, on a chunk of rock in the middle of nowhere. Ferris Clark wasn't with his comrades. He was on his own.'

'So Hans Dietrich pitches up in the middle of the night, breaks into the weather station and kills him?'

'Yes. But first he manages to extract the D Day weather forecast, perhaps by torturing him. And that's exactly the point at which Ferris Clark tricked him. Gave him the wrong forecast. Told him the weather was going to be so bad that there was no chance of any Normandy landings taking place.

'It's incredible, really. True bravery. Ferris Clark deserves every bloody medal under the sun. Deserves to be in all the history books. He must have known he was going to be killed. And he must also have known that the outcome of the war depended upon the D Day landings. And so he tricked Hans Dietrich.'

'They get the forecast. They kill him. And once he's dead - ?'

'Stage two of the mission. Hans Dietrich's plan is to fly to Nevada in his Blohm and Voss plane. Land on the lake. Kill the scientists.'

'But how come he's carrying Ferris Clark's address?'

'They'd done their research. They knew what they were doing. We're talking about the elite of the elite. Hans Dietrich was intending to use the house as his base, I'm sure of it. It makes sense. He knows Ferris Clark's dead. He knows he has no brothers, no sisters, no parents. There's every chance the house in Green Diamond will be empty.'

There was a pause. Karin poured herself another glass of wine. 'But he never made it,' she said. 'Hans Dietrich never made it.'

'No. He never made it. He ended up in the Greenland ice. Naked. Frozen. And perfectly preserved.'

'So how d'you account for that?'

Jack thought for a moment. 'D'you remember me telling you about the Arctic frog? The way it protects itself in winter? Releases glucose into its body, like anti-freeze.'

She nodded slowly then smiled. 'You're telling me that Hans Dietrich is an Arctic frog?'

'Not exactly. But everything points to the fact that something similar happened. He must have taken some sort of chemical, I don't know what. It's the only possible way his organs could have been protected in the way they were.'

Karin nodded. 'It still doesn't answer why he was naked.'

'No. That's the missing link.'

'But that's why they got you to Nevada in the first place.'

Jack got up from his chair and walked over to the window. Then he turned back to face her, placing his hands around her waist.

'This is what I can tell you,' he said. 'Hans Dietrich didn't commit suicide. I'm sure of it. And he didn't drown. He was dead when he landed in that freezing water. But he wasn't murdered either. There was no struggle, no cuts, no bruises. So what does that leave? An accident. It was some sort of weird freak accident. It's almost like he tumbled into the water, already dead, already frozen, and was then sealed into the ice.'

'But naked?'

'But naked,' repeated Jack. 'But naked. But naked. It's the question that keeps going round and round in my head, but I still can't get the answer. To be honest, the only way I'll ever find out why Hans Dietrich was naked is by winding back the clock. And that's something I can't do.'

GREENLAND, 3AM, JUNE 5, 1944.

C lic-clic-clic-clic-
He was dimly aware of a high-pitched clicking noise coming from somewhere outside. His eyes were blurred to a dark mist and his heart was thumping in his throat.

He felt mud run through his innards and then his bowels emptied themselves onto the floor. There was an acid feeling in his throat. He wondered if he had been sick.

Clic-clic-clic-clic-

There it was again. He knew that sound. Even though the hypothermic shock was blunting his brain, he had some vague sense that the roof top anemometer was spinning wildly out of control, its little metal cups snatched by the Arctic gale.

Clic-clic-clic-clic-

And then, as he lifted his eyelids a fraction, he got a sudden jolt into the here and now. Towering over him was a man with steel blue eyes and a face that could kill.

* * *

Hans Dietrich had been staring down at Ferris Clark for the better part of ten minutes. He had been almost unconscious when they'd dragged him inside, his breathing coming in faint gasps. But now the stifling fug of the cabin was beginning to stir him.

He pulled a packet of Epstein cigarettes from his jacket pocket, drew one into his mouth, lit it with a cool blue flame. Then he breathed out a long cloud of smoke. He watched the eyelids tremble, noticed the fingers clench tightly in on themselves. He knew from experience that the pain would only get worse. Soon his organs would be stabbed with frostbite and his brain would expand into the casing of his skull.

He knelt down slowly, hitching his trousers at the knee. And then he took his half-smoked cigarette and held it, very deliberately, next to the exposed flesh. It sizzled and there was a piercing scream.

'I see we understand one another.'

Ferris Clark writhed in pain, twisting his head from side to side. And then his lips began to tremble. Hans Dietrich turned to Streckenbach, snapped an order. 'Pen. Paper. Get it down.'

Streckenbach crouched on the floor and listened intently. As he did so, he started making notes.

Ferris spoke faintly and in gasps, yet he was curiously coherent. The information seemed to spill from him like an automaton. Force Eight. Pause. Low cloud. Pause. Visibility poor.

While Streckenbach noted the information, Ulrich was attempting to reset the frequencies on the radio transmitter. He knew how it worked. A Timson Model HT5, battery operated, single tube. At first it produced no noise at all, but as he twisted the dials and shifted the frequency towards 2410 kcs it started to emit a series of high-pitched whines.

'It's coming.'

The whine became a solid whistle.

'Getting it. I'm locking onto the Tirpitz. *Hallo – hallo – Sturmhauptführer Joachim Ulrich hier – SS Panzer Division Totenkopf.*'

A crackle from the transmitter then a faint voice from the receiver.

'*Ja*! Herr Ulrich, we hear you. Heil Hitler! Funker Eberhardt, battleship Tirpitz.'

Streckenbach pulled up a chair and began reading out the

weather information. Ulrich meanwhile transmitted it down the line, requesting that Eberhardt repeat it back to him so he could be sure it was noted correctly.

'Urgent, Eberhardt. Stop. Top secret. Stop. Inform Berlin. Stop. Inform the Kriegsmarine. Stop. Inform Army Group Three. Stop. Heil Hitler.'

Hans Dietrich glanced out of the cabin window. The snow had stopped and the sky was the colour of slate. It was almost dawn.

* * *

The Blohm and Voss seaplane lifted sharply from the ice field, its nose tilted high towards the sun. Hans Dietrich gazed down on the purity below. He could see the glacier stretching to the sea, its shafts of ice translucent in the sunlight.

The trace of a smile curved across his face as he relived the events of the previous few hours. Streckenbach and Ulrich had bound Ferris Clark, gagged him, tipped him shrieking off the icy cliff top. He'd bobbed up and down in the frigid blue water, once, twice, then sunk like a stone.

As Hans glanced out of the cabin window he was struck by the immensity of it all. The land far beneath was a vast sheet of bluish steel stretching into infinity. Even the horizon, warped convex by the earth's curvature, was icy-white.

He swallowed three capsules of Pervitin and followed it by drinking off some of the glucose, thinking of Doctor Fiedler as he did so. Wonder drugs, *huh*. Good as useless. Had they really prevented frostbite? More likely it was their Arctic gloves and boots.

He groped his way down to the rear of the plane, twisting the handle to the cabin-cupboard at the rear. On the top shelf he saw the three piles of American clothes, neatly stacked and ironed. Dressed in those, they'd look like regular Yankees.

Nevada would never know.

He started to undress in the confined space of the cabin, pulling off his fur-lined Stromso jacket and knocking his arms against the shelf as he did so. He had to twist his knees upwards in order to remove his trousers. *Pervitin.* Alright then, he'd see if it protected him from the cold. He pulled off his vest, catching a glimpse of his tattoo in the mirror as he did so. He noticed that he wasn't shivering, even though it was freezing. Perhaps Fiedler was right after all. Bastard. He removed his Arctic stockings, socks and underpants. And then he was naked.

He was about to reach for the jeans when the plane gave a strange shudder and then lurched violently to the right.

* * *

Strapped into the cockpit, Streckenbach and Ulrich were wrenching at the controls, struggling to bring the seaplane back under control. The bank of storm had appeared from nowhere. One moment they were flying through smooth clear sky, the next there was a blurred white mist advancing towards them at incredible speed. It enveloped the sun, turning its light to a dirty fuzz. The sky was stained the colour of tea, the land below snatched away.

Ferris Clark. They both spat out his name. He'd forecast fine weather for their entire route southwards. A tail wind over Greenland, that's what he'd said. High pressure stretching far to the south. He'd not mentioned an Arctic storm.

Another block of freezing air smacked hard at the plane, tearing the nose and pushing them upwards from behind. They plunged into a moment of free fall and their stomachs were sucked into their throats. *Bastard Ferris Clark.* And then the plane was dashed into a dense wall of freezing air.

* * *

If only he could get his clothes on.

Hans Dietrich was gripping at the shelf, hanging on with both fists. He cursed Ulrich up front and then reached once again for the jeans. But as he did so there was a far more serious jolt that lifted the plane out of the clouds. Everything was momentarily weightless. Then it was rammed so hard into a bank of air that the propeller shuddered and screeched. There was a shredding noise, like metal being ripped in two, then a sickening rattle as the propeller was torn to splinters. Shards of wood and metal were studded into the cockpit and tail.

Assaulted by the storm, the plane was punched through the snowstorm, fuel draining into the sky. Hans Dietrich was jammed on his side, naked, wedged against the exit, fighting to get himself onto his feet.

And when it all happened, it did so in a split second. There was a sudden flash of light as the door gave way beneath him. Next thing he knew, he was plunged into a knife-blade of ice, falling through the void at incredible speed, spinning, twisting, tumbling headfirst through freezing emptiness.

He had a vague notion of the white sheet below him, a dim awareness that his feet, legs, arms had locked to steel. A tremendous blast of air from beneath him halted his free fall for a moment and held him suspended in the void. His last thought was of the mission he had failed to complete. Then there was white in his mind and white in the sky. When he plunged into the glacial waters below, he was unaware of anything, past or present.

FINIS

ACKNOWLEDGEMENTS

I am grateful to the late David Howarth whose book *The Sledge Patrol*, a colourful account of Greenland during the Second World War, was the genesis of this book.

Thank you to my literary agent, Georgia Garrett; to my French publisher, Vera Michalski; to Rob Kraitt at Casarotto, Ramsay and Associates.

Many people have helped me along the way: thanks are due to Tony Saint, Christine Kidney, Jeremy Trevathan, Nat Jansz, Masha Bozunova and Mark McCrum.

Thanks to Laura Bamber for designing the cover, and to Danny Gillan and Jane Dixon-Smith for the layout.

A heartfelt thank you to Marie Lossky for ensuring that the American characters speak like Americans and to Rita Gallinari for copyediting the book so thoroughly. Any remaining errors are entirely my own.

Lastly, a huge thank you to Alexandra for the excellent advice and constant encouragement.

Lightning Source UK Ltd.
Milton Keynes UK
UKOW02f0840031114

240941UK00002B/7/P